AMEFYRE

BOOK THREE

R. A. SANDPIPER

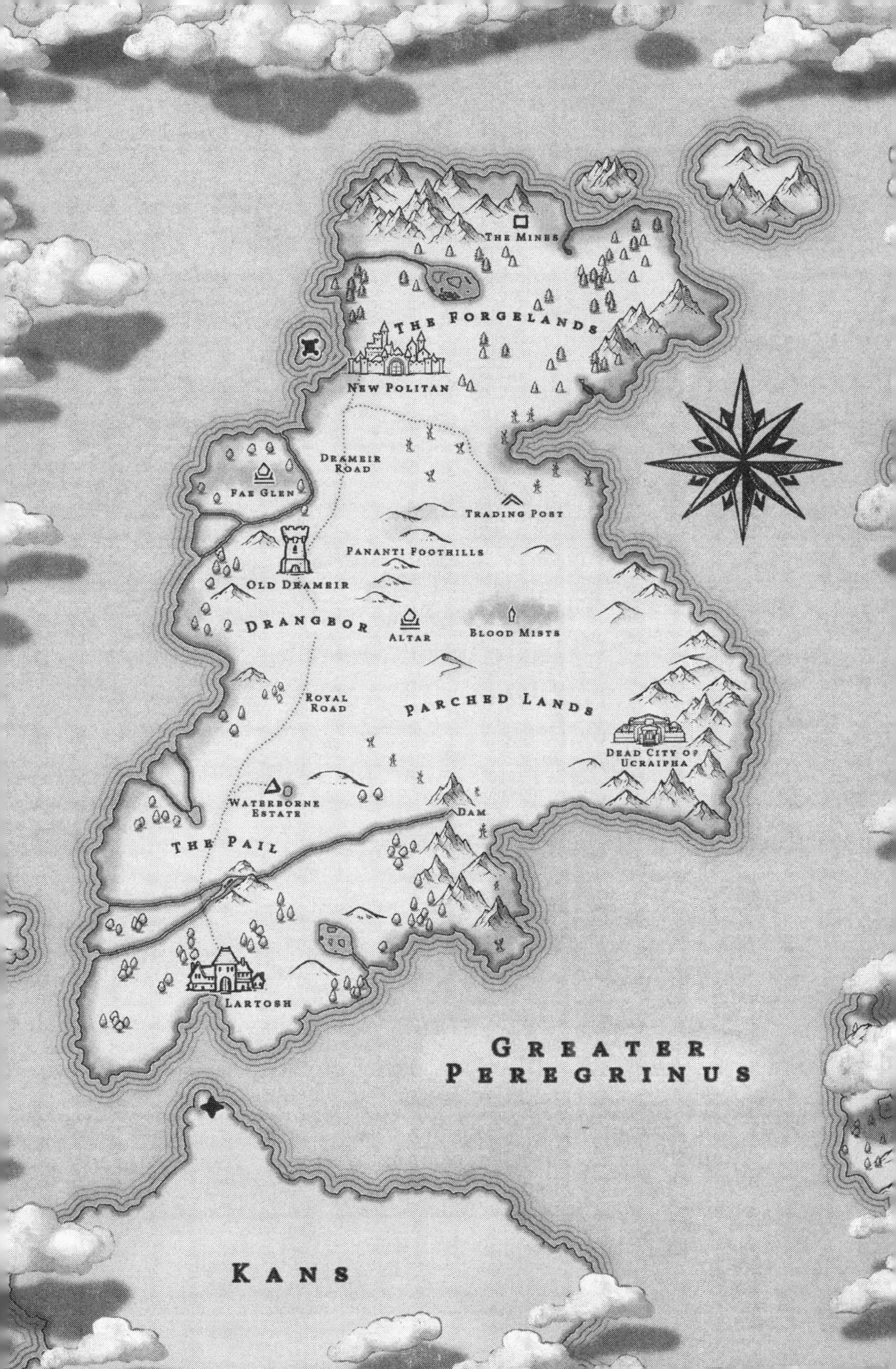

The Mines
The Forgelands
New Politan
Drameir Road
Fae Glen
Trading Post
Pananti Foothills
Old Drameir
Drangbor
Altar
Blood Mists
Royal Road
Parched Lands
Dead City of Ucraipha
Waterborne Estate
Dam
The Pail
Lartosh
Greater Peregrinus
Kans

The story, all names, characters, and incidents portrayed in this production are fictitious. No identification with actual persons (living or deceased), places, buildings, and products is intended or should be inferred.

Book Cover by [saintjupit3r]

1st edition [2025]

To Rick,
For never letting me down.

1

There were many things I would miss about the Glen, but the all-consuming purple was not one.
Unknown author, est. 2nd-5th century

Suri sat up from the straw mattress as the key clicked in the lock, relaxing a little when a head of long hair appeared around the door, the part of her waiting to see him coiled tight as a spring.

Aisha gave her a knowing smirk as she closed the door behind her. The Blood Witch's daughter, and usual resident of Akdaria, had arrived the other day, somehow already knowing they needed her. "Sorry. It's only me."

Suri couldn't resist asking. "How is he?"

"More himself every hour." Aisha pulled open the dingy curtain in the corner of the room, frowning. The window was at street level, only inviting a narrow light made grey by the rain.

Once they realised they were somehow alive, and Kol wasn't going to become some Death God's puppet for the rest of eternity, they split up. It would be tempting fate to have the entire Life Court sitting like ducks in the basement of a single brothel. So instead, they sat in the basements of several different establishments.

"Good," Suri said. She lay back fully again, relieved as the skin around her back loosened. The raked teeth of the longtooth had gone deeper than even she thought, and if she lived long enough, they would scar in two long jagged lines.

"He wants to see you."

Her heart thudded. "Then let him."

It had been a day and a half since she had returned his soul to him and with it, his life magic. But he'd passed out almost straight away after, succumbing to a long overdue rest. Only Esra stayed with Mother Edi, his presence the least likely to alert the other street urchins who swept through her home.

Aisha watched over Suri and Nadrian from the basement of a butcher shop at the edge of the Tangle. The numbing agent on Nadrian's wings was slowly wearing off, and he was still badly injured otherwise. He moaned in pain from the other room half the night and she groaned herself the other half.

Aisha strode to her side, laying the back of her hand on Suri's forehead.

It was a relief to have another set of hands. Mother Edi's were long weary from keeping them all alive after the arena, and Aisha was better than the rest of them anyway. Better even than Viantha, who had arrived alongside Aisha and had a surprising amount of innate skill with healing. She'd volunteered, apparently. Suri had not seen her; Viantha had clearly restricted her budding ability for those who had not kidnapped her, namely, Kol and Scilla. An old curl of jealousy flared, but Suri couldn't fathom the will to truly think ill of her when she'd healed Kol better than she ever could.

"I must tend to you first," Aisha said, gesturing for her to flip onto her front. "You're still warm."

"It's stuffy down here," Suri replied into the pillow, as she gritted her teeth.

Aisha narrowed her eyes. "It's freezing."

"Some of the time."

Aisha touched Suri's shoulders with the back of her hand. "You have a fever. But the wound looks clean. How bad does it hurt?"

"On what scale?" Suri asked, a sardonic edge to her voice. "A lot?"

"Sorry, stupid question," Aisha said. "Stay still."

Aisha's method of life healing was different. Suri had learnt to find her heartbeat in her body and draw them back to her heart. Aisha, by comparison, held her hands out, fingers splayed, several inches above Suri's back and closed her eyes, falling into some sort of trance.

After a minute of concentration, Aisha opened her eyes and folded her hands back. Her voice wavered a little. "All done."

Suri rolled her shoulders and felt the difference immediately. The stinging pain was still there, but it was now accompanied by the itchiness of a wound a week old. "Thank you," she said genuinely. "How did you get so good at this?"

"Mother says I had a natural affinity for healing as a child." Aisha's voice dropped. "That's why she cast me out."

Suri thought of the girl's mother, Waris. She'd met her on a visit to the Blood Mists she wasn't keen to repeat. The woman was a true witch, with ancient blood magic practised in ways ready to turn even the strongest stomach. "She cast you out?"

"Sort of," Aisha said, with a smile. "Her tower is a place of pain inflicted, not pain removed. She could see how it hurt me to see her work. She only discovered I could heal because I aided a mist-touched rider."

"Did you heal him?" Suri asked. Touching the mists was a death sentence, everyone knew it.

Aisha shook her head. "He died shortly after, it would have been kinder for me not to act."

"And then she sent you to Akdaria."

"Eventually, yes. She wanted me to see more of the world, and use my talent somewhere where life was valued more."

"But you're still close," Suri said. "If she told you to come here?"

Aisha shrugged. "It's not quite *telling*. I am of her blood, and blood is her way. Sometimes she sends me things in my dreams. Visions, or hints of knowledge. She shows me what the blood shows her, and allows me to interpret it myself."

"What did she send you?"

"An image of a Northern city, and me outside of it. I left the next morning."

Suri nodded. "Do you know when I can leave?"

Aisha frowned. "I'd like you to stay in bed for two more days at least."

Suri sighed. "Can I see Kol?"

"I'm not sure that would be—"

"Am I contagious?" Suri interrupted, rolling onto her side with a grimace.

"No," Aisha said reluctantly.

"So, I can have visitors." Suri studied Aisha's face.

The reply was guarded, uncertain. "I'll let him know."

Suri scanned Aisha's tight-lipped smile, the grey pallor across her cheeks. "What are you not telling me, Aisha?"

Aisha sighed. "He knows what you did."

"Ah," Suri said, falling back onto her bed.

Aisha grimaced.

He knew what she had done. From Aisha's expression, it was clear the man was livid. She allowed the events of the past week to wash over her once more, the flashes of memory she'd already replayed too often to count in the last two days.

After Kol had martyred himself, choosing to ride into the city of New Politan to warn of Queen Lera and Rasel's plan to launch three massacres within its walls, Suri rode in another direction. She bought a glamour from the Fae King Xianyu, a pure Fae creation allowing her to temporarily kill Kol and trick the terms of her blood bond. If Suri killed Kol, she could ask for whatever she wanted. But only Fae magic was strong enough to kill him, and bring him back, and it came with a price.

She had forced the glamoured potion down Kol's throat in the Northern arena, to all eyes killing him. In exchange for the completion of her bond, she had asked for three things. First, forgiveness for everyone in the arena, second, for a meeting between Kol's court and the Northern court. And finally, a house in New Politan which she and Esra could call home.

Kol had come back to life, unbeknownst to the world, in the hidden refuge of Edi's basement. But the glamour had cost her. Dearly. Suri had sold her very soul for it, bottled and stored in the Fae Glen's Aviary of Souls.

Kol had clearly discovered the price she paid for the glamour. He knew she was soulless now, as he had been all the while she'd known him. Maybe he had also discovered she nearly died trying to retrieve his own soul, diving into Sotoledi's dark world to restore it to him so he could come back as himself.

"He's angry," Aisha said.

Suri raised an eyebrow at Aisha's nervous lip bite. "I'm sure."

"It's not funny, Suri. I've never seen him this mad. He's been angry before, but this was something so much worse. I thought Sotoledi had stolen his body back." Aisha looked pale.

Suri's brief moment of humour died at the mention of Sotoledi, the pagan Death God. "I'll explain it to him."

Aisha blew out a breath. "I think you're the only one he'll listen to. Viantha said he nearly tore Scilla's head off just for mentioning it."

Suri groaned. "I did it to save his damned life."

"I don't think he sees it that way," Aisha said. "Be careful."

Suri opened her mouth to carve a retort, then stopped. She met Aisha's dark eyes, and nodded once.

Aisha studied Suri's body once more, then leaned back and stretched to her full height. "I'll let him in."

"He's here?" Suri breathed, her heart jumping in her chest. He'd been waiting this whole time? And she hadn't let him in?

Aisha smiled. "He asked to see you. I wanted to check if you were ready."

"Ready?" Suri echoed. She'd been asking to see him for the whole time she was here.

Aisha winked and opened the door. She was barely a woman grown and puppeteering them all as readily as anything. Waris had taught her more than she thought.

A deep voice spoke from behind it as soon as Aisha slipped from the room. Suri did not catch the words, but then she saw him.

Kol strode past Aisha into the room, scanning the bare dusty shelves, the grime-encrusted single high window and scattered cobwebs with a frown. Then his eyes found her. They blazed with a hundred emotions, half of them surprisingly kind.

His hair was washed, his stubble shaved clean. There was something of a wildness to him which felt different, as if he was learning how to be a person for the first time. His hand on the door was to claim it rather than grip it, his movements were jerky. But he seemed himself. More than himself, she realised.

His skin glowed. It was faint, perhaps only noticeable to those like herself who had studied every pore of his face more times than she wanted to admit. But beyond the usual pearl skin there was something of a sheen, an effervescence, that signalled Diophage's magic. Here was the Son of Life.

Alive and well. Because of her.

A small noise escaped her as she pushed herself back up, and he caught it. Anger swept across his wide mouth and brow.

"Hello," she said.

He swallowed, his throat bobbing. He glanced at Aisha, still in the door, staring between them with a twinkle in her eyes. As soon as she noticed Kol's look, she disappeared. He pushed the door closed, his hand shaking slightly as he held it against the wood and waited for a couple of breaths.

Then he strode towards her. She moved back on the bed, sweeping her knees round to sit cross-legged and braced herself for the coming storm, expecting him to berate her.

She sucked in a breath as his black cape whipped behind him, his eyes holding a fierceness which felt foreign and new. She'd forgotten how intoxicatingly intense his presence was, addictive even as it fried every nerve in her body.

Then he dropped to his knees in front of her, and hung his head.

She barely had a moment to feel shocked before he spoke.

"Suri. I—I have thought for a full day on what I would say to you. It has felt like a week, and I still find I don't know where to begin."

Suri swallowed, her mind scattered from his sombre tone.

"I am so, so deeply sorry," he said.

"Kol," Suri said, more from surprise than any real want to reply. He jolted his head up and she saw that this fearsome anger was little more than self-directed loathing. "What—"

"You should never have had to do what you did. It was a terrible thing, for it to even be on the table. And to lose your soul." He choked on the word. "For you to lose your soul in order to get this bargain. To nearly lose yourself retrieving mine. It is something I could never repay."

"I don't want you to repay it."

His eyes narrowed. "I need to. I need to find some way to repair all the hurt I have caused you. I promise I will get your soul back."

"Kol—"

"Let me see your back. Aisha said you were hurt."

Suri thought to argue, but his face wasn't having it and she figured he'd see at some point. So she sighed, but obliged, reaching behind and pulling up the age-softened grey shirt which sat loose over the injuries, gathering the fabric in front of her until half her back was exposed.

Kol ghosted a hand over her back, touching only the very sides, far away from the cuts. Even then his touch was a feather, as if she was an inch from breaking. "I will tear them apart."

"I killed the cat already."

"You know that's not what I meant."

Suri dropped her top and turned to him. "If you truly believed Thandul and Shaedon had plotted to blow up *your* city, how would you have reacted? What would you have done to them?"

Kol gritted his teeth, and the answer shone through as plain as day. *Worse.*

"Exactly," she said. "I'm surprised they honoured the blood bond at all."

"There's more to blood magic than seers and Bloodhounds. And far more hounds than those you've seen. It's not a balance even a King would want to upset." He shuddered. "Ask Waris some time about it."

Suri grimaced, thinking of the dancing corpses littering that blood witch's lair. "I'd rather not."

"Gods, I am so sorry, Suri." Kol's expression softened. "I'm sorry I couldn't help you. I have lived without a soul for decades, and now when I am whole, it is because you cannot be. It's a sick joke."

"We'll find a way," Suri said, with a smirk that didn't reach her eye, the movement more from memory than mirth. "Maybe it's some cosmic balance. Our lands need at least one horrible soulless monster at all times. It's my turn, clearly. Maybe I'll get a nickname, too."

A ghost of a smile traced his lips, too. "Lady of Death. The Demon Queen."

Her brief humour abruptly ended. Those were *his* nick-names: Lord of Death, The Demon King. For him to flip them, it almost sounded like they were partners. *His* Lady, *his* Queen? Is that what he meant? She glanced at his near black eyes and saw the mirth drop from them, too.

He changed the subject. "Will you accept my apology?"

"For what?"

"For putting you in a position where you had to save me?"

She raised an eyebrow. "Can you assure me you will never again need saving?"

Kol furrowed his brow and his wide mouth pursed. "I suppose I cannot."

"Then I will not allow you to apologise for it, and I will not accept your apology," she said. He opened his mouth, but she didn't stop speaking. "I did what was right. Right by the world, to bring the Son of Life back so you might bring life magic back to the world. Right by my brother, as that deal forgave all of our crimes too, and gave him his house. Right by your court. By you."

Kol shook his head then raked a finger through his curls, and the mannerism was so quintessentially him it made her stomach clench. "And yourself? To become this, to enrage and steal from Sotoledi? You must know he will come for you. You have lost yourself in saving me."

The words made her shudder, but she shook the fear from her head. Sotoledi could not harm her. Not now, not if she kept her amefyre on and blocked him out. This was a price she was willing to pay, and it didn't have to be permanent.

Suri reached her hand out for Kol's and he gripped hers back immediately. She noticed then his ragged nails, something his healing had failed to disguise. Chipped and torn, as if he'd tried to claw his way out of his cell.

She rubbed her thumb over his hand, hesitantly. "I've been lost my whole life and alone for half of it. Then I lost my soul. Yet somehow, I feel I belong now, more than ever. I'm part of something. You gave me that when you trusted me, and along the way, Nadrian and Scilla trusted me, too. I would give up my soul again today to have people who would look for me in the darkness. Not because they want anything from me, but because they believe I am worth it."

Kol steeled his jaw, his eyes starry.

Suri looked at the floor, unable to meet his gaze. He looked at her as if she was something greater than the sum of her parts, but she knew whatever altruism he saw in her was only a reflection of her selfish desire to keep him near. "We need you. All of us.

The world, your court. *I* need you. Don't apologise for letting me save you when I did it to save myself."

Kol lifted his other hand to her chin, brushing his thumb across her jaw. He raised her head lightly. She swallowed back the fearful lump in her throat and made herself meet those dark eyes again.

He stared at her with more heat and brightness than she knew possible. He was glowing again, fully this time, shining out rays of pure light and reminding her what it was like to hold his soul. How it had been enough light to penetrate for miles in that dark place. It was like staring at the sun, but she didn't pull her eye away.

Kol rubbed her cheek again, a smile forming. It had been one of her favourites. That weird feeling of joy tried to rise up, before it was quelled, as if a candle snuffed in her chest. "Thank you."

Suri scoffed. "You're welcome."

"I meant my promise, though, I will get your soul back. We'll leave as soon as you're well enough to travel to Xianyu's. There must be some price, some bauble I can find in payment."

She nodded. "We can pay the price together."

"You should know," Kol said. "Jem sent word from Akdaria."

Suri froze. "What is it?"

She held her breath, the fear lancing through her.

If Jem had sent word, surely it meant he was still alive. Kol gave his soul to Sotoledi eighty years ago in exchange for the lives of those lost in the Wrath, but there was a catch. Those he brought back were trapped on the island of Akdaria, and attempting to pass through Sotoledi's Gate would kill them. Suri had taken

Kol's soul back, and none of them knew what effect that would have on the deal.

"Everyone is alive," Kol said, and her relief came out in a gasp. "They knew something had happened though, as a woman got her blood."

Suri frowned. "She wasn't having it before?"

Kol shook his head. "No, for the whole time, everyone was locked, unchanging. We think they are now ageing once more."

"Is that a bad thing?"

"Some enjoyed their unchanging bodies, others hated them. At least now, there is a natural order restored. A sense of the cycle of life back, some normalcy."

"What of the Gate? Can they pass through?"

"I don't think anyone has yet tried," Kol said, then he smirked. "But Agata is already inundated with requests from the women. They haven't had to worry about children in decades."

Suri replied with a wry levity. "Don't tell them it was me who brought the curse of blood and babies back upon them, then. They will mutiny."

Kol chuckled. "Now, there's something I need to do."

"What?"

Kol tilted his head. "A royal message arrived at Edi's. They must have followed us there after the arena. The meeting you requested is at dawn tomorrow."

"So soon?" Suri said, seeing the light fading outside the dirty window. It was twilight already.

"They don't want to give us any more time to recover than we've already had. We're weak, on the back foot. It's what I would have done, too."

"Are you going?" Suri asked.

"I want to," he said, rubbing her cheek idly again. It made her heart jump each time, and she wasn't sure if he was aware he was still doing it. "But it is a rare commodity to have the world think you dead. I want to use it. See how Lera acts, thinking I'm gone. See what pieces move."

"If you're not going to the meeting, what is it you need to do?"

He smiled, and it dazzled her. She hadn't realised how much of the warmth of his smile had been sucked from him when he had no soul. Now, it transformed him. Was that what she was like? A distorted version, smiling through frosted glass, sucked of the little joy she'd ever had? The thought chilled her.

He rocked back on his heels and his hand dropped from her face, and she felt chilled ever more. "Two things. First, I *am* going to the meeting." She furrowed her brow. "I'm just not going as me."

"What is that supposed to mean?"

He winked. "You'll see."

Something inside her knotted tight. His wink had awakened the lust she'd tried to bury, but her body betrayed her when he toyed with her like this. "And the second thing?" she asked, her breath catching in her throat.

"You might not have specified a time for the meeting, but you did specify one thing: the meeting is with Kol's court. Nadrian is, for all official purposes, my Master of Trade. Scilla is my War General. They can go."

"So?"

"You can't nearly die for a meeting you don't even get invited to." His eyes glowed. "We need to make you a member."

2

It was my time to leave, the walls were too constricting and my science too little respected.
Unknown author, est. 2nd-5th century

The moment they walked into the Royal Quarter, four guards flanked them.

Nadrian raised an eyebrow at Suri. "I suppose it's just the three of us?"

The grey spring sky was lightening by the minute, but the night's chill felt as wintery as ever. She was glad again for the lined green cloak Xianyu had given her back in the Fae glen.

A sleepy Nadrian had greeted her outside the butcher shop and together they'd met up with a resigned Scilla. All three of them looked much further away from death than they had two days ago.

Kol was nowhere to be seen.

She took another look at each guard, assessing their faces, expressions, checking for some signal that Kol was amongst them, glamoured to resemble them, and saw nothing to alert her. Maybe when he spoke of attending unseen, he didn't mean anything as extravagant as glamours, maybe he meant he'd monitor them through seeing silk.

She shrugged. "I suppose so."

The Royal Quarter was subdued at this time of day, with no need to hustle for the best prices and no work better done in darkness. They might have been a week into spring, but frost still clung to the evenly tiled roofs, and nested in the empty flower beds latched to the storefronts. New Politan slept on, waiting for the true end of winter, which would take another few weeks.

Before long, they reached the Royal Square. It was giant, fit for fetes of thousands in that one area alone. At its centre, surrounded by a narrow moat, was a small tower accessible only via a manned bridge. In that stone tower sat the Gate linking New Politan to its castle, remotely located on a nearby island.

To Suri's surprise, King Thandul stood on the stairs, his hands clasped. His greying hair had been freshly oiled, his clothes pressed and then arranged artfully, with his pinned cloak splaying over one shoulder. He even wore all of his garish rings, coating his fingers. Yet his face betrayed what the rest of his presentation could not. He looked old, and tired.

"Guests," he said in a flat voice, as they reached the bottom step of the bridge. "You are welcome."

"How gracious you are," Nadrian said.

A flutter of wings thudded from behind Suri as something oddly heavy landed on her shoulder. She darted her head round and flinched.

A runtish bat sat on her right shoulder, its head flicking one way and then another, not looking at her. She caught its eyes anyway, and they were blood red. It settled itself, grabbing more firmly onto her shoulder, its claws finding purchase on her cloak and the skin underneath it.

She struggled not to react or cry out, conscious not to draw too much attention to herself. A bat, really, Kol? Surely there were eight hundred options less conspicuous than this.

Thandul cleared his throat and Suri jolted her eye back to the King. But he was looking at Nadrian, still. "A private audience was requested. By the nature of royal private audiences, we will, of course, still be attended by a small personal retinue. Two Bloodhounds will also be present to ensure everything goes as it should."

"Naturally," Nadrian replied, bristling. "Just as you recall that Suri requested you treat us as distinguished guests."

Thandul's hand shook at his side, and he clenched it into a fist. "You imply I would seek to hurt those under the protection of blood magic. Do you think me a fool?"

"Gods, no," Nadrian said. "Fools are far more entertaining."

Thandul paled, and then his cheeks blossomed in a combination of embarrassment and anger. His lip curled, but he calmed himself. "Enter."

Nadrian and Scilla climbed the stairs. Suri followed, conscious of the strange weight of the bat on her shoulder. The guards hadn't questioned it, perhaps thinking it was some custom. She realised that perhaps it *was* some sort of custom, one she wasn't aware of. Was a familial bat some kind of token, did it mean anything?

She was so woefully unprepared, and decided to act like it was nothing.

At the top of the stairs, Nadrian and Scilla bowed. Suri didn't want to dislodge the weird Kol-bat on her shoulder, so instead she bobbed in an awkward curtsy.

Thandul did not return the gesture, only waving towards the Gate. It was a doorway of stone, holding a black void. Dark and impenetrable, as water in the middle of a moonless night. "After you."

Nadrian nodded, and stepped through the Gate and disappeared. Scilla hesitated, before taking the step herself.

Suri was alone now, both her companions swallowed through to its twin. Within the space of a single step, the void would transport them, little more than black air holding a fold between this place and another. Though to Suri, it never felt like air, it was thicker than that. It pulled at her stomach, as if she was falling.

"Wait," Thandul said, recognising her for the first time. He scanned her from head to toe, eyes snagging on the bat before training on her face. "The invitation was for members of Kol's court, girl. The blood bond was sealed to those words."

Suri swallowed. "I am a member of Kol's court."

Thandul frowned, as if he would refuse her, studying her dress and the strange bat. Then he shrugged with a deep weariness she rarely saw on men. "If you are not, blood will out."

King Thandul had led the Forgelands for decades, and had always been known as a proud and vain king. Whilst generally respected, as much as any rich man could be, he was always distant, a figure carved in stone who rarely appeared to his subjects. Here, staring into the void, he seemed defeated.

She took a breath, glancing at the bat as if to give Kol a second to warn her if anything bad was likely to happen. The bat seemed disinterested, glancing around the square.

That was as good a sign as any.

She stepped through the Gate and that same feeling swamped her senses. A tug in her stomach, a twist deep in her body. A sensation of hollowness, a scream so distant it was almost silent.

Then she was through the other side, standing with the others on the balcony overlooking the main ballroom, the bat still there and unperturbed by the travel. The air was stale, carrying with it a scent of old ale and soaped floorboards. The fallout of last week's Winter's End still marked the room, with red streamers hanging from the chandeliers and a fresh stag's head pinned above the throne. It oozed dark blood, its eyes bulbous and mouth ajar.

"Please forgive my son's lack of manners in not greeting your party today. He awaits us in the dining hall."

Nadrian sniffed, likely ready to say something that would turn Thandul's face an entirely new shade of purple.

"I imagine he has been quite overwhelmed by the changes in the last few days," Scilla cut in, dipping her head. "Your Grace."

"Quite," Thandul replied.

The Northern King led their party through the castle, and Scilla shot Nadrian a look of warning which he duly ignored.

As soon as they were out of the ballroom, everything they passed was new to Suri, yet it all felt a harmonious extension of the ballroom with the same dark, rich colours in the tapestries and the same hardy stone floors. Yet now, this, which was so distinctly northern, no longer felt like home. The heavy walls and furnishings didn't soothe her. She felt entombed by it all.

She missed Akdaria. The once hopeful longing for its greenery, the bittersweet desire to return home, twisted in her broken soulless body to a pitiable yearning.

"Strange pet, you have." The voice was little more than a wheezing hiss.

Suri swung her head to see a Bloodhound, head cocked as he stared at the bat on her shoulder. His pallid skull reminded her of something long dead and she nodded once, turning back forward.

"I knew someone with a blood bat once," his voice croaked. "She said it was the only one left."

Her shoulders tensed. Why would Kol disguise himself as something so rare? Couldn't he be a fly, or a rat, or anything a little less strange?

"Probably to con you into buying it for a silly amount of coin," she said over her shoulder, avoiding having to look at his creepy face again. She wasn't sure what it was exactly, but the Bloodhounds didn't feel like people. It was like seeing one of Waris' reanimated corpses.

"Perhaps."

She trained her eye forward, not looking at bat-Kol, or acknowledging the Bloodhounds at her back.

Then Thandul stopped, and two guards opened the thick double doors to his left. He stepped over the threshold, and their party followed.

A thick indigo rug covered half the floor, and a large dining table sat atop it, covered in a sickening display of food considering the hour. A plump plucked pheasant sat centre stage, adorned with peaches and assorted herbs and greenery. Suri glanced at the others, but they didn't seem too confused by the feast laid out for a dawn meeting. She pitied the cooks tasked with braising a bird through the night.

The Prince sat at the head of the table at the far end from where they entered. He had eaten half a plate of food already, and pinned Nadrian with a glare the moment they walked in.

"Be welcome," Thandul said.

The three attendants in the dining hall bobbed. Two of the attendants were clearly kin, a boy and a girl with button noses and red hair so alike they could be twins. The third, a tall boy with mousy brown hair, stood at Shaedon's side, holding a polished silver carafe.

Shaedon did not stand when they entered, nor bow. Instead, he tapped his finger on the top of his goblet, and his attendant rushed to refill it. The Prince's eyes glazed over the rest of them, before focusing in on her. His lips were stained purplish and his skin looked grey, and she guessed that for him this dawn meeting was coming at the end of a long night without slumber. A night full of wine, from what she could tell. "What's she doing here?"

Her golden blood bond pulsed at her chest, a hint of uncomfortable warmth.

Aisha had bought some vaguely presentable clothes for them from the Merchant's Quarter, which fit as well as could reasonably be expected without tailoring. For Suri, that meant she was once again garbed in Northern colours and style, the red corseted dress equipped with a full and heavy skirt built for the colder climate. Once again, she missed the tunic with the flowing trousers she wore in Akdaria. The air here felt too breathy, as if there was nothing to it, no thickness of substance or heart. It didn't help that Shaedon's sneer seemed to find every fault in her; her defensive posture, and the way her dark hair escaped its braid. The boots she chose to wear instead of a heel.

Thandul's tone was firm. "She is here as a member of Kol's court."

"What, then," Shaedon seethed. "Some sort of jester. That act you put on in that arena... all part of one big joke at our expense. Only an idiot would be stupid enough to kill the leader of her own court. And she's here with a fucking rat on her shoulder. It's probably diseased."

The anger swept over her so quickly it was hard to smother. Her hand flicked for a weapon that wasn't there and her eye caught on the sharp fork sticking from the rump of the pheasant.

Then the bat moved on her shoulder, its claws pinching back into her skin. A warning?

"Careful, handsome," Nadrian snapped, as Suri took a deep breath. "I wouldn't poke fun at our new Mistress of Coin. She bites."

Shaedon choked as his face reddened. "A backwater thief, the Mistress of Coin? Now that is surely a joke."

Yes, she wanted to say, *it was*. But her bond flared hot again, and she grimaced.

Kol had offered her a number of titles to choose from.

Mistress of Beasts. This one she objected to out of hand, as it would require her to have knowledge of horses, of which she had none, and besides, she was still far too scared of the creatures.

Ax's role was offered, too, formally denoted as the Master of Messages. Spy master, in all reality. Her penmanship was far too shoddy to be sending missives far and wide, and worse, she couldn't think of his birds and messages without picturing his severed head rolling in the wood chips.

Mistress of Coin, though. It made her smile. For someone with less than three days to her name where she carried more than fifty silver, it seemed comical enough for her title to suggest she managed the coin of an entire Kingdom.

Now, seeing the look on Shaedon's face, it was the right choice.

Thandul interrupted, with a nervous look to the Bloodhounds. "Shaedon. These are our distinguished guests. Remember the bond."

She realised then why the Bloodhounds were there. It wasn't to scare them, or to try to provoke their cooperation. At least, not in entirety. They *had* to be there. They were adjudicating… whatever this was. The deal had been bound in blood; if the King or Prince were to subvert the terms of their agreement or to renege on anything, the magic would flare.

It explained why her mark had heated up again when the Prince spoke to them as he had, because he was supposed to treat them as guests. Treating them poorly at this meeting would constitute *them* breaking the blood bond. What would happen then? Would the Bloodhounds take Thandul's hand after all, as he initially wagered?

Shaedon clearly knew it, too. He gritted his teeth and stared at the floor for a moment, and when he pulled his chin back up, his eyes were forcefully neutral. He stood, bowing to her. "I apologise, daughter of the North. I don't believe we have been formally introduced. Pray, would you do me the honour of giving me your name and titles?"

There was a slither of malice in his words, an insinuation that, of course, she had no titles. Her bond didn't flare up, though. It made sense, in some strange way, that the bond allowed for diplomatic aggression and threats hidden in words. The same honour was long bestowed on real distinguished guests. Daggers hidden in pretty wrapping.

Suri smiled. He had to be nice to them, at least outwardly, no matter what she said. "I gave you a false name before," she said, her voice sickly sweet. "You knew me as Edi, shadow killer of the Tangle, when you sentenced me to my exile. Now you can know me again."

Shaedon stared at her.

She met his gaze without flinching. "My name is Suri Hillsend. Backwater thief, kidnapper of princesses, murderer of many. Mistress of Coin in the Life Court, and the new Seer of Time."

Shaedon's face went white, then a little blue, but he had the good sense not to say anything. Thandul stiffened, and looked at Suri in a completely new way.

"As the Seer of Time," Nadrian drawled. "She is under the protection of the Fae Glen. She is also under my personal protection."

"You have claimed your birthright, then?" Thandul asked.

Nadrian frowned. "Not as such. Xianyu remains the steward of the Glen. But as one of its princes, I am as bound by our oaths to the Seers as you are bound to this meeting."

Suri was unused to hearing Nadrian be so serious. She could see it troubled him to discuss the Glen, and she thought back to the moment in the arena, when Thandul had taunted him. *A cowardly heir whose actions caused the deaths of all his siblings.*

"Sit, let us discuss this around the table like men." Thandul stood by the opposite end of the table, leaving three places on each side to pick from.

Despite her desire to be as far away from both these *men* as possible, she figured leaving an empty seat between her and both the Forgelands' regents might be seen as rude. She studied the table, assessed Shaedon's sour face, and selected the seat to Thandul's right. Scilla took the middle seat directly next to her, in front of the bird, and notably also a distance from Shaedon.

Nadrian, however, swept his red hair back and noisily pulled out the chair to Shaedon's right, diagonally across from Suri. The two redheaded men were a warping mirror of each other, and were it not for Shaedon's impressive attitude, she might think they were related. Though, if Nadrian were to release his constant glamour, he would outshine his moody tablemate even further.

The attendants moved into action, offering food and filling their cups with wine. The boy with the mousy hair paused beside her, and she glanced up as he filled her wine, his lips twitching at the bat on her shoulder.

After serving Suri, he didn't move away, lingering behind her. She tensed. Had he been ordered to watch her? She supposed she didn't have the best history at these sorts of events. The last time she was at a fancy party in the Forgelands, she killed a man in the middle of the ballroom. But, she reasoned, she had actually been helping Thandul there, if by accident, so all of this guarding was distinctly unnecessary.

Thandul raised his goblet and they all followed suit. He took a deep swig of wine, and put his cup down, and they drank, too.

The silence was weighty.

"Now, will you tell us your reason for demanding such an audience?" the King asked.

Scilla glanced around the room. "I understand the need for your immediate men-at-arms. The Bloodhounds, too, and a taster, if you believe they are needed. But any others can leave. There are sensitive matters to be discussed."

The boy behind her made some small noise. Almost a choke.

Shaedon bristled. "But—"

"I'm sure you are more than capable of pouring your own wine, prince," Nadrian interrupted, tapping the prince's hand.

Shaedon tore his hand away, standing abruptly. His chair pitched backwards, and the girl grabbed it to stop it from falling over entirely.

The room held its breath as one.

Scilla's hand clenched on her cutlery. Suri gripped the armrests of her chair, ready to move at a moment's notice. Nadrian did nothing. He didn't look outwardly nervous, merely pinning

Shaedon with a pitying look. But she saw through the glamour, saw how his wings poised for action.

The Bloodhounds too, had moved, both of them taking a solemn step away from the wall. She had no idea what they would do if displeased, but from her brief taste of their speed, she really did not want to find out.

Thandul raised his hand, shooting his son another look. Shaedon's jaw quivered, taking in the room and the reaction of the Bloodhounds. He glared down at Nadrian and slowly sat again.

"It is not a matter of the Prince's autonomy. All the attendants cannot hear a word. Deaf, all," Thandul said. Again, Suri heard a scuffle from behind her. She whipped her head around to see the mousy boy drop his gaze to the floor in an instant. He had this distinctly odd look of forced solemnity, like a child forced to mourn for an elder they never met. There was some hidden mischief there. "Those two, from the explosion at the mine. And him, from birth," Thandul continued, loosely pointing at the boy studiously focused on the rug. "Do you still object to their presence?"

Suri realised a couple of things at once. The first, that she was a complete idiot. The second, that the boy behind her, who seemingly had just worked out he was supposed to be deaf, must be Kol.

So, what, in the Trio's name, was the fucking bat on her shoulder?

She saw Nadrian staring over her shoulder at the boy. A near invisible smile gave away that he'd come to the same conclusion as her. He didn't seem as confused by the bat, though.

Scilla paused. "If you believe them to hold no threat, they may stay."

The boy, or Kol, relaxed. Suri didn't know how she hadn't felt it before. Even now, with her senses so muted and her amefyre blocking Sotoledi's influence, there was something coming *back* from the boy's body that was hard to ignore. A hum, a presence. She sensed the tension from him like a ripple, and then it disappeared.

Thandul let out an aggrieved sigh. "Now then, why are we here?"

Nadrian waved towards Scilla.

Scilla dabbed her mouth. "Kol had nothing to do with, nor no knowledge of, the proposed attacks in New Politan."

Thandul didn't seem surprised. "Do you have proof of this?"

"Proof to the negative?" Nad jumped in.

Thandul raised an eyebrow.

Scilla shot Nadrian a look. "No, we do not have proof that confirms Kol's *lack* of involvement. Axri'don was acting as his own agent, bought out by another."

"That is convenient when both Axri'don and Kol are gone. You speak of the dead, I am concerned with the living," Thandul replied.

"We would tell you a story of what really happened, and you can decide which tale is more likely. That Kol would launch an unprovoked assault on your population, or that Lera would."

3

The Drangborian hills are more than refreshing, and every stride fills me with a sense of true purpose.
Unknown author, est. 2nd-5th century

"No," Thandul said yet again, as Suri rubbed at her forehead. They'd been here nearly two hours, and it turned out wine first thing in the morning was beyond an awful idea. "We cannot agree to that."

"What will you do, then?" Scilla said. "Just sit here as Lera creates a second Wrath, and kills every soul in the Parched Lands? Will you pluck birds and drink wine as she forms the world to her making?"

"These are stories and rumours," Shaedon replied, but his voice shook. "Nothing more."

"Witness the story, then," Scilla said, looking between both of them as spit flew from her mouth. "If you will not fight at our side, if you will not act, then agree to watch."

Thandul put his cup down with force. “Do you think me blind? I see all that happens in our kingdom and the kingdoms beneath us.”

“I don’t mean watch from your stone castle,” Scilla replied, with far more poise than Suri could have claimed in that moment. “If Lera declares war on us, as we believe she will, then we would ask you to ride to our city. Not to fight, not to speak. But to observe it all. See what she is truly like, beneath the veil.”

Suri nodded. *Asari ith vulturis.* To beware the harpy, they had to see her for who she was, know the evil she intended.

Thandul paused, considering this. Shaedon, too, did not chime in with some immediate dismissal. Scilla waited for their words, knowing they were reaching the end of the Northerners' patience.

Suri held her breath. Maybe they had finally made ground. Even Nadrian leaned forward, though he’d lost faith in the meeting near an hour ago.

King Thandul leaned back. “We make no promises to witness at your city.” Suri deflated and Scilla’s lips tightened. “My final offer is this. If Queen Lera launches a war at your feet, we will not stand with her.”

Nadrian groaned. “That is it, then. You offer us neutrality.”

Thandul didn’t react to Nadrian, only looking at Scilla. But Scilla wasn’t looking at the King, she instead flicked her gaze to the serving boy standing behind Shaedon’s shoulder. A moment passed, which Nadrian distracted the regents from with an ungracious slurp of wine, and then Scilla met Thandul’s gaze anew.

“Fine,” Scilla said wearily, standing up. “If that is your final offer, we will accept it.”

King Thandul stood, also, and the two approached one another. Again, the Bloodhounds stepped, and Suri turned nearly fully in her chair to observe the pair.

They stared at each other, shook hands, and it was done. Within seconds, the meeting was promptly and summarily dismissed.

The three of them, alongside the strange bat, left the castle without hesitation. Suri sighed as they moved back through the Royal Square, relieved to be in the fresh morning air.

Thandul seemed pensive, but hardly willing, and Shaedon refuted every single word. They had left on barely greater footing than when they arrived.

Beyond that agreement of neutrality, all they'd agreed was that Esra was permitted to stay in the North. None of the sworn members of Kol's court were welcome in the city without express permission, brought by written request to the King by Esra or another chosen representative. They had to leave by tomorrow night or they would be arrested the following dawn. What they would be arrested for didn't seem to matter, and clearly their forgiveness to all past crimes wouldn't extend to newly invented ones.

In swearing fealty to Kol's court, Suri had already lost the welcome of her childhood home forever. Rage hummed in her blood, and she tried to think with clarity, to linger on the good in the situation. Esra was safe. He would have a house here and be treated with respect. They had come out of the meeting alive. Gods, they had come out of the last days and *weeks* alive. Her back was healing, and she hadn't succumbed to Sotoledi in his lair. Kol hadn't been caught out or noticed, and he was whole again. They hadn't convinced the North this time, but they had a genuine audience, and they had sown the seeds of uncertainty in Thandul's mind at the least.

She should be feeling fine. Hopeful, even.

But instead, every foul look Shaedon had given them twisted and replayed until her mood was jet black.

The guards stopped following them at the edge of the Royal Quarter and the bat flew off of her shoulder without a second glance.

She scowled up at it, rubbing at her shoulder. "What was that thing?"

Scilla scoffed, her brow raising. "You don't know? You invited it in with you!"

"I thought it was Kol," she said, bluntly. "And then I saw *him* and realised."

Scilla slapped her hand over her mouth, and Nadrian choked on a laugh until it burst from him like a dam. Scilla chuckled as Nadrian worked himself into a greater and greater fit of laughter.

He glanced up at her through teary eyes and then started cackling again at her angry expression. "You thought—Kol—would somehow morph himself into a blood bat," he said, pausing to laugh. "For hours?"

Suri rolled her eye, finding no humour at all. "I don't know how glamours work."

Nadrian's laugh only got louder and even Scilla let out a guffaw. Suri just glowered at them. Eventually, after what felt like an eternity, he straightened and breathed shakily in and out, rubbing tears from his green eyes. "It takes me a lot of energy each day to maintain this one, and all I'm changing is my wings and taking the edge off my features. I think if I tried to morph myself into a bat, I'd either have to sell my soul for that level of magic, or it would last about half a second."

"So, what was it?" Suri asked.

"It belongs to Waris," Scilla supplied.

"Waris," Suri echoed. She'd had a blood witch's spy scrabbling over her shoulder for hours.

Nadrian smiled. "She must have been nosy. Not a lot of blood bonds like that get fulfilled these days."

And, of course, the bat wouldn't have settled on the shoulders of the two people that actually knew what it was. It had to land on *her* shoulder. She wondered if Waris had told the bat to land on her, as some kind of odd mockery, or whether the bat had decided to make her a laughing stock of its own volition.

Suri scowled at the ground, and then turned from the pair of them.

Scilla spoke to her back. "Suri, what is it?"

"Nothing. I'm going for a walk."

"I'll come with you."

"No," Suri spat, with more venom than even she intended. She took a deep breath and contained the rage that shook across her entire body. "I need to go alone."

"That's not a good idea," Nadrian said from behind her.

The rage came back, swift and fast. She stopped dead. She closed her eye as she resisted the urge to scream in their faces. When the murderous urge lessened, she looked back at them and the concern on both their faces only irritated her further.

"Please, just leave me alone. This is my home. It's a few hours. I'll be fine."

She didn't give them enough time to reply. She simply turned and left, spine rigid and toes curled.

Her shoulders loosened when she realised they weren't following her, and something like disappointment joined the festering of hatred withering endlessly in her stomach.

The streets were colder than ever before. The morning ticked towards noon and everyone was in the street. A man yelled at a teen for falling asleep in his wheelbarrow, a woman dragged her kid along by the wrist.

Distracted, Suri tripped over a cobble and stumbled into a damp wall. Her vision swam, and she pulled off her eyepiece, suddenly feeling that phantom itch. She stuffed the fabric into her pocket, resenting the fine clothes almost as much as herself.

Her disfigured face finally matched the Tangle. It was who she was, no point in hiding. She'd never been able to hide from anything here, as much as she had always wanted to.

The cobbles blended into the walls and those in turn blended into the sky and she was hit by how grey everything was. This was where she was made, a body forged in shadows and stained walls. A world of foul smells and leering glances. No wonder Sotoledi found her; she was carved out of every dark place there was. A gutter girl through and through, fit only for death.

Her black mood continued as she wandered through the Tangle. Her feet tried to take her to Mother Edi's but she didn't let them. Instead, she forced herself to walk into the darkest parts of the web, snaking down tight alleys.

She didn't know what she was looking for. A fight, maybe. Something to challenge her, someone to see nothing more than what she always was.

Instead, she saw a doorway she recognised.

A long-abandoned bakery on the far edge of the Tangle, piled up against the city wall. Destined to fail, of course, no one with a coin in their pocket or a good place to be would come here.

She herself had only visited once when it was open. At least, she thought she did. It was one of those memories that hazed around the edges, uncertain if she invented it from her brother's story or truly experienced it. A sweet cake hot to the touch, a round man slapping her hand away, a muffled shout.

When the family moved on and the faintly sweet smoke stopped billowing from its roof, Esra dragged them down there.

Suri stepped through the doorway.

Bare shelves, dusty floor. The soot still sat in the mouth of the large brick oven. She moved past the cold counters and dead insects on the windowsill, and pushed open the stiff wooden door to the storeroom, then to the next door. She walked through, and it was like she went back in time.

Nothing about it had changed. Frozen for the last ten years.

There, on the far side of the room, two rusting knives lodged in a faded painted wooden box, one off-target, another dead centre, splintering the wood. A straw bed covered with dirty cloth waited in a corner to her right.

And then to her left, only one pace from the entrance, a dark brown stain on the floor. Clacker's blood, long dried. Tasting the staleness of the dusty air was the only way she separated herself from feeling ten years old again.

"Look who's back."

For a second, she thought it was Esra.

She turned, and the coil in her chest tightened ever more. That part of her that could still feel Sotoledi's influence throbbed. "Geren."

He stood in the storeroom with three men behind him. No, she corrected, three boys behind him. He clearly hadn't dismissed his fan club of teenage children in the last two months. One of them might have sixteen winters behind him, but the other two looked closer to twelve.

Geren had put on weight, and he did not wear it well. His clothing pulled at its seams, and his coin pouch hung under his belly like the bell of a goat. It was a sign of wealth, certainly, but it was also an advertisement of that wealth, and therefore dangerous. Rings clad his fingers like some mockery of the King's own jewellery, only his were gaudier somehow.

"Suri." Geren's study lingered on her missing eye and the rich cloak about her shoulders. She saw him note its weight, its likely value. "You look ridiculous."

She snorted. "Have you seen yourself?"

Geren took two steps forward and his shadows moved with him. "Do you think you're better than us now? You're a rat. You've always been a rat."

Suri didn't step back. There was no exit behind her, after all, there was only through. She paused, waiting for that familiar trickle of fear to come. She was outnumbered four to one, and even if half of them were kids, she knew how vicious children could be. She only needed to glance at the bloodstain by her feet to prove it.

But the fear didn't come.

In its place, there was only anticipation. An accumulation of dark energy inside her which seemed to say, *this is what you wanted. This is what you came for.*

She wanted them to come at her. She wanted them to try.

Geren cocked his head, mistaking her silence for nerves. He stepped forwards once more until he was three steps from her. "Nothing to say?"

Suri breathed in and out. She could taste their sweat and body odour.

Gods, she wanted to kill them. She wanted to tear them apart.

And worse, she wasn't sure she'd succeed, she just wanted to hurl herself against something again and again. Tear it and let it tear her back. Did she want to punish them, or herself?

Before, her mind would snag against anger and she would allow herself to pause on it, revel in it. But now there was nothing else to look for. Jagged edges of negative emotions, with a wasteland of nothing in between. Hope was somehow foreign. Justice: estranged.

She fluttered her eye closed, forcing herself to not give in to the horrid urge. "I'm leaving."

"Oh, are you?" Geren mocked. She opened her eye again to see him looking back at his cronies. "Does she look like she's leaving?"

One of the younger ones laughed. "No, boss."

Suri strode forward, setting her sight on the storeroom door behind them and ignoring the itch in her hands.

Geren put his arm out and she ducked low and swerved under it. She made it under and past his first henchboy, but then a grubby hand grabbed harshly at her collar.

He wrenched her back, and she went with it so as not to strangle herself.

She whipped her body around, staring daggers at the boy as several more hands grabbed at her arms. “Don’t fucking touch me.”

“Who do you think you are?” Geren asked, leering down at her. “You get one cheap dress and luck out in the arena and you think you’re a fucking princess?”

She spat on the floor at Geren’s feet. “One more chance to let me go.”

Geren laughed. He wasn’t scared. He should have been.

“I warned you.”

Her voice came out as a shudder as her eye fluttered and she let Sotoledi’s influence creep across her body, as she had at the altar and in Rasel’s manor.

Suri clutched the hand at the back of her neck first, twisting it around so quickly she felt the snap under her fingers. She ducked as if pulled down by a puppeteer, eye closed as the swoop of air above her confirmed she had narrowly avoided a firm punch to the face. She twisted, her body moving unnaturally, dodging a kick to the ribs. She jabbed once. Twice. She punched into a gut and tore her fingers around, claw-like, as a white face loomed in front of her.

If they were screaming, she heard nothing over the thudding in her ears.

Suri stared upwards, and it was only the pressure of the floor at her back that made her realise they'd knocked her down. A bloodied face snarled at her, a flick of a knife in his hand.

She smirked and thrust her hands upwards, gripping the very air in front of the knife wielder. He choked, and the glint of metal fell to the floor as he pawed at his neck.

Their voices penetrated through the barrier of beating blood in her head as she pulled herself back to her feet.

"Her hands!"

"Black magic."

Some ran, but not all. There was still a target, there was still flesh. A man grappled with her, his ring-laden fingers at her neck as her own fingers squeezed his. They tumbled, one having the upper hand, then the other, both losing air. It only made the pummelling in her head louder. Every inch closer to death brought more of a smile to her face as they danced on the edge of the ultimate victory.

And then voices, more footsteps.

An order. "Stop them. Grab them, both."

"But—"

The same voice again, yelling now. "Now!"

Stronger hands than Suri could resist wrenched her backwards, locking her in a vice-like grip and tearing her from Geren's would-be corpse. They dragged her down the corridor and into the main room of the dilapidated bakery.

Two adult men held her as she thrashed against them. They did not let up. She glared at them, recognising neither.

Another two dragged Geren out, and he did not struggle.

He looked bad. A split lip, a darkening above his right cheek which would blossom into a horrible black eye, and tight red marks on his neck. The noise in her mind lowered enough for her to realise she had caused it, but not enough to care.

"That's better, isn't it?" It was the voice from before. The one who had given the order. A woman standing somewhere behind her.

Geren tried to smirk at the woman, but it came out as a pitiful grimace. "May, thank the Trio. This little bi—"

"Shut him up, please," May said.

The two men holding Geren didn't blink, one of them held Geren up as the other launched a fist into his stomach and Geren crumpled to the floor with a gasp.

May strode over to him and patted him on the head before turning to Suri.

Suri stopped struggling. The woman was short, not quite at Suri's shoulder. She had mousy brown hair and a nose dotted with freckles. Her jaw was tight and her arms corded with muscle. She'd seen some years, with ten maybe on Suri's own twenty-one.

So, this was May. Shit.

She glanced at May's scarred fist, imagining that going straight into her stomach. Suri had somehow come out of this fairly unscathed, other than the bruises already forming at her neck, and she wanted to keep it that way. It didn't seem likely that the infamous woman before her would let her walk free.

Suri went limp in the men's arms.

As soon as their grip changed, she threw her body forwards. One lost his hold immediately, but the other didn't, and redoubled his grip, and she fell to the floor as his fingers dug into her upper arm so tight she screamed.

May's voice betrayed no surprise. "Hold her still. Don't break her damn arm."

The other hands came back and pulled her up.

Suri bared her teeth at May, snarling like a yowl of a kicked cat. Geren groaned as he clutched his stomach.

May crossed her arms, staring at her. "Breathe."

Suri stared back, the breath falling out of her in pants. All the while, the murderous rage hummed quieter. Her blood came off of its boil and her fingers relaxed from their white-bone grip on nothing but air.

"You know who I am, don't you?" May asked, cocking her head.

A legend, as far as backwater Tanglers could be legends.

They called her the Tanner, though not to her face. Rumour had it she once skinned a man alive, and hung his flesh over her door for a week. To her face, she was May. The leader of the biggest gang in the Tangle, the same one Esra used to be a part of. Until Suri murdered Clacker, one of May's right-hand men.

Of course, May thought it was Esra who killed Clacker. As a child, Suri would lie awake telling herself that in a way, it was better that the King's Justice found Esra, and not May. At least in the mines, Esra had a fair chance of survival. In May's hands, who knew?

"Take her with us," May said.

Yes, Suri knew who she was. And it was time to find out if the rumours were true.

4

There is another in this town like me, another Fae disinterested in the Glen's bounty. He is odd, and I find him grating.

Unknown author, est. 2nd-5th century

Suri sat in a windowless room in an unfamiliar corner of the Tangle.

She'd caught several curious glances as May's men dragged her down the side streets and into this place. It was an orphanage once, and now it housed the largest gang in the Tangle. That didn't seem odd to Suri, growing up in a gang was pretty much the same as an orphanage, after all.

The room they sat in now must have been a broom closet in a former life, with nothing inside but two chairs nailed to the floorboards and a small table between them.

Two men stood behind Suri, ready to strike if she dared to breathe funny. She had to give it to the Tanner, her men were clearly loyal.

May sat in the chair across from her, her back to the near door, studying Suri with hazel eyes and an unfathomable expression. The table, also nailed down, held dark stains she guessed were blood rather than food-based. The perfect private torture room.

"What do you want?" Suri asked, and the question came out tired, not abrasive. A horrid sense of fatigue had washed over her as soon as she'd dropped her hold on Sotoledi.

May's gaze was serpentine. Her round face held eyes that were impossibly quick, noting everything. "I was waiting to speak to you. I followed you today since you entered the Merchant's Quarter, waiting to corner you. Did you notice?"

Suri grated her teeth together. May had been following her all day. Great.

May's mouth quirked. "I'll assume not, then."

The only useful element she could draw out of it was that May didn't seem to want her immediately dead. Maybe there was some elaborate torture planned in connection with Esra, or some other unknown crime. But she'd instructed her men not to break her arm and she'd brought her here. There was something she wanted, information, or money. She sighed. "What is this about, May?"

"When I was eleven, a man assaulted my mother," May said quickly without a flinch. "The man who did it was a noble and friends with the King. When no justice came, my father found his own. He tracked the bastard down and took his hand.

The King's Justice imprisoned him for life. My father, not the rapist."

Suri's hands shook a little on the table as she tried to follow this odd direction. "I'm sorry."

May shook her head, not unkindly. "I don't want your false pity, I'm telling you this because you need to understand. In his imprisonment, he refused to let himself get weak. He trained each day in his cell and eventually, the King saw an opportunity to use him. A few years into his imprisonment, my father became one of his gladiators. Thandul gave him a deal. Kill enough people in that arena, and he would be finally free."

May drummed her fingers on the table. Just one hand, and just the once, but it was the closest to something betraying a nerve that Suri had yet seen from her.

"He wrote to my mother all the time," she continued. "He couldn't provide for her, and the King gave no reward for his continued fights, but every week without fail, a letter would come. She wasn't able to make money of her own and nor was I, since we were the family of a criminal. No one would look at us with anything other than contempt. When I was sixteen, we'd used our last coin, and fell into nothing in the Tangle.

"I built a name for myself. I built a gang from nothing. Within five years, I had the biggest gang in the Tangle. It was enough to support my family, but my mother hated it.

"She died two years ago, when my father had been held for some seventeen years. She died with her last memory of him as a captive brute. After she passed, he still wrote to me, but not as often." May paused now, her mouth pursed as she tracked Suri's expression. "Two days ago, your friends killed him in the arena. He'd been a gladiator for nearly twenty years."

Her stomach flipped. "Shit."

It was an inelegant sentiment but it slipped out. Suri didn't know what she was expecting, but it wasn't that. May still looked calm, though, as Suri glanced around the room for anything she could use in a struggle.

Suri thought again about apologising, but it would be fake. She wasn't sorry that they had killed May's father, she couldn't be. It was kill or be killed. Every Tangle kid knew it, and if May didn't accept her apology before, she sure as Death wouldn't take it now. The thought of the lie died on her lips.

The silence stretched fifty heartbeats.

"Did you kill Clacker?" May asked, licking her lower lip. "All this time, I believed it was your brother acting to protect you. But seeing you in that arena, the way you acted, the way you spoke. It was you, wasn't it?"

Suri stared back at May, and knew she was going to tell the truth. She was fucking tired of the masquerading, and tired in general. Her head was pounding, and the truth here might spare them coming after Esra when they were done with her. "He tried to kill Esra. I didn't have a choice."

May studied her mouth and her brow. Suri studied her back, impressed that the woman could be so terrifying with rosy cheeks and freckles.

Of all the things likely to happen today, she didn't have the Tanner murdering her on the list. But then again, she went to the Tangle looking for a fight. She probably deserved to be skinned for that stupidity.

She would fight if given the opportunity to do so. But she doubted that May would let her fight fair. One click of her fingers and the men behind her would have her immobile. Another and she'd be dead.

May's expression softened. "I am in debt to you."

What?

Suri twitched. "I—What do you mean?"

May's mouth curved just a smidge. She pulled up a knee, holding it between her interlocked fingers in front of her in a strangely casual way. "He had hundreds more to kill before he would have won his freedom. He never would have survived long enough to fulfil it. He would have died a slave to the kill. A criminal. But the conditions for your blood bond. You asked forgiveness for every person, living or dead in the arena. That included my father."

May dropped her knee, staring into Suri's eye with something approaching respect. "You gave him back his honour, you absolved him of his crime."

Suri couldn't fathom it. What the fuck was going on? May had brought her here to what? Thank her for killing her beloved father? Her mind raced as she tried to work out what to say. *You're welcome?* No, that sounded glib, as though she had done it on purpose.

May seemed to see right through her. "I'm not stupid enough to believe that was your intent, but the result was the same. My family name has been cleared. I received an official pardon with a royal seal on his behalf."

Suri gave a half-shrug. "You're welcome."

Shit, it did sound glib.

"So, I might not like you. But I owe you. Name your price, and we can both move on from this." May smirked.

This was what the meeting was for. May had dragged her to a windowless closet to tell her she could pick a damned favour? If this was how May treated those she owed, she was horrified to imagine how she treated those who wronged her. Suri swallowed, realising perhaps that was the idea.

It was uncomfortable to have the Tanner of all people offering her something. Ask for too much and provoke her ire. Ask for too little and provoke the same.

But the favour she wanted rose in her mind immediately. "Protect Esra."

"Esra. The brother," May mused. "What am I protecting him from?"

"I don't know yet." May cocked an eyebrow but Suri continued, not letting it deter her. "He's back in the city, and he's soon to have a nice house in the Merchant's Quarter. That's public knowledge now. And he's injured. That's also public knowledge. Someone in the Tangle will try to take what's his. I don't know who. I would have guessed your gang but now, maybe not."

May narrowed her hazel eyes. "He's paid several times over for that crime already. I have no bad blood with him. I'll ensure my people do not act against him."

Suri blew out a breath. It was a huge weight off to even hear that, one less heavy chain tugging at her soul, one less darkness threatening to pull her underwater. But it wasn't enough. She had unlocked the worry now.

Esra would be here in the Forgelands for the rest of his hopefully long life, if Suri had anything to say about it. She couldn't promise the same for herself. Even with the aching gap of a soul, she remembered the feeling she had in Akdaria. Remembered Winter's End and playing by the pools and that almost oppressive heat clinging to her. She missed the community of it, missed the lack of fear. It had begun to feel like home, and maybe if she went back, she might not feel so empty inside.

But leaving Esra here, unprotected, after just getting him back. She couldn't do that. If they were to ever have any life here, she needed to know no one would dare to touch him and she might not always be around to help.

So, Suri took a risk. "I want more than that. Watch out for him. Not around the clock, but don't let him get sticked by a gang. If you hear something, you warn him, or you stop it yourself. If something happens to him, I will blame you. You protect him."

May stared back at her and there was an intensity in it impossible to look away from. A calculation, too. Not just of her requested favour, but of her as a person, as a woman, as a fighter.

It occurred to her then that May could be scared of her, too. She noticed the way May's gaze dropped to her hands. The twitch in her shoulders which almost looked like a shudder. May had seen Suri earlier. She couldn't fathom what she might have looked like in that state, but it hadn't *felt* human.

May shook her head. "You ask for too much. I saved your life today, and my people will leave your brother alone. That is all you are owed, all I will give you."

Suri took this in, and knew it was more than fair. The woman had no duty to her, and Suri had no bargaining chip. She opened her mouth to respond when something thudded hard against the door.

May stood and whipped around, her arms raised in front of her. The door was still closed, but it rattled hard on its hinges. A muffled voice came from the corridor.

May backed around the table towards Suri as the two men inside glanced at each other and approached the door. One braced the door while the other stood by its opening, his well-crafted knife ready to move as he stared at the door.

Another thud, and a dragging sound.

The Tanner pulled Suri out of her seat, gripping her arm tight. "Know anything about this?"

Suri shrugged. "I have a couple of suspects. Today has been a day of surprises, though."

An almighty thud hit the door and it came down in an instant, smashed completely from its hinges. The force of the burst threw the man on the other side of it halfway across the small room, his body rolling over the nailed down table until he groaned on the floor.

The man waiting with the knife had time for a breath, before he choked, his knife falling from his grip as he reached up to his neck.

Standing in the doorway, looking oddly unassuming, was the glamoured mousy Kol. His eyes darted straight to her. Whilst his face was morphed, his features plain, his stature smaller, his expression was just as deadly. "Found you."

May didn't look scared. "And who might you be?"

The man to the left of the door still lay gasping. Kol didn't appear to be killing him, but he wasn't letting up either.

Kol's eyes fell to their arms, where May still held onto Suri. His jaw twitched. May dropped her grip, noticing the warning look on his face.

"He's the reason you're going to agree to protect Esra," Suri said, rubbing her arm.

"Suri, let's go," Kol said, ignoring May and still keeping that one hand stretched towards the man on the floor. He raised his other hand out to her, palm upwards. An invitation.

Suri took a step towards him.

May grabbed Suri's shoulder, tugging her cloak down as she did. "Who the fuck do you—"

Kol saw Suri's neck. The vein below his jaw bulged, his mouth tightening. Kol's eyes darkened, changing from the warm brown of the boy to the near black she was used to. When he spoke, his voice started to betray the glamour, too, flickering deeper with every word. "You hurt her."

He moved his other hand from the writhing man, as May shifted, ready to lunge.

"Wait, stop," Suri said, tugging May's hand from her with a huff. "It wasn't her, she didn't do this. She helped."

Kol paused. As did May.

There was a moment of stillness. Suri stepped towards Kol, and May didn't stop her this time. Suri put her hand into Kol's and he gripped it immediately, something in his shoulders unlocking.

He pulled her to the door. Suri stood her ground, turning to May.

"You have interesting friends," May said, glancing at her two men who both rolled in pain on the floor.

"Yes. One of many. Do we have a deal?"

"We're leaving, right now," Kol said. In his glamoured form, they were more or less the same height, and she heard every spit of his venom. He was so mad.

Suri didn't look at him, she stared down May.

May sucked in her bottom lip and then let out a breath. She nodded, holding Suri's eye. "Fine. We have a deal."

Kol whisked her from the room and down the corridor, stepping over two more doormen groaning on the floor. He spoke into her ear, and the voice was entirely his own. "You are in so much trouble, little thief."

5

My castle will be a humble one, a cottage away from the smoke of the town and the politics of the Seat.
Unknown author, est. 2nd-5th century

Kol pulled her out of the building.

He didn't pull hard, but his pace left no room for her to do anything but move after him. Those still standing in the Tanner's orphanage stared at them, but none stopped them. She didn't even want to imagine the look in Kol's eyes; the instinctive step back of every person said it all.

Finally, Kol pushed through the front door and out into the street, his hair already darkening, his shoulders broadening.

But he didn't stop.

He didn't stop until they were around the corner, and then he glanced to either side before pushing her into a stone alcove. It smelt bad, as if someone had been sheltering in the alcove for a few days. Musty, sweaty and faintly sour. She didn't even have the chance to wrinkle her nose before he was with her, pressed up against her in the alcove.

The tendrils of black enveloped them, spreading from his hands to everywhere around them in the blink of an eye.

They were in the shadows. In his shadows. And he was fully himself again, looming over her, his presence sticking in her throat. Her throat was dry, her heart racing.

His feral gaze pinned her. One hand gripped her waist, and she felt the restraint as he flexed his hand against her. His whole body was on a knife-edge, nothing but tension.

"Who did this to you?" he asked, his black eyes locked on her neck where she suspected angry red handprints laced its skin. "Give me a name."

"You don't have to do that."

Kol chuckled in a pained way. "I'm not doing it for you. I'm doing it for me. Someone fucking *hurt* you. Tried to kill you, from the looks of it. And I can't have that person *breathing*. I want to tear them apart."

Suri nodded. She understood it, she'd felt the exact same way. "I almost tore him apart myself," she said, and her voice was soft. "I gave into it. To *Him*. I'm not sure what I did."

"I found the boys in the bakery." He scanned her body, his grip tightening. "Is this yours?"

Suri glanced down at herself, seeing the blood coating her. Her stomach turned. "No, it's not mine. Are they alive?"

His eyes flickered. "Yes."

Suri shuddered. "That's—That's good."

"Why was she offering you a deal? What did you give her?"

"Nothing, she owed me a favour."

Kol dropped his grip on her waist, taking a deep breath through his nose. He raked his hand through his hair with a groan, leaning forward as he put his hand on the wall behind her head. His breaths were heavy, his eyes closed.

"What's wrong?" Suri asked.

Kol's grip on the wall above her head became white-knuckled. "I had no idea what I was walking into there. I didn't know if I'd find you tortured, or dead. I'd prepared myself for everything. I was ready to kill every person in that building, Suri. I can't just shake that off," he said with a strained voice. "I want to heal you, to channel the light and take the pain away, but I can't hear Diophage over all this rage."

Suri gripped the front of his shirt and felt every muscle of him tense to stone. "Just breathe, breathe here with me."

He kept his eyes closed, the breaths shaky. "It's pent up inside me, so much darkness. So much fucking darkness and now my body is craving it. I know that group didn't do this, and yet so much of me wants to kill everyone in sight."

Suri didn't speak.

He opened his eyes and stared at her. "I thought it would go. I thought when I had my soul back, when the life magic came back, Sotoledi would release his claws. But he hasn't. It's still there, he's still there, everyone I've ever killed is a tally in his favour I can't erase."

She nodded. "How can we fix it?"

Kol barked a laugh. "That's it?"

"What do you mean?"

"Nothing," he said. Then he shook his head. "I keep thinking I'm going to say the one thing that scares you off."

Suri stared up at him. At his expression that she hadn't been able to identify before. It was fear. He was afraid, afraid of losing her. Something bright tried to make its way to the surface and died, strangled within the blackness of her soul. "You can't scare me off."

"And that's why you terrify me." He lifted his hand off the wall and dragged the back of a rough finger down her cheek. "You know I'm a monster. And you're still here."

"I'm worse." Suri dropped her gaze to the floor as her words from the arena echoed in her mind. His tally might be more, but her mind was a pit of nothing. She'd always been selfish. She'd never been a hero, and even when she somehow did the right thing, it was never intentional. It was a consequence of her trying to serve herself. He killed, yes, but he had a higher cause. She was a lost fucking cause.

His finger pulled up her chin. She met his black gaze to see him staring at her mouth. "If you truly believe that, you're crazier than I thought."

"How can we work through your darkness?" she asked, staring at his mouth right back.

He stared at her, his eyes pitching even darker. Then he looked away and sighed, his hand still touching her jaw. "I don't usually fight it, Suri. I don't usually have that part of my mind telling me to be good, telling me to focus on hope and light. I don't know. I usually give in to it."

Suri pulled her bottom lip into her mouth. She wanted to give into it, too. "There are many types of darkness."

"What are you saying?"

Suri swallowed. Remembering when He first spoke to her and her whole body felt electric. How He spoke to her in the carriage, how His darkness caressed her legs. He encouraged murder and torture. But that was not all. "When Sotoledi first started speaking to me, there was violence. But there was other darkness, too. Impulse. Desire. Lust."

"Suri," Kol said, his eyes back on her mouth and his tone a warning.

"What if you gave into that instead?" Suri asked. "We could work through your darkness together."

"Do you realise what you're saying?" he asked, leaning down towards her. He swiped his thumb over her lips. "Offering?"

Her knees nearly buckled. Her mouth was so sensitive that the faintest touch had her opening it. His thumb dipped between her lips and he groaned, pushing her back against the wall.

She sucked in a breath. "I don't just speak for the noise of it."

Kol growled. "Suri, you can't do this to me."

"Is that a no?" she asked breathily.

"You think I am capable of saying no to you?"

"If you do not want it—"

"Want?" he cut in. "Want, little thief?"

He grabbed her hips and shoved her harder against the wall, his fingers digging into her side.

She gasped as his lips came down like judgement. They were so soft, pressing against her mouth, and she let him in immediately. They groaned against each other as their mouths gasped hot and greedy breaths and clawed for more. More. More.

Kol pulled back from her, rubbing his thumbs against the skin near her hips as he bent his head to her neck. "*Want* is a word for good food and revelry. To imagine I simply *want* to fuck you is to imagine a starving man only *wants* a meal. I do not *want* it, I fucking crave it, you, all of it. I would claim you under every phase of the moon. I would ruin you in your finest dress in the softest sheets, I would worship you against a dirty wall."

Suri's head fell back, and he latched his mouth to her neck as her mind spun into stars. "This dirty wall?"

She felt his smile upon her collar. "This very one," he said. "Would you like that?"

She reached her hands into his curls. "Gods, yes."

Suri scratched his scalp and Kol made a noise which was almost a purr.

"My concentration might drop. I might lose my grip on the shadows." He punctuated his thoughts with open kisses on her neck. "Someone might see us."

Suri's legs weakened, and Kol held her even firmer. "I don't care."

Kol snaked a hand into her hair, gripping her head. "No?"

"No," Suri said. "I want you."

Kol moved his face back and stared at Suri. His cheeks were flushed, his mouth perfect and red. "Those are the magic words."

"Then take me."

His eyes were black. "Not here."

Before she had time to mutter a protest, Kol swept her into his arms and carried her so fast in his cloak of shadows he was almost running. And then they were through a wooden door, and Kol was kicking it closed behind him.

Suri stared around to see a dimly lit empty stables. She had time to clock a broken wheelbarrow and several clumps of hay before he had her against another wall. She gasped as his lips pressed at her neck once more, as he teased her head back with one hand and grasped at her left breast with the other.

"What was wrong with *that* dirty wall?" Suri asked, her fingers fumbling with his cloak.

Kol pulled it off, dragging it from around his shoulders. He paused a step away from her, staring at her chest as she breathed heavily. "You might not mind being seen. But I mind people seeing you. Only I can see you like this."

"Come here."

Kol smirked, but obeyed, closing the gap and unfastening her cloak, letting it drop to the floor. She tugged at his shirt, pulling it out of his trousers as her hands snaked under the fabric. Kol hissed as her cold fingers traced his stomach.

He released the ties at the front of her dress, dipping down to kiss her mouth as he did. Her hands explored the hard planes of muscle and skin, tensing under her touch, as he pulled her corset off and threw it to the floor.

Kol lifted her by her thighs and she wrapped her legs tight around him, her core hot against his middle. Her mouth attacked his neck, the wet kisses trailing from below his ear to his collar.

He laid her down on a pile of straw and she gazed up at him, waiting for him to pull off his shirt and reaching up to him with one hand in a lazy attempt to do it herself. Instead, he just stared down at her, her red dress bunched up to her upper thighs as her legs parted.

He wiped his lower lip with his thumb. "Mine."

Suri's breath caught. "Take it off."

Kol pulled his shirt off. Immediately she saw the jagged cut at his side, where her knife had slipped between his lower ribs. Scabbed over, the line raised and pink. It was going to scar. *She* had scarred him. Her black thoughts swelled, and he hissed as she dragged her finger over it. She pulled her finger back immediately, grief and guilt swelling.

"It didn't hurt," Kol said, grabbing her hand and placing it back onto his chest. "Your hands are cold."

"I'm sorry," she said, and that same itching thrum came back as her thoughts swirled ever blacker.

Kol bent over her, his shoulder flexing as he lowered himself and kissed her cheek. "If stabbing me keeps you alive, I give you permission to stab me as much as you'd like."

A ghost of a smile flickered on her face, then died. Kol kissed her mouth again and distracted her from her spiralling emotions. She kissed him back desperately. He lowered himself further over her onto his elbows and nipped at her lower lip. She wrapped her legs around him again, one hand scratching lightly over his shoulders.

He untied the front of her dress, and in less time than it took for her to gasp, his thumb teased at her nipple. She arched her back as she moaned into his mouth, reaching for his trousers.

She had them partly undone when he grabbed her hand and stilled it.

Suri met his gaze and saw the hesitation there. "No?"

Kol raised himself back up, rubbing one hand over his face. He looked down at her, flushed beneath him, and then shook his head. “I’m not fucking you without a soul.”

6

I visited it today, and it is perfect. I have already decided where I will place my books.

Unknown author, est. 2nd-5th century

Shock like cold water flushed across her. "What?"

Kol rocked back onto his knees and his voice was stronger this time. "I'm not having sex with you until we get your soul back."

Suri pushed herself up. Embarrassment and rejection followed the shock, and she crossed her arms over her chest. "You're not serious."

"Completely serious." Kol looked down at the floor. "I don't want this to be about release for either of us. And as much as your body might enjoy it, your mind doesn't. It's not the same. You don't get the same rush. It's a weak imitation. Trust me, when I fuck you, it will not be a weak imitation."

Trust me. The words rang in Suri's head.

Because he would know. Because he hasn't had a soul for decades. Because all the soulless sex he's clearly been having has done nothing for him.

A sweeping sensation of further embarrassment came over her. Before, in the cabin. He hadn't had a soul then. He'd brought her to climax with his tongue, with no soul. Had he even enjoyed it? Was that a weak imitation, too?

All his reticence made sense now. He hadn't wanted to because it wouldn't have been fun for him. Gods, she was stupid. He always knew it would be bad.

She pulled her dress back into position and plucked straw out of her hair and didn't look at him. "I get it. We'll have to find another way to deal with the darkness."

He stepped towards her. "Suri—"

A muffled noise came from his discarded coat. Suri looked at the garment in alarm as Kol sighed. He knelt next to it and flipped the coat over, finding something in his pocket as the noise came through again, louder now.

A voice. Seeing silk.

Kol held the silk in his palm, staring down at it and away from Suri. "Nad—"

An angry Nadrian cut him off. "Where are you? I've been trying to contact you for two hours."

Kol raised an eyebrow. "What's going on?"

"I've left the city. Rumour is Lera's travelling to Lartosh."

Any light left in Kol's face vanished. "She's going south? Why? I was sure she'd come here to gloat over my corpse."

Nadrian sighed. "Yeah I thought that, too, which is why I've been trying to talk to you. Something big must be happening."

Kol gritted his teeth, already tying his shirt. "You're right. Maybe it's time I actually speak to the Guilds."

"I'll ride ahead, and start sniffing around the leaders for a meeting, see who might be open to it."

Kol nodded. "Be careful."

"Obviously," Nadrian said with a snort. "Are you bringing our favourite Seer?"

"I don't know." Kol turned to Suri, still sitting in the hay. He appraised her expression, his eyes strangely vulnerable. "Am I?"

Suri stared up at him, her mind racing. Go to the Pail? Now? Was that a good idea? What about Esra?

"She's there? Good. It might be a good idea, having a Seer on our side. People fear Seers. You saw how Thandul and Shaedon reacted, it might help them to respect us," Nadrian said.

Suri sighed, speaking loud enough for Nadrian to hear. "I can barely do anything."

"They don't know that," he replied, his voice remarkably chipper.

Suri thought, but she knew from looking at Kol that she already had her decision. "I'll come. If Lera's making another move, I want to be there."

The voice came back through the silk. "Good, Kol would just be stressing about you the whole time if you didn't."

Kol rolled his eyes. "Thanks a lot."

"Anytime." She heard the smile on Nadrian's face.

The scene they walked in on in Mother Edi's room made Suri want to leave. There was something intimate to it, with candles scattered across the floor, the warm amber light bouncing off Viantha's nose and Scilla's cheeks. They knelt facing one another, Viantha's skirts blocking the view of whatever they focused on.

Scilla shifted when they entered, moving a fraction away from Viantha as she nodded to them. "Are you two hurt?" she asked, narrowing her eyes. "You look like you've been in a fight."

Suri shrugged, impressed at how even here, Viantha's floral scent filled every room. "That's because I was. Kol came to get me."

Scilla frowned. "And then you dragged him through a haystack?"

Suri instantly glanced at Kol. His clothes looked rumpled and his cheeks a little pink, and there it was, a telltale piece of straw sticking out of his even more unruly dark hair. She went cold with embarrassment. "I—"

"Pretend I didn't ask," Scilla interrupted, speaking a little too loud. She pointed in front of her clumsily. "Look at this."

Viantha wore a dress of the softest yellow, like a buttercup not fully bloomed. Even the small patches of dust and dirt only seemed to complement her loveliness. Suri glanced at Kol and noticed he wasn't looking at the woman, but at what was before her.

Three cracked pots sat on the floor. One, a dead plant. But the two nearer explained the floral scent as both overflowed with life. Red closed cup flowers with closely knitted petals populated one, and in the other, wide lilac flowers faced brightly into the world, hundreds of smaller petals spiralling outwards.

Viantha stared down at them, fiddling with the metal flower at her neck.

"You did this?" Kol asked.

She nodded.

Scilla's eyes sparkled. "Do you have the strength for the third? Can you show them?"

Viantha bit her lip. "I'll try. Plants aren't usually my area."

Kol knelt beside Viantha, and Suri's gut clenched. Scilla moved the two pots of flowers away with something approaching reverence, and perhaps it was, the flowers some evidence of their faith in the Pagan Diophage. Even if now she knew Diophage was no god, but an ancient Fae who had cheated death, he still created life magic, or honed it into what it was now. He was a saint to them, if not a deity.

Viantha placed her fingertips on the clay and closed her eyes. Something caught in the air, almost a breath over the candles, and the air felt fractionally warmer.

Kol made a small noise, and Suri narrowed her eye.

Then the plant started to grow. The brown tendril stretched as if suspended in sleep and then yawned back into life. It reached upwards, the colour shifting as it did, to a vibrant green. It crawled up as if there were a sun in that very room with them, shoots branching off of the stem, then leaves, and finally buds.

Viantha's breath faltered but she continued, her eyelids tensing and jaw clenching. The buds continued to shoot and grow, and then they started to unfurl. Like the hatching of an egg, the white petals spread and life began in that very room. The long almond-shaped petals were waxen and delicate, the half a dozen petals opening like fingers on a hand with the pollen buds reaching out from the middle.

Suri felt no wonder. Jealousy writhed in her belly as she watched the magic with the detachment of observing a housemaid polishing a vase. The feat meant nothing to her, but it clearly meant everything to Kol.

She pushed herself back up to standing, leaning against the table she'd bled on many times. Wonderful, perfect Viantha. If their guess was correct, she was one of the Daughters of the Earth, prophesied to bring life back to the desert. Maybe Kol could fuck her instead.

"Beautiful," Scilla said, her attention still riveted on the flower. "What flower is that?"

Viantha opened her eyes, and her breath caught. She swallowed as she removed her hands from the pot slowly. "I believe they are a type of lily."

"Incredible work," Kol said with a nod as he stood. "It is nice to know we have found one Daughter. Now we just need to locate the others."

Viantha nodded. "Any ideas on the how?"

"None." Kol sighed. "Let us hope more of you are from the Pail."

"Why?" Scilla asked, brushing her hands on her dark trousers as she also got to her feet.

"Lera's moving south," Kol explained.

Scilla frowned. "What? She's not coming here?"

"Apparently not."

Scilla shook her head. "That doesn't make any sense."

"Exactly," Kol sighed, before repeating Nadrian's own sentiment. "Which must mean something big is happening."

"I'll come with you."

"No." Kol held a hand up as Scilla instantly went to protest, giving her a look which allowed no argument. "You're Viantha's protection. We need to keep her safe for the prophecy, and I'm trusting you to do it. Get her back to Akdaria."

Scilla paused before nodding. "You got it."

Viantha remained on the floor, staring at the plant. "My estate is on your way down. Stop there for a night or two, save yourselves from camping out in the woods or in some bawdy inn. I'll send word."

Great. They could sleep in Viantha's huge manor. How generous of her, to remind them of her status, her importance, and what she sought to inherit.

Kol nodded, his expression warm. "Thank you."

Scilla addressed Suri. "What of your brother?"

Her acidic jealousy dampened ever so slightly at that. She hadn't really thought about it, or truly comprehended that by going south, she would have to say goodbye to her brother yet again. "I'll speak with him," Suri said. "He's staying here. I've made a deal for his protection."

"With who?"

Suri scratched the back of her head. "May. She's a gang leader in the Tangle."

Scilla jaw slackened. "The Tanner?"

"You know her?"

"I know *about* her," Scilla said. "Barsen and I came here enough times over the years to hear most of this city's sordid rumours. You've trusted the man skinner?"

Suri shrugged. "Her dad was in the arena. I asked for a pardon for everyone living or dead, and that included him. Her family's name has been restored and she offered me a favour."

Scilla blinked. "Nicely played."

"Kol made a well-timed appearance that helped seal the deal," Suri explained.

Kol didn't smile, only shaking his head, a hint of his earlier anger flaring back up. Scilla only nodded, and returned her attention to the plant pots.

Suri broke the silence. "I've also been thinking."

"Your ideas often get people killed," Scilla pointed out, with no hint of humour.

Suri sniffed and ignored her. She instead looked at Kol, pointing a finger at his chest. "Didn't you say that magic loves a survivor?"

He eyed her wearily. "Yes."

"Maybe the reason I have any sort of life magic in me is because of everything I had to survive in the Tangle. Maybe other kids are the same," she said, gesturing vaguely at the room they were in. "I'm sure half of them are just as fucked up as me and have Sotoledi whispering at them, but Diophage might be there, too."

Kol pursed his lips. "It's not a bad idea. But how do we test it? Do we go up to all the children and ask if they've ever grown a plant?"

"I've got no idea." She wasn't sure why she was even suggesting it, but the thought had occurred to her and she wanted to help even if she wasn't fully sure why anymore. "But there must be a reason the priesthood grabs so many kids from around here. The melting pot of it all, it must trigger something."

Scilla nodded, now.

And Kol seemed deep in thought. "Edi might have an idea of who to approach. I'll get Aisha to stay and work with her on it."

"Esra can help," Suri said.

Kol looked at her with a contemplative expression she couldn't quite understand.

"Do you want me to heal those bruises?" Scilla offered, gesturing to Suri's neck. "I'm getting better at life bonding now."

"I'll do it," Kol said quickly.

"Are you—Are you in the right space to?" Suri asked.

"I'm fine now," he replied, moving towards her and looking at her neck.

Suri smiled with only her mouth. "Go ahead, then, oh great Son of Life."

He smirked and placed one hand on her neck, nearly encompassing the entire thing. She shivered even though his hand was warm, and he stroked her jaw with his thumb.

"Much more calm," he murmured low enough so only she could hear.

Suri swallowed as he stared down at her neck. He closed his eyes for a moment, and she felt the tension and pain fade.

7

It is such a relief to have a place of one's own. I wake at the hour of my choosing, read all I desire, and do little else.

Unknown author, est. 2nd-5th century

Suri tucked a finely crafted piece of metal into her pocket as she descended into Mother Edi's basement the following morning. She'd played with it all the way back from the sewers, rubbing her thumb over the silver as she used to with her coins, pleased it was still there.

As she rounded the corner, she saw Esra, cleaning the perpetually filthy table with his good arm. He looked up and noticed her, smiling. She winced as he carefully straightened and turned, and she noticed how he held the table to support him, favouring his working leg.

Her brother greeted her with a hug, careful not to hug her too tight. "How are you? How's your back?"

"It's not too bad now." It was the truth. When she flexed her back, she could feel the tightness of the scabbing, but even with every hour, it was easier to move. In a couple more days, it wouldn't be anything more than another ugly scar, and she had made her peace with those. She was still alive, after all. "How's your leg?"

Esra grinned. "I don't understand it, this life bonding stuff, but I'll try not to question it. I would have loved it up in the mines. I tore my shoulder years ago, and even that's healing now. I haven't felt this good in a long time."

"I'm glad," she said, but it came out flat. She *was* glad, but the only thing she could feel was sorrow and regret that he had to live so long in pain.

"When are you getting your soul back?" he asked, studying her face. "Can I—Is there anything I can do?"

"Kol and I need to go to Lartosh to work out what Lera's doing. Then we're going to the Glen to pay whatever stupid price Xianyu concocts for my soul."

His brow furrowed. "You're leaving, then?"

"Later tonight," she said. "You'll be fine, here?"

"Suri, you've got me a house, healed me, and absolved me of all my crimes. You've done everything you could do for me and more. I just wish I could help you."

Esra pulled her in for another hug, and something eased, like the tightness in her chest had been unbuttoned.

When he released her, she explained her theory on the children of the Tangle, and he agreed to help Aisha and Mother Edi in any way he could.

"You never know," he said with a grin. "Maybe I'm the next prodigy."

"Shame you're not a daughter."

He chuckled. "It's always women that get all the fun."

She swatted his chest. "And it's always men that think that."

Suri knocked on Mother Edi's door and stepped inside.

The kid sat upright on the table, staring at Suri as she waited by the door, watching the older woman tie off a bandage. At maybe seven years old, she was buck-toothed, with blonde hair stuck up in tufts as she gazed in wonder. "You're the one who killed the longtooth. Took its tooth from its mouth."

"That's me."

She pointed at her leg proudly. "This is a dog bite."

Suri gave an exaggerated wince. "Nasty."

"Do you still have the tooth?" she asked as Mother Edi tapped her knee.

"I don't, no."

A crestfallen expression dropped across her small features. "I would have worn it every day." Then she hopped down from the table and walked out of the room, staring up at her as if committing her to memory, before dashing up the stairs. Suri shook her head.

Mother Edi turned her glassy-eyed stare in her direction. "Here for the Time Circle?"

Suri nodded. "Can you teach me?"

Mother Edi shuffled over to her Time Circle. It was strange to think it had always been there, something Suri had dismissed as nothing more than a basin made of stone and surrounded by puddles of wax. "After Cthanda passed, it took me many moons to discover I was the next Seer."

Suri stepped up beside her, breaking off a small piece of dried wax and rolling it between her fingers. "How did you find out?"

Mother Edi smiled. "I was brushing Ruben and thinking of her. Cthanda became one of my dearest friends as she carried Kol to term. We tried to protect her. We couldn't." Her voice held no devastation. Now it was only the facts.

Suri squeezed the wax between her thumb and forefinger and it crumbled to the floor. "You saw the relics in Ruben?"

"I did." Mother Edi swirled the top of the stagnant water in the basin with the tip of a wrinkled finger. "This is the way it is supposed to be, I believe. The old Seer of Time teaches the new. But I was never taught. Cthanda barely knew her own power. I think she flung her memories into that horse by accident. She thought of them so hard they had to find somewhere to lodge."

Suri frowned. "But what am I supposed to do? How am I supposed to help?"

Mother Edi let the water settle. "There is value in seeing what is, and what has already come to pass. Many decisions that are yet to come would change if people understood their own history."

It was so vague that Suri couldn't help the bubble of frustration that rose up. "So I am supposed to be an advisor? There are so few relics left. What more is there to learn?"

Edi was ever constant. "Relics and Time Circles open the window, like a door into that first moment. From there, it is possible to wander from time to time, ever deeper. But be careful, Seers have become lost that way too. The Fae spoke of a Seer who got lost in the past, unable to travel back up to her own time."

Suri stared at Mother Edi. Travelling through relics? She'd never heard of such a thing. She assumed they were static. "You can travel through the relics into other times?"

Mother Edi only nodded, her furrowed brow filled to the brim with wrinkles.

Suri grabbed her hand. "How?"

Mother Edi patted her hand. "For you, Time is a muscle. One you've never used before, so it stumbles under any weight. But you can strengthen it."

"How?" Suri repeated.

"Start with the Time Circle. Get to that place in your mind where you can find people easily."

Suri nodded impatiently. "And then what?"

Mother Edi sighed and the noise rumbled through her body. "Relics are based on memories attached to deeply powerful emotions. Those that locked them there did so for a reason, because they wanted that specific moment to live for an eternity. I found it easiest to travel when I could understand the emotions of the relic. Music helped."

"Music?"

"Whatever settles your mind," Mother Edi pulled her hand away, frowning. "Though I do not think it is natural for a Seer to be without a soul. It is to be heartless and unfeeling. You cannot be a conduit for memory when you have nothing of warmth."

An icy feeling crept over her. Rejection, again. Of course, she would be a terrible Seer. Everything she tried she seemed to fail at. Terrible thief, even worse murderer. She wasn't a Daughter, and now, she'd ruined her chances of helping anything by selling off her soul.

If her success at being a seer was intrinsically linked to her emotions, she was fucked. She couldn't feel half of them now, and when she could feel positive emotions, she didn't exactly have a wealth of experience to draw from.

Suri huffed out a breath. "They chose the wrong Seer, then. Even with a soul, I have never known warmth."

Mother Edi studied her. "I refuse to believe that is true."

"I know me," Suri shrugged.

Mother Edi flicked a finger at her face, and a drop of water hit her cheek. Suri gaped at her and Mother Edi only shook her head. "I know you, too, child. Find your warmth."

When the knock came on her door a few hours later, Suri had napped at Aisha's request, and gathered all her possessions together. "Come in."

Kol strode in. "Have you got everything?"

Every time she saw him, it made her breath catch. She wondered when that would stop happening, but it didn't seem likely to be soon. He was so huge and imposing, but when he looked at her, it was so much softer.

She nodded. "Mostly, but I didn't manage to get any new clothes."

She wore the red dress Aisha had found, and she had the repaired grey outfit from Xianyu. They both were probably not the best for days on the road, but it would have to do.

"What?" Kol said, looking at her meagre pile of clothing. Annoyance twinged at the corners of his mouth. "Why not?

You can't wear your dress when we're riding for days. You need riding trousers at least, and something nice enough to meet the Guild Leaders."

"You think I don't know that? I tried. We'll have to get something on the road."

Kol crossed his arms. "What do you mean, you tried?"

Suri flopped back onto the bed, staring at the ceiling. "None of the seamstresses would serve me. They know who I am. They know I'm from the Tangle."

Kol's voice went cold. "They refused you?"

"And they weren't polite about it," she sighed. Then she shrugged. "I'll ask Mother Edi for whatever spares she has going and maybe we'll find something to buy in Lartosh."

"Come with me." The danger in his voice made her look at him again.

His brow was tight, his jaw locked. His eyes burned, but his gaze was elsewhere. Kol was livid.

She pushed herself back up. "Where?"

He pointed to the door. "We're going shopping."

Suri stood hesitantly. "I don't want to get turned away again, Kol."

Dark eyes met hers. "They wouldn't dare turn you away. Not with me."

A small smile crossed her lips. "But you're supposed to be dead."

Kol's answering smirk was deliciously wicked. He reached out his palm, offering his hand to her with a bow. "Trust me, my lady."

Suri couldn't help the momentary feeling of excitement. It lit up her body with something other than stress and sadness and rejection, searing her with something *good*. She put her hand into his.

Kol glamoured himself as they walked in the streets.

Nothing too fancy. His shoulders were slimmer, his stature smaller, his features less perfect, and his jaw less sharp. In his own mind, he must have believed himself ordinary. Yet Suri noticed many appreciative glances in his direction despite the changes.

"I don't see how this is going to go any differently."

His answering grin was chaos. "Oh, it will."

Suri rolled her eye at the ambiguity. She approached a seamstress's door, though not one she went to earlier. She wasn't quite up for that. "Here goes nothing."

She stepped into the shop and the lone woman sewing in the back of the room didn't look up immediately.

Suri swallowed as she felt Kol come in behind her. "Good afternoon."

The woman's head lifted, a pleasant smile on her face. It dropped the moment she saw Suri, and then dawned into shock when she saw Kol. Maybe even a hint of horror. "Well me—" She shook her head vigorously and dropped into a nervous curtsy. "Gods above, my Prince. I mean, your highness. What can I—What do you need? I am your humble servant."

Suri turned her head and nearly jumped out of her skin. Behind her, instead of Kol Aubethaan, was Prince Shaedon. For a second, Suri searched past the Prince to check he hadn't just come in at the same time. But then something flashed in

Shaedon's eyes that could only be described as Kol's brand of mischief, and Suri relaxed.

Kol looked the perfect image of the Prince, with nary a red hair out of place. He had depicted the Prince as he had been at dinner the other night, complete with blue smudges under his eyes, though he had made his clothes somewhat less rumpled. He inclined his head towards Suri. "I'm here for clothing for Lady Suri."

The seamstress was still gawping at him. "The Lady—" Then she stopped, tilting her head and then pointing at Suri. "Oh, yes. Of course, quite right. What can I do for you, my lady? Dresses? Shirts? Skirts?"

The glamoured Kol stepped forward, running his fingers over fabric with a calculated disdain. "She will be riding south for several days. She'll need some sturdy riding clothes first."

The seamstress bobbed again. "I have several such items in the back." She motioned to Suri. "Let me take your measurements, so I know if I need to adjust them."

Suri stepped forwards, turning to face Kol as the woman pulled out a string and wrapped it around Suri's waist, her fingers fumbling and jittery. He waggled his eyebrows, and she barely held back a tut.

Then the seamstress straightened, her face stricken. "Can I offer you anything? A drink? I have wine, or some tea from the Pail if that's to your liking. Or I can go out for ale? Do you drink ale? I'm sorry, your highness."

Kol waved a hand in a bored way, even as Suri saw his eyes dancing. "Wine will be fine for me. My lady?"

Suri swallowed with a shrug. "Wine is good."

"Wine, it is. I'll be back in just a moment." The seamstress ducked into another rushed curtsy, before running from the room. Suri heard her in the back room, yelling out for someone. "Carrie. Carrie!"

Once she was firmly gone, Suri gaped at Kol. "What are you doing?"

Kol grinned, but it was strange to see it painted on Shaedon's face instead. It didn't twist her stomach as it usually did. "Well, I was hoping to drink some wine and watch her dress you up."

Suri scoffed. She stared at him once more, looking for pieces of Kol and finding very few. The posture, the quirk of his brows. "The Prince?"

He shrugged. "I can probably maintain this glamour for an hour tops. If I had one of Agata's concentration potions, it would be longer. Being a specific person is always difficult, distorting my features is easier. With this, I can't let anything slip. People notice quickly when something seems off." Then he stepped towards her, trailing a finger along her waist where the seamstress had just pulled the string. She shivered. "But you clearly have a thing for men with titles, so I thought you'd like it."

Suri swallowed. "How'd you figure that?"

Kol's smile was a little forced. "You must have flirted with Rasel, he seemed a bit infatuated. And you've tortured me long enough."

She raised one eyebrow. "This is torture?"

"No." He smirked. "This is my reward."

A bustling of skirts and footsteps caused Kol to take a couple of steps back. He folded his arms over his chest as the seamstress hurried back into the room holding a bundle of clothes.

The seamstress bobbed into yet another curtsy, at least her fourth by this point. "My sister will be here in just a moment with the wine, your highness. I'm not sure we have a vintage suitable for you, though."

He smiled. "I'm sure we will make do with your humble offering."

The seamstress blushed. "So, it's just travelling clothing she needs, your highness?"

Kol shook his head. "She'll need one formal dress, too."

The lady's eyes went wide, and Suri saw her hands shake. This woman was so incredibly excited at the mere idea of a dress. Kol could not have bestowed his princely charm on a more wanting worker. "Of course, did you have anything specific in mind? I can make a divine red and gold dress. It would be my honour to befit her in your colours."

At that, Kol's jaw clenched. It was subtle, but Suri saw it immediately. It was such a Kol mannerism; the tension painted across his mouth at the idea of this woman befitting her in Shaedon's colours. He opened his mouth but Suri was faster.

"Not red," she said.

The seamstress furrowed her brow at Suri. "No, my lady?"

Suri shook her head at the seamstress. She felt the weight of Kol's gaze from the corner of her own. "Black."

The seamstress frowned. "Black, are you certain?"

Suri dared to glance at the Prince. Kol stared back with the most self-satisfied and devilish smirk, a trace of the real him coming through it. Her cheeks heated. "I am."

The seamstress clasped her hands together. "Of course, my lady. Black. Any style?"

Suri looked to Kol for answers, but he didn't appear to have any. He stared at her body ravenously. She made a vague gesture, keeping her voice as normal as she could. "We don't have time for you to make a dress from scratch. I have business which requires me to leave the city tonight. Do you have any black dresses already?"

The seamstress paled. "I might have one or two, but I warn you my lady, they were intended as funeral wear. I can do my best to make some quick alterations to make them more appropriate for a formal occasion?"

"That would be great," Suri replied.

The seamstress nodded. "Give me just a moment to find something. I can't thank you enough for choosing us today." Bobbing again, the seamstress whirled back out of the room. She muttered to herself as she moved into the backroom. "Where is that fool girl?"

Suri followed her movement out before turning back to her disguised Kol. It seemed he hadn't looked away from her for a moment. Her breath caught, and his eyes darkened to a shade which was decidedly more Kol.

He took a single step forward. "Black, eh?"

She tucked a lock of hair behind her ear and smirked at him. "Do you like the idea of me in your colours, your highness?"

He growled and closed the gap, but didn't touch her. "I don't like you flirting with me whilst I wear another's face," he said, frowning. "I'm becoming jealous of myself somehow."

Suri laughed. "I don't have a thing for Shaedon."

"Good," he purred. "His head can stay on his shoulders another day. Just don't touch me when I'm in his skin."

She held her hands up in surrender. "I won't lay a hand on you, your highness."

He took a step back, taking her in. Something in his gaze seemed to change. He shook his head, only a small motion, more to himself than to her, but she saw it. Something had shifted between them, and the moment had died.

A new girl came into the room with a silver tray bearing a matching carafe and two glass goblets of blood red wine. The girl also dropped into a curtsy then kept her head down, putting the tray on a small table near them. Kol picked the cups up and passed one to Suri without meeting her gaze.

He cleared his throat, and the serving girl jumped. "Carrie, is it?"

The girl stared at her prince with moonlike eyes. "Yes, your highness."

He smiled, taking a sip of his wine. "Let your sister know my lady will be needing pockets. Lots of pockets."

Carrie nodded, and fled from the room.

Suri stared at Kol as he gulped down his wine. Her heart hurt, and she didn't understand it. What if she never got her soul back? Would she always be this to him? A distant, untouchable thing, to admire but never embrace. She hated it, and sadness curled in her belly like a sleeping cat.

8

The grass around me never gets repetitive, the water is sweet and cold, and the hills in the distance are ever-watchful over me.

Unknown author, est. 2nd-5th century

It was a good thing Nadrian rode out ahead, because they travelled very slowly. They couldn't risk riding Ruben. Even if people didn't know he was a Roanhadham, people did know the Lord of the Wastelands rode a huge dark steed. Taking him would have drawn unnecessary attention, but any normal horse couldn't comfortably support the weight of two people on a long journey to the Pail.

So they were on two horses, which meant Suri had to actually ride hers.

Kol had found her an older horse with a docile temperament requiring very little direction. Still, Suri struggled. Growing up, she had no reason to spend time with horse nor hound and now, they were alien, and her respect for their natural wildness made her hesitant to drag them to her bidding. He was a good teacher, though, which Suri appreciated and felt aggravated by in equal measure. She had to bite back every snarky response to his patient tutelage, and wasn't always successful.

It wasn't plain sailing for Kol, either.

"Once we get further from the city, it'll be easier," he said, his voice a little strained as they passed through a small wood just outside New Politan. "I'm not used to glamouring so heavily. No wonder Nadrian was always napping. Once there are fewer people on the roads, I can drop it."

But ever since they'd left the city just before dawn, there seemed to be a steady stream of people. As soon as they passed one group of merchants or travellers, another lot would appear on the horizon, and because of it, Kol's glamour was near constant, keeping his features dull and his body small.

She could see how weary he was growing by noon, and they hadn't travelled fast by any measure. She found the slow pace painful, her legs still unaccustomed to it and her mind tired from constantly pulling the mare's head away from every clump of grass.

"If you're going to be glamouring this often, we should have a code word."

He furrowed his brow, clicking his tongue at his own horse. "What do you mean?"

"What if you walk into a room and I attack you, not recognising you? Or how do I know it's not someone else pretending to be you?" Suri asked, dragging her eye across him.

Kol smirked. "You think someone might try to pretend to be me?"

"They could exploit it."

"Exploit what, exactly? Most people think you hate me. You did murder me, after all."

"Axri'don was working for Lera. He might have told her the truth."

"And pray," Kol drawled, "what is the truth?"

Her cheeks heated and she stared at her hands on the reins. "Let's just drop it. If you don't think we need a code, fine."

"No," he said. "It was a good idea."

Suri glanced at him to find him already studying her. Even with his ill-refined features, there was a heat in that look that made a shiver pass down her spine. "What do you suggest?"

"A phrase. I'll say something in the Old Tongue, and you'll know it's me."

"What will you say?"

He thought for a moment. And then nodded. "*Nen alerisee f'ith sotele.*"

Suri rolled the words in her head. She didn't recognise it at all. She attempted to repeat them back. "*Nen alerisee f'ith sotele?*"

He corrected her pronunciation with a small smile.

"What does it mean?"

"It means I am the real me."

Suri sniffed. "That's what it translates to?"

Kol winked. "It means the handsome man has returned."

"Oh, great," she said, but a small smile crept onto her face despite herself.

When they eventually stopped in a small town along the Drameir Road, it was barely evening, and Suri could barely walk. Kol was in an even worse state, his face almost grey with concentration.

The innkeeper shot a worried look at Suri as they paid for a night's stay and whatever food was hot. Suri gave him a wan smile that she was certain was equally unconvincing, and followed Kol up the stairs.

The room was fairly small. A double bed, a small chest, and a fireplace with an old rug in front of it. Kol stepped inside and dropped the saddlebags looped over his shoulder by the door. Suri put her bag of clothes down near the chest.

They both stared at the bed, and her heart raced despite her exhaustion.

"You take the bed," Kol said, before striding to the rug and sitting in front of the fire.

Suri almost flinched with the chill of the words. She scoffed. "Don't be stupid. There's more than enough room."

"I know," he replied, throwing some wood into the fireplace. He breathed in and out, letting the glamour fade with a shudder. His shoulders filled back out, his jaw sharpened, his nose more angular and his brow stronger.

Suri stared at his hulking figure as he fiddled with the tinderbox. Then she stared at the bed. It didn't make any sense. A childish part of her felt rejected again. What had she done wrong? He didn't want to be anywhere near her. "We've slept in the same bed before."

Kol's voice was drained beyond all measure. "I remember."

Suri waited for any sort of explanation, and when it clearly wasn't coming, she sighed. "Fine, suit yourself."

Kol just stared at the fire as she tugged her hair from the braid she'd had it in all day. She rubbed her fingers into the back of her scalp in soothing circles.

What in the Above was going on? She'd seen him tired before, but he'd never been this disconnected from her. He held the flame underneath the wood until it started to catch and didn't look at her once. At least when he was angry, he wasn't this ambivalent.

She swallowed. "I'll bring up our food."

Downstairs, the innkeep passed her two bowls of some meat stew, with two hunks of pale floury bread balanced on top. She nodded her thanks and made her way back up the stairs.

When she returned, Kol was still staring into the growing fire with that same detachment. She passed him a bowl, and he shuddered from the warmth of it.

"Thanks," he said.

Suri pulled off her cloak and boots, and sat on the bed in her dress and stockings. Kol never looked around. They ate in silence, only broken by the noises of them blowing on the stew to cool it. The food was good, the meat likely rabbit, though she didn't have the palate to know for sure. It was hot, salty and lightly spiced, and she felt the warmth seep through her bones. But she couldn't fully relax. She kept staring at Kol, sitting on the damned floor.

When Kol was mopping up the last of his stew with the end of his bread, she couldn't hold it back anymore. "Why didn't you get two rooms?"

"Sorry?"

She put her bowl down on the floor by the side of the bed, sitting in the middle of it with her hands clasped. "If you knew you didn't want to share a bed with me. Why didn't you get two rooms?"

He shrugged. "I'll sleep better knowing you're safe."

Her heart jumped, and that coiling sensation of lust came back to her. "You'll freeze on the floor."

"I'll ask for another blanket."

"I don't get it." Suri scooted to the edge of the bed, only a few feet behind him. She let the fear spill out. "You won't even look at me. Did I do something?"

Kol groaned, dropping his head into his hands.

Suri's heart sank as her throat thickened. What was so wrong? Why wouldn't he speak to her? She clearly wasn't wanted here. His words from before swirled in her head. He must have regretted inviting her along. The broken, cold-hearted girl he didn't want to touch.

She should have stayed in the North. Even if she was banned from the city, she should have stayed out there, near Esra.

She stood up and took a step towards the door.

Kol swivelled and grabbed her ankle. He stared at her foot, his whole body tense. "I'm not annoyed with you."

"Then why?"

He finally looked up at her, and his expression was haunted. "I need to keep a distance from you, at least until you have your soul back."

"This is about my soul again? What, you're not even going to look at me now until we get my soul back? What if we never do?" Kol flinched. "Am I damaged somehow, without my soul? You don't like me without it?"

He choked, speaking under his breath, but still loud enough for her to hear. "She thinks *she's* the damaged one."

"What does that mean?"

"It means that I haven't had a soul since I was your age," he said in a tortured tone. "And with my Fae blood, I was barely an adult then. Now I have my soul back and I can feel things again. I taught myself to feel without a soul over decades. Smile, even laugh sometimes. But now I'm whole again, and I feel it all."

Kol laughed, but it held no humour. "I knew I felt something towards you before. But now... Being around you makes me happy. Happier than I've been in maybe my whole life. You've seen all of me and you want me, and I've seen all of you and I want you, too. You're strong, you're fiercely loyal."

Suri reached towards his hair, that pain in her starting to unravel. "Kol—"

"No." He caught her wrist. "I can't sleep with you in that bed."

"But—"

"I can't sleep with you. I can't even be with you when you're like this. Not until you understand how you feel."

Suri blinked. "I don't—"

"Just as I thought you were starting to hold affection for me, too, you gave up your soul. You did that for me. I know it means something. And I heard what you said in the arena. How you trust me. How you want to mean something to me, how you can't stay away."

Suri flushed. She didn't think any part of Kol was hearing her at that moment. He was feral, more beast than man, so deeply under the influence of Sotoledi's thrall she had convinced herself there was no way he had heard it. But he had. Gods.

"You've got your wish. You are all I ever think about," Kol said.

Suri didn't know what to say.

Kol stared at the floor. "But I've changed. I have joy back. I want more. It would kill me if you get yours back and regret what we've shared. I need to know how you truly feel, if any of this is real."

Suri blew out a breath. The intensity of the moment left her on a precipice, but she couldn't fall off its edge. She didn't know how. It was too much. She stood on the cliff, looking down into something utterly terrifying as the wind buffeted her from every angle.

She didn't know how to act or how to speak, and so she stayed firmly still, letting the world move around her. She wanted him so much. He wanted her, too, so much that he wouldn't let her near him. Because she was broken.

There was nothing she could say to convince him. He was right. She was damaged, unable to feel everything. It wasn't fair for her to ask anything of him, even though she craved the calm he gave her.

When she eventually spoke, her voice sounded distant even to her own ears. "So, what do we do?"

Kol sighed, utterly weary. "We find out what Lera is doing. Then we go to Xianyu, and we get your soul back."

Suri swallowed. "And until then?"

He glanced at her and the turmoil was gone. Only resignation remained. "Until then, I'll sleep on the floor."

The next day passed painfully slowly. Kol still treated her in the same friendly way, teaching her how to ride more comfortably, giving her instruction when she needed it. But he stopped touching her. He wouldn't even help her onto her horse, and whilst he offered her a hand when she jumped down, he would barely look at her.

It didn't help that he was constantly exhausted, the roads busy with tradesmen creating a near constant stream of faces. The weather was fair, and clearly the world had waited until the end of winter to peddle their wares along the city roads, which gave Kol no respite from his glamour.

By the end of the second day, they reached the fork which would take them towards the Parched Lands instead of Drameir. Immediately, the traffic on the road more than halved. It was less direct than going through Drangbor, but the trade-off for safety was immeasurable. It was best that they weren't studied too hard, and the guard patrols of Drangbor were an unnecessary risk.

When they stopped for the night, though, Kol's mood seemed lower than ever. With no inn to rely on here, they slept on the ground under the stars. Suri woke several times as the stars swirled above to see Kol staring out at the road, unable to sleep.

When they set out that third morning, his eyes were bloodshot. They rode harder that day, with fewer pauses.

The vegetation faded to nothing, and they reached the border of the Parched Lands around noon. The heat crept up through the morning, and it was now uncomfortable, with the next two hours into the desert proper only going to get worse. They kept their pace, though, and Kol kept his glamour up. She wondered why he didn't drop it, with no one around them it seemed surely safe, but he was relentless in its upkeep.

Sweat soaked her body by the time they reached the first tower. They approached slowly, and a guard in a white tunic came out, hand lazily on his pommel. The guards at the top of the stone tower stared at them, and an archer took aim.

The glamoured Kol held a hand up and then dropped down from his horse.

"Stop right there," the white guard said. "What is your business in these lands?"

Kol checked behind them, looking to the empty road at their backs. Suri saw his shoulders finally relax as he dropped his glamour in a breath and grew several inches taller. He must have been waiting until he knew for certain his lands were still safe and manned.

The guard jumped back and then pulled his faceguard down as if it would help him to see better.

"Lord Kol." He gaped. "We thought—Gods, we were told you've been killed."

Kol rolled his shoulders. "It is nice to see you, too, Stone. And it's best if people continue to think that."

"Of course, my lord. I understand." The bewildered look in his eyes suggested otherwise. "Is there anything we can do?"

"Just some water and oats for the horses." Kol waved back in the direction of Suri and the horses. "We won't stop long."

Great. He was in an even worse mood today, not even looking at her as he lumped her in with the livestock. It wasn't lost on her that he didn't ask for food or water for them, only for the beasts. She swung her leg over and dropped down from her mare, only stumbling a little on her painfully stiff legs.

He glanced back. "We'll be moving on soon."

Suri glared at him. "I heard you. I'm just taking a minute."

Kol nodded, before moving into the guards' tower to speak to one of his men. Perfect. The most words they'd exchanged all day.

Suri walked in an awkward circle near the tower, her legs enjoying the stretch as she fielded looks from curious guards. He hadn't explained her presence, but at least from the lack of chains it was somewhat obvious she wasn't a prisoner. So much for being part of his court.

The horses drank, and Kol tied the bags of oats onto the saddles and mounted his horse again. She sighed and reluctantly mounted hers. Then they were off once more. She kicked in with her ankles and the mare plodded forwards.

Kol waited until she levelled with him and then nudged his own steed forwards. "You are riding well today."

Oh, he was deigning to speak to her now? Fantastic. She kept her eye forwards. "Thank you, my lord."

"Cute." Kol's tone was curt, matching her own. "We'll rest at the outpost tonight."

Suri's chest seized as panic clawed at her and her ears rang. Something cold gripped her despite the growing heat of the sands.

The last time she'd been at the outpost, she had arrived as an exile. Filthy, bruised. Two of her fellow cage mates had died before they even reached it. They'd sold her and humiliated her.

Kol had watched.

Her anger bubbled up so immediately, and so red hot, that it supplanted all anxiety. But to him, she said nothing. "As you wish."

9

He visited today, although I did not invite him. He remarked upon my books, and I entertained him only so long as was polite.

Unknown author, est. 2nd-5th century

When the first buildings fell into sight through the haze of dust on the horizon, it wasn't the punch to the gut that Suri expected. Even when that first terracotta swathe of fabric rippled in the wind, it didn't suck the breath from her. Their horses plodded ever forwards, and soon enough, they were through the sandstone arch.

But any small hope Suri might have had dissipated as they walked through the streets. They had arrived in the afternoon, and the emptiness brought her no calm. It was the same as when she arrived in the cage, but now she knew that the city's residents were only sheltering from the sun and the vultures would descend when evening fell.

Kol was oblivious to her growing panic. "We'll be safe here. You can choose your own lodgings for the night."

Suri looked at him as they weaved through to the main square. "You won't be staying with me?"

He didn't look back. "No. I won't lie on your floor again, don't worry."

Did he think he was doing her some favour by leaving her alone here? He would rather spend the night without her now they were in his home. Suri swallowed back the lump in her throat as they reached the main square.

Kol dismounted and swiftly tied up his horse outside an inn. Suri dismounted her own horse and he tied the mount up, barely paying her any mind. Then he reached into his pocket and put a small pouch into her hand. "Here."

She opened it and looked inside. Several gold pieces glinted back, and she shook her head. "This is far more than I'd need for one night."

"You're Mistress of Coin now. You should get used to handling my money." The jest was accompanied by a tired smile which didn't reach far into his cheek, much less to his eyes. He met her eye then, only for a second. "Oh wait, stand still."

Suri obeyed. It was easier to stand here, surrounded by the musk of their horses and the smell of her own sweat than to look around and see the post they sold her against.

Kol reached into another pocket and pulled out a small piece of metal. It was a pin, carved of metal and then blackened. A carved plant, only small. Barely sprouting. He clasped it to her riding jerkin.

She rubbed a finger over it, thinking of the similar jewellery she carried in her own pocket. She'd meant to return it before, but hadn't found the time. Her resentment at him stifled any want to give it to him now. "A royal pin? I thought my title was only for the meeting."

"You're a member of my court now, Suri, like it or not." Then he smiled at her, and it seemed halfway real. "Stay wherever you'd like, and relax."

Her breath caught. Relax. Here? "What will you do?"

Kol stared out across the empty square. "I'll catch up with Gwin about how the mines have been. The storms are still increasing and I know he's worried."

At the mention of Gwin, her heart seized ever more. Did he have any idea the torment her mind was in? Did she want him to know? She looked for any salvation, any distraction. "Can I come?"

Kol shook his head. "No, you're fine. It won't really be very entertaining."

She swallowed and held onto her horse's saddle. "Have fun."

"We leave in the morning."

She nodded, and he left.

He seemed more relaxed than he had in days as he walked away, no longer needing to hide. These were his people, this was his home.

Rationally, this was just a town. A collection of walls. Buildings. People. Scilla had told her that even if she was sold here, she would have always had a choice and would not have been a slave.

But as she turned from her horse and really took in the square for the first time in months... She still froze the moment she saw that post.

She could picture with horrible recall where their cage had sat. Where the slaver had dragged her out and attached her manacles to the wooden post. Where he had called her a northern beauty and sold her for so little.

How the bidding had increased, but how she was eventually sold. To Kol, but only by proxy. He bought her, thirty feet from her, for eight silver.

Eight *silver*.

The gold in her pouch battled against the reminder of how much she was really worth.

Her heart pounded in her chest as she walked towards that post. It stuck out from the ground in such an ordinary way. Just a piece of wood. That's all it was, really. But every step she took towards it reminded her of how she was nothing. No one. Sold.

When she got to it, she swallowed as her mind whipped like a storm. Her hand shook as she reached out to touch it. The wood felt like wood. The metal loop nailed to it was hot in the desert air, and a little rusted.

It was nothing. Just material. But she couldn't stop her body from feeling like it was curling up, dying. She wiped the tear that fell down one cheek away with the heel of her palm. She sniffed as her throat thickened. Gods.

She wondered what would happen if she was sold again now?

Soulless. One-eyed. Was she even worth the clothes that she wore? The boots on her feet? Everything ached as her chest seized against the pain and fresh tears spilled. Every breath was heavy, pulling against the weight of the hole inside her.

Suri crouched as the tears abated. She took a few deep breaths, the heat of the sun making her woozy. She clutched the post to keep herself from falling as her vision narrowed.

Was she going to faint?

Then a voice came from a few steps away. "You resemble a woman in desperate need of respite. Mayhaps in the form of some most delicious libations and the liberation of song."

"Something like that," Suri said, still struggling to think. She turned her head to the man who had addressed her. Her vision swam for a moment and then resettled. He smiled at her playfully, wearing a waistcoat and tails in an alarmingly bright shade somewhere between green and blue. His hair was curly, his face clean. But it was his voice she had recognised above anything else. She straightened. "Maggory?"

He blinked, taking her in again from head to toe. Nothing of recognition passed across his face. Yet he noticed her pin and his eyes widened almost comically. He gave her a wide grin. "My reputation precedes me, it seems. How is it you have come to know of my moniker?"

Maggory. Her annoyingly verbose cage mate, who had been sold to some inn. She knew him in an instant, even if he was now cleaner.

"As you said," she responded drearily. "Reputation."

"Well," he said, shrugging it off. "I cannot claim to have had the pleasure, most esteemed one. What might I call you?"

Was she so changed? She had lost so much of herself since then. Was she still the same person? "Suri," she said, lacking the conviction to lie today. "You can call me Suri."

"Suri," he said, tasting the word. "The cogs in my head still click against nothing. No matter, perhaps my name is growing larger than my pockets would suggest. I would be honoured to have your company in the establishment just yonder, so I may pick the threads of the yarn that has you looking so contemplative."

Suri smiled without mirth. He only wanted her company because he had seen her pin, and likely the pouch at her side, and wanted to prey on whatever foul mood she was in by dragging her to buy some drink. She shook her head. "I'm sor—"

"Miss," he said, interrupting her. "You're standing in the blazing sun, playing with a slave post, and if I may say so, your complexion is looking rather pale. I am bound by the laws of honour to get an ale into your waiting hands."

Suri really looked at him then. He had the same ridiculous air and pompous posture, but his smile was sympathetic and his brow furrowed. This man was concerned about her. There was genuine kindness in the way he dipped his head, a kindness which made her feel even worse and one she deeply wanted to reject.

But instead she heard herself saying, "Lead the way."

"With the utmost haste," Maggory said, and he reached his elbow out for her to take.

The inn was made of carved sandstone, with blue wall coverings in shades of ice and midnight. Some fell like tapestries, others served as curtains across small alcoves providing a little privacy from the rest of the clientele.

At this hour, it was mostly empty. A few patrons sipped from clay mugs or green-dyed glass, but they chose to sit around the bar, leaving all the tables empty.

To Suri's relief, Maggory led them to one of the alcoves. He motioned to one of the bartenders to bring them drinks.

When they sat down, he waggled his eyebrows at her. "So, what's it like working in the Lord's council? Any sordid gossip?"

Suri stared at him, then looked at the table in front of them, examining the rings left by mugs over the years.

He held his hands up. "I see that was not the place to kick off our engagement. Please allow me to redirect the nature of our conversement. Tell me, have you heard the story of the Woman from Nowhere?"

Suri raised her gaze.

"I gather from your confounded expression that this is a new tale to you. Allow me to unfurl it."

And he did, weaving a story of a woman centuries past, who could appear and then disappear as if made of the air itself, with no name and no family. The ale arrived as his tale began, and both were welcome distractions. The ale was cold and soothed a dull ache she hadn't realised she was holding onto, and the inn was a new location, somewhere distinct enough from the square outside that she could almost forget where she was. And his story, too, transported her to somewhere else.

She found herself smiling when the story called for it, even faking a laugh at the natural pauses in Maggory's dramatic retellings. By the third ale, and the third story, she found herself far more at ease.

Suri told him a little of herself, how she was a born Northerner. He asked her about what had happened in the arena, and she could tell even her abridged version captured his attention and memory. Kol had revealed himself to the whole town by riding in unglamoured, and word of it would spread fast. She figured there was no harm in acknowledging his present existence, though she warned Maggory to repeat the story to Kol's subjects only. Oh, she knew he would exaggerate it, but it was hard to imagine how he could exaggerate anything quite so terrible as the truth. She skipped over the mechanics of the poison and any notion of feelings, so at least that would not make it into any story or song.

Then a woman walked in. The inn had filled up considerably already, and where the sun had once peeled through the gaps in the curtains, it no longer did. Still, she recognised the woman's gait and her keen gold-lined eyes, toying with all they locked onto.

She tapped Maggory's mug, then nodded towards the woman. "That's Daiyu."

Maggory grinned. "You are most correct, honoured guest. She has some of the finest men and women one ever did lay eyes on, if you're looking for that flavour of diversion."

She stared at the woman. That was to be her fate once, bought for the trade of skin and perfumed nights. Daiyu would have succeeded in buying her flesh had Kol not wished to spite her further.

Suri finished her ale and put a few silver coins down on the table as she stood. "Thank you for your company, and the diversion."

Maggory shook his head so emphatically she brought her gaze back to him. "No, no, no. Thank *you*, esteemed patroness. Your choice to sit with me this evening has been most inspirational. I shall write an epic poem to attest to your great beauty."

Suri snorted. "I wish you luck."

Then she strode up to Daiyu, with no small trepidation, and introduced herself.

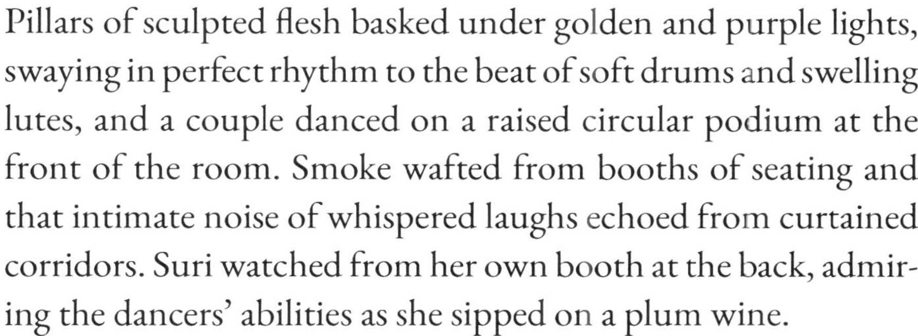

Pillars of sculpted flesh basked under golden and purple lights, swaying in perfect rhythm to the beat of soft drums and swelling lutes, and a couple danced on a raised circular podium at the front of the room. Smoke wafted from booths of seating and that intimate noise of whispered laughs echoed from curtained corridors. Suri watched from her own booth at the back, admiring the dancers' abilities as she sipped on a plum wine.

Daiyu had happily led her here at her request and she found it oddly calming to see in person, and the drink helped to further loosen that knot in her belly.

The women were healthy and fit, the men virile and strong. They laughed with each other and the patrons that came in treated them with respect and appreciation.

Until Kol came in and ruined it.

He swept into the room, lacking his usual grace. Even so, his presence commanded the room in an instant. The man spinning on the podium froze for a moment, before regaining his composure and the musicians faltered a few beats.

Suri tried to ignore that her own traitorous heart still skipped a beat every time she saw him. Any thought that he might not have come there for her evaporated the moment he started scanning the back of the room instead of the stage.

He found her quickly and stalked towards her, stopping in front of her, his arms crossed and his figure so wide he blocked out all the lamps around the stage. "So, this is where you've been spending your time."

"How do I know it's you?"

"We're in my fucking outpost."

Suri raised a brow. He wasn't glamoured, and even if he had been, she knew it was him. But he had come to her with an attitude, and she wasn't going to hold back on her own.

He snarled a lip. "*Nen alerisee f'ith sotele.* Answer me."

"Yes, I have spent some of my time here," she replied, happy her hand did not shake as she took another sip of her wine. "Something to say?"

Kol glowered at her. "If it was your intention to hurt me, you could have chosen to do it less publicly."

She blinked at the frost lacing every word. It made no sense. How was she hurting him by having a few drinks and sitting here? It was his damned idea to come to the outpost. What did he want her to do? Sit in her room alone all day? He was busy, after all, on business which did not include her.

Suri pursed her lips, placing her glass down with a thud. "Hurt you?"

He shook his head, his shoulders tense with unexplained rage. "I understand my rejection must have offended you, but to fall instantly to drink and then into the arms of a paid stranger. Clearly, it *does* mean that little to you. Was it always about the sex?"

Suri did not contain her shock, and the anger followed behind it like lightning. "How dare you."

Kol didn't flinch, only glaring down at her.

"Look at you, so noble and righteous," she spat. "Ready to lash out without a moment's pause or context." Suri stood up fast and used the surprise of it to launch her hands forwards. "Fuck you."

He stumbled a step backwards, not expecting her push. She could see his confidence faltering, but it wasn't enough.

"Get out of my sight," she said, her rage cutting like a knife. "I have never been so lonely as I have felt in your company the last few days. You've got your wish, I finally agree with you. You're right, oh benevolent *Lord*, we're better off at a distance."

Kol took another step back, and she could see his anger flare and dispel as his confusion took over. "I don't understand."

"No, you don't." Suri barked a harsh laugh, all noise and no joy. "Do I look bedded?"

Kol scanned her from head to toe. She narrowed her gaze at him as he swallowed and dropped his arms to his sides. If she wasn't imagining it in the dim light, his cheeks looked a little pink.

"Now let me ask you another question," she said, stepping up to his face and pushing him again. This time he expected it, but still stepped back once more. "Do you remember the last time I was here?"

Kol's eyes widened. He glanced at the door, as if recalling what happened outside of it.

She crossed her own arms. "Yes, you remember it well. The last time I was here, I was chained to one of those posts outside and the people in this outpost bid for me and tried to buy my flesh. For a time, I thought my life would be spent within these very walls. Forgive me if I try to understand what would have happened to me had you not intervened to worsen my fate."

Kol reached for her. "Suri—"

Suri pushed him back another step, not allowing him to touch her. "I don't resent you for it. I killed your friend. But this isn't a place of comfort for me. I was hungry, I was thirsty." She pointed to the door. "This is where I was sold like cattle. I have eight gold in this bag, gold you gave like it was nothing. I was sold for eight *silver*." Her voice cracked, and the anger gave way to the unstoppable sensation that she was about to cry. She kept talking before it overwhelmed her completely. "A person. Eight silver. I could buy myself ten times over with your coin and have money left. Can you even fathom how sick that is? Nothing has made me feel so worthless as this place did when I was here."

Kol's face was as white as a sheet.

Suri reached into her chest pocket and pulled out the brooch she'd recovered from the sewers back in New Politan. A spiralling sun carved with tens of curling spokes of silver. It was Cthanda's, and she no longer wished to carry it. She grabbed forwards and was almost gratified when Kol flinched, but she only reached for his hand, pressing the cold metal into his palm. "Here. I meant to give this to you before. Take it, and leave me be."

She strode past him, her fingers tingling from the warmth of his palm. Then she turned back, the breath shuddering out of her body, hitching as she gulped in some perfumed air. He stared down at his palm, stuck rigid.

In for a silver, in for a gold. "You have ignored me for days. I am lonely, and every part of me feels fucking empty. So please, do not chastise me for drinking. I'm trying to keep it together."

Then Kol surprised her.

He dropped to his knees before her. The musicians must have been watching, because she could have sworn they missed a beat again. He either did not notice, or did not care, as he only seemed to see her.

Kol stared up at her, his shining eyes full of remorse. "I'm so sorry. I didn't think."

She acknowledged his apology with a small nod, even as her stomach clenched at the sight. "I'm going to rest. We have a long day tomorrow."

She walked for the door. But she had not gone more than two steps before he called her.

"Suri?" His voice was soft, but she turned immediately.

He was still on his knees.

"Yes, Kol?"

Kol studied her. "Can I sleep on your floor?"

10

Despite the town's charms, I find the market to be dreary. There is nothing of art, learning, nor true innovation to be found.

Unknown author, est. 2nd-5th century

"Where are you two?" Nadrian asked a couple of days later, his perpetual snark seeping into every word. "Actually, if your pace is due to your nightly activities, spare me the gory details."

Kol sighed as he tied the seeing silk around his right eye to give Nadrian a window into their movements. Their horses plodded beneath them through a steadily thickening lush forest, following a scrubbed small dirt path through the trees, the terrain too unpredictable to go any faster. "We just passed into the Pail, and we're closing in on the Waterborne estate."

"Two days out, then?" Nadrian guessed.

Kol glanced up at the purpling sky. "If we hit the Royal Road by dawn, we could reach you by nightfall tomorrow."

"Good," Nadrian said. "Both the Metal Guild and the Magic Guild want to meet."

"Magic, too? I thought Manthi was allied with Lera," Kol replied.

"So did I," Nadrian said. "But she is open to a conversation."

"Do you think we can trust either of them?"

"Hard to say. Manthi sticks to her word, though she doesn't often say her word until most of the coins are laid on the table. Metal are fickle, too. I always found Nonlos an odd pick as he largely keeps to himself, and in the ten odd years he's been in charge, he only comes to Guild meetings with strictly enforced attendance. People say he's small-minded. If you appeal to his ego well enough, he might be reliable."

"Have the rumours hit?" Kol asked.

"The rumour of your death arrived before I did, Kol. There are faster wings than mine in this sky. Most of them don't have to hold up such an alarmingly attractive man."

A small laugh escaped Suri, and it was a relief to feel something other than tension for a moment.

Kol, however, was focused. "What's the consensus?"

"Most believe it, but some say they won't be celebrating until they see a body."

"And the harpy?"

"Lera seems to be keeping her head down. I haven't worked out where she's staying, or what she's doing," he noted with frustration. "From what I've heard, Lingyun might be with her, but I can't say for certain. I can only assume one of the Guilds is sheltering her."

"Probably Dellon. He's an oily little vole," Kol said, his jaw flexed.

Nadrian paused. "If you plan on confronting him, don't forget to invite me. I want to write poetry from your threats."

Kol smiled despite himself. "Your poetry is terrible."

"Tell that to my companion from last night."

"Yes, I'm sure it was your fine stanzas that drew him in and not your copious booze allowance and fine clothing," Kol quipped sardonically.

"They come for my wealth, they stay for the rhyming couplets," Nadrian said, and then his voice became far less wistful. "Be careful. I haven't worn my pin here, and I'm exhausted from having to glamour my face as well as my wings. People are wary and see more than they should. As much as some believe the head of the snake is gone, they're still nervous and they're waiting to see how our court is going to retaliate."

"They should be wary of the snake in their very city," the Son of Life growled.

Nadrian made an appreciative noise. "Maybe you should be the poet."

Kol clicked his tongue. "Goodbye, Nadrian."

They weaved through thicker and thicker trees as the light faded, following paths led by hunters and animals alike. Suri found the forest quite peaceful; the simple soundscape of leaves, birdcalls, and clanking pots in the saddlebags provided a homeliness the desert did not.

Eventually, they hit the edge of a lake and the horses stopped, stooping their wide necks to drink beside one another. Suri scanned the black water, likely freezing from the recent winter. On the distant shore Suri could see a manor, its figure dark against the mauve sky but its windows candlelit and warm.

Kol stared out, too. “The Waterborne estate.”

“Looks cosy,” Suri said. She tried to inject some wit into it, but after twelve hours of riding she was barely able to do more than stay upright.

“It is now that Viantha is the heir,” he replied. “The place felt like a crypt before.” Kol clicked his tongue and pulled his mare up. “Nearly there. You’ll have a stable and everything.”

A tired smile drifted onto Suri’s mouth. “Are you talking to me or the horse?”

“With the way we smell, I wouldn’t be surprised if they left us in the hay.”

“A warm barn with a roof would be a welcome bed.”

“Don’t tell our hosts that,” Kol said, turning back to grin at her. “You’re a lady now.”

She was about to retort that she was no such damned thing when an arrow sliced through the air, nicking the back of Kol’s horse.

The next moment, his mare bolted with a disgruntled noise as her own mare reared, braying. Suri fell back, tipping out of the saddle and flipping down to the floor, landing in the soft mud near the river bank. She pushed herself into a crouch as her mare ran into the trees.

She scanned the darkness, pulling a knife from the pocket just above her riding boots. Kol and his horse were long out of sight, and the woods were eerily silent.

Another arrow whistled. Twisting at the last second, its bolt pierced the side of her right arm. She needed to move, she was a sitting duck by the water.

Suri pushed upwards and sprinted into the trees in the same direction as her horse, away from wherever the arrow had come from. She grabbed her arm as the pain lanced through it. It wasn't too bad, the cut wasn't deep, but she couldn't risk being hit again.

"Suri!" Kol's yell was somewhere beyond her, deeper into the night.

She swallowed, about to yell back when she heard the tell-tale sound of a sword sliding from its sheath behind her. Suri whirled around, raising her knife as the sword came clattering towards her. It was a lazy strike, not expecting to meet resistance, from a man wearing all black and an unpleasant sneer. His next strike was more intentional, but she had her balance back, and as he cut towards her neck she rolled away, yelling out as she did. "I'm here."

It might bring more men down upon her, but it would also bring Kol, and he was far more dangerous than these useless excuses for human breath.

The man grinned with yellow, stubby teeth as he advanced towards her again. "Not for long."

His sword arced towards her. It was a nice manoeuvre, but a slow one. It gave her time to roll again, this time right towards him.

She nicked him across the inner thigh, and he whirled, his next strike an inch from taking off her scalp as she ducked underneath it, falling back. Her cut was true, she was sure it had pierced that place where the blood was fullest, and the wound would kill him in minutes. Though, that wouldn't help if he killed her in seconds. She rolled again, dodging his obvious downstrike into her chest as she kicked up hard at his grip and he dropped his sword.

Suri was at his neck within a moment.

"Don't kill him," came the voice behind her as Kol thundered into the space behind her.

Suri relaxed the pressure on the knife. She looked at Kol, the tension in her stomach unravelling when he appeared unscathed. "It's you?"

He nodded. "*Nen alerisee f'ith sotele.*"

Suri blew out a breath.

"Yes," the man gasped. "Yes, please. Don't kill me, please."

"Who are they?" Suri asked, her blade shaking against the man's jugular, her hand twisted in his greasy hair, wrenching his head back.

"That's what I'd like to know. I killed the three who jumped me." Kol stared at her. "Are you hurt?"

"The archer caught my shoulder," Suri said. "I think he's still out there. Back left treeline from where they first clipped you."

The man gasped. "Please, lady. Please."

Kol's eyes blackened. "Stay here."

When Kol left, the man twisted, trying to catch her off-guard. She pressed the knife into his neck, carving a thin line of red. He stilled.

Less than a minute later, Kol returned, holding two severed hands. "He won't be firing any more arrows."

Kol threw the hands at her yellow-toothed man, still dripping blood as they hit off his tunic and fell at his knees. Suri admired the severance, both cleanly sliced off at the wrist.

She smirked. "Unless he learns to use his feet."

Kol shrugged. "He's also dead, so that might be hard."

The man in Suri's grip groaned.

"Who do you work for?" Kol asked, crouching in front of him.

"I work for the Demon King," he said, sniffling. "Kol's black guard."

"How interesting," Kol said, glancing up at Suri. "And why would the Demon King's appointed guard be out in the Pail attacking random civilians?"

He shook his head. "Please, good sir, I just follow orders. The Demon King's evil knows no boundaries."

Kol nodded sagely. "True enough. So, who gave you the order to pretend to be the Demon King's lackeys?"

His eyes went wide, the whites of them catching in the moonlight. "Sir?"

"Was it Queen Lera?" Kol asked.

His mouth opened and closed like a fish.

Kol stood. "Let me see how much of this I guess correctly. You were once a common sellsword, perhaps a highwayman, making a passable living attacking travelling merchants along the Royal Road. Then one day, you get a royal invitation. The great Queen Lera, inviting *you* to dine with her? Surely, too good to be true. She makes you an offer. You can continue doing what you love best. Murdering, looting, pillaging. As long as you wear black, maybe a touch of silver, too, and don't forget to tell everyone how horrible the Demon King is."

The man swallowed. "Listen, I don't know nothing. I do as I'm told."

Kol sighed. "The sad thing is, I think you're telling the truth. Are there any more of you?"

"Only five," he said. "Only five. If you've killed," his voice wavered. "If you've killed the other four, then that's it. Please, sir. Have mercy."

"Thank you for your cooperation," Kol said. "Mercy is not my call to make. That rests entirely with the beautiful woman whose hands you don't deserve to have anywhere near you right now."

"You're done?" Suri said.

"I am," Kol said.

She sliced his throat without a second thought, and let his body fall to the floor. It *was* mercy, in a way. He would have bled out in ten minutes from the blood loss. She was really sparing them the pain of listening to him wail.

"Good choice." He stepped around the body and pulled her towards him by her hips. His fingers peeling away the torn fabric at her shoulder to look at the wound. "I want to bandage this. Let's get you to the manor."

11

Once more, he visited. This time I pretended not to be in, despite the telling plume from my fireplace.
Unknown author, est. 2nd-5th century

A footman opened the manor door as they reached the stone steps. It was a fine house of dark stone with a uniform hedge all around it. The windows showed glimpses into large halls with high ceilings, and torchlight shone from its two battlements. The footman stared at the pair of them. “It is a late hour for guests. And ones without horses?”

Kol had glamoured himself until they could be sure of welcome, but no one could mistake the commanding tone of his voice. “We were accosted by highwaymen in the woods around your estate. Our horses have bolted, and it’ll be easier to find them come morning.” The footman’s eyes widened. “We are courtiers of the Lord Kol. Your lady may have written ahead to warn you of our arrival.”

The footman swallowed, apprehension blossoming at the mention of Kol, but he opened the door to them readily enough. "Of course, come in. The ladies Ressa and Viantha are not home, but I will send for the housekeeper at once."

"There's no need to send for me, Foxton." A young woman appeared in a comfortable pale green day dress, with honey-coloured hair in loose waves to her hip. Her cheeks were dotted with freckles and her front teeth were a little crooked as she grinned at the pair of them. "Get in, then. You're letting in an awful draft, and I somehow have the bones of a crone already."

The entryway opened into a wide hall framed by a sweeping stone staircase, with plush blue rugs covering the floor and a fire crackling pleasantly in the hearth.

The footman took their cloaks, and the young woman gasped upon seeing Suri's shoulder. "Are you alright, my lady? I'm no doctor, but I can mix up a salve and wrap it with some clean cloth?"

Suri glanced at Kol. "I don't want to be any trouble."

Kol rolled his eyes. "If you could pull something together, Millie, I'll apply them myself."

"Of course, sir," Millie said, then stared at him again, her gaze narrowing. "How do you—"

Kol grinned and released his hold on the glamour. "Good to know you're still kind to your guests when you're not trying to impress me."

Suri ground her teeth as Millie jumped back with a gasp then hit Kol lightly on the arm. "Gods, Kol. Next time, warn a girl when you're going to do black magic in her damned doorway."

He chuckled. "If I ever do black magic around you, Millie, I'll let you know."

Suri tried to ignore her rising jealousy, but she hated how familiar they were with one another. It was another part of his life Suri wasn't in, another reminder of how cold she was by comparison.

"How do you seem even taller? What do they feed you in that desert?" Millie muttered, before gasping again. "Where are my manners? You must be starving. I'll get the cook to make up some dinner."

Suri's stomach rumbled, her hunger and exhaustion overtaking her annoyance. "Food sounds good."

"Take a seat in the drawing room," she said as she backed away, waving her hand to a door to the left of the main hall. "I'll check on your rooms, too."

Kol and Suri nodded at her retreating form, and then fell into padded armchairs beside another fire in the drawing room. They both moaned at the feeling of the warm comfort after the long day on the road.

"She seems friendly," Suri said with a yawn.

"Millie's great," Kol said, sounding equally exhausted.

Her jealousy flickered once more, but it was hard to concentrate on it when the cushion was so soft beneath her.

Despite their need for rest, as soon as Millie returned with the food, they set upon it like wolves. The venison was tender and the vegetables ripe. Millie returned a few minutes later with a pot of something, some clean cloth, and a bowl of steaming water.

Kol knelt next to Suri's chair. "Sit still."

Suri didn't mind that instruction at all. "Yes, sir."

His eyes darkened, but he focused on her arm, using a wet cloth to dab the blood away and clean the wound. "Does it hurt?"

"A little."

"I should have noticed them before they ambushed us," he said, staring at her arm as he admonished himself.

"Don't do that. Neither of us noticed them, and I'm barely hurt."

"Yet you seem to get hurt every time you're with me," Kol said, applying a thick layer of the salve to the cut. Suri fought a flinch and he frowned.

"I've been getting myself into trouble long before I met you, Kol," she said, before changing the subject. "Have you spent much time here?"

"I've visited a couple times in the last year," he said. "I was here when you used the silk to tell me about the ceremony at the altar."

She recalled seeing him walking through dark corridors. "Oh."

Kol wrapped her arm with a dry cloth, tying the knot tight. Suri grimaced, and he rubbed her arm, meeting her heavy-lidded gaze. "All done."

"Thank you," she murmured.

He nodded, still rubbing his thumb over the bandaged cut. She shivered as they stared at each other. He dragged his tongue over his bottom lip, and she followed the movement, biting her own lip. Kol made a small noise, almost clearing his throat, and dropped the eye contact.

Suri felt instantly ridiculous, her mouth dry and her thighs clenched. She blinked and stared down at her hands as Millie came back into the room.

"Your rooms are ready," she said in a sing-song voice. Then she paused, taking them in with a gulp. "If you're done?"

Great. The tension was that palpable. Both of them sprang up, standing beside her.

"Perfect," she said, mirth light in her eyes. "Just this way."

She led them up the staircase and along a corridor. Even in the darkness of the night, attention was given to keep each space warmly lit, and plants sat near every window they passed. "I didn't have Ressa down as a gardener."

Millie looked back with a small smile. "It's Viantha who is the lover of plants."

"I suppose that makes sense," Suri said. Viantha was born to be a Daughter of the Earth. Or one of them, whatever the prophecy actually meant.

"Do you know the Lady Viantha well?" Millie asked.

Suri choked as Kol smothered a noise from behind her. "I can't claim to know her well. We are acquaintances."

"You are lucky, then," Millie replied. "She is a fair and kind woman."

Suri had no reply to that as Millie pushed open a door on the left and then stepped across the corridor to open the door exactly opposite it.

Millie turned to the pair of them and smiled again. "These will be your rooms. There are hot coals at the end of the bed, clean water, towels and linen. There is also a bath waiting for both of you."

That must have been what Millie dashed upstairs to check on. She took one whiff of them and ordered two fresh baths poured at once. Suri smirked at Kol, ready to make some quip, but he was looking straight ahead. So she just nodded at Millie, weary once more. "Thank you."

Millie passed Kol a small pile of clothing and then passed her another folded pile.

"Yes, thank you, Millie," Kol echoed.

Suri stared at one door and then the other. It struck her they hadn't spent a night with a wall between them in days. There was something cold about it, the idea of stepping to the door and nodding a goodnight to Kol. It was so formal again.

She hesitated.

Kol didn't seem to have the same reservations. He strode through the door on the left and closed the door behind him with little more than a cursory glance in her direction.

Oh.

Suri nodded awkwardly to Millie before walking to the right. "Good night," she said. Millie dipped her head, and Suri closed the door.

The room wasn't lavish, not like the ones in the Seat of Drameir, but it was so much more comforting. Again, plants filled the spaces which she imagined would catch the light of the day, and copper-toned rugs warmed the floor. There was a charming small double bed with a duck-egg blue embroidered bedspread. The exhaustion of the day fell upon her as soon as she looked at that bed, and she craved sinking into it more than almost anything.

But it was the bath that caught her attention more. The steaming water caught in the candlelight as the moonlight fell through the one open set of curtains. She peeled off her sweaty riding gear and sank into it with a small amount of grace and a large amount of relief, keeping her injured arm out of the water.

Once she was clean and mostly dry, Suri put on the nightdress Millie had given her and got into bed. Her feet were toasty as the coals warmed its sheets. The pillows were cushioning and the mattress was firm, but not too firm. She was perfectly comfortable.

Then, she lay there.

And lay there.

No matter how she moved, she couldn't sleep.

Every moment, she looked at the door, waiting for it to knock or open.

Kol was all she could think of. His eyes as he rubbed her arm earlier. The way he held her hips after she'd killed that man, and how her own stomach had clenched when he said he'd already killed three.

That perfect smile.

Gods, it was insufferable. It was Sotoledi's influence, she decided. He was exaggerating her lust. But even as she rationalised it, she couldn't get away from the need to be in the same room as him more than she needed air.

She strode to the door and listened. Nothing. She opened the door, just a fraction, part of her believing he might be sitting in the corridor as he had in the Glen. But nothing again.

An empty corridor had never made her so sad before. She closed the door again, her breath coming quick. Every part of her body pulsed to see him, to touch him.

Damn it. She took a deep breath and grabbed the candle. She opened the door once more and stepped across the corridor.

She stopped outside his door. It seemed stupid again. He was probably fast asleep. Her hair was falling in damp waves and her nightdress was almost sheer. He'd seen her in less, yes, but this still felt new and inappropriate. He didn't *want* her. Not right now. How many times did he have to tell her?

Suri swallowed and stared up at the ceiling. She breathed in and out once more, and then raised her hand to knock.

And the door swung open.

Kol stood naked from the waist up, a towel tucked around his hips, his dark hair wet, a few strands falling over his face. His brow was creased, and for the split second before he fully registered her, he looked angry. And then his determined gaze dropped to hers, and his expression transformed. Surprise, joy, and then something of a smug arrogance that irritated her and melted her in the same moment.

"Hey, little thief." Husky, low.

Suri swallowed against a suddenly dry mouth. "Hey."

He smirked. "Forget something?"

Suri weighed it in her mind. The embarrassment, the possibility of rejection, the sheer need to be around him. She knew it was irrational, but she honestly couldn't fathom sleeping in another room, even one as delightfully presented as hers had been.

Shit.

She closed her eye for a long blink and then set him with a determined look. “Can I sleep on your floor?”

His arrogance cracked. He studied her hair, the way her damp tresses likely made the white dress ever more see-through. Her cheekbones lit by candlelight and bare feet on the floorboards. She wondered if he could see how fast her heart was pumping. It must be visible, it felt on the brink of explosion. “Get in here.”

Suri slipped through the door and placed her candle next to his on the small table just inside. Even that felt intimate somehow.

She glanced around as he closed the door. The room was a near mirror of hers, with a pale green bedspread instead. He hadn’t even tried to sleep yet, with his bed still perfectly made. From the wet footprints by the bath, he must have only just got out.

Kol paused by the door, his back resting against it as he stared at her. His midnight eyes seemed to linger on every part of her, burning through her with an unrivalled intensity. Something breakable hung in the air, teetering towards the floor.

Her cheeks flushed, and she covered her strange embarrassment by striding to the small couch under one of the curtained windows.

“What are you doing?” Kol drawled.

Suri fluffed up a pillow and sat down. “I can go get the blanket from my room.”

Kol rolled his eyes. “I’m not actually going to let you sleep on the floor.”

“What?”

“Get in the bed, you idiot.”

"I can't take your bed—"

"I won't be able to sleep tonight unless you do. Get into that bed, right now."

Suri swallowed, but followed his instruction. She pulled the covers back and settled herself onto one side. When she looked back at him, he had pulled some light trousers on, and they sat sinfully on his hips. She felt her blush spread, knowing that if she'd looked around at the right time, he would have been there fully naked before her.

Instead, he stared out the one open window, his fingers clenched tight around the back of a chair. She recalled one of her first impressions of him. She had thought he was like marble, a statue carved by some divine thing. Now, in the moonlight, his body rigid and his firm torso bare to her, she saw it again. The shadows in the room hid the line of amefyre punctuating every ridge of his spine, so all she saw was the man, and he was achingly handsome.

"Did you know I was outside?" Suri asked.

"What?" His grip whitened and she saw a muscle in his arm flex.

"Did you know I was outside your room, just then?" she repeated. "Or were you coming to my room?"

Kol smiled without looking at her and she glimpsed only a hint of it. But his voice was pained. "What do you think?"

Suri's heart hurt. "Please sleep in the bed."

Kol groaned. "Suri—"

"I know," she said. "I know that you don't want to be around me right now. I know it's painful for you because you have no idea what I'm feeling. I don't know what I'm feeling either. I *can't* feel anything. I can only feel the bad."

Kol turned to face her, his arms crossed over his wide chest.

"But I can't watch you lie on a damned cold floor again, or contort yourself onto that tiny excuse for a couch. You can paint my reasons as any dark emotion you want. All I know is, if you don't sleep in this bed, I'm getting out of it, too."

He stared at her, marking whether she meant it, mapping her every tell. Then he swallowed. "Fuck it."

He strode around to the other side of the bed and pulled back the covers, setting himself next to her. He was wide enough that even on either side they were almost touching. She turned towards him, staring at him with something akin to relief. As if all the negativity had lifted from her body.

"Happy now?" he said, with a raised eyebrow. She smirked joylessly as he groaned, covering his face with his hand. "Poor choice of words, sorry."

"Good night, Kol."

He smiled. "Good night, Suri."

She let her eye close and was unconscious within the minute.

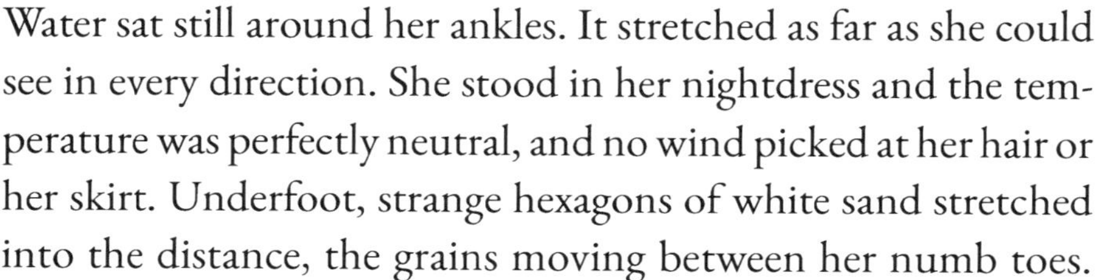

Water sat still around her ankles. It stretched as far as she could see in every direction. She stood in her nightdress and the temperature was perfectly neutral, and no wind picked at her hair or her skirt. Underfoot, strange hexagons of white sand stretched into the distance, the grains moving between her numb toes.

There was no sun, and yet orange and pink lanced the sky as if one was setting.

Suri had an odd sensation that she was waiting for something. She turned, looking for something, anything. The water moved, but she couldn't feel its resistance. After two full revolutions, a woman appeared in front of her.

"Hello again, Seer," she said, her golden hair hanging in a loose braid over one shoulder, laced with small white flowers. She was young, looking younger even than Suri, but she hooked Suri with a gaze a century old.

Kol's mother, locked in her beautiful youth in the fragments of the past.

"Cthanda," Suri said. "Where are we?"

"We are nowhere," Cthanda said.

"Is this a relic? Are you truly dead?"

"I showed you my death, did I not?" Cthanda retorted.

Suri swallowed, but it felt wrong and unnecessary. "Is Diophage dead?"

Cthanda smiled, and it gave a playful innocence to her face. "What is death really, but another journey the soul makes? You would know about that."

"Do you know who the Daughters are?"

Cthanda stepped forwards, her flowing dress tugging against the water. "Thank you. For saving my son's soul."

"The world needs him."

"The world needs you, too," Kol's mother replied, tilting her head. "My son can bring back Life. But a time will soon come when you will have the chance to stop Death."

Suri nodded, the motion slower than it should have been. "I know. We need to stop Lera from bringing back Sotoledi. Stop her before she gets to eight massacres."

"You are a Seer of Time. Everyone else must work to form what is to come. Your gaze should be to what has already passed."

"But how?"

Cthanda smiled. "Learn from the past, go back and observe what came before, and maybe you can change the future."

Suri narrowed her eye. "Change something in the past, you mean?"

Cthanda's face went cold, her mouth rigid. "No, your role is to observe. Only to observe."

"Observe what?"

Cthanda reached out her hand, her palm facing up. "With relics, you can see the past. Your own, and others. With Time Circles, you can see the present. Use it."

Suri furrowed her brow. What good was witnessing the past if she could not do anything about it? She reached forwards and her hand went straight through Cthanda. "I don't understand."

Cthanda's mouth was a hard line. "Really try to reach me. Breathe. Focus."

Suri tried, but the world around her only grew blacker as her head began to pound and the water at her feet went cold. She breathed deep to try to refocus herself, but the moment slipped further away.

In one final attempt, Suri reached out once more, expecting her hand to pass straight through Cthanda, as it had before.

But it caught, like pushing her fingers through hair, and in that resistance there was a flash of something.

The pavilion on the summer solstice, the moon hitting its structure as Diophage appeared from the fountain to see Cthanda. Then it pulled away, back to the strange limbo of ankle-deep water and salt.

She had barely opened her mouth before she was pulled back again.

Back, back. Cold, darkness.

Then she gasped and woke up.

Suri sat bolt upright, hands fisting on the sheets beneath her. Kol groaned, his arm shifting around her. At some point in the night, they had become tangled in each other, and his arm now sat like a comforting weight across her middle. She blinked, taking in the dark room. It wasn't yet dawn.

She breathed heavily for a moment, realising her forehead was clammy with sweat. She pulled the strands of hair back, her whole body shaking.

What was that place?

Was it a relic? Inside herself? Or Kol? It didn't seem like a relic. It wasn't a memory, surely, as Suri had never heard of such a place existing. So how would Cthanda have trapped that place in Kol, if it was no place she could have remembered?

Suri didn't understand any of it. Why would she bother to show Suri that she could go through that relic to the other relic she'd seen before? What use was that to her? She'd already seen all of Cthanda's relics. She remembered them, and besides, if she really needed to see them again, she could just see Ruben. There must have been a reason, but for the life of her, Suri had no clue what it was.

But soon, the warmth of Kol's body pressed next to her, and her need for rest overtook her once more, and she fell back into a fitful sleep.

12

What does he mean by it? Leaving a tome such as this on my doorstep. It is not one I have seen in town.
Unknown author, est. 2nd-5th century

Lartosh was a city set against steep hills, rising and falling in paved streets down to the bustling port. From their approach, they had seen most of it already, the curving road casting new vistas across the city with every hill passed. Even at twilight, though, she could tell it was also a city of colour and vitality. The port in the distance sprawled the full length of the city, dotted by huge ships and fishing boats alike. Sailors crammed on, like ants from this distance, waving arms and hauling loads. The buildings were warm, not built of the grey slate of Drangbor or the white and grey stones of the North. Here, the roofs were terracotta clay in hues of orange and red, and yellow flags hung from every building.

Suri asked about the flags, as they weren't anything she recognised.

"Lartosh has a ceremony at the end of every fortnight," Kol explained. "Representatives of one Guild will march through the city, dancing and waving their flags, visiting every other Guild. Their flag is shown until the fortnight is up, and the next will take over."

She turned to him. "What's yellow for?"

His shoulders were slumped and his hold on the reins loose. "Yellow is the Construction Guild. Food is green, Magic is purple and Water is blue. Metal is white and silver."

Keeping his glamour up all day as they traversed the Royal Road had taken its toll. Despite Millie's insisted-upon breakfast and the generous lunch she gave them, they were both flagging when they hit the stable at the edge of the city.

Foxton had tracked down both their horses in the night with the saddlebags still intact. Millie graciously offered two of their own horses as replacements, and given Kol's mare had a cut across her back from the fray, they decided to leave both of their mounts at Viantha's estate to rest. Thankfully her new mare was equally soft-tempered, and Suri handled the change well enough.

Kol paid the stablekeep and hopped down from his white horse, giving her face a stroke. Then he turned to Suri, holding his hand out to her.

She looped one aching leg around and grabbed his hand with both of hers as she dropped down to the ground.

He squeezed them, staring down at her. "You rode well again today. It must be painful, your legs aren't used to it."

Suri shrugged as her thighs quivered. “Pain, I can do.”

“I’ve noticed,” he said. “But you don’t have to. If it’s ever too much, we can stop. You just need to tell me.”

Suri nodded. “I will.”

He was still glamoured, and he looked so oddly human that she could see his vulnerability even more now. Her muscles ached, but he was hurting too.

Kol gave her a tired smile and, still holding her hand, pulled her out of the stable. “Let’s find an inn.”

There was a moment, as they walked through the city gates into a brand new place where the salt wrinkled her nose, like a pair of lovestruck newlyweds hand-in-hand, with his human face matching hers, that they could have been anyone at all. They were possibility itself, and they didn’t have to prevent an evil queen from committing atrocities that would reawaken a death god, they were just a man and a woman, in a city she’d never been to before, looking for a place to stay. He glanced at her as they walked, and the lantern light hit his uncertain smile.

Suri knew what she *wanted* to feel. Hope. Exploration. The joy of discovering something new and shiny that was just for you. The child she had once been couldn’t have fathomed that this was her life; Esra safe and protected, she herself a rich woman and a core member of a Lord’s court. And this Lord next to her, holding her, falling for her.

Yet the skin touching hers was just skin. The city was pretty, but it was just a place.

Kol dropped her hand as he pushed open the door of The Tarrying Juggler. Suri paid the innkeeper for three nights, and they went immediately to their room. There was no suggestion they would even ask for two.

The door closed, and Kol became himself again. He picked up his silk from his pocket, called for Nadrian, and confirmed they were in the city.

"Good," came the overly loud reply. Either he was somewhere with a strange echo, or he was drunk. "I know where Lera is. She's holed up down by the docks, in one of Dellon's fishing warehouses."

"Perfect."

"What now?" Nadrian asked, his voice a little slurred. Definitely drunk, then.

"Organise a meeting with Nonlos and Manthi tomorrow. Let's see where their loyalties lie."

"Oh," Nadrian said, excitement filling his voice. "Are we doing 'The Xianyu'?"

Kol rolled his eyes. "Yes. We're doing 'The Xianyu'."

Whatever the fuck 'The Xianyu' was, it involved more waiting than Suri wanted.

Suri shifted again, her thighs somehow aching more today as she checked the other door, though she was certain she was already looking at the right one. Nadrian should have been out by now.

Kol was across town, waiting outside another door. Nadrian had been there earlier, meeting Nonlos. Now, he was in a meeting with Manthi, in the building across the road from where Suri watched from an upstairs window.

The sun was warmer here, though the sea air brought with it a sharpness and more than a little tang.

Cthanda had come to her a second time last night, and as before Suri pulled herself briefly into that solstice night before it faded. She needed to know what it meant, but didn't want to talk to Kol about it yet. Something about admitting she was haunted by his dead mother didn't feel appropriate. She'd much prefer to talk to Mother Edi about it, and she wondered if there was a Time Circle somewhere nearby. Either way, she had no answers and she was tired.

Nadrian left, glancing briefly around him, but he didn't look upwards and didn't notice her. Then he was gone, weaving down the street and out of sight.

Finally, the real work would begin. She stared at the door, waiting.

Only minutes after, a boy left through the door. He wore a dark blue thick woollen top and matching cap, with brown trousers and scuffed shoes. There was nothing to signify him as part of the Metal Guild, dressed alike to every other Pail boy she'd seen.

Suri studied him for a second, fixating on his slightly imbalanced gait from the loose buckle on his left shoe, his hat's exact shade of blue and the way his ears stuck out from under it.

Then she was out of the building and after him. She followed from as safe of a distance as she could, falling back when there were few others around, keeping closer in the crowds. He didn't lose his hat, which helped her find him more easily.

At the docks, a crush of people swarmed the main thoroughfare down to the water. Returning fishermen collided with citizens descending like gulls for the freshest produce, and she readily pushed herself into the crowd, muttering unfelt apologies as she wormed her way through without a backwards look.

The boy with the blue hat and the stuck up ears also tried to push his way through the group, but was trapped in the tide of people. She brusquely shouldered past him, not stopping as she made her way to the water's edge.

On the dockside, she glanced around her. The boy had made it past the crush, and darted quickly now towards a warehouse building. Exactly as they had guessed, delivering the message straight to Lera.

Suri spoke into her silk. "Manthi's boy is entering the warehouse at the docks."

Nadrian came back immediately. "Did you get it?"

Suri clenched her hand, feeling the paper crumple. It had been too easy to slide it out of his pocket as she went past. "I got it."

Nadrian made an appreciative noise. "What does it say?"

Suri ambled down the path, in the same vague direction the boy had gone, but with a relaxed gait. She opened the note and whispered it aloud. "'*Word is they plan to sacrifice twenty maidens to bring K back to life. Be careful.*'" She shook her head. "Nadrian, what the fuck?"

"I'm just as annoyed as you," he replied, the glee bleeding into every word. "Twenty virgins and *four* goats. They always forget the goats."

Suri waited until she saw the boy duck into the building, and then turned back to the docks. She would pause here, and then meander back, stopping at a few places to throw off any tail of her own.

Kol spoke then, clearly listening in. "So, Manthi failed the test then."

"Seems like it," Suri said, keeping her voice low in case he was still following someone. "Anything your end?"

"Nothing, no movement," Kol said. "Nadrian, dare I ask what you told Nonlos?"

"I told him we sent your dead body on a ship to Kans for burial, but the ship mysteriously disappeared into a strange green fog."

Kol tutted. "A ghost ship?"

"Everyone loves a mystery."

"Did he buy it?"

"He seemed to," Nadrian said. "Though he wasn't what I expected."

"How so?" Kol asked.

"He was quieter than the rumours gave him credit to be."

Suri stared out at the water as a shiphand squawked at a burly man who almost dropped a heaving barrel of silver-blue fish. "Do we trust him, then?"

Kol's sigh came through the silk. "I'm not sure how much choice we have. Ressa is the only one listening to us right now. We can't beat Lera with four Guilds against us. This is the gateway to the Shale, and then to Kans. If we can get the Pail to turn against Lera, it could cut her off from Dabri'yon's support." He paused. "Nadrian, set up another meeting with Nonlos. My Mistress of Coin wishes to meet him."

13

I mean to confront him about it, to demand why he left such a book with me. I have read it twice, but he has not come again.

Unknown author, est. 2nd-5th century

Back at the *Juggler*, a man found her in their room. She immediately tensed and stood, but he held up a hand. "*Nen alerisee f'ith sotele.*"

Kol had glamoured himself again, this time even more than his usual de-chiselling. He had blunted every aspect of his appearance, made every feature as dull and unassuming as possible.

He dropped his glamour, and gave her a sad and tired smile. "I was practicing. That is the face I will wear tonight."

Suri stared at his true face, lingering on his wide mouth and large nose, and found she had missed it.

He gave her a slightly confused look. "Tonight, we're going to meet Nonlos. I'd like you to lead the meeting."

She glanced down at the floor, studying the grooves in the wood, embarrassed to have been caught in admiration. "I'm not sure I would know how."

"You don't have to do much," he reassured. "I just need to make him out, understand his motivation for entertaining us and maybe why he hasn't sided with Lera. As much as he is our greatest opportunity, he is also a mystery. I can't risk revealing myself to him unless we believe he is trustworthy."

"And you will be there, too?"

"Yes," he said. "I will pose as your guard. If you believe him to be worthy of trust, you can give me a signal, and if I agree, I'll reveal myself."

"Must you show yourself? Surely it is too great a risk," she replied, looking up at him from under her lashes.

Kol stiffened a little, and his hand moved at his side, almost as if he would touch her. Then he dropped his hand back and looked to the window with a sigh. "They believe us weak right now, and no one would rightly side with us if they think our entire leadership is in disarray. If they know I'm still alive, that we are still strong and unswayed by Lera, they may consider an allyship."

"How am I supposed to find out if they are worthy of your trust?" she asked.

Kol smiled at her. "You ask them questions, little thief. Like a normal person."

Suri rolled her eye, but her stomach clenched at his smile. "Why couldn't you task this to Nadrian? I am hardly your most diplomatic courtier."

His grin only widened, and the knife edge they walked on grew thinner. "Be that as it may, I like my decisions to be supported by a majority, where I can. And despite your lack of airs, I do believe you to be a good judge of character."

"I hated you for ages," she pointed out.

He shrugged. "You came around."

Suri scoffed. "That's what you think."

Kol let out a noise that was close to a laugh. It was an achievement, if a hollow one.

Suri took a large breath and released it. She had an overwhelming need to leave, and fast. Being around him was getting more and more difficult. Every moment breathing the same air as him had her in turmoil, but closing the gap and acting on her desire would only hurt them both. "I'll do it, but I'm going to need some time to prepare myself."

"How so?" Kol asked, oblivious to her torment.

"They're expecting to meet a lady of your court. A woman who by all accounts, murdered you," she said. "I'll need to look the part."

He held up his hands. "Do what you must, I'll meet you at sunset. Don't be late."

Suri nodded, and pushed past him, leaving the room in a hurry without a backwards look. He made a noise, but she did not turn.

She should never have come here. Xianyu might have offered her a deal if she'd visited him instead. What good was she here, really? Sharing a room with him, a bed with him, was killing her from the inside as much as it was killing him.

The fresh air outside the inn calmed her slightly, but that ever-beating restlessness would not leave. The sooner they had Metal on their side, and exposed Lera's plot, the sooner she could get herself to Xianyu's and fall at his feet for her soul back. She just had to get through the next couple of days.

After a trip to the city baths to wash off Lartosh's salt in a perfumed private room, Suri made her way to a seamstress in the city. Here, no one knew her face. Instead, they saw her well-made riding clothing, clean hair and proud chin, and figured her to be some noble-born traveller. The experience was vastly different to the North, and she welcomed the invisibility of it.

When the seamstress had pulled her into her black dress and applied the stain to her mouth and powder-sheen to her face, it was twilight. She thought of the Glen then, and its perpetual purple light, as she travelled through the lilac streets to their meeting point, *The Veiled Promise*. From the outside alone she could tell it catered to a higher clientele; someone had polished the sign and tended the flowerbeds with fresh white blooms.

Suri stepped into the inn as the bard played some jig, letting a draft of cooler air into the clammy room. Many pairs of eyes turned to her. She caught their initial glances of bored curiosity, and clocked those whose eyes returned to her for a second, longer, look. The bard's song changed to a ballad as she strode to the bar.

Behind it, a blonde woman knelt down, her hair escaping from its long plait. “One moment,” she said, cranking something on one of the ale kegs. She straightened, face flushed with exertion as a studied smile painted across her face. Then she clapped eyes on Suri and froze. “Gods’ grave.”

Suri raised an eyebrow. “Hello.”

The woman swallowed and ran two fingers down her plait, smoothing it. “Sorry for my rudeness, my lady. You took me by surprise is all. We don’t get too many ladies who look like you coming in here.”

“Look like me?” she asked, meeting the woman’s gaze head on. One-eyed women?

The blonde woman blushed, her voice stuttering. “Ones that look so regal, of course. You aren’t a Queen of some kind, are you? You look fit to be a King’s consort.”

The powder dusting Suri’s cheeks masked her blush. “Nothing of the sort. Do you have Icebolts?”

The woman nodded with vigour. “I don’t make many, but I think I know the method.”

Suri nodded. “Thank you.”

The woman stared at her for a fraction more, then whirled away, plucking bottles off the shelves behind her.

Suri turned, and as she did so several patrons turned away and pretended to be looking elsewhere. The seamstress in the Forgelands might have done too good a job when she selected a dress popular in the Pail. With its tight bodice and slit up to the knee, she was something to be stared at and not really seen. Even the bard gave her furtive glances from his perch in the corner as he sang a melancholy tune about a hunter ensnared by a nymph.

One man, more emboldened, did not look away. Good-looking and close to her own age, with honey skin and a narrow build. She met his look with calculated disinterest, waiting to see if he would cower. Instead, he leered at her exposed leg.

How banal.

The noise of glass on the bar behind her made Suri swivel, and she grabbed her drink and paid the girl. She took a long drink, and turned back to find the man approaching. Suri ignored him, even as she set her shoulders and prepared for the worst.

He swaggered up to her with the gall of a man who had never heard 'no'. The coins clinked in his velvet pocket, and his waistcoat was finely tailored. As he reached her, he smirked in a practised way that other women must have at some point tolerated. "My lady, might I join you for a drink?"

She blinked. "No."

His smirk faltered, and his confidence soured. "My lady. Are you—Did you hear what I said?"

She looked over his shoulder as a man stepped into the room, one she'd seen in her room not hours before. He was tall, though only normally so, and his features were handsome even when softened to appear more normal. Kol.

The creep before her cleared his throat.

She gave him a cursory look, already bored of his presence. "I heard you, the answer is no."

The tips of his ears blushed red as he choked on his words. "Perhaps, I should have introduced myself."

Suri took another sip of her Icebolt. "I have a feeling you are going to, regardless of what I say."

Kol had completed his scan of the room and apparently had not found her. She took a step to move past her irritating obstruction, and several things happened at once.

Kol caught the movement and his eyes fell first on her skirts, then landed on her face with nothing short of astonishment. Then, the narrow man grabbed her wrist, forcing her to look at him. Kol saw that too, and his jaw clenched. She shot a warning look to him, keeping him from stepping in.

"I am Eshanlan," he said, in a whiny tone.

Suri stared at her wrist in his hold and noted his amefyre ring. Three small square cut gems positioned in a rough triangle shape with two below, and one centred above. Clearly a Guild heirling. She narrowed her eye. "And which Guild do you represent?"

He puffed his chest up, glad to have been recognised in some capacity. "I am heir to the Construction Guild. And you are?"

That explained the trumped up attitude then, and the ring, which now resembled bricks. She's heard some rumours of Thanlas' second child—the only legitimate one, by all reckonings. She pulled her wrist from him, and he dropped it without remorse. He had a self-satisfied smile, as if certain that now she knew of his importance, she would simply *have* to spend time with him.

She threw him an asinine smile to ensure he was watching her mouth as she leaned over her drink and then spat directly into it. She handed it to him, his wide-eyed gaze focused entirely on the glob spinning on the surface of the drink, and not at her hand at his side. "Leaving. Enjoy the drink."

Suri strode past him before he could think to touch her again, and walked up to Kol.

He leant against the bar, his gaze trailing up her bare leg as she moved towards him, the darkness in his eyes so inherently him. He reached his palm out to her with a small bow. "Handled with grace, as ever, little thief."

She placed her hand in his, and he reached it to his mouth. She shuddered slightly as he pressed a kiss to her knuckles. "Let's leave."

"Gladly," he agreed, turning her around and pressing a hand to the small of her back. Half the inn stared at them. "I leave you alone for an afternoon and your beauty nearly causes a brawl."

"Most of them are only looking," Suri observed.

Kol guided her back through the room, close enough behind that she could feel the warmth of his breath. "Still," he said. "I'd rather leave before anyone else tries to take what is mine."

"And before the Construction boy notices I just robbed him blind," Suri added under her breath.

Kol's hand slid around to grip her waist as he pushed the door open to the night. "You are a nightmare."

Suri hid a laugh with a black gloved hand as Kol escorted her out into the fresh air. He led her around the corner before stopping to study her from head to toe, his trailing eyes as slow as pouring gold.

Her hair was oiled back, the dark tresses pushed behind her ear. Her eyepatch was replaced with a silver fabric sash across her face, tied elegantly at the back of her head. Her skin glowed with a powdered luminosity and her lips were painted blood red.

Kol devoured her with his gaze. "Suri, you look..."

She swallowed, and twirled just once, staring down at the black gown. "Exactly as one expects of the Lord of Death's court."

The back of his finger caressed the skin above her breast where her brands would normally show. The seamstress had painted over them with some skin-like mixture. Kol swallowed thickly, his throat bobbing. "I'm not sure I want to let you in there."

"But I have a meeting to attend, your highness." Suri saw his hand flex at his side as she mocked him with the title.

Kol looked up to the sky. "I've brought this upon myself."

Suri smiled, a fragment of real mirth clawing to the surface. "You have."

Her Lord took a moment to compose himself, and then he, too, smiled. He held his arm out for her, and she took it.

14

Winter has set in, and there are no callers to my door. I asked after him in the town, but I dare not return his own impertinence.

Unknown author, est. 2nd-5th century

Kol had already assumed his subservient role, positioned behind her, as they stepped up to the threshold of Nonlos' house. It was an unassuming townhouse at the edge of a lavish park, with candlelight coming through the gaps in thick curtains.

He touched her side and she looked back, catching his gaze. "You ready?"

Suri nodded, and allowed herself one more breath before she knocked. A minute passed before the door opened. She glanced at the doorman, before blinking and ducking into an inelegant curtsy. His moustache was twisted with hair oil and matched with a small tuft of hair below his thin lips, his long blonde hair already fading into a fine grey, pulled back with a silk tie. His dress robes were in a mauve-brown shade, and buttoned over his portly shape.

This was no doorman.

Nonlos inclined his head. “Please come in out of the cold.”

They stepped inside and Suri shivered at the change in temperature, rubbing her hands together. The days had been warm enough, but the nights dropped quickly.

She used the act of taking off her wrap to take in as much information as she could, her eye darting around. Again, inside, she saw no doorman nor a waiting party of serving staff. The hall was modest but well-sized, a fire burning in the hearth. Something of it felt like a trick, a play at normalcy which was finely executed but surely could not be genuine.

He took her wrap himself, and she noticed his strange lack of jewellery as he hung it over a waiting wooden holder.

“Welcome both,” he said, his watery gaze drifting over Kol before fixing his attention on her. “My name is Nonlos. I must say we are surprised by your visit, my lady, so soon after your fellow courtier. We could not fathom what more there was to be said.”

Suri nodded. “I understand it might seem strange, but Nadrian’s visit was little more than an introduction. I hope tonight will cover more ground.”

His hazel eyes tightened ever so in the corners, the only tell of his discernment. It was clear he was as keen to make them out as they were of him. “Let us dine, then. Will your man be joining us?”

“He will, if that is amenable.”

Nonlos nodded and gestured towards an ajar door.

Suri swallowed, and followed him. "You said 'we', just then," she said. "Will someone else be joining you?"

Nonlos did not reply as he pushed open the door.

Behind the door, the ascetic charade of restrained and sparing wealth continued. The dining room, whilst comfortable, with high-backed carved wooden chairs and a large polished table, held little graces of his peers. The food laid out consisted of freshly baked loaves of bread, a couple of local hard sheep cheeses, pickled fish, pear fruit and a carafe of deep plum-coloured wine. This was a Guild Leader, and yet his candlesticks were pewter, his tablecloth simply hemmed and with no embroidery, and the walls bare of tapestry.

The only jewel in the room was the beautiful woman sitting at the helm of the table. She stood when they entered, ducking her head. Her neck was shapely, her hair a thick wave the colour of burnt sweetnuts with dark features carving across her tanned skin.

Suri guessed her to be around forty, with Nonlos maybe ten years her senior. She was dressed in a simple way, with a white shift and woven belt without any of the golden filigree Suri had noticed on the town's nobles. When the lady looked up, her dark eyes pierced Suri with such intelligent beauty, Suri dipped her head just to escape them.

Nadrian had never mentioned a wife, nor had Kol suggested he had someone in his life. One small glance at Kol showed him to be just as wrongfooted by the lady as Suri was.

Nonlos made his way to the woman, touching her shoulder with a warm familiarity uncommon in noble society. "This is my wife, the Lady Allis'don."

Allis'don. That was a Kans name.

Marriages between those on the continent and those from Kans were unusual. She'd heard of one man from Kans marrying a Tangle barmaid, but he'd lived here most of his life, and it was a love match. Suri didn't know of any leaders in her lifetime marrying across the Shale, and had even less of an idea what it meant politically.

Suri dropped into a curtsy, using the moment to regain her composure. "My apologies, Nonlos. I had no idea you were married."

He gave Suri a strained smile. "We were wed only this year."

She floundered, standing rigid as a stone as she tried to decipher the way forward. She hadn't been expecting a wife, much less a Kans wife, and had no idea what to ask. The urge to look at Kol swelled, but she suppressed it. This was important. She had to do this for him, to discover if he could risk exposure.

"My name is Suri. I am the Mistress of Coin in Lord Kol's court," she said. Then she straightened her shoulders, trying to think of a question. Then she met Nonlos' wife's eyes once more, and the question bubbled up without bidding. "You are from Kans, Allis'don?"

Allis'don lifted a brow, and Suri realised then she had dropped Allis'don's title of lady completely. Axri'don had explained the ending 'don' already marked him as nobility, and she'd assumed the same went for the women. Suri glanced at Nonlos. Was this some faux-pas? Or a test?

"I am," Allis'don confirmed.

"What brought you to Peregrinus?" she asked, trying to think of anything to say to quell the horrible nervousness in the room. "I hear the weather is much fairer across the Shale."

Allis'don narrowed her eyes. "What brought Axri'don to Peregrinus?"

Suri breathed in sharply, his name so rarely spoken in the last weeks that she had almost blocked it out. But Allis'don named him without fear, knowing and seeking a reaction, and clearly succeeding, as in an instant, Suri was back in the arena watching his head roll through the dust as the acrid smell of burning hair filled her nose.

Nonlos took a seat at his wife's left, pouring himself a glass of the wine.

Suri clenched her hands, the only tell of her horror. "You knew Axri'don?"

"There were only a dozen noble houses in Kans. Now, there are perhaps six. I know the names of those who survived." Her words hung in the air, and Suri heard the unfinished sentiment. *And those who didn't.* "Please, sit."

Allis'don opened her hands, suggesting the seat to her right, or the one beside her husband. Suri knew her role was to learn Nonlos, and his motivations, and so she took the seat beside him, leaving Kol to amble around to sit at Allis'don's right.

Suri cleared her throat when they sat, the silence penetrating. *Ask questions*, Kol had said. Gods, she wished he had sent anyone else. "Why Lartosh, then?"

Allis'don smiled without warmth. "The Guilds fight in plain sight. It is what I understand."

Suri blinked. "You do not trust those who fight in the shadows."

"That which is done in the night is often dark," she said, her voice deadpan.

The moment swelled between them, and then Allis'don cut herself a hunk of bread and placed a healthy slice of cheese atop it, garnishing it with a small spoon of some berry compote. The lady from Kans took a large bite, the berries spilling a little onto her pretty rose mouth.

Nonlos poured both Suri and Kol a glass of wine and she thanked him in a small voice. No serving staff here either, then. Normally, Suri would take that as her sign to tuck right into the food, her mouth watering at the crumbly cheese. But she waited to be prompted.

She couldn't help but feel she was messing this all up as she took a birdlike sip of wine. Seeking reprieve from Allis'don's intensity she looked at Nonlos. "The wine is lovely," she said quietly to him, even though she had hardly tasted it, so consumed as she was by the tension. "Is it local?"

Nonlos smiled, the first she'd seen from him, and it transformed his face entirely. "You have a fine nose. This is an eighteen-year vintage from the vineyards not ten miles east of here. I always think you can sense the locality of the wine, and smell when it lived in the same soil you sit upon."

She nodded, faking interest. "Oh, I quite agree."

Nonlos' enthusiasm only increased as he addressed her. "This one is from my personal cellar. I could give you a tour?"

She wanted to smile at his eagerness, but checked herself even before the void inside her did. Suri could not help but feel like the real battle of the night was not winning Nonlos, but deciphering his wife. Staying in this room was the only way she would get the answers she needed. "Perhaps later."

"Of course," Nonlos replied.

She gave him a forced smile. "I feel bad that I did not know you were married."

"In truth, it was a small ceremony."

Nonlos' reply was evasive enough to give them their answer. She wondered if they had eloped, if the marriage was a secret until recently. She could sense an unease from Kol which suggested there was more to it, something beyond her measly understanding of their politics.

Allis'don swept a finger over her mouth, and then addressed Suri with such directness it made her straighten in her seat. "Why is Dabri'yon meeting with your Queen Lera?"

She took a sip of wine as her heart pounded. "We are still trying to understand that ourselves."

"You must have some knowledge of Queen Lera's plans, if you seek to enlist us in your war against her," she said.

Allis'don had seen right through them, then.

Could this be going any worse? The woman was clearly not one to hold back, and being pinned in Allis'don's sights was enough to make anyone squirm. Fearless, questioning and quick. Oddly, she found herself respecting it.

Nonlos, too, seemed a kindly man, not at all like the assertions put on him. His reclusive nature seemed much more to do with his character and his fiery choice of wife, than of any pride.

Suri nodded. "It is Lera who seeks war against us, not the other way around."

Allis'don placed her hand over her husband's. "And what of us? Did you come here to make us change our minds, too?"

Suri took another sip of her wine. Kol had trusted her to do this, to make out their characters and understand if they can be trusted. She had a lifetime of assessing marks, knowing who would be an easy target and who was far too aware. This woman was cunning and clever, and expecting trickery. She was no flower to be won with gifts. This needed more than that, this needed honesty.

"I came here to understand your motives." Suri stared at her unwaveringly. "To see if I could trust you with the truth."

Allis'don narrowed her dark eyes, and it only exaggerated her fierce beauty. "Understand this, lady. I detest Dabri'yon. That your Priestess Queen works with her makes me detest her, too. This does not make us friends, however. We have a saying in Kans. Those who hunt your predator—"

Kol cut in. "Have even sharper teeth."

Suri's eyes shot to Kol and she noticed him leaning forward, his expression clouded.

Allis'don did not flinch at the interruption, only nodding as some of her vitriol faded. "You are familiar with it. I can save the breath of the childish lesson."

Nonlos flipped his hand and squeezed hers. She smiled faintly at him, and there was no doubting it anymore. Nothing of this was for show. These two were genuine in their love, their way of living.

For the first time that night, Kol met her eye. Suri returned the gaze, and he cocked his head just a fraction, asking her a question. Suri nodded, and she saw his exhale.

They were doing this. They were choosing to trust them.

"Lord Nonlos, Allis'don," she said. "May I introduce you to my guard?"

Allis'don narrowed her eyes. "What is going on?"

Suri swallowed. This was it. She met Kol's gaze and saw him giving her a small smile, and it grounded her. "The Lord Kol."

Kol stood, and Lord Nonlos joined him, standing so fast his chair tipped backwards. Allis'don's eyebrows arched as Kol released his hold on his glamour.

Kol's shoulders broadened, filling his tunic and shirt as his face morphed into the one haunting her days and nights. He was so beautiful, she'd flinch from it if she could. Instead, she stared just as readily as the strangers around her.

Lord Nonlos's face had turned red. "What manner of unkind trickery is this?"

"Husband," Allis'don said warningly, taking pains to control her expression. "Sit."

He stared at his wife, uncertain and protective as he gripped the table with white fingers.

Suri swallowed, still sitting despite the alarm blaring in her body. "Please, let him explain."

Kol stared at the Metal Guild Leader and his wife. "Allis'don, Lord Nonlos. I apologise for the manner of my arrival. I am Lord Kol, and I am glad we can finally meet."

"Speak," Allis'don said, her hands folded in her lap as if this were a normal occurrence at a normal dinner. Suri envied her composure.

Then Kol started talking, and didn't stop. He explained everything about the massacres, starting at the altar, covering their discovery of Rasel's plans, everything that had happened in New Politan and now their coming here, to understand Lera's next move and who was in her pocket. He notably left Suri out of it, only mentioning her involvement in bringing him back to life through the use of a glamour. Suri's quest for the return of his soul and the loss of her own, were omitted from the tale.

Once Nonlos had sat back down, the two had listened in silence, Allis'don's only reaction was to tense her hand at the mention of Axri'don's murder.

As soon as it was over, Suri and Kol joined the silence, waiting for one of the two of them to say something. Call him a liar, throw them out on the street.

Instead, Allis'don's first question was to her. "And what of your story? The news travelled that you were the one to kill the Demon King. "

The illusion was up, their roles laid bare.

Suri spoke as herself, not looking at Kol for approval nor lacing her words with false sweetness. "I killed him. But I also saved him. I am sorry for his masked appearance tonight, but we all must wear masks to survive."

Allis'don scanned her one grey eye, her high chin and steady hands. "And below your mask, who are you?"

Suri did look at Kol, then. He stared at her already, not in warning but in languid want. She smiled. "I am his equal."

The room sat in waiting for several breaths. Then Allis'don cleared her throat, and they all looked at her as she stood.

Their chairs groaned backwards as the three of them followed suit.

Allis'don pinned Kol with a wary look. "I was sorry to hear of Axri'don's passing."

Kol nodded. "Thank you."

Allis'don motioned to her husband. "We have much to discuss, and it is best you leave us now. Thank you for meeting with us."

"Thank you for seeing us," Kol replied, and made for the door.

Suri bowed to them both and followed him out. Nonlos came after them, silently handing them their warmer layers and opening the door for them.

And then they were out in the cold of the night again, not one hour after they had entered. Kol looked down at her with mischief on his mouth, and offered her his arm.

Once they were safely around the corner, she nudged into him. "What did you make of them?"

Kol blew out a breath. "Allis'don is a force to be reckoned with. Nonlos is keeping her hidden for now, but she will force him to take a stand against Dabri'yon sooner rather than later."

Suri nodded, agreeing with him. The life they may choose to lead in private may be quiet, but that woman was anything but. She was a war waiting to happen.

Kol nudged her back. "And him?"

Suri considered her words. "I believe his kindness was genuine."

He stopped them under the light of a streetlamp. "You like them, don't you?"

"I do," she confirmed. "Do you?"

"She was abrasive, intelligent, and saw right through me with only the barest modicum of respect." He ran his fingers through his hair. "So naturally, I like her."

Suri raised an eyebrow. "You do seem to have a type."

"Women who talk back to me, wither me with a glance, and look profoundly beautiful in black." Kol's tongue wet his bottom lip, and his desire was written as plainly as if carved on stone. "It's a problem."

If Allis'don had been wearing black, the comment might have passed as general, but with every trail of his eyes against her chest, waist, hips, it became decidedly less so. Yes, it was a problem, and one she had lost any ability to resist.

15

A great storm tore my roof apart. When I ordered its repair, I heard a tale of him. He is a traveller through Drangbor, rarely settling for more than a cycle. I have put it from my mind.

Unknown author, est. 2nd-5th century

"Are you hungry?" Suri asked as they stepped back into their room. They'd both barely eaten at the Metal Guild.

Kol's eyes darkened as he stared at her dress again. "No," he answered eventually. "Are you?"

She swallowed. "No."

He flicked his eyes to the bed. "Tired?"

She followed his look. "A little."

He nodded, his jaw clenched, and the pause that followed it was heavy.

Yesterday they'd done barely more than pass out, but now it felt different: the air charged. She thought of what she might say to get him to look at her again. She wanted him to touch her so badly it hurt.

"Will you help me with my dress?" she asked.

His black gaze burned through her, the constellations in his eyes drowned out in the wake of tortured contemplation. Then, he raked his fingers through his hair and gave her a curt nod. "Turn around."

Her chest pulsed with the force of her heartbeat. She turned, every hair on her body raised, every pore in her skin aching to be touched.

His breath ghosted across her shoulders and she couldn't stop herself from shivering. His hand moved into her hair and she sighed as he loosened the clip and dropped it to the floor. He weaved his fingers against her scalp, unknotting the tension there. She realised the error of her request immediately.

This was going to be a sweet torment. Him touching her, but not enough, not where she needed him.

He leaned down to her ear. "I enjoyed your company tonight, my lady."

She shuddered then, and he pressed a kiss to the skin where her neck met her shoulder. All coherent thought and prospect of reply died, and she bit her lip to keep herself from moaning. It was a slow kiss, followed by three peppered up to her jaw.

Suri turned, hoping the next might fall on her lips.

But Kol only tutted, turning her shoulders back. "Now, now. I'm helping you with your dress."

He touched her gossamer short sleeves as if to make the point, and swept the sleeves from her shoulders. She moved her arms out of them and the gossamer layer fell down, leaving only the corset to cover her chest.

Kol played with the corset strings. His tongue touched her shoulder, and he licked up to below her ear. "You are delicious."

"Kol."

He untied the corset string and pulled the corset wide. She gasped as the corset fell down, leaving her breasts exposed.

"Did you want something?" he asked.

"Touch me."

Kol made a noise as his fingers drifted around to her front, playing with the skin under the swell of her breasts. "Say that again."

"Touch me, please," Suri whispered.

Kol's hands came up, cupping her breasts from behind her as his thumbs rolled across her already hard nipples. "Like this?"

Suri hissed as he played with her, his mouth at her ear again.

"Yes," she moaned, falling back against him.

He let her fall against him, his hands still on her as he leaned down to press a kiss on her hair. Then he dropped his hands.

Swivelling, she looked up at him. He stared down at her, his gaze blacker than her dress and his cheeks heated. She touched his leg, and he swallowed as she drifted her touch slowly up his thigh.

She reached the thick bulge pushing against the fabric and ran her hand over it. He hissed, and grabbed her hand. He held it there, tight against him, and rubbed into it once, before shaking his head and dropping her hand.

He stumbled backwards, shifting his trousers. "I'm sorry. I can't. This was a mistake."

And then Kol fled from the room without a backwards glance.

What?

The moment the door closed behind him, a prickly sensation of coldness swept across her. The room was too dark. The spring air was now wintery. She sat there on the floor and tried to fathom what had just happened.

Her blood was too hot, and she reached down in the dark, cold room, pressing her hand to where she needed the relief. Her other hand rested on the bed, holding her up as she breathed heavily, her breath coming in pants as she pushed back against her own hand, rubbing herself in fast circles.

Climax came fast, and she cried out, working her body until she fell over the top of it, moaning out her pleasure. For a second, she forgot about it all, she was pleasantly numb from everything. And then too soon, the pleasure ebbed away.

Suri dropped to her knees on the uneven floorboards, her skirts falling back around her. She understood what Kol meant then, when he said it was a weak imitation. There was pleasure, yes, but one which barely clawed to the surface before it was pulled below.

She wondered what she had done wrong. He would tell her it was for her own good, but she knew she wanted it. All he was doing was hurting them both.

Her mood spiralled as she sat there, waiting. The sting of the rejection was so acute she felt paralysed by it as she sat there for what felt like an hour, staring at the door, waiting for him to compose himself and come back.

Suri must have fallen asleep at some point, as she woke to the dawn light filtering in through the curtain she'd never drawn. She sat up from her crooked position, curled up into a ball at the end of the bed.

Kol was nowhere to be seen. Part of her expected to wake up to find him stubbornly passed out on the floor. But he was still gone.

He'd slept somewhere else. Left her alone for the night.

A new wave of rejection struck her. This one hurt even more. Him denying her advances she could understand, but to leave her in a foreign city alone? She thought they had an understanding. She might not be able to feel the joy and hope and warmth his presence should elicit, but she certainly felt far worse when he was gone. Did he not need her, as she needed him?

Suri pulled off the rest of the dress, red marks from the linings of the fabric covering her waist and legs. She pulled on her riding gear, cleaned and left folded by the innkeep at the door. She didn't know where she would go, but she had waited for him all night, and would not wait any longer.

Had he gone to Nadrian? Or, a darker part of her asked, had he gone somewhere else? Had he sought out someone whom he could have sex with, without their soul being a question? She did not want to think it, but they'd never explicitly said anything. There was no agreement between the two of them. He did not belong to her, not truly.

She ate breakfast alone and stepped out into the city. Being lonely in one's own city was an affliction in itself, but to be lonely in another was so entirely worse. Everything was unfamiliar, everyone a complete stranger.

Seeking out Nadrian felt like a fool's errand, so instead, she walked down back towards the pier. Maybe there was something she could learn about Lera, whilst avoiding the gnawing sensation in her heart.

She couldn't kill Lera, not now that Suri was so connected to Kol's court.

At best, if they didn't connect the murder back to her, Lera could become a martyr of her faith. Her secret Fae son, Lingyun, would continue her legacy, using Dabri'yon to organise the massacres, and Sotoledi would still return.

At worst, she would be caught, and Kol would be blamed for killing Lera.

But just because Lera was off the table didn't mean there was nothing she could do.

The streets snaked down, and the morning brought with it thicker smells and louder voices than she had found yesterday. Despite the liveliness in the air and the morning sun peeking through wispy clouds, Suri felt more grey than she had in days.

Women yelled fish prices, all claiming to have the freshest catch. Men lugged barrels and ropes and crates from ship to shore. Children ran around underfoot, cheeks streaked with dirt as seabirds squawked overhead. Brown waves lapped against green wood and she could taste the salt as she strolled down the seafront, meandering with little purpose towards the same warehouse that the boy had scurried into yesterday.

Then someone yelled out behind her. More than just the usual grumbles of the crowd, this was a full shout.

Suri whirled as someone slammed into her shoulder at full pelt, knocking her off balance. She caught herself from sprawling over completely, scraping her hands on the dirty cobbles below.

The barger kept running, a shabby brown cloak hiding them from identification. Suri tapped her pocket as she scowled after them.

Shit.

She patted her pockets again. Definitely empty.

Damned thief.

Suri launched after them, their cloaked head still visible as they barrelled down a jetty in the distance. There was no way she was going to let this idiot walk away with Kol's coin. They'd picked the wrong fucking target today.

She pushed through the grumbling morning crowd, darting around wagons as she kept the pickpocket in view. The cloaked figure reached the end of the jetty and ran across the very last gangplank, and Suri caught the glimpse of a bare white foot as they disappeared into the cabin of a small ship.

Suri smiled. A dead end. Clearly, they weren't expecting a chase, running straight for where water was the only exit. She ran along the jetty, feet pounding against the wooden planks as she stared down the narrow-hulled ship at the end of the line. It was greening at its sides and worn from years of use, but the rope tying it to the dock was new.

As she approached its gangplank, the ship appeared empty.

Could it be some kind of trap? Had someone recognised her, seeking to lure her out?

Behind her, she heard raised voices and the telltale noise of metal unsheathed from a scabbard. Suri swivelled to see a group stepping onto the far end of the jetty. Several guards surrounded a woman in a deep black cloak, one holding a sword to a scrawny fisherman's chest as he berated his folly.

Suri studied the woman in their midst with a crawling sensation of unease. A curl of her golden hair spilled from its hood, even as the woman kept her head down. Suri caught the curve of her cheek and the way her steps glided across the wood.

Queen Lera. Only fifty steps away.

Suri spun so her back was to the Queen, pulling her hood up. She herself was twenty paces from the end of the line, where wood met the endless sea. Of all the timing in this rotten world, now would be the time she was stuck between the harpy and the unwelcoming ocean.

Glancing back, the Queen didn't appear to be coming for her. Lera walked with purpose but not urgency, flanked by guards focused on shoving nearby sailors back from the Drangborian Queen.

If the Queen didn't know she was here, Suri sure as all Wrath wanted to keep it that way. But she could hardly walk back down the jetty *towards* Lera. Suri pondered the water on either side of her, lapping in cold slaps against the wood, its depths murky. But that was sure to drag attention from the approaching guard, seeing a fully-dressed woman splashing into the water.

In the space of a second, Suri scanned the nearby ships and barrels for any potential hiding spot and then glanced back over the gangplank.

She ran across it, following the path of the thief. Any potential trap awaiting her here would be easier to manage than the Queen's discovery. She slammed through the door to the small cabin, hoping to surprise the pickpocket.

But the room was empty.

A small table sat with a handful of chairs around it, and no other furniture adorned the space. Is there any way the thief could have left when her head was turned to watch the Queen? No, the only way off this vessel was back past her, or diving into the sea.

Then she saw the telltale scrap of brown fabric. A patch of the thief's cloak, trapped in some wood panelling. She never would have known there was a compartment or cupboard behind it if the cloak was not showing. A silly mistake.

She opened and closed the door at her back, mimicking the sound of her leaving. Then she crept towards the panelling, her feet light on the vessel, using the creaking of the ropes and the churn of the sea to further disguise any sounds.

She reached the panel and put her hand to it. Then she wrenched it open, ready for the scrap that would surely follow.

An empty large cupboard sat behind it. Well, not entirely empty. The cloak sat in it, and her pouch of coins sat on the floor.

Suri whirled around, again expecting a trap.

There was nothing at all. No one moved towards her.

Where was the thief? Why would they leave their cloak and her coins?

She grabbed up the pouch, counting the coins by feel. It was all there. This made no sense. Why steal from her just to leave it here?

A noise came from outside the cabin. Footsteps on the gangplank. Raised voices. Shit. Someone was coming aboard.

Suri scanned the room. There was no other exit. Just the door back out through the cabin.

Fine.

She turned back to the cupboard and wedged herself in. Once she was through the opening, the space inside wasn't too tiny, but her knees were still pressed up to near her shoulders. She pulled the cloak's edge fully inside and then closed the cupboard with her fingertips.

Everything went dark, and there was a moment of silence as Suri breathed hard. The door opened and she switched to breathing through her nose as several people stepped into the room.

"You've secured the ship?"

Her voice was as sharp as ever.

Fuckery. Queen Lera.

16

The spring has been a strange one. The welcome solitude now rings of loneliness, and it is not a feeling I am well-used to.

Unknown author, est. 2nd-5th century

A man cleared his throat. "It's clear. It usually ferries people from here to Kans, or around the coast to Tinashel. There's no trips planned for a few days because of the winds."

Suri had no idea if this was a stroke of extreme luck or deep misfortune. She supposed it depended on if they caught her.

She couldn't see a thing, holding her legs in the pitch black cupboard as the retreating tides swayed her slightly and the small of her back protested at her horrid posture.

More steps hit the gangplank. The voices in the room went silent. Boots walked past her cupboard. Suri held her breath, but they didn't pause. Once more, the door opened.

"Summer has not hit your shores and yet the smells are as ripe as ever."

Another woman. Bold, to step into a room with Queen Lera and immediately comment on how badly the place smells. Where were the titles, the introduction?

The accent was decidedly one of Kans, Suri picking it up easily after her evening with Allis'don.

"I cannot lay claim to the smells of Lartosh. Were you seen?" Lera sounded annoyed but not surprised. Whatever their dynamic, it was one of equals, or at least time-wearied allies.

"I made all efforts not to be. This is a strange sort of meeting place."

"Everywhere on the shore has Guild ears."

"I thought you had won all the Guilds, Lera'yon," the voice dripped with disdain. Lera'yon. Definitely from Kans.

A woman from Kans of equal footing with Queen Lera... This had to be Dabri'yon.

"Not all. Water and Metal still prove stubborn."

It was too much of a coincidence. Suri sat in a cupboard on a random ship, and it happened to be the meeting place of two queens. Had the thief *led* her here?

It made little sense. Who would do that? What would they gain? Was this some anonymous ally they didn't realise they had, who knew exactly where these queens would be meeting, and where to hide?

Suri corrected herself. It made *no* sense. But what was the alternative explanation?

"Fine. Is the Great Altar Gate working?"

"It is, at last," Lera replied. "We had to change the exit point, as we did not have enough... power to get to our original destination."

"That's four of your eight, then. One in my lands, two powered pairs in the North, and now one at the Altar. What news from the miners?"

Suri's stomach clenched. They spoke of the eight massacres needed to bring Sotoledi back as if they were discussing invitations to a party. The Altar Gate working *at last*, Lera had said. How many priestesses had she murdered there to finally bring that to life? And the mine, too. The explosion killed hundreds up in the snowy capped hillsides and mountains of the Forgelands.

"The Northerners blame the Demon King for the explosion," Lera said.

"Ah yes. Him. What news of your dark prince?" Dabri'yon asked.

Suri's blood ran cold.

"We heard a rumour he was killed," Lera replied breezily. "But my advisors aren't sure. If he *is* dead, it might not be a permanent condition."

As always, Lera was too quick. Knowing too much, guessing the rest.

The reply held no emotion. "We should act fast, then. Strike while the snake is healing."

Insanity, she considered, to be here in this nest of queens and vipers alike, and have the Life Court be spoken of as the snake. Their looking glasses must be so full of their reflections they could not see their own scales.

Suri heard a clicking sound.

"Guards, leave us."

Lera's demand hung in the air, and the room was near silent. Suri kept her breath as measured as possible, but her heartbeat clamoured in her ears. Had they noticed something?

A sigh. "All of them?"

"All, Dabri'yon."

So it was Dabri'yon after all. A pause settled in the room, and then a scuffling noise. A hinge creaked and a door clicked closed. Heeled steps on wood made their way around the table.

She wondered if they had even the faintest suspicion of her, the third party to their discussion, the former slave Lera had once invited as a guest in Drameir, the thief she had drugged and plied with promises, and the one who had ruined her massacre by killing the conduit.

Lera spoke, and Suri's musings were silenced by shock. "I've set a plan in motion with the Food Guild. Dellon will cut the sand dweller's access to food tomorrow. He predicts their stores won't last them more than a week. They might be able to get something from Water, but soon they will begin to starve."

What? Her thoughts reeled in shock. All her reason for staying her hand nearly flew to the wind in an instant. But she held herself back, biting hard on her hand to suppress the horrid rage blooming in her chest.

Lera meant to starve them all? Wrath and piss.

A coward's way out, then. She wouldn't face them in battle, but weaken them barbarically. It would not work, the world would not allow it, surely. If only she could prove this, prove what she was hearing right now, but she could not risk making a single noise. She thought of the silk, and for a breath cursed herself for leaving it behind, but in the next, she realised it was a blessing. If Kol spoke even a word to her right now, they would surely hear it.

"That holds a lot of risk," Dabri'yon replied, her voice still level. "You will be accused of this crime. We sit at four, you are too hasty to take this step now."

Suri listened, hoping Lera would end this terrible plan.

"Dellon will claim a shortage, some error. There is nothing that can truly prove my hand in it." The clopping noise of heels against the floor again fuelled Suri's rage ever more. "And they cannot flee. I mean to make a statement in favour of the Forgelands, declaring the explosion an act of war against a valued ally. Then I will annex his city. They will be weak, and Kol's court will be forced to surrender to me. If they do not, they themselves will create the final act in their world's destruction."

Cut off the food, and annex the city. The effectiveness of the plan fell on Suri as an executioner's axe; they would die within their own cliffs and walls, without a blow falling.

Dabri'yon's reply was appreciative now. "A massacre without violence. Clever. But there is no Gate there to capture your work."

"That is where we have been wrong. You should know, Axri'don is dead."

Suri tensed again, her shoulders flexing forwards.

"That is good news. My scribe won't have to forge his sister's hand any longer. His family can be as dead as they ever have been. What of it?"

The callousness of Dabri'yon's response cut into her bones. She could sense the genuine relief, how much of a chore it had been for Dabri'yon to forge those letters. It proved their theory: Axri'don's betrayal was to help his family. It was in a way a small comfort to know he died believing them to be alive somewhere, rather than discovering his actions had been for nothing.

"Before your countryman died, he confessed that Kol already created a Gate," Lera supplied. "That is why the Altar Gate failed to make a connection to the Wrath, because the bastard had already done it. We are at five, from the Demon King's own doing."

No. No. Lera knew? For the love of every God real and fake, was there anything they could shield from her? Akdaria was the only safe haven away from Lera's touch, the unknown thorn in her side, the refuge of so many souls.

"I see. Where does their Gate lead?"

Suri gripped her own hands so hard they began to lose feeling.

"Axri'don would not say. Even when... pressed. I expect the Gate is most likely within their dust-ridden city. If Kol's court stays within the city walls, we will connect his people's shrivelling deaths to their own Gate again. If they fight, the sand-dwellers will not last a minute against my army."

Suri didn't have the capacity to feel relief. Their ignorance of Kol's Gate's exact location, and where it led, was nothing to the fact they knew it at all. If they managed to get in, they would scour the city for it, searching high and low for it. They could not be allowed to reach Akdaria. She would die to protect it, she knew that now.

"And if his court surrenders, after all?"

"Then we will have no true resistance left on Peregrinus," Lera said. "The rest will fall in line, and if they do not, we can summon him then, instead."

"If enough men starve, you will be at six," Dabri'yon drawled. "If instead, they fight and die upon your swords, you will still be at six. If any of their courtiers remain, if the dark prince lives, you will have rather played your hand by attacking the desert folks now, when we are still short two massacres."

They discussed the horrors of war like a game of dice.

"I have a plan for the two that remain," Lera said. "If they do not surrender, the battle in Old Ucraipha will be the eighth and last."

"Tell me, then, Lera'yon," the Kans Queen said.

Lera paused before responding. "The numbers of the dead could be lower, if those lives are worth more."

"What decrees the worth of a life?" she replied, almost in bemusement.

"Its span, for one."

No. Surely they could not know of Akdaria, and its frozen inhabitants?

"You mean the Fae." It was silent for a moment. "Is the Glen not well defended with deep wards?"

"Leave that with me," Lera responded. "The plan is already set in motion. The Altar Gate has its twin close to the Glen. Once it is done, the ceremony will link them, and we will have our sixth."

Suri's mind reeled as the information hit her like a rain of blows. Lera had set a plan to kill the Fae in the Glen. Who did she mean to kill, and how would she evade the wards? To hear Xianyu speak of Lera, she had thought them close. Did he know?

And yet, it was an unwelcome relief, to know the target was Xianyu's home, and not her own. Lera must not know of the city of century-old people just on the other side of Kol's Gate, and Suri was determined to keep it that way.

Lera's plan seemed barely to require Sotoledi, bringing Kol in line through starvation or the annexation of the Old City. Suri wondered, then, what the Death God had promised Lera, for her to be so adamant on his return, to be willing to massacre the Fae to quicken his coming. Eternal youth? Some greater glory yet? Maybe he had vowed to help her bend all of Kans to her bidding, too.

"And the seventh? The one which bridges this Fae slaughter and your sand-bathed finale?" Dabri'yon pressed.

"I would not call you without need," Lera said pointedly.

"I would hope not," Dabri'yon replied. "You know many in this land would see me dead."

Suri thought of Allis'don, and could not help but agree with the Queen of Kans.

"And you know once Sotoledi is back, he will rid the world of your enemies, just as he promised," Lera continued.

"You are stalling, Lera'yon."

The pause lasted long enough for Suri to worry they would notice her again. It was hard to control her breathing when everything was spinning.

"How many troops can you spare?" Lera eventually asked.

"To annex Kol's city?" Dabri'yon questioned in her lilting tone. "How many do you need?"

"How many can you afford to lose?" Lera rebutted.

"You expect him to fight back?"

Suri fancied she could hear the smile in Lera's voice when she replied. "History will reflect that they attacked us first."

Her room at the Tarrying Juggler was not empty when she returned.

Kol paced the floor, unglamoured, speaking in hushed tones. The moment she entered, his head swung towards her. His palm quivered, his eyes were almost black and his expression nearly as feral as it had been in the arena. "Forget it," he said. "She's back."

The afternoon sun beat into the room as she stood there taking him in.

After the Queens left, Suri must have waited over an hour, stewing in the horrid swirl of everything said, before finally summoning the courage to leave her cupboard. She'd taken a convoluted route back, checking over her shoulder every other second as her stomach cramped with waves of nausea.

Kol threw the seeing silk down on the bed and stormed towards her. To her credit, Suri did not flinch, even as he towered above her, his breath flaring his nostrils. "Where have you been?"

She folded her arms. "That's a long story."

"Why is it always?" Kol asked, frustration strangling his voice. "Why couldn't you stay put?"

Suri scoffed. "Why couldn't you? You left me. I stayed here all night."

"You know why I left," Kol seethed. "You didn't have to run off for some strange revenge."

"It wasn't revenge," Suri said, glaring up at him. "Not everything is about you."

Kol barked out a cruel laugh. "And yet, everything becomes about *you* when I have to find you again."

Suri turned away from him, embarrassed at her own anger turned to sadness in the span of a second. She didn't want to cry. "I didn't know when you would be back."

Kol took a few breaths, and then he touched her shoulder. She blinked furiously until the tears felt further away, and then turned.

Some of the anger had fallen off him. He swallowed, his eyes still laced with irritation. "I'm sorry I left. I went downstairs to clear my head, and then Nadrian found me. He told me you probably didn't want to see me."

"And you believed Nadrian."

"For my faults." His jaw flexed. "Where were you?"

Suri forced a smile. "At the docks. I know most of Lera's plans. And I think we have a secret ally."

Kol looked so baffled it was almost comical. "What?"

Suri shrugged. "I just eavesdropped on a meeting between Lera and Dabri'yon."

"You're kidding." Kol raked his hand through his hair and finally stepped back. "Tell me everything."

And so she did.

17

I saw him today, out in the hills. In the distance, little more than a shape. I admit, it excited me, to think I might soon be able to confront him.

Unknown author, est. 2nd-5th century

Kol sat on the bed in stunned silence for half a minute. He'd seemed most perplexed by the disappearing thief. "I have no idea who would want to help us like that."

"Or even know about it?" Suri questioned. "Could it be Al-lis'don?"

"Doesn't seem like her style. Barefoot, you said? Maybe she caught wind of it and sent someone?" Kol suggested.

"Still, couldn't she just leave a note?"

Kol shook his head. "It's bizarre."

"What are we going to do about the massacres?"

"Even hearing that question doesn't feel real," Kol said, his hand flexing against the bedclothes. "You should have taken seeing silk with you. I don't like that I wasn't able to contact you."

Suri sighed. "I know I should have. But I suppose it was for the best. If you'd come through the silk during that meeting it would have been a disaster. I'd be with the fish at this point."

"Fine," Kol said, but he didn't relax. "Maybe take your own advice and leave a note to say you've left of your own volition."

Suri raised an eyebrow. "What if I left of my own volition and *then* got kidnapped? Then you wouldn't know to be worried."

"I know you're being glib, but I am not. Every time I can't find you, I think the worst," Kol explained.

Suri couldn't hold back the bite in her reply. "You wouldn't need to find me if you didn't run away. I was only alone because of you."

"Suri."

Suri breathed out hard. "Kol."

A moment hung between them.

And then Kol laughed, genuinely, with enough mirth to shake his whole body. It hurt her gut to see it. "Gods, we're impossible."

Suri smiled a little despite herself. "Maybe that's what we do."

His eyes lit up, and she saw the constellations caught in them as he stood and stepped towards her. There was so much less anger in his body now, and yet she was more inclined than ever to flinch or run away.

He reached up, tenderly brushing her cheek with a thumb. She shook beneath it. "I like that. That something could be ours."

Suri's mouth went dry as Kol leaned down and pressed a small kiss to her cheek. It was barely anything, a brush of his mouth against her skin, and yet her head felt foggy and her heart thundered in her chest.

She swallowed. "What now?"

Kol managed the wisp of a smile himself. "What, since Lera is about to declare war on me and annex my city with thousands of troops, cutting us off from food and water while she murders some Fae? And then force my hand somehow to throw the first stone and cause the final eighth massacre that'll summon an ancient half-dead half-deity Fae?"

"You somehow made it sound worse."

Kol's smile faded as he grabbed her hand. "Let's find Nadrian. He's not going to like what I have in store for him."

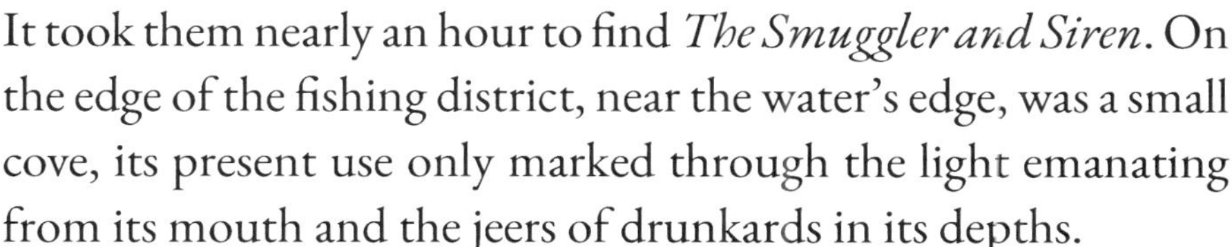

It took them nearly an hour to find *The Smuggler and Siren*. On the edge of the fishing district, near the water's edge, was a small cove, its present use only marked through the light emanating from its mouth and the jeers of drunkards in its depths.

A rowboat sat disused on the sands before the cove, tied to the rocks. It wasn't necessary at this hour, the tide was low, and they made their way inside, the damp rock beneath strewn with foul-smelling seaweed. Further in, and higher up, the noise increased, and the rock below them was largely dry, with the moisture now coming from the dripping stalactites that threatened to behead Kol. She was fine to walk beneath them, and she led him around the corner, where the inn finally materialised.

From this angle it appeared to be half of the hull of a large ship, the wood impressively sturdy and free from too much rot, a doorway carved from one of the cannon holes. "He really finds some interesting places," Suri said.

He ducked another rock icicle and shook his head. "He lives to torment me."

Kol adopted his glamour and they stepped inside, barely getting through the door from how busy it was. This was clearly no secret to the locals, with bodies packed into the strange hull as far as the eye could see. Which wasn't very far, as the place was small to say the least.

Nadrian found them before they had to barge through half the patrons, making his way carefully through the cluster of men in front of them with three overflowing mugs of ale held to his chest.

"Welcome to *The Smuggler*," Nadrian said.

"What a place," she replied as she grabbed a mug and knocked back a gulp. Gods, it was horrid, barely a step above sea water. She took another sip and nodded to him in thanks.

Kol grabbed one and together they shuffled to the side where they could at least breathe, leaning over a table which was little more than a few planks of wood nailed into the hull. "Why did you pick here?"

"You can't leave Lartosh without trying out some of its local watering holes," Nadrian said with a lascivious wink which indicated more than a slight double entendre.

Kol hadn't touched his mug. "I don't think we should be drinking."

"You know when you speak to me in that tone, it only makes me need a drink more," Nadrian said, taking a sip.

Kol frowned. "You're going to need to fly. With Suri. Tonight."

That made Nadrian put his mug down. "Where?"

"It's a long story," he said, echoing Suri's own opening line.

Nadrian just stared at him. "Where, Kol?"

"The Glen."

"I refuse," Nadrian replied without a moment's hesitation. "I want Suri's soul back as much as the next man, but why can't you go on horseback?"

Kol shook his head. "This isn't about Suri's soul."

"Then why am I taking her?"

"Okay, it isn't *just* about Suri's soul. She's a Seer, they can't bar you entry to the forest with her beside you, and if you get her soul back whilst you're at it, I won't complain," Kol said.

He looked between them. "What's going on?"

Suri chimed in now to put him out of his misery. "Lera has a plan to murder a number of pure Fae."

Nadrian looked behind him for somewhere to sit, but there was nowhere. So instead he just opened and closed his mouth, then sighed. "Shit."

Suri nodded. "She says she has some method to get into the Glen, and that a plan is already in motion. Apparently, a much smaller number of pure Fae need to die in order for it to... count."

"Balls and fuck." Nadrian groaned and slapped his hand on the table. "So I have to go, because if I leave you to ride up there, they might all be dead already."

"Pretty much," she said.

"Do we know how she is planning on killing them?"

Suri shook her head. "No clue. Could be bombs, ritual slaughter, assassins, poison..."

He held up his hand, looking a little ill. Or maybe seasick was a better term. "I get the idea."

Kol waited a few seconds before he spoke. "Will you do it?"

The Fae Prince's expression was a myriad of things Suri had never seen before. A flicker of shame in his mouth, nervousness in his eyes with a doubtful pallor to his skin.

Kol said nothing, only waiting.

Nadrian gave her a smile which was more of a grimace as she touched his hand. "Face down my dear old stepfather who may or may not have been responsible for the deaths of my siblings and mother? Save all their lives for the greater good?"

"That's what I'm asking," Kol said.

He sighed. "Xianyu won't believe that Lera would hurt him."

"Maybe he's not the target, but the Glen is. Make him believe it," Kol replied.

Nadrian hummed. "And maybe we can extort the tip off to get the killer's soul back."

Kol glanced at Suri. "It's worth a try."

Nadrian swallowed, then nodded. "Fine. We'll go tonight as soon as it's dark enough. We should be there by tomorrow night."

"Thank you."

"It's the right thing to do. What will you do?" Nadrian asked.

Kol launched into the explanation of everything Suri had relayed, and Nadrian's face got increasingly grey as the story continued, and every new facet came to light. He finished up with another helpfully depressing summary, "So, Lera is going to declare war on us imminently, and try to annex the city."

"Is there a plan?" Nadrian asked.

"I'm going to send a missive to the North. It's time to put them to the test, see if they will ride south to bear witness. I'll speak to Ressa about emergency provisions, and hope we can get them through to the city before Lera's troops arrive. Then I'll ride back. We'll have to pull everyone within the walls. I can't leave hundreds of our people out in the desert when the Queen's Guard descend, I doubt Lera would have qualms about using the outpost as an easy massacre. Oh, and I'll need one of your seeing silks, since you'll be together."

Suri narrowed her eye. "What for?"

"I intend to give it to Allis'don," he said to her. "They do not trust us enough to ride to our defence now, but I will warn her of Dabri'yon's involvement. If they are willing to let us show them the truth when Lera's troops arrive, that is half the battle."

"Is that safe? Giving them our silk? They could spy on us forever," she said.

"It isn't safe. But the Guilds work on a basis of needing four leaders in accord. With only Ressa to defend us, Lera could convince the rest to condemn us as war criminals. We need to win Nonlos, or at least keep him neutral or we'll be at war with the Pail, too."

It made sense, but it felt strange knowing they were giving away silk which could be used against them. Information was a weapon, and they were giving unbidden access to themselves.

"All the same," Nadrian said to Kol, handing over his own piece of fabric on their behalf. "I'd be mindful to hide your silk if you don't want eyes on you."

"I do that anyway," Kol said, pointedly glancing in Suri's direction. Heat flushed to her cheeks. "Do you not?"

Nadrian grinned. "And save you the chance for the show of a lifetime?"

Kol spluttered, and Suri nearly laughed.

Nadrian glanced around before speaking in a lower tone. It didn't seem like this was an establishment for any ranking Guildsmen to frequent, but this was still their territory, and there was always a reward for those with an open ear. "And what of Dellon's intention to starve us?"

"The man is terrified of me, so Lera must have promised him something stronger than his fear of death," Kol mused, matching his quietness. "We will outlive Lera's prediction by a few weeks at least. Perhaps that will be enough to sway her from her siege."

"We could just kill him," Nadrian replied. "Maybe his replacement would be more amenable to our way of thinking."

"If we kill a Guild Leader, or are blamed for killing one, we will lose all the Guilds," Kol said.

"What, so we just allow Dellon to cut us off?" Suri asked in frustration.

Kol leaned over the table and they mirrored him, their faces huddled close. "Lera is going to do everything she can to paint us as the villains in this war. I will gladly kill her soldiers, but I will not let her win by killing the men she dangles as bait in front of us. She wants us to retaliate against Xianyu, Thandul, and Dellon. She wants any excuse for this war. She has hated me since before I was even in this world, and she will hate me until I am out of it. If we are to end her, the people must think it is just. The world must see what she is doing to us."

It was impossible to argue with him when he became this. When he showed himself as the true Son of Life, as their King.

Nadrian nodded, but still looked a touch despondent. "How are we going to win, though? She has us backed into a corner."

Kol didn't even blink. "We win by stopping the massacre in the Glen. We win by not starving when it is convenient for her. We let the North and the Guilds see that we are not fighting back, let them watch their righteous Queen annex and siege an innocent city. She will not get three more massacres without showing herself as the harpy we all know her to be. The tide will turn."

Nadrian smiled sadly. "I wish I had your optimism."

"It's not about optimism anymore." Kol grabbed his shoulder. "It's survival."

There was nothing more to be said. The plan was as watertight as the aching ship around them, but it was the best option they had, and they would not go down without a fight. All of them would die for the cause, and the grim reality of that set in.

Kol released the Fae Prince and turned to her, cupping her chin lightly between his thumb and forefinger. "You'll be safe with Nadrian."

Suri nodded. "I know."

"I'm telling myself." Kol pointed to him. "No funny business."

"None?" Nadrian replied with a chest-clutching gasp. "But that's what I do best."

"Behave." Kol met her gaze with that same warmth he bestowed only on her. "And you. Go get your soul back, if you can."

A ghost of a smile traced her lips. "I'll just offer them Nad's."

He grinned. "Not a bad idea." His eyes creased at the corner, the concern back in the tormented star-flecked brown. "Take care of yourself. And then come back to me. Come home."

Home.

It was only now, as she had to leave him for the first time in over a week, that she realised she needed him more than anything. And not just from lust or any other dark urge, but she needed him like a drowning man needed something to grab onto.

But that wasn't what he wanted to hear from her. He didn't want to be her life raft, he wanted to be everything. As much as she wanted to tell him the words he needed to hear, she knew he wouldn't believe them until she had her soul back, and she knew she wouldn't trust them until then either.

So it had to wait.

Her breath hitched. "Try not to die."

There was a shadow of sadness in his answering smile. "And you, little thief."

18

He visited again. I riddled him with every manner of question on his gifted book, and he responded to each with equal fervour. He has read it three times. I asked him to visit again.

Unknown author, est. 2nd-5th century

"Dawn is breaking," Nadrian said. "I'm too tired to glamour us both. We'll need to find somewhere to hide until the evening."

Suri blinked and murmured something agreeable. She was long awake but her eye had fallen in and out of focus in their long night's flight, and she'd almost forgotten their destination entirely. She'd drifted asleep as he'd carried them fast across the undulating wheat fields of the Pail, already growing heartily in the early spring. The sleep was unexpected considering his arms were like a vice under her knees and back, but she'd clearly needed it.

Now, they neared the border of Drangbor, and she stared across the slate-trimmed hills, the weight of Nadrian's bag on her lap keeping her cloak in place and protecting her from the worst of the cutting winds. Nadrian seemed little affected by the cold.

Then she saw something she recognised, even from their height. Remains of something that had once been a hulking house, now charred with soot and reduced to a ghostly stone building.

"That's the ruins of Rasel's manor. I know a place near here."

Nadrian grunted in assent, and Suri directed him as best as she remembered. She scanned the canopy of trees until she saw that small clearing and the top of a dilapidated well. "That's it."

Nadrian squinted down, hanging in the air above it in the lightening grey sky. "The tiny overgrown hut?"

"Yes." Suri sighed as Nadrian groaned. "What were you expecting? A royal welcome in Drangbor?"

Nadrian swooped in and landed. The place seemed even more wild than it had been a few weeks prior. The spring rains had brought the grasses to their knees, and the mud squelched beneath their boots.

She shouldered the bag as he rolled his shoulders, the Fae's only visible complaint from having to carry her all night. "Sometimes I just hope for places that are less... damp."

Suri pushed the door of the hut open, checking for any signs of habitation. A thin layer of dust coated the surfaces, everything seemingly untouched since she'd left. She dumped his bag onto the table and turned back to Nadrian, waving her hand in. "That's your inner Crown Prince talking."

He grimaced and strode past her. “Don’t remind me.”

“Should I try to find something to eat?” Suri asked, thinking of the Drangborian barricade not too far from here. “Steal from some guards, maybe?”

Nadrian shook his head. “You’re too known now, it’s too risky. People hear tales of the Northern thief with the blood bonds. I’ve got a few provisions in my bag which will have to keep us until the Glen.”

Suri leaned against the table. “Get some rest, then. I’ll take the first watch.”

Nadrian glanced around them. “I don’t think we need to keep watch here. I appreciate the thought, don’t get me wrong, but we’re in the middle of nowhere.”

“I managed to sleep a little… on the journey,” she said, heat tingling her cheeks as she tried not to admit how she’d fallen asleep in his arms.

Nadrian grinned. “Oh, I heard the snores.”

“Shut up,” she said, slapping his chest. “Besides, there’s only one bed.”

The Fae Prince raised an eyebrow. “You came here with Kol, right?”

Suri shifted on her feet as she nodded, bracing herself for the inevitable ribbing.

Nadrian pushed open the door to the small room with the still rumpled bed, and tutted. “The gods cursed me when they bestowed on me such an incredible imagination.”

Suri had never wanted to sink into the floor more.

Nadrian pointed at her. “I’ll sleep first, but use your time effectively. Seer practise.”

"There's no Time Circle here."

Nadrian scoffed. "Because that's the only way to connect with time."

"Do you have a relic I can read?"

He shook his head. "No, but you don't need me. Try making one yourself."

Suri opened her mouth and then closed it. "Making a relic. In myself?"

"Why not? You're not that tired, after all." He winked. "Would be helpful to have a Seer of Time on our side who could actually do something."

Suri took a light step towards him, ready to slap him again, maybe this time in the face. "Is that right?"

Nadrian backed into the bedroom with his hands raised. "Don't hit the steed, o' soulless monster. You need me."

Suri rolled her eye. "Go to sleep."

Nadrian grabbed the door. "And you, practise."

Then he closed it, and she found herself alone again.

She stepped around the room, her finger brushing along the table. She looked at the fireplace, long dead, and the stool where she'd soaked up the water from Kol's hair.

Suri sighed. Practise.

How?

She sat cross-legged on the floor and breathed in and out. Anger and rage was her route to channelling Him, and the only times she'd felt a whispering of anything else was when she was in an entirely different mental state. Not quite calm, but driven. In the desert, it had been nothing but her and the sand and her own determination. When she had read Ruben's relics, she was also alone, riding towards a fate she didn't understand.

She didn't need anyone else to do this and she knew that, but it didn't help with the how. It was one thing to find something someone else had captured. It was wholly another to capture something within herself. What memory would she even hold onto?

Suri allowed the last time she was here to wash over her, remembering when Kol had picked her up and thrown her down on the bed, how he had pushed her to her limit and beyond it. She memorised every part of the layout of the room, picturing it happening right now, in front of her. Breathing in through her nose, she closed her eye.

Every detail played in her mind; the weather outside, the feel of the fire, the brush of her underwear against her hip, his dripping hair.

She opened her eye. For a moment, she saw it. Instead of the dawn light, the window showed only darkness, and the fire crackled in the hearth. Herself, topless and lying back against the table as Kol held the flesh around her ribcage.

Suri gasped and stood, and within a blink, it was gone. The cabin was dusty again, and the morning light filtered in. A creeping sensation of failure trickled up her back. Waris wasn't even a Seer of Time and yet she had relics inside her. Suri was supposed to be powerful, and she couldn't trap one memory, let alone even make it strong enough to revisit for more than a second.

Mother Edi had said it was a muscle and it wasn't supposed to come naturally to her, but Suri hated that. She'd never taken to things she couldn't do well the first time: there was an inherent vulnerability in it. Though, she reasoned, if she never admitted to Nadrian she'd tried, no one would know she was a failure but her.

So she sat back down again, and she tried. Again and again. Sometimes when she opened her eye, the memory she wanted surrounded her. Sometimes it did not. When she succeeded, the sensation was fleeting, and often if she imagined a memory in an open space, she could still feel the cabin floor beneath her feet, and not the rubbery flesh of the leaf pools. She spent hours trying and only found her mood worsening with each failed attempt.

Suri had just found herself in the City of the Damned; Kazem placed two overflowing shots of Gold Dust on the bar. But the purples were grey, and when she breathed in, instead of the incense and sweat she recalled, it was dust and cobwebs.

"Suri?"

She turned, but the voice wasn't coming from where a hazy version of Nadrian nodded at her. It was coming from behind her. She blinked, and she was back in the cabin.

Nadrian looked at her with a furrowed brow with his hair stuck up at a funny angle. "Where were you just now?"

Suri sighed. So much for failing without observation. Admitting it might be easier than faking lunacy. "I was trying to follow your advice. Practising."

To his credit, Nadrian simply nodded without judgement as he moved to sit at the table. "Any luck?"

Suri gave him a sour look. "Of course not, I have no idea what I'm doing."

"What memory are you using?"

"I've tried several," she responded, embarrassment sweeping through her as she recalled her first attempt. "I can't get anything to stick for more than a couple of seconds."

"Where were you just then?"

"At Kazem's bar."

Nadrian smirked. "There's your answer. That's nowhere near a strong enough memory. Unless drinking with me really made such an impression."

Suri rolled her eye. "I don't see what difference it makes."

Nadrian's green eyes flashed. He looked like he wanted to say something, and then he just shook his head and pulled a pipe out of his pocket. "You're even crankier than usual somehow, just get some sleep."

"If you know something, say it," she said, crossing her arms.

He studied her. "I don't know much. But the relics I *do* know about, were created out of a place of true strength." Suri flinched, but Nadrian shook his head. "I'm not calling you weak, killer. I'm saying that relics need you to feel so strongly about their creation that the memory lives on by itself. You have to feel it so much that it gives the moment a life of its own. And you can't do that."

A crushing disappointment hit her. Mother Edi had said a similar thing. Suri nodded, feeling powerless once more. "I can't make relics without a soul."

Nadrian grimaced. "No, I don't think you can."

Evening rolled over the hills as Nadrian slowed above a small patch of trees. The green valleys and hills of Drangbor expanded and contracted beneath them, the grey shale breaking from the hilltops and purple flowers dotting the landscape almost as often as the cloud-like sheep.

His arms tensed around her as they descended. "I haven't been back here in years."

Suri hadn't even noticed that the copse of trees below them was *the* copse of trees, as it looked much the same as any other. But as they hit the ground, the wind shook through the branches in such a familiar way, almost like the trees were sighing or calling out in greeting. Yes, this was the Glen.

Kol had spoken to them on their travels, though only briefly, to tell them he'd seen Lera's troops gathering in the distance, where Drangbor melted into the Northern edge of the Pail. He'd ridden hard, clearly, to be nearly in the Parched Lands already. It was lucky he had left when he did, any later and he might have been stopped.

She turned to the Fae prince behind her. Nadrian tucked his wings back, no glamour attempting to hide them or soften his features. He was fully himself, Crown Prince of the Fae Glen.

If she had not known him well, the tension around his green eyes could be read as annoyance, and the slump to his shoulders little more than exhaustion. But no. Nadrian was terrified.

Suri swallowed, uncertain if she should acknowledge it. He wasn't looking at her at all, he didn't even seem to be looking at the Glen. There was something else, a faraway look filled with regrets and nostalgia.

"Do you want to lead the way?" she asked.

He composed his features into something far more blank. "No. I think the trees will be more open to your entry than mine."

Suri nodded and walked across the field, glancing back to ensure Nadrian was actually following her. She had been here alone before, but she was desperate then, and knowing now that Xianyu was entangled with the deaths of Nadrian's family, it seemed more irresponsible than ever to stroll in there alone.

The trees trembled as if in a light wind, but the air was still. The waxing crescent moon shone down its pale light upon the branches, casting them aglow in silver. She could not yet see the small insects lighting the trees within.

Suri stepped to the edge of the treeline. This was it, the Glen was warded. If they were not welcome, they would soon know.

The shrub before her swayed to one side, inviting entry into the forest.

A hand clapped onto her shoulder.

"On second thoughts, I should go first," Nadrian said. "I forgot you were mostly human. I'm used to travelling with less breakable people."

Suri huffed, but stepped back. "This whiplash between being a powerful Seer and a feeble human is beginning to grate on me."

Nadrian scoffed. "Don't be bitter. You only accept being a Seer when it serves you. And trust me, feeble human is probably the safer call right now."

He moved past her, and the shrub which had bowed to permit her entry snapped back upright.

"You are not welcome here, son of Fae."

The voice was silken and girlish. It sounded like it was coming from the bush itself. No voice she'd ever heard before.

"But she is?" Nadrian called.

"She is a Seer."

"I am a Prince," he said.

"You claim a title you do not want."

"She doesn't want hers either," Nadrian whined. "And you're letting her in."

"Master's orders," the voice replied. "Step inside, and you will regret it."

"I know he's listening," Nadrian said. Then he took three steps back and yelled at the forest. "Xianyu. King Consort and Steward of the Throne. I know you can hear me. Speak with me yourself."

The narrow willow to the right of the shrub shifted. Its bark knolls twisted and stretched, pushing outward slightly. A nose, eyes, and then the mouth protruded until Xianyu's face appeared in the tree bark. "There's no need to yell, Nadrian."

"Stop playing games with me, and drop the wards."

"Three days ago, my advisor warned me she could sense death on the horizon. Ill omens in the skies. And then you appear, demanding entry to the Glen," Xianyu said, his mouth gaping into the tree. "Tell me, would you let me in, should the situation be reversed?"

Nadrian sighed. "You were always good at tasting a lie. Listen when I say this, and tell me what you think." He stepped up beside the tree. "I do not come here seeking harm against you or the Glen. That is not my purpose."

Xianyu's face in the tree paused. "What is it you seek?"

"To discuss those who do seek harm upon you, and to negotiate for the release of Suri's soul."

Xianyu's face in the tree hovered for a moment, and then it started to retreat.

"I tell the truth," Nadrian said at the tree.

But Xianyu was gone from the bark, and the willow was just a willow once more.

"You know it, you hear it in my voice," he called, yelling once more.

A silence descended, the copse unnaturally quiet, the wind slowing its path through the myriad of thick green.

"He's gone?" Suri asked.

"Seems like it," Nadrian said.

"What now?"

Nadrian didn't reply, simply staring into the Glen with an irritated look on his face. Suri sighed. What a waste. They'd come all this way to warn Xianyu, and now he would not even see them.

Then the shrub sighed. Suri jumped back a step, forgetting about the sentient bush at her feet which had once again bent to the side.

The childish voice returned. "Are you coming in or not?"

19

He returned, and this time with a new book. He means to stay in the town until the harvest.

Unknown author, est. 2nd-5th century

The pig was the first thing she saw when the ballroom peeled into view. Roasted, golden, slathered with a red glaze, with a dripping peach sitting in its waiting gob. The room was set up for a feast rather than a dance, with the whole pig the centrepiece. Around it, fruits and vegetables of every jewel tone covered the table, with steaming buns and other cut meats filling any empty space.

Maybe seventy Fae encircled the feast, and many of them turned to stare at Suri and Nadrian, but her own eye was drawn to the Fae King waiting across the small moat.

Xianyu was dressed in a red robe, the colour close enough to blood to make Suri nervous. It appeared at first glance similar to the Bloodhounds, but even a second's appraisal showed it to be far more opulent, with hanging gold and silver chains lacing from his shoulders across his chest. Rubies adorned his fingers as he reached his hand to Suri in a perfunctory act of grace.

Suri bowed her head to him. She wore her riding gear, and Nadrian wore the same rumpled grey tunic and black trousers.

Xianyu scanned the pair of them and clearly found them lacking. "Welcome to our humble feast. We *were* about to celebrate some new and old friends, but now it seems we have even more."

"What's the occasion?" Nadrian asked.

Xianyu gave him a tight smile. "A celebration of our Guilds." He twitched his hand towards Suri and she stepped forward and took it, allowing him to guide her off the dais. His grip tensed around her as he spoke quietly enough that his other guests would not hear. "Always a pleasure, pretty Suri. Though, it is rare to be surprised by the same guest so... frequently."

Suri grimaced. "We would not have come if it was not necessary."

The Fae were paying Suri little mind, thankfully, and she could now see why. All of their whispering was focused on her companion.

Nadrian stepped down beside her. He had not yet bowed, or greeted the King. The scales of their warring statuses hung in the air like threatening rain. The Prince that should be King, and the one that reigned in his chosen absence.

Xianyu appraised him. "Welcome back, Prince."

Nadrian stared back, his green eyes flashing with an emotion Suri could not place. He swallowed, then dipped his head. It was a tiny motion, but it was deferential nonetheless, and she felt the collective sigh of the room. "Xianyu."

Xianyu flitted his eyes between them. "Will you join us for our feast?"

"I do not think that wise," Nadrian said, dropping his voice to barely a whisper even though the Fae around them had started chattering once more. "This revelry itself could be the intended scene of the massacre."

Xianyu's face turned from curious to black anger. "Massacre. A very deliberate choice of word. Not murder. Not assassination. Massacre, you say?"

Nadrian's jaw clenched. "The sixth, by our calculations."

Xianyu put his hand onto Nadrian's shoulder. "With me."

Suri flinched at the grip. From a distance it looked almost friendly, but from beside them, she saw the way his fingers dug into the redhead's flesh. To his credit, Nadrian did not cry out.

"As you say," Nadrian replied with no mischief lighting his eyes.

Xianyu called over his shoulder at his guests. "Please, amuse yourselves. Eat, drink, dance, if you would. I will be back in just a moment with our two additional guests of honour."

He pulled Nadrian through the side doors and out to the balcony. There were three Fae there, who disappeared back inside. Suri followed the men into the perpetual twilight, her whole body ready to pounce. The two were on the cusp of a fight, that much was clear. What Suri thought she might be able to do between two winged Fae, she had no idea, but her instincts forced her to be ready for anything.

Xianyu shoved Nadrian, hard. "Explain."

Suri stepped forwards as Nadrian stumbled back, but he only shot her a warning look. He breathed out, righting his tunic.

"We have reason to believe Queen Lera is planning a massacre within the Fae Glen, imminently."

Xianyu's eyes flashed. "Queen Lera has been a friend to my reign. She would have no motive to kill anyone here. What evidence do you have?"

"I heard it myself," Suri said.

The Fae King appraised her. "Heard what?"

"I heard the Queen herself state an intention to kill pure Fae, and that she had found a way around the wards."

His cheeks paled. "Did the Queen give a reason as to why?"

Suri nodded. "She explained that less Fae needed to die for it to count as a massacre. There is a Gate nearby and she intends to link the deaths. Your deaths."

Xianyu looked at her for several seconds, then turned from them both, walking to the edge of the balcony and placing his hands on the stone.

Suri glanced at Nadrian and they shared an uncertain look. The three of them all stood in the silence.

Then Xianyu spoke. "It is not true."

Suri opened her mouth but Nadrian got there first, barking out a laugh. "You are joking, Xianyu. You could taste the truth of what she said. Do not deny it."

Xianyu spun around. "What Suri just said was true, what she believed she heard may not have been."

Nadrian sighed. "What are you talking about?"

"I believe that Suri heard what she thought she heard. Whether Lera actually has such plans, is not for any of us to know. She herself has told me otherwise."

"And you believe Lera?" Suri said, her voice incredulous.

Xianyu narrowed his eyes. “Careful, both of you. You are in my court, and whilst you may have come with admirable intent, it does not mean I tolerate contempt.”

Nadrian stepped forwards, ignoring his words entirely. “Are you so blinded by love that you could not think Lera capable of treachery?”

Xianyu growled. “I know her to be capable of treachery. I have seen her treachery myself. She has shown her true self to me time and time again, over a century. We have known every ugliness the world could claim, and once she has succeeded, we will rule this world together.”

All of Suri’s breath left her body.

Nadrian staggered back a step. “You are supporting her? You would see Sotoledi back?”

Xianyu’s shoulders dropped, and he looked infinitely tired. “This world is divided. It needs strong leadership and a clear goal. Sotoledi is not a monster, and neither is Lera. With Dabri’yon and myself, we can bring a unified vision to Peregrinus and Kans. Peace.”

Nadrian shook his head. “At what cost?”

Xianyu clenched his fist. “The massacres now will save decades of wars.”

“Even if those massacres are of your own people?” Suri asked.

Xianyu flinched. “Whatever you heard, she would not do such a thing. She would lose me if she hurt the Fae.”

Suri found herself suppressing a scoff. “Maybe she knows that. Maybe she wants to replace you with someone who cares less for your people.”

"Nadrian is the only heir left. She would hardly want him in charge," Xianyu dismissed her.

Suri narrowed her eye. "And if Nadrian were to die. Then the lineage would fall to your own firstborn."

Xianyu reddened. "Do you think me a simpleton? If she meant to raise Lingyun to unseat me, she would have married me and planted him in my court. But she has kept him from claiming his right as my heir. Few here know that he would be the next."

Nadrian shrugged. "Enough for him to claim it. Of course she kept him at her own side, so she could poison him with her own plots until he was ready."

Xianyu looked ready to swing at Nadrian.

Suri held her hands up. "Think about it. Please. What does Lera care more about? Having you as an ally and—a friend—or holding onto her power?"

Xianyu scanned them both, his lip quivering. Suri held her body tense, ready to jump into whatever was about to happen. Nadrian had his usual painted boredom on his face, but she saw the set of his shoulders as clear as day.

The Fae King flicked his hand at them. "You have made your points. There is nothing left to discuss, I would like you both to leave immediately."

Nadrian glanced at Suri. "And what of the other matter?"

"Her soul, you mean?" Xianyu said, his voice incredulous. "If it was trade you were after, you should have made your case for that before you threw your accusations and insults. If you're right, and Lera means to kill me, you'll get your damned soul back soon enough. Now leave before you disturb my guests any further."

He spun on his heel and left the balcony, pushing open the doors and striding back into the ballroom.

Nadrian and Suri stood in the mild air staring at the closing door.

"Well, that went horribly," she said.

Nadrian dragged his fingers through his hair. "That it did. At least we tried."

"You can tell Kol."

"Oh, great," he replied. "I'm sure Kol will be delighted to hear how I fucked up ever retrieving the soul of his lady-love."

Suri's stomach clenched. "It was equally my fault."

"Thanks." Nadrian stood there, his green gaze disappointed and full of ire. Then he sighed and offered her his arm. "Want to steal some food before we go?"

Suri faked a small smile. "I'm starving."

Back in the ballroom, most were deep in their cups and filling their plates, but Xianyu kept his gaze locked on them as he murmured to his Queen. Nuo offered him a bite of the meat on her plate, and he bit it from the fork without looking at her.

Nadrian didn't look towards the steward royals, focused entirely on the table in the middle. He wasn't attempting subtlety at all, dragging them both to the middle of the room. "Fuck eating those rations again."

Suri tried to ignore the weighty judgement of the King and walked with him. They'd grab a couple of plates, eat quickly and then leave. Xianyu had asked them to leave, that much was clear, but would he risk telling them they could not eat in front of everyone? No, they would eat.

They reached the first dishes and stood behind two jovial Fae. The two women were both wingless, but had other signifiers of their blood.

"The wine is delightful," one said, her tongue the same deep purple shade as her eyes. "Xianyu has outdone himself."

Her companion was tall in a way only a Fae could be, close to seven feet, with limbs so perfectly elongated that she looked terribly graceful even leaning down to speak. "It's been sent specially from the Pail, I hear. Three hundred bottles gifted from the Guild cellars."

Suri froze, and looked at Nadrian. He tapped her arm and shot her a quick look. She read it without issue. Quiet, listen. He loaded a pile of fluffy golden potatoes onto his plate, and then covered them with a red jus. She followed suit, both of them icily silent as they listened in.

"True wine is so much more fruity than our own," Purple-Tongue admired, taking a drink from a crystal glass. "Though the effect is less potent."

The tall one laughed. "Have a few glasses and I think you'll find the effect stimulating enough."

Nadrian continued filling his plate, taking a small spoon of everything with idle attention.

The two Fae stopped before the pig, already half carved down to the bone in the short minutes they'd been gone. The tall one watched as Purple-Tongue served herself. "Strange that Xianyu is serving pig, I thought he hated pork."

"It's Queen Nuo's favourite," Purple-Tongue said over her shoulder as she placed cuts of the meat onto her plate. "I imagine we will have much of it this year to celebrate her three hundredth cycle."

Nadrian cleared his throat as they turned to leave. "Excuse me," he said.

"Yes?" The tall one said, spinning on her heel. She choked on her sip of wine. "Prince Nadrian, my stars. Are you well?"

Purple-Tongue's cheeks went a pretty shade of pink which complimented the silvery dust shimmering across her cheekbones.

Nadrian nodded, gesturing to her goblet. "I am, thank you. Could you tell me which of our lovely Guild Leaders sent this gorgeous shipment of wine?"

"The wine?" The tall one blinked. "Oh. I believe Lord Dellon sent it. And then, of course, the food came courte—"

"Thank you," Nadrian interrupted, before grabbing Suri's arm and pulling her away just as she was about to spear a slice of the meat. "Enjoy the merriment!"

"And you," the tall one said in bewildered awe.

Nadrian dragged Suri away from the table and she struggled to keep her piled food balanced.

Once they were halfway to the dais and out of the near earshot of the other tables, he spun to her. "Are you thinking what I am?"

Suri nodded. "It's the wine."

"Shit." Nadrian scanned the tables. "How many people have already had some?"

She looked around, now noticing the two huge wine barrels. They were clearly well-used, a small group clustered around each. On the tables, most places had a glass before them. Thankfully, the Queen didn't. But Xianyu did. "A lot. What do we do?"

Nadrian blinked rapidly. "Destroy it? Make everyone throw up somehow?"

Or they could do nothing.

The thought rose with a selfish spurt. Xianyu had told them to leave, and both of them knew that if Xianyu died, all the souls he had collected would be freed. Inaction was a quick solution. But it would be a massacre. A massacre they hadn't even tried to prevent, and one which would bring Lera one step closer to victory, one step closer to Sotoledi coming back. No. They had to do something, if only to spite the harpy. "We have to tell Xianyu."

"That's one of your worst ideas, yet."

"And somehow forcing everyone to throw up with no explanation is a better one?" she asked.

"Fair point." Nadrian took their plates and put them down on a small side table. "The food will have to wait."

Suri stared after the steaming plates with a small pang of loss. It was a cruel fate trying to be a good person. "Let's go make another scene," she said.

Nadrian shook his head in disbelief. "And Kol thought he was giving us an easy job."

20

The weather grows warmer, and so does my heart. He comes near twice a week, and I find myself waiting for his arrival. It is a kind thing to have a friend.

Unknown author, est. 2nd-5th century

Xianyu's face bloomed red as they strode directly towards him. He did not stand, only gripping his Queen's hand as she looked up from her plate and gave them both a curious look.

It hit Suri then that the only thing standing between Queen Nuo's own children being the next heirs of the Glen, was Nadrian himself. If all of Zulra's line died, surely they would become the throne's true holders. Was it safe for Nadrian to be here? How had his siblings really died?

Two men, clearly human, sat on either side of the royal pair, and they took in Suri and Nadrian's approach with apprehension. The room around them fell quiet as all strained to overhear the conversation.

Nadrian raised his hands. "I apologise for overstaying my welcome, Xianyu. But we would request one more word with you."

"What more could you have to say?" Xianyu raised his wine glass to his mouth. Suri jolted forward, her hand reaching out, and the Fae King straightened, pulling his hand back. "What is the meaning of this?"

Nadrian shot Suri a look. "Xianyu, we have reason to fear that tonight's revelries might hold some danger."

Xianyu clenched his jaw.

Queen Nuo stared between them. "What is going on here? What danger?"

It was the first time she'd properly been up close with the woman. She was like an ice princess, trapped in time. Her eyes were the colour of a winter lake, a turbulent white-blue, her hair the finest pale blonde and her rosy skin so smooth it was impossible to believe she was three hundred years old. Her pink wings were insect-like, thin and wide, not built to carry anything.

Xianyu put his goblet back on the table and Suri breathed out. She hadn't seen if he had already drunk any, it might be too late. "Our surprise guests believe there is a murderous plot unfolding."

Nuo's face barely changed. "What evidence do they have?"

"None," Xianyu replied.

"Your wine is from Dellon?" Suri asked.

Xianyu gritted his teeth. "It is."

"He is allied with Lera," Suri said quietly.

Xianyu barked out a laugh. "Gods above, girl. I know." He clapped a hand over the shoulder of the man on his right, who flinched. A young man with ruddy cheeks and blue eyes which might have been quite striking were it not for the immediate comparison to Nuo's. "This is Dellon's nephew. How many glasses of this fine wine have you imbibed tonight?"

He stuttered. "None more than would be appropriate, I'm sure, your grace."

"A number, boy."

"Three, perhaps," he said, his ears reddening.

"And how are you feeling?"

He swallowed. "Very well, your grace."

Xianyu shot the pair of them a meaningful glance. "Is the matter settled? Dellon's only nephew drinks the same nectar as us all."

Nadrian and Suri shared a look of complete confusion and a small dose of embarrassment. Nadrian cleared his throat. "Perhaps—"

"No," Xianyu said, speaking loud enough for half the room to hear. "You have made a complete spectacle of yourself, as you always do. In a way, I am glad of it, you have shown to those here who have longed for your return who you are. Still a boy, playing pretend. I hope everyone here has realised how little you have matured in your absence from this court. Go. Or I will make you."

Suri glowered at him, waiting for Nadrian's quick retort as her own rage built. But nothing came. Nadrian had frozen beside her.

Shit.

Xianyu's expression was steady, but she saw that minute twitch of his mouth. A smug satisfaction.

Suri's anger rose like a wave of blackness. Her own fingers twitched and she knew that if she had wanted them, the black tendrils were a mere thought away. A flick of her hand and she could wipe that arrogance off his perfect face. Instead, she breathed, her nostrils flaring. "And your court has seen how you treat those who only seek to save you. He came not as a rival, but as a friend."

Xianyu's face rippled, but Nadrian caught her attention more. The red-haired green-eyed joker was like a statue beside her. He needed her right now.

She gripped his hand and felt him shudder. "Let's go."

He nodded once and they turned, walking towards the dais hand-in-hand. The feast room was silent, their footsteps against the marble the only sound.

They had miscalculated, it seemed the wine was not poisoned. It was an error, but one which was well-intentioned. They needed to go before her black mood spiralled further.

Suri took deep breaths, trying to contain her rage in a body that never felt big enough to hold it. Her emotions were always too great for her, expanding out and hurting everyone she touched.

And then behind them, someone coughed.

Suri jumped a little, but the pair kept walking. Another cough, this one much louder, a choking and racking noise, echoing in the quiet.

She stopped and turned.

The Queen Nuo's pretty face bulged, her cheeks as white as the fluffy potatoes as she coughed indelicately into a white cloth. All eyes were locked on her as Xianyu murmured something, his face more nervous than she'd ever seen it.

There was no wine in front of her and Suri hadn't seen her take a single sip of the stuff. But perhaps she'd had a taste earlier.

Another started coughing. It was Purple-Tongue. The other patted her back as around the room Fae erupted in fits of coughs. There was no discernible pattern, only half of them seemed to even have a goblet before them.

Someone called for water, another for medicine, and several Fae ran from the room with purpose. Nadrian broke out of his stupor and stared around the room with horror.

Queen Nuo stood up, walked two miniscule steps clutching her stomach and throat, and then collapsed onto the floor. Already, there was a blonde Fae at her side, popping the lid off a stoppered vial of a milky-white substance and opening her mouth.

At the same head table, Dellon's nephew burst into fits of coughing, as did the man at the other side of the Queen Nuo. Their suffering was the shortest, their humanity granting them that gift, at least. They coughed no more than four times before they both died. Dellon's relative fell dead into his plate, his face pushing into a pile of soft vegetables. The man at the other side fell backwards, his twitching corpse hitting the floor beside the icy Nuo.

Xianyu looked up from his wife's side as the blonde Fae male kept trying to force the white potion down her throat. Even across the room, Suri saw how Nuo convulsed, and how the Fae

King searched the room desperately, as if he would find the cure in one of the alcoves.

Then Nadrian ran towards him. Suri's body seized, but he only crouched beside Xianyu, and asked how he could help.

She moved slower, her head feeling foggy and vision blurring as she took in the scene. All around her Fae writhed on the floor, faces various shades of red, white and blue. She counted maybe thirty down. A couple of Fae returned with fistfuls of those stoppered vials, others with water, the silver carafes sloshing over the side and onto the marble. Suri saw the tall Fae put her fingers down Purple-Tongue's throat.

When she reached Nadrian, he spoke to her and she couldn't understand him. "What?"

He repeated himself. "Do you know what's causing it?"

Suri shook her head. "I don't think it's the wine, but... I don't know."

Xianyu cradled his wife's head in his lap, brushing her hair back from her face with true tenderness. The blonde Fae sat back, staring at the Queen, the half-empty vial shaking in his hands. Suri noted his pale colouring, his horror as he reached out and touched the Queen's hand, and deciphered that he was likely one of her sons.

Queen Nuo, however, was clearly already dead.

Then Xianyu went as white as a sheet. "The pig," he whispered.

Nadrian looked to the table. "The pig?"

"A gift from the Magic Guild," he said, his voice disconnected as if it was the tree speaking to them again, and not the man himself. "Lera knows I dislike pork. She's a diplomat through and through, she would have advised Manthi to send a gift everyone likes. I thought it was an oversight."

Nadrian sucked in a breath, echoing him. "She knew you didn't like it."

The sick realisation dawned then on Suri, too.

Tears glazed Xianyu's eyes, and then he hacked out a single cough. "She wasn't trying to kill me, after all. I guess that is some small comfort. How she thought I'd forgive her for it, I don't know. What joy is there to being a shepherd with no flock?"

The blonde Fae grabbed Xianyu's arm. "Father, let me help."

"Who would have guessed I would have tried the meat?" he asked rhetorically, ignoring his son. There was an odd twinkle in his expression as he coughed once more, and a tear fell down his cheek. "Gods, I am a fool."

"Open your mouth," the blonde Fae instructed, immediately standing beside Xianyu. To the room at large, he called out. "Bring water and farrowfell to the King."

All around them the room was filled with sobs and coughs. The Fae who hadn't fallen now looked to their King, realising they could lose both their monarchs. Xianyu opened his mouth obediently, and the blonde poured the rest of his vial into the King's mouth. Xianyu swallowed, before his body shook with another wave of coughs.

"How much did you have?" Suri asked. "Maybe you will live."

Xianyu smiled. "If I know one thing about my Lera, she does not leave things to chance. Good luck, Seer. Treat your soul more kindly this time."

Another Fae who was undoubtedly Xianyu's child fell beside him, clamouring to help as the King's coughs increased. Three more arrived with water and vials, and quickly they were surrounded.

Nadrian fell back off his knees, pushing away from the scene and allowing those left of the court to crowd their King. Suri stumbled back a few steps herself, a wave of nausea hitting her as she stepped on the arm of a dead Fae. Nadrian pulled her through the balcony doors as she breathed hard, her skin feeling too hot.

They staggered out into the night air and leaned over the stone balcony. Nadrian's complexion was equally white as he heaved in gulps of air. Queen Nuo, dead. Xianyu dying.

She didn't know how to feel about the Fae King. He was stubborn as the Gods, and aligned with Lera. She should hate him for that alone, but she knew he loved deeply and love made people blind. In his way, he had always helped her, bestowing both gifts and patience. He didn't have to accept her deal for the glamour, and he had, glamouring the potion, too. He was the only reason they had the deal that freed both Kol and Esra. Xianyu might not have been the best man, but she truly believed he was doing what he thought was right.

And now he was dying. Gods. She didn't even know how to process what had just happened.

Suri heaved, her gut rolling as she retched over the side of the gardens. Nothing came out, her body spasming and contracting in some poor imitation of a true death. Nadrian rubbed her back, but Suri couldn't get her mind off the feeling of the dead Fae's flesh rubbery under her foot, and Xianyu's expression when he discovered Lera's plan.

It was sick, it was all sick.

They stayed like that for a while. Her, breathing over the side, her head pounding. Him, touching her back and staring out at the mauve-tinged world.

Lera had picked her poison carefully, trying not to kill him. She wondered if Lera did that out of love, or if she simply believed Xianyu was an easy person to manipulate.

"Suri," Nadrian breathed, dragging her out of her rolling thoughts. "Look."

She raised her head as a pink light shot up into the sky. Across the gardens, beyond the fountain and the twilight flowers, beyond the shrubbery and the silk mollusks Xianyu had shown her, a light came from the Aviary, deep in the Glen.

It twirled in the air, a small golden circle like the stars above but glowing in the twilight sky. It paused for a moment, tumbling and freewheeling, and then it flew away.

Then a blue light. Then green. Small flares shot out of the dark tower in the distance, curling and zipping, before shooting off in all directions. More and more lights poured from the roof of the Aviary, until the sky was nearly full of souls.

Horror and awe met her in equal parts, and Suri's limbs froze as she understood what it meant. She looked to her companion, his face a rare picture of sombre assessment.

The lights of hundreds of souls reflected in Nadrian's eyes. "The King is dead."

Then a beam of light came barrelling straight towards them, and Suri barely had time to gasp before her soul hit into her chest.

21

He has explained to me his true ambition, of his dedication to preservation. I did not know there was such a possibility.

Unknown author, est. 2nd-5th century

Suri sat up and her head pounded with the rush of blood.

"Woah," Nadrian said. "Take it easy."

She clutched her head in her hands and let out a low moan, her fingers tingling. When the pounding sensation lulled, she raised her head, slower this time, and blinked.

The room around her was fairly dark, a handful of red-waxen candles adding to the purple light filtering through the brown gauzy curtains. She lay fully-clothed atop a bed in its centre, and Nadrian sat in a blue armchair across from her, a wan smile on his lips.

"What happened?"

He shrugged. “The massacre happened. Oh, and your soul collided with your body, and you passed out.”

Shit. Xianyu was dead.

And her soul was back. She rubbed her chest, expecting to feel some kind of extra weight. But she was still herself, still nervous and saddened by Xianyu’s death.

“How long have I been out?”

“An hour or so.” Nadrian moved to her side and passed her one of their travelling biscuits. “Better safe than sorry.”

She wrinkled her nose, longingly remembering those steaming potatoes, but took a bite anyway. “You didn’t have to stay here with me.”

Nadrian let out a large sigh. “I wish I could claim it was purely for you. The Fae have been hounding me the moment the light show ended. You’re my most convenient excuse right now.”

Suri swallowed the bite. “Why? Do they blame us for it?”

He sat on the edge of the bed. “Worse.”

She stared at him.

Nadrian looked pale with horror. “They expect me to be next.”

Her eye went wide with alarm. “They think you’re going to die.”

“No,” he groaned. “They want me to be King.”

Oh.

Suri swallowed. “Shit.”

Nadrian smiled. “Thank you.”

“For what?”

“For not saying congratulations.”

Suri grinned then, and it was the first true smile she'd had in ages. She noticed the lightness of it, then. How the humour wasn't pulled away, how she didn't have to fight to keep it there. "What do we do?"

"I don't think I have much of a choice."

"Of course you do."

He gave her a pointed look. "If I say no, they might ask Lingyun. He's Xianyu's eldest son."

Suri scanned his green eyes. "I thought not many of them knew."

He broke the eye contact and stared out at the purple sky beyond the windows. His mind was somewhere far away.

She sat up, fluffing the pillows behind her and leaning against them.

Eventually, he spoke again. "It's not just that. The wards are already losing power. They need me, need a ruler, now."

"Why?"

"The wards are powered by the souls in the Aviary," he explained. "Soon, anything or anyone will be able to wander into the forest, and not long after that, the glamour of the forest will drop entirely. The Glen will be laid bare."

Suri realised what it meant. "Lera is probably sitting by her Gate right now, celebrating her successful massacre and waiting for the castle to appear."

Nadrian sighed. "Thanks for that image."

Suri smiled slightly, then asked the question she'd been wondering about since Thandul spoke to him in the arena. "Will you tell me the story?"

"What story?"

She had a feeling he knew exactly what she meant, but she explained anyway. “Why you left this place? Why you never came back? You’re the rightful King.”

Nadrian flicked his hand. “Because I never wanted it.”

Suri said nothing, when he glanced in her direction he could see her sat, waiting for the actual story.

He rolled his eyes and spoke, directing the story to the window rather than her. “Fine. I’m old. Older than Kol by about thirty-five years. I grew up with Lera and Cathie. Well, sort of. Lera is ten years younger than me, and Cathie was fifteen years younger, but I spent time with them both when I was your age. Given my nearest sibling was fifteen years *older* than me, I enjoyed playing big brother for once. The girls lived on the outskirts of the Glen, and even as a teen, Lera was insufferable. She thought herself better than everyone, better than me, and I was a prince. The youngest prince, sure, but I was in line for the Fae throne, and she wasn’t in line for anything besides a decent dowry.”

Nadrian clicked his tongue. “She wasn’t just proud, mind you. She was conniving, and completely disparaging of the Fae’s ways despite being more narcissistic than half of us.”

Suri resisted the urge to ask what half of that he placed himself in, allowing him to continue the story.

“When the Wrath happened, I was only a few years into manhood, by Fae standards, and Lera was still a young woman. Cathie... Cathie was barely a woman. Your age now, but with her blood, she could have lived to two hundred. I was angry. Beyond angry, I was... incensed.” Nadrian’s voice cracked, and he paused before continuing. “She’d never known a day’s hardship before she was forced into that brute king's court, but she had a generosity of spirit which was ageless. She was innocent, through and through. And I'm not talking about virtue, I'm talking of justice and everything that should be stood for in this world.

"After her murder, I demanded that my mother, Zulra, do something. Lera had her claws deep in Volker, and the Fae didn't want to upset the King of Drameir. That, I could have at least understood, in my grief. But then, Xianyu arrived. A Fae of another noble line, well-respected by her court. He knelt on the floor and begged for Zulra to assist Queen Lera. He said Lera had been horribly transformed by the Wrath, and it was there I first heard his version of the truth. That Cathie was a fallen woman and a pagan witch, and Lera had stepped in to heroically defend their world against her. If she hadn't acted, the whole world would have been caught in the Wrath, not just the Eastern Kingdom. I remember laughing at him," he said, his voice quiet. "I remember being the only one who did so.

"Then he offered his soul in payment, hoping to trade it for a permanent glamour to turn Lera back to her true form. I begged her to refuse him. She did not. She accepted the exchange. The Fae value beauty highly," he explained. "Vanity is not a fault, but a way of life here, and Xianyu knew that. He appealed to it, calling them to help a beautiful Fae now trapped in tragic ugliness forever. It was clever, and it worked, but I could not stand to be there for even a moment longer, and I left the Fae Glen that night."

A tear tracked down Nadrian's cheek. Suri knew she should comfort him, but she felt he needed to get it all out.

When he spoke again his voice was a little stronger. "First, I went to the Parched Lands. I'd heard rumours of Cathie's son, and I wanted to offer my assistance in protecting him. I found them, after a time, when Kol was taking his first steps. But those guarding him didn't want me bringing them any unwanted attention. That was my first time meeting Edi, and she was as much of a battleaxe then as now. I get it, a Fae Prince lurking around when you're trying to keep the child hidden isn't ideal. So I was adrift once more.

"I didn't know how long I would stay away from the court. Originally, I believed only a handful of years. A drop in the ocean of the lives of the Fae, you understand. But as years passed, and I heard word from the Glen, I no longer wished to return. My father died a couple of years after I left. He was four hundred, and a man with little patience and a poor habit of consuming far too much. It was not untimely. A few years after that, Zulra remarried."

"To Xianyu," Suri supplied.

"Yes," he confirmed distantly. "It was then I decided to stay away a while longer. I visited Kans, and spent fifteen years in its lands. I was lazy, enjoying my adulthood in drunken stupors, pursuing frequent lovers and infrequent adventure. I was on the boat back when I discovered the news of Zulra's death. She was only one hundred and eighty. Not only that, her tragic *accident* killed two of my siblings as well. Enamis, my oldest sister, was sixty years older than me, and used to read to me and plait my hair. She was more of a mother to me than Zulra. I suspected foul play, then, but I did nothing. It is one of my foulest regrets.

"Knowing that my mother was dead, and Xianyu held the throne, I had no desire to return home. It wasn't as if there was a throne to storm in and claim: two of my siblings still lived. So instead, I travelled back to the Parched Lands, where I found Kol."

A wisp of joy flitted to her. "How old was he then?"

He shook his head. "In his early twenties, I'd guess. He'd given his soul to Sotoledi a few years before, and he was out of control. I pulled him back from the darkness, taught him to control it." His face darkened. "Then my remaining two siblings died. She wasn't even subtle this time. They were poisoned."

"So you were the last?" she asked.

"Yes. The fifth in line, now the rightful fucking heir."

Suri furrowed her brow. "And you still didn't return?"

Nadrian gripped the bedclothes to his side. "I suspected something was amiss after my mother. And I did nothing. And then the rest of my family died. All of them. They fell exactly how Lera wanted, so that Xianyu could stay on the throne and pander to her for the rest of her forsaken life. I was the only one left, and I was terrified I'd be next."

She saw the guilt and shame of it written on his face.

"And then, when a few years had passed and I thought myself ready to return, I found I couldn't do it. How could I? How could I come here and look these people in the eye?" His eyes were wild with defeat and uncertainty. "Their absent prince who hadn't stepped foot in the Glen in twenty five years. The man who had run away and lived a life of nothingness. Who was I to command any respect? To claim I had any greater right than

Xianyu because of the woman I came from? I couldn't do it. I couldn't go back."

His palpable anger at himself consumed him as his self-flagellating tone filled the empty space around them. "That's all of it. My tale of woe. I'm a coward."

Suri waited, and when nothing more came forward, she spoke softly. "It wasn't your fault, Nadrian."

He chuckled. "What does fault matter now, when the result is the same? Xianyu is dead, too. The people here mourn him as a fair and just leader. And now they look to me, their wayward prince, to save them, as I never have before."

She stared at him. "What are you going to do?"

Nadrian stood, moving to the window. He stared out at the endless twilight as its magic faded even then, to the spire of the Aviary in the distance. When he turned to her, she saw something glint across his face she'd seen before. Something of the true him, the one that would die for his friends and risk everything for his court.

He shrugged at her, as if it was nothing, when she could see it was everything. "I can't let them down again."

22

My own science has grown under his tutelage, just as I aid his with mine. He knows near enough the names of every mineral.

Unknown author, est. 2nd-5th century

The Fae walked in a slow procession. The dead were already gone, moved into the forest, and soon their bodies would disappear completely. The Fae believed they changed in the night, morphed and reborn as a sapling or a flower. Nadrian had his own beliefs, which revolved around a rumoured small population of wolves.

Still, the deaths of the Fae were usually seldom and gradual. The forest had not been littered with thirty bodies, including two rulers, ever before. She hoped the Fae were right, and there would be thirty new trees in the forest, and not five fat wolves licking their claws.

The procession of those still living was close to two hundred Fae. Not all had attended the feast, and the distraction of their own arrival had meant not everyone had started eating. It was a small relief that perhaps there was something good from their coming.

Nadrian snorted softly at her side as they moved towards the Aviary.

"What is it?" she asked quietly.

All the other Fae glided across the path, their footsteps holding an ageless grace Suri couldn't emulate on her best day. Both the men and women wore flowing gowns, the fabric sweeping down to the floor in one swathe of elegant fabric. There seemed to be no code to the colours, but each looked as ethereal and ancient as the twilight forest itself. As they moved, they hummed a melancholy tune, one of woe and regret. Some harmonised and others didn't, creating an unnerving discordance which somehow perfectly matched the feeling in her gut.

Nadrian leaned towards her. "I'm imagining explaining this to the others."

Suri let out a strangled laugh, and marvelled at the sound. It had twisted from her but there was nothing trying to pull it back. The strange mirth she felt stayed, no tide tried to wrench her back to the hollow darkness.

The Fae shot them a curious look, and she pressed her lips together. This was half-funeral and half-coronation, and the tone was far from joyful, yet she found joy nonetheless.

Nadrian chuckled. "The King and Queen dead along with anyone who enjoys pork. You have your soul back, and I'm about to lose mine."

She laughed, unable to resist the dark comedy of it all. Then she stifled it and shot him a look. "Wait, you're losing your soul?"

Nadrian nodded. "The Aviary is soul-linked to the monarch. All the soul glass chambers will connect to me. That's why they were all released when Xianyu died. It'll be my duty to collect more souls to create a stable power source for the Fae."

Suri's joy faded. "You can't."

"Hm?"

"You can't give up your soul, Nadrian. You... your joy and laughter is who you are."

Nadrian didn't look at her, choosing to look straight ahead. "It's not so bad. The Aviary is a kinder mistress than the glass you were locked into. It's not pulling a part of me away... it's more, grounding me here. So long as I stay in the Glen, I will be whole. Mother even believed her emotions were strengthened here."

Suri swallowed. "And what of the Life Court?"

His face dropped. "I'll come with you, of course. I am loyal to Kol. We will fight Lera and end this together."

"And after?"

Nadrian watched his feet as they stepped along the stone path past the glass walls that housed the seeing silk molluscs. He did not speak for several steps, and she wasn't sure he would reply, or that he had even heard her. Then he gave her a sad smile. "I'll visit when I can."

Her heart dropped a little.

Every time something went well, there was some tragedy to pull her back to reality. And somehow, barely seeing Nadrian felt like its own tragedy. He had become important to her. He always had a funny word to say and sometimes a kind one, he'd never coddled her nor been sickly sweet in his attentions. Their mutual respect, their friendship, it had been hard earned on both parts.

They completed the rest of the journey to the Aviary in silence, matching that of the surrounding Fae. The procession mounted the small hill to the spire, and in turn they all stepped inside.

Nadrian and Suri were the last to enter. The glass chambers were all empty and lifeless. Before it had seemed alive, with the souls creating pockets of dizzying light in the many hexagonal prisms locked into the walls all around the Aviary. Now, it was flat and cold. The light in the glass chamber buried in the floor was gone, too. She realised now that it must have been Xianyu's soul. Now it lay open and empty, waiting for its next King.

The Fae waited too. They stood in a circle, with a gap in the middle for Nadrian to stand.

The blonde Fae from yesterday waited a step away from the crowd. She heard his name spoken by the whispering Fae. Sanjuine. Xianyu and Nuo's eldest. The man who might have been the Crown Prince himself, if Lera had succeeded in wiping out Zulra's line. His eyes were red like the blood bat's, and his light golden skin complimented his curling honey hair. In his right hand, a bone knife. In his other, a small vial.

Nadrian stopped in the doorway, and she stopped beside him.

The Fae began to sing. Softly, in aching low notes, the words trembled with reverence, voices melding as if their very nature compelled them to unite.

Sanjuine beckoned to him. "Step forth, Nadrian, son of Queen Zulra. Give us your soul, and with it, your eternal protection of all Fae who live in our Glen. Both King, and Servant, as it must be."

Nadrian shuddered and took a step forward. Suri glanced around the circle of Fae. This was their celebration, their moment, and she had no part in it.

But no sooner had she started to move, did Nadrian touch her arm. She stopped, giving him a curious look.

"Please," he said under his breath. "Stay with me."

Suri studied him for a second. His back was so stiff he looked frozen once more and blatant fear addled his green gaze. She nodded and placed her hand in his. His lips twitched in surprise. She gave it an encouraging squeeze. "To the end."

He smirked slightly, then dragged in a shaky breath. "If this is my end, something has gone horribly wrong."

"And I'll fight them for it," she said, nudging his shoulder with her own.

Nadrian stepped forwards, and she stepped with him. "Of that, at least, I have no doubt."

The Crown Prince, and her dear friend, stepped into the middle of the room, setting his feet over the glass chamber with grim determination. She stayed on the stone, but he kept his hand in hers, gripping it tightly. If any of the Fae thought it odd, none spoke nor raised a brow. They kept singing, and Sanjuine closed the distance between them.

Sanjuine touched the bone-knife to Nadrian's sternum. She felt her heartbeat dance as the Fae quieted until it was quiet enough to hear the smallest shuffling of a cape.

Sanjuine bowed his head to Nadrian. "Will you protect the Glen with your own soul, as your mother did before you, and hers before her?"

Nadrian nodded. "I will."

"Will you strengthen our Glen by finding new souls to keep our wards healthy and keep our lands hidden, and help us against those who would see harm befall us?"

This time, Nadrian's voice was a little stronger. "I will."

"And will you rule us with honour, grace and respect?"

Nadrian's voice rang out, bouncing and echoing off the many empty chambers. "I will."

Sanjuine nodded. "Will you accept this knife, as it pares you from who you once were, and carves you into who you must be?"

Nadrian closed his eyes, clutching Suri's hand.

She breathed raggedly, so deeply scared, but she had to let him do this.

A single tear fell down his cheek. "I will."

Then Sanjuine pushed the bone knife deep into Nadrian's torso. He cried out, holding Suri tight with one hand, while his other hand clutched to his middle. He fell to his knees, breathing as he stared down at the hilt buried in his chest.

The Fae sang once more, this time a battle cry. The words were in the Old Tongue, spoken loudly and quickly. They stomped their feet as Nadrian's blood soaked through his tunic and he gasped from the pain.

Stomp. Stomp. Stomp.

Red pooled around his knees. His face white as the bone-knife, he turned to Suri in a wordless gasp. Then he collapsed onto his back and dropped Suri's hand. His back arched as he gazed up at the Aviary ceiling, the light fading.

"No," she said softly, and leapt forwards, but arms pulled her back. Three Fae held her as she struggled.

Nadrian bled out on the floor as the Fae only got louder and louder.

"He's dying," she gasped, writhing in the iron grip. Why weren't they stopping it? Surely, this was enough. Take his soul now, heal him.

She was about to cry out and scream for someone to *do something*, when she saw it. A green light fell out of Nadrian and into the chamber underneath him. It flickered weakly. Sanjuine moved immediately, crouching next to Nadrian and parting his mouth before pouring the vial into it.

The Fae kept chanting and stomping, and Suri dragged in a deep breath. The green light had faded to nearly nothing. Please. He had to be fine.

Nothing happened for several seconds, and Suri deflated in the Fae's arms until they stopped bothering to hold her. She sat on the floor, staring at Nadrian.

The green light flickered once more.

And then it blazed.

Nadrian gasped as his green light filled the chamber.

The Fae erupted into cheers as Sanjuine helped Nadrian sit up with a smile on his face. Nadrian looked around, bewildered, as if he had completely forgotten where he was and what he had been doing.

The Fae applauded and whooped, and he held up a hand in a modest gesture. Suri's heart pounded with some emotion she couldn't place.

What if it wasn't him? What if he looked at her, and all that light that once belonged to him was gone? She couldn't imagine Nadrian any other way. What if he looked at her and she didn't recognise him? It was so selfish, she knew that.

Then his green eyes fell on Suri. His playful smile widened into a shit-eating grin. "Fuck me, killer. You look like you've seen a ghost."

She let out a strangled noise, somewhere between a cry and a laugh, and launched herself towards him. His blood soaked into her clothes as she hugged him, and she didn't care at all. "I'm happy you're still you."

Suri pulled back and looked down at him, wiping a tear off her cheek with a sleeve. His eyes shone just as they had before, and maybe brighter than ever, with the light of his own soul bouncing in them.

"Me too," Nadrian said, and he sniffed back his own tears.

Sanjuine stood and offered a hand to Nadrian. Suri moved back once more as Nadrian took it and got to his feet on shaky legs. His green light refracted against all the empty glass chambers, creating hypnotic patterns and dancing emerald spots all the way up the tower.

The Fae all cheered once more as Nadrian lifted his hands to the sky and stared up at the Aviary.

"Crown Prince Nadrian, he is no more," Sanjuine said, calling out to all that could hear. "From now until his last day... He will be the Servant of the Fae, the Protector of the Glen, and the Keeper of Souls. Long live King Nadrian!"

And this time, Suri's voice was just as loud as any of the Fae. "Long live King Nadrian!"

23

I have decided my own ambition. It came from a small thought, that I would desire to be near him, wherever he was, always.

Unknown author, est. 2nd-5th century

"What are those lights?" Suri asked, pointing as the wind buffeted her face. She'd braided her hair back before their flight so at least that wasn't whipping her. "Is there a city there? I thought we were approaching the foothills."

They'd been in the Fae Glen only one full day and left in the same evening glow they'd arrived in, giving Suri an eerie feeling they'd not truly left. If Lera's word was true, Dellon had cut the Parched Lands' access to food yesterday, which only added to her growing unease.

It was a cold night even at ground level, and they flew high as soon as they left the Glen. The higher they flew, the smaller they looked in the sky and the less effort Nadrian had to put into glamouring them. But it was freezing up near the clouds, and Suri's teeth chattered as she pointed.

The dark grass beneath them faded into purplish dunes, but at the place where the two would meet, instead of the foothills, there was a dark mass populated with light.

"There's no city here," Nadrian said, his tone nervous as he dipped a little lower. It was night, so even a particularly large bird in the sky shouldn't be too obvious to any would-be stargazers. They flew ever nearer, and the light became torches and fires and tents. "Shit."

It wasn't the light of windows in hundreds of houses. It was people, camped on the foothills. So many that the light bled into the night as far as the eye could see. Shadowed figures around a fire, the clanging of pots and jeers from beneath orange fabric tents, horses upon horses tied up at posts.

Suri sucked in a breath. "Lera's army?"

"Must be."

She blinked as the wind dried her eye, trying and failing to count how many tents there were. "There has to be thousands of people here."

"There are more by the Pail's border, and then Dabri'yon's troops, too."

Suri set her jaw and finished his thought. "Kol can't fight this."

"I don't think a fair fight was ever Lera's intention."

Suri reflected on Lera's words from that strange moment in Lartosh. *The sand-dwellers will not last a minute against my army.* "Fuck."

Nadrian pulled higher into the air as they flew over the war camp. They coasted over it, and soon there was nothing but purple dunes below them.

"How are you feeling?" Suri asked.

"Stop asking me that," Nadrian replied.

"That answers the question. You're crabbier than usual."

Nadrian sighed. "I feel the same way I did when we left the Glen. Colder, emptier. Like I'm flying away from a lover."

Suri frowned. It was strange to hear him categorise it in that way, to hear how the stripping of emotion felt like losing a loved one. To her, it had felt like a boot on her chest, pushing her underwater.

Then she smirked up at him. "I didn't realise you and Sanjuine had got to lover status already."

Nadrian rolled his eyes, but she saw the mirth catch on his face. "Shut up, Seer, or I'll drop you."

Suri laughed, and the sound danced from her like the bells of Winter's End. Soulful, free and celebratory.

The old city had been a dusty carcass, an empty husk sheltering little more than a stables, a manned towering entrance, and the treasured Gate hidden deep within it.

Now, it was something else.

Sand still piled against the buildings, most dilapidated and covered with debris and wood, but the city hummed with people. Those closest must have already heeded Kol's orders, and made their way into the protection of the mountain-shielded lost city.

As they flew towards the city gates in the morning light, she noticed the guards along its rocky top had doubled.

Nadrian gripped her a little tighter, raising his voice over the winds. "It's going to be a quick descent. I need as few people to see us fall as possible. You might want to close your eyes. Eye. Shit, sorry."

Suri nodded, and clutched onto him. "It's fine. Do it."

Nadrian swept in over the city and then he pulled his wings in, and the two of them plunging like a stone. She did not close her eye. They fell straight down, the buildings rising up to meet them, readying themselves for the imminent splatter.

But Suri wasn't scared. She was exhilarated.

The wind whipped into them as they fell ever closer to the sandstone, the dots turning from bustling insects to people. They dropped closer and closer to the buildings and her stomach flipped as her breath fell in a wordless gasp. She trusted Nadrian wouldn't drop her and they would land safely, and that thread of belief turned the freefall from fear to joy.

Then Nadrian billowed his wings, and slowed them. They didn't stop immediately, falling as the air caught in his huge gold wings. And then, just like that, they were past the roofs, and he landed on his feet, as lightly as if he had just jumped a few feet down.

A few curious gazes looked their way, but most blinked and kept going.

"Do none of them see your wings?" Suri whispered.

Nadrian released her and checked the coast was clear. "They see what they want to see," he explained, flexing his shoulders. "Their mind looks for the logical explanation, and us jumping down from a ledge or window is more plausible than flight."

Suri nodded. "Where to?"

He led the way, navigating the city with ease as she followed. "The ruins of the castle."

"Why?"

Nadrian gave her a lop-sided grin. "If Kol was going to establish himself anywhere in the city, it would be there. He has a flair for the opulent and dramatic, if you hadn't noticed."

Suri's heart thudded as the nearness of it all locked in her chest. The nearness of him.

So much had happened. The massacre would not be a fun thing to explain. Nadrian's loss, and his crowning, another thing entirely. But consuming her more than that, she had her soul back. How would she feel? Seeing him again?

What if she felt nothing? He had waited on her emotions to come back to prove what they had been doing was real. That it meant something, that the two of them *were* something. Perhaps it didn't mean anything, and the mask over her true feelings was really masking nothing at all.

More than that, she was terrified she *would* feel something, of her heart soaring. Gods, she didn't know what it was like to give her heart to someone who could break it. She had avoided it all her life, only allowing love which was safe and familial, always taking lovers at arm's reach and pushing them away before she could feel a thing.

She trusted Kol. She liked him. She was attracted to him. Before she lost her soul, she knew she could see herself loving him some day, and now, she found she missed him. She longed to see him again. She longed for *him* to see her.

Nadrian thankfully left her to her thoughts as he weaved them through the city. He looked conflicted too, his gaze hard yet distracted and his teeth gnawing into his lip. Much had changed for them both, and she found herself grieving the loss of his soul more than she had grieved her own. Even at her brightest, she had never been full of life. Hers was an ember quickly dampened, his was a blazing fire now in coals.

The air was hazy, filled with the steady dust of constant footfall on the sandy streets. She covered her mouth with her cloak as they avoided the bustling streams of people. The main paths had been freshly swept, but the constant flow of new groups entering the city churned the sand and dirt into the air. Each carried their worldly belongings on their backs, and a guard stepped in to help a mother carry a bag into an abandoned house, her two young children clinging to her skirts.

They passed a large crowd gathered around a stall where guards appeared to be handing out generous food packages. Suri winced. If they couldn't stop the food blockage, everyone here would starve in a matter of weeks, and no one knew. Were the guards aware that the food was scarce? Were they rationing yet, or acting normally to prevent a panic?

She noticed the hierarchy of the guards again, one she'd noticed in the outpost, too. Those in red largely helped with cleaning, carrying, and signposting the new arrivals. Those in black handed out the food and stood guard up on the roofs and atop the city walls.

Then there were those in white. Rarer, a couple seen at the city wall, one or two passing along the streets.

Six in white guarded the entrance to the huge building ahead.

It seemed Nadrian had been right about where to find Kol.

Wide, low steps led up to the huge fifteen-foot entrance doorway. It was one of the few parts of the city well intact, with hulking dark wooden doors cast with portraits of nymphs and beasts in clever relief upon its frame, telling some long-forgotten story. Nearly one hundred citizens lined up outside the door, with the guards letting some in every few minutes.

"Do not push," one guard called out. "The Lord Kol will see as many of you as he can. He will have another audience session tomorrow at noon."

"I guess everyone knows he's alive now," Nadrian said, grabbing Suri's hand and pulling her past the line.

A few citizens grumbled as they stepped past the queue, but one look at their faces and pins and their expressions changed from annoyance to something akin to awe.

The guards at the door bowed and let them in without hesitation. And it wasn't just because of Nadrian, they seemed to know her, too, but how, she hardly understood. Maybe the rumours of the one-eyed woman at Kol's side had become so widespread that she was famous now in her own right, or Kol had told the guards to await their arrival. Either way, there was more than respect in their eyes. There was fear there, too. She wondered how many of them believed she had genuinely tried to kill their lord.

Still, no one stopped them as they stepped into the vast antechamber within. It was lucky to be standing, with the stone support pillars more like strange rocks, half-formed things cut off at the torso. Someone had swept the sand to the far corners, but it still piled up at the edges of the room, a constant reminder of the Wrath.

A citizen's voice echoed against the high stone walls, the windows mostly shattered, though some small panes of the stained glass mosaic at the back had survived. The daylight filtered in, supplemented by a large fire in a hearth to the left, and several braziers.

Their own boots on the stone floor echoed alongside the hushed whispers of the couple dozen others waiting for their turn to speak.

Then she saw him. And instantly, she knew she was in trouble.

At the end of the chamber, sat on a stone throne clearly dragged in from somewhere else, was Kol. Her breath caught in her chest and she could feel her heartbeat in her stomach and pulse in her fingertips. She clenched her hands into fists at her side to keep them from shaking.

Just seeing him flared an unadulterated fear she'd never felt before.

She'd never placed enough value on herself to truly fear death. It had always been a close companion, something haunting her like a shadow, ready to catch her the moment she faltered. It was more than an eventual inevitability—it was a constant. But this, looking at Kol, his fingers steepled in front of a contemplative mouth, real fear lanced through her heart.

His brow was furrowed as he listened, his shoulders tight and the hollows under his eyes darker than usual. He had not noticed them enter.

She needed him like air. Looking at his face lifted her whole body; she felt weightless, and yet anchored. Fear alone did not express the horror that this might be taken from her, that he might reject her or leave her.

Oh, fuck.

The throne wasn't raised, the seat sitting on the same floor the citizens stood on, giving the strange effect of them speaking down to him. Though, she thought, Kol would somehow make sitting cross-legged on the sandy floor look regal.

The citizen had just finished explaining how their well was unexpectedly full, as their settlement had lost a third of their population to disease and storms. "I do not blame you for our misfortune. The Parched Lands have been a haven to my family when we were ousted for treason from Lera decades past. I only wish to offer that water now, should the war keep us here longer than expected, and resources be scarce."

Kol's brow relaxed a little. "I thank you for your generous offer, Munis of the Eastern Plains. There may come a time when we need that water." He waved a hand towards one of the men in white to his right. "Speak to my guards about the location of the well and I will ensure we send good men to retrieve the water before the enemy forces arrive."

The citizen nodded several times, and then hesitated.

"Is there more?" Kol asked.

"No, your grace," he said, his ears reddening. "Only that—Do you think we will survive it?"

Kol sighed and stood, rubbing his face. He addressed the man, but raised his voice enough that all could hear it. "I wish I could give you the reassurances you all crave. I want them, too. There are people I am worried about, people I would lay down my life for. All I can tell you is, we are stronger than they know, and we will fight this the right way." The room was silent, hanging on his words. "We will be smart and defensive. I will not send a single man or woman into a conflict I do not believe we can win. I promise you this: I will give everything I have to keep as many people safe as I possibly can."

The man's blush faded, and he nodded at Kol, meeting his gaze head on. "Thank you, your grace."

Kol gave him a pained smile that only touched one side of his mouth and sat back down. The citizen left, and the others shuffled forwards.

Nadrian took the moment to walk towards him. Kol caught his movement, and flitted his attention to them. His dark eyes trained on her immediately, and he appraised her fully from head to toe, searching her for something. His gaze reached her face and softened. She saw the weight fall from him as a genuine smile broke over his face. He stood up again, back ramrod straight and the tired slump of his shoulders gone. She couldn't tell if it was the sunlight falling in shafts through the window behind him, or if it was magic, but he glowed.

Kol wafted a hand to the guard and murmured that he needed a small break, and strode to them without a second look.

No. He strode to *her*, his steps long as he closed the distance.

She couldn't help closing the gap herself, stepping forward to greet him. Kol cupped her face in both hands, his thumbs caressing her jaw. He breathed out, touching his forehead to hers as she grabbed the front of his tunic, holding him in place.

"Did anything—You must tell me. Are you well?" Kol asked. His breath washed over her, loosening the muscles in her body better than any stretch.

"I am well, Kol. I am well," Suri replied, her mouth dry and her heart pounding faster than she had ever known.

She used to know home to be a place. She'd believed the North to be her home for so long, simply because its icy walls had been her world. Then she thought her home could be Akdaria, because its humid branches had shown her wonders and kindness.

Now, she knew home was always people. New Politan was home because Esra had been her home. Akdaria had been her home because of Axri'don and Jem and Nadrian and even Scilla. But being here, in his touch, in his embrace. Home was wherever Kol was.

She was completely screwed.

He gazed down at her with his deep brown eyes. "*Nen alerisee f'ith sotele.*"

She smiled up at him, unable to help it. "I know it's you, you idiot."

He made a surprised noise, caught off-guard. His gaze shifted from warm relief to something of a study, taking in her wide smile and focusing on her silver eye. "And how do you figure that, my little thief?"

"No one else is quite that bossy."

"Is that so?"

"Yes. It is," she said, staring up at him.

"She's got you pegged," Nadrian laughed, looking between them with no small dose of curiosity. "Are you going to hold me like that, too?"

Kol stroked Suri's jaw once more, then released her with no embarrassment. She missed his touch immediately. Even here, when there were thirty odd pairs of eyes watching them, he was all she could see, all she wanted to be around.

He clapped Nadrian into a hug. "Welcome back, old friend. It is good to see you."

"And you, my lord. We have much to discuss," he said into Kol's ear, loud enough for only the three of them to hear. "Can you wrap up here?"

Kol pulled back and looked between them both. "Yes. Meet me in the tower. I'll let Scilla and Viantha know you're coming. I'll make my way there as soon as I've seen those already here."

Nadrian smiled. "Be quick. I have an appointment with the leaf pools and a long drink."

Kol smiled, but then he looked at her and the smile dropped. His gaze was curious. He swallowed and his throat bobbed and his hands twitched nervously at his side. "I won't be long."

Suri and Nadrian walked out, and this time the stares were trained on her, both guards and citizens taking her in anew.

Nadrian nudged her as they exited the castle and stepped down the stairs. "Do you know what you're doing there, killer?"

Suri glanced at him when they reached the bottom of the stairs. He appraised her with a calculated look. Not an unkind one, but trying to work her out all the same. She puffed out a breath, the anxious energy morphing into a delayed shakiness. "I think I finally do."

Nadrian scanned her expression, and a smile tugged at the edge of his mouth. "Perfect. Now all you need to do is tell him."

She returned the small smile even as her heart spiked. "I will."

An unexpected cool breeze tickled up her spine and Suri shuddered, turning to its source. It was never cool at this time in the Parched Lands. But there was nothing there, just a crowded street. She rolled her shoulders, the tingle of ice still making her uneasy. "Did you feel that?"

"Feel what?" Nadrian asked.

Suri blinked, checking once around her again. She was too goddamn paranoid. "Nothing."

He studied her as they walked. "How long have you had that code phrase with Kol?"

Suri took his offered hand as he guided them around a cluster of women. "Since we left for the Pail. Why?"

Nadrian shrugged from just ahead of her. "Do you know what it means?"

Suri smirked and nodded. "The handsome man has returned."

The Fae King snorted and then shook his head.

"What?" Suri asked.

"Nothing," Nadrian said. "Just. You were right. Kol is an idiot."

Suri laughed. "I'll drink to that."

"Gods." Nadrian let out a moan as they ducked into a much quieter side street. "I'd kill for an Icebolt."

"Let's go home, then," Suri said.

Nadrian smiled and crooked his arm so she could take it like a lady. "Let's."

She put her hand on his arm and they walked like that to the Gate hidden under the city.

24

To think of a design for the world: that is easy. To realise it, near impossible.

Unknown author, est. 2nd-5th century

The humid air on her skin held a reassuring weight and the sun peeling in overhead found the small gaps in the leaf canopy, hitting their faces with its small rays and welcoming them back to Akdaria.

They moved along the path, the lanterns dry and dark at this time, but the tinted orange glass still marked their route as surely as the worn path underfoot.

An unexpected sight greeted them as they reached the top.

Scilla and Viantha approached from the wooden bridge to the scout's hut.

Nadrian waved. "Well met, ladies."

Suri's stomach tightened at Scilla's navy general tunic. It was her battle outfit, the one she'd worn when she ordered Suri's eye to be carved from her head. A wave of nausea rose and fell as she recalled what she'd tried to block out. Scilla strode towards them, her eyes tired but her expression warm. "Heard you were coming back, thought you'd like a greeting party."

Suri smiled, but it was wan at best.

Nadrian bowed, doffing a non-existent hat. "You thought correctly."

She turned her attention to Viantha as they closed the distance. Somehow, the woman she'd kidnapped in a sewer and then left stranded on a rooftop was easier to look in the eye. Maybe it was selfish to seek refuge in the person she herself had hurt, or maybe she just liked that Viantha was the only one who still looked at her with true hesitation. Viantha's blue untrusting gaze cut to the core of her, reminded her of the monster she always knew herself to be.

The Water heiress looked stunning, her pale pink dress overlaid with a glossy golden layer which met in the centre of her waist and fell away. With matching golden pins in her dark hair, she was a walking sunrise.

The two women reached them, and Nadrian swept Scilla into a hug. The general embraced him back just as hard. When they pulled away, Scilla studied them both. "So you survived the Glen, then?"

"More or less," Nadrian said, his voice light. He pointed to Suri. "Well, her more. Me less."

Scilla processed this, trying to decipher the meaning.

Again, an icy chill crept up Suri's back. This time, she whirled round fast, knowing immediately something was wrong.

A flash of a cloak moved on the stairs.

"Shit." Suri reached for her knife and moved to lunge at him. But she wasn't fast enough.

His hand was already there, a claw in the air, and the ice lanced the platform under her boots, freezing her in place along with the others. He pushed his hood back with his other hand and smiled at Suri, white-blonde hair carefully braided back from his face, leaving only one wispy strand falling towards his narrowed blue eyes.

"For a place supposed to be secret, you two did a shit job of checking for a tail."

Rasel Waterborne. The man who drugged her and tied his own life to hers, marking her chest in its second bond of blood, one she hoped would remain unfulfilled for decades to come.

Suri held the blade up by her head, cocked, pointed. She didn't dare throw it. Not yet. If she missed, her only weapon would be gone. If she hit too well, he might die, and if he died, she died with him.

That was the nature of their bond, a pact of death laid upon them before the Seer of Blood like some dreadful facsimile of a marriage. She could kill him, right this moment, but then her blood would compel her to follow after.

He had come here though, willingly. Maybe he *wanted* her to kill him. Her lip curled in a snarl. "What the fuck do you want, Rasel?"

Before he had time to reply, water slammed into him—the moisture from the leaves, the bark, and the very air. In a second, he was soaked from head-to-toe, but it didn't stop. He spluttered, looking more confused than worried. "Whatever this trick is, sister, stop it. I'm not here to kill you."

Suri turned her head, her body locked in place.

Viantha stood on the far edge of the platform, her feet also welded to the floor. Her arms, though, were trained outwards, towards her brother, a look of reviled disgust painted on her pretty face. "Lies."

Clearly, Viantha had no intention of finding out what he wanted to say. She pulled more and more water from the humid air and forest around them. Soon, Rasel wasn't just covered in water, but a layer of water had formed around him.

From his feet upwards, water encased him within seconds. The water swelled and bulged, and Rasel gasped in a breath and pinched his eyes shut just as the water covered his nose and mouth.

Still the water kept coming, the air thick with it and waiting upon the water princess' command. Suri didn't know what to say, hardly had time to think as the water expanded around him, smothering him in a bubble of water. Now, it raised him from the ground, as Rasel started to writhe in his watery prison, one hand over his mouth as he struggled to hold his breath.

"Viantha, stop," Nadrian called, still stuck. Rasel's focus had dropped from the magic pinning them, but the ice stayed firm for now. "If Rasel dies, Suri dies, too."

Rasel held his breath, but his face turned red and then a little white as he struggled to hold on. His eyes burst open, and he stared at his sister with nothing short of terror. The bubble held firm around him and his feet kicked into nothing.

Viantha grimaced, as if she had forgotten, but she didn't stop. "Maybe it's for the best. You trust her, but is that worth more than ending my brother, once and for all?"

"Yes," Nadrian said without hesitation.

Viantha frowned. "He is a disease. She is perpetuating him."

"I'm sorry," Suri said. There was no defence she could raise. "I'm so sorry for what I did to you."

"A convenient time to apologise," Viantha said, but a trace of uncertainty pulled at her mouth.

Suri nodded. "You're right. I should have said something before. Your brother deserves to die. I would forgive you, if you did it."

Rasel gasped, the sound muffling into a high-pitched submerged squeal as the water encasing him filled his mouth.

"Fuck that," Nadrian growled. "We did not go to all that trouble for you to die because of that weasel. Viantha. Stop. I am sworn to protect her. She is the Seer of Time, and she is my friend. If you mean to kill her, I *will* hurt you."

Rasel choked in his bubble, clutching his neck.

"Vi," Scilla said, pulling at her icy restraints. Viantha flinched. "Don't."

Viantha blinked a couple of times, her arms shaking. Rasel made a small, desperate noise. Then she sighed and dropped her arms.

Rasel dropped to the floor, hard. The water splashed and spread, falling around him and through the cracks in the floorboards. He spluttered, holding his chest as he hacked up water.

"Why the fuck is he here?" Suri asked. The shock of almost dying, and the adrenaline of not, made the question come out strangled and fast.

"Well, he had the jump on us," Scilla said. "And he immobilised us instead of killing one of us. So your guess is as good as mine."

"I still can't move my bastard feet," Nadrian said, using his hands to attempt to pull his feet free of the ice.

Rasel leaned over on all fours, coughing less now. He looked up, his eyes bloodshot and filled with rage, as he stared at his sister. "You're always the thorn in my side. Not this time."

The prince raised a shaky hand. Viantha shuddered out a pained breath.

The ice spread up Viantha's body faster than Suri had ever seen. She would be entombed, a sculpture like Manira had been in the desert.

He was going to kill her.

Nadrian swore as he wrenched once more, the ice crunching around his feet as he loosened it. Suri raised her knife. She might only get one shot at this. One throw, and if it went well, they would both die. But Viantha wouldn't.

Cull the disease. Be the good guy.

Suri took a breath in.

But she wasn't first.

Vines struck into Rasel's body, hitting him from every angle. Thickened branchlike arms met smaller ivy roots, all latching to the ice wielder at once. Some pummelled into him, some wrapped and stretched. Rasel's concentration on his own magic dropped again as the vines wrenched and snarled, hauling him up until he was tied at each hand and foot, suspended from many entangling vines.

Suri blinked as she lowered her knife, unable to comprehend what had just happened. She turned, face pale with shocked confusion.

Viantha took quick breaths, rubbing at her chest. Nadrian's ice had finally broken, and he stood facing entirely away from the ice prince. Both of them stared at the general with awed disbelief.

Scilla. Her hands pointed towards Rasel, the rage in her face morphing into complete surprise. She stared down at her fingers like she'd never seen them before.

Suri's voice shook. "Did you just—"

Scilla looked up, her mouth parted. Her body shook, her breath was unsteady. "I don't know. Maybe. I think so."

Suri didn't know what to think, or how to feel. Scilla had just pulled vines out of the air somehow. How?

Awe warred against a little of her old jealousy. Suri had been trying to get a grasp on her time magic for weeks, and now Scilla had discovered a powerful magic almost without thinking. But where that salted envy would have consumed her before, she let it fall away as the feeling of mystifying wonder rose to the top. Scilla had magic, magic far beyond the shadow magic she'd previously seen.

Viantha's expression was hard to read. "You have life power."

At these words, something inside Suri unlocked. Scilla had controlled plant life. If that was life power, that could mean she was a Daughter of the Earth, too.

Scilla turned to Viantha, studying her with hawkish eyes. "Are you hurt?"

Viantha shook her head and a faint blush bloomed near her cheekbones. “It was painful, but I’ve had worse from him. I’ll be fine.”

Scilla nodded, opening her mouth to say something, before nodding again and dropping her eyes. “Good. Good.”

Nadrian snorted. “Rasel is strung up in plants like a prize fool and you’re not even going to talk about it?”

Scilla huffed. “It was probably just an accident.”

Viantha touched Scilla’s arm. “I can train you to control it.”

Scilla stared back at the Water Guild heiress.

For a time, they had all believed that there was only one Daughter, whom Kol, the Son of Life, was destined to fall in love with. By all odds, that Daughter was Viantha. But Mother Edi had corrected their translation, to say there were multiple Daughters, and the definition of *love* was far from fixed. If Scilla was a Daughter, too, then maybe it was true after all. Maybe Kol wasn’t prophesied to fall for another, maybe he could be hers after all.

Either way, it was a new power on *their* side of the battlefield.

Nadrian rubbed a hand over his mouth taking them all in with a mixture of wonder and amusement. “I regret praying for an exciting life. Never a single shred of peace with you lot.”

Suri flipped her knife back into her pocket, nodding her head to where Rasel struggled to no avail against the knots of the vines. “Now, what do we do with him?”

25

The stick of summer bears the threat of the looming season. There is no language to express my fear of his upcoming departure.

Unknown author, est. 2nd-5th century

"What if we don't have to fight Lera's army when they arrive? What if we can entangle them all in vines and stop the march that way? They would be useless."

Scilla groaned at Nadrian's eager suggestion. "Great plan, except for the fact it relies on me doing that again. I have no idea how I did it the first time."

Suri leant against the wide table, still reeling from what had just happened. After they'd called the guards to cut Rasel down and clamp him in silverwood, they'd all made their way to the tower, needing a safe place to talk more than they needed a drink. With any luck, Rasel was already locked up in the canopy prison.

Nadrian blinked as if it had only just occurred to him, his ring of smoke coming from his mouth in a surprised circle as he leant back in his armchair. "Oh. True."

Scilla played with the edge of the roll of seeing silk, her gaze locked onto the table. "I'll try to recreate it."

Nadrian shrugged. "I think you were trying to protect Viantha. Maybe you just need something you really want to protect."

Viantha tensed, her small fingers curling around the side of the bookcase.

"Nadrian, you know I love this city. I would die before I saw it lost to the Queen. I want to protect it. But our plan can't rely on me," Scilla said, her shoulders locked.

"Yes, maybe it's better to rely on powers that have already been tested," Nadrian said. "Viantha suspended Rasel in water. Maybe she could suspend the army too, with an air bubble around their heads so they don't die?"

Viantha's response was cutting. "You don't have any idea what you're talking about."

"Ouch," he said.

"Look, this isn't only about practice. It's about sources of power," the Water princess explained. "When Scilla saved me, she pulled most of those vines from the trees around her. When I drowned Rasel in that bubble, I used the water in the air and the dew on the leaves. Where do you expect us to find walls of plants in the dust of the Parched Lands? A wall of water? It would have to be created from nothing. And then controlled, held. It would take an army of people like Scilla and I to even attempt it."

The strange energy in the room deflated as the reality hit. If the power could be used, it wasn't going to be straightforward.

Someone cleared their throat from behind Suri.

"What if you didn't need to create the water?"

She spun around to see Kol standing in the doorway. He'd asked the question to Viantha, but the moment she turned, he glanced at her. There was something uncertain in his expression. He looked jittery, his fingers tapping against his other arm as he folded them.

"Lord Kol?" Viantha said.

Kol ran his hand through his hair, focusing studiously on the princess. "What if the water was there, and you only needed to manipulate it?"

Viantha frowned. "It would still be a large undertaking. I'd need help."

Kol nodded. "I have sent for Ressa. She's on her way."

Viantha paled and her hand clenched against the side of the table. "My mother is coming?"

"Yes," Kol confirmed. "As soon as she's destroyed the Dam."

Suri blinked. There was only one dam she knew of, and it was heavily protected by the Guilds. "The one in the Pail?"

Kol smiled at her with something approaching reluctance. Then he moved to the table and rolled open one of several large maps. It depicted the Eastern Kingdom as it used to be, with the city of Ucraipha marked on the eastern border. He ran his finger over a snaking line of blue near the city. "This city used to be framed by a river, with a large bridge arcing over the river bed. The bridge is rubble now, but the river bed still lies sunken around the city. In the years after the Wrath, when the world discovered that even the river wasn't enough to grow anything here, the Guilds built the Dam, keeping the water where the people were." With a fingernail, he tapped where the Dam was now, drawing their attention to the hills separating the Pail from the Parched Lands. "There was no one with enough influence to stop them. In the first decades after the Wrath, to be sent to the Parched Lands was a death sentence, with only a handful of unmanned and dusty wells to cling to."

Suri grimaced as Kol paused to let that sink in. Everyone had been so ready to give up on the Eastern Kingdom entirely.

"When I became the land's keeper," he continued, "I negotiated a deal with the Water Guild: gems for water. But the Guilds would not release the Dam. Until now, until Ressa. She finally has full control of the Dam, and its removal. If the water comes back, it should find its same path again, and with everyone evacuated, it's the perfect time. I hope one day, it'll forge new life here. But until then, it'll stall Lera. They won't be expecting it, they'll have to construct bridges for the troops, or use Rasel to freeze it."

Nadrian smirked. "They won't be using Rasel for anything."

Kol's eyes narrowed. "Explain."

And he did, explaining how Rasel must have followed them through the Gate. How he froze them, claimed he didn't want to kill any of them. How Viantha nearly killed him, which caused Kol to look sharply up at her, and then how Rasel's own attempt on his sister's life was thwarted by Scilla. Finally, Nadrian explained how Rasel was now locked in the upper prison.

Kol growled. "You left him alone up there? But what if—"

Nadrian sighed and interrupted. "He's in a cell, with guards ordered to watch him around the clock, and with nothing in his room capable of killing him quickly. They're also ordered to make sure he actually eats and drinks. He's as safe from his own death as we can make him."

Kol lifted his hands to his mouth as he looked around them all. "Good." He met Suri's eye head on. "When he was drowning, when he was being hit with the vines, did you feel anything?"

"Like what?"

"Did you feel like you were drowning, did you feel any pain? Anything at all?"

"No," Suri replied.

Kol smiled, and it was his most dangerous one. "Even better. The blood bond only works for death, then. You can't feel his pain."

"What are you going to do?" Suri asked.

He ignored her question, instead giving Scilla a once over. "How are you feeling?"

Scilla shrugged. "A little shaky, as if I just sparred for an hour."

"The magic has taken it out of you," he replied, "but you're strong. If I could have wished life magic on anyone, it would be you."

Suri's heart hurt. She could see how much he meant the words, how his hope for their future wove so deep into everything he did, and it only made her crave his touch more. Gods, she just wanted to talk to him now. She needed to know if he still needed her as he had before. Her own need clawed at her as she drank in his warm expression.

Scilla allowed herself a small smile, before she ducked her head. Ever restrained, ever the general.

Suri folded her arms as she stepped closer to the map, closer to Kol. "What does it mean? Is she—? Is Scilla a Daughter of the Earth?"

The room exchanged looks. The Son of Life, and the Daughters of the Earth, bonded by love. Who would be bonded by love? Scilla and Viantha?

Viantha stared at Scilla, whose own gaze was directed to the table legs with an impressive focus.

"I don't think we know enough yet to rule anything in, or out," Kol replied. "Is it only creation that counts, or is life manipulation enough? We're guessing. Aisha sent word that she cured a man with lifelong seizures. Perhaps, she's a Daughter, too."

"Maybe there's five Daughters," Nadrian mused, standing up with an excited flair in his eyes. "Ten, even."

The tension in the room dropped slightly at the mention of other Daughters. Scilla nodded, and Viantha leaned back against the bookshelves behind her.

"The prophecy can wait," Kol said. "The focus right now is to stop Lera before she gets to eight massacres."

"We saw Lera's troops at the Pananti Foothills. Dabri'yon must be approaching through the Pail. Any chance the Guilds will stop her?" Nadrian asked.

Kol shook his head. "Ressa might be with us, but Nonlos isn't ready to make a stand yet without more evidence. But I spoke with Allis'don."

"Through the silk?" Suri asked.

He didn't address her directly, nodding to the room at large. "After my warning in Lartosh, she wrote to the remaining great houses across the Shale. They seek proof against Dabri'yon for their own politics, and have hidden their men amongst her ranks. If some trickery occurs, at least the houses will be aware."

They all sat with this. It was progress, but so slow. All anyone would commit to was watching, and it frustrated Suri to no end. For leaders, they were certainly benign in their approach to war.

But there was more to discuss. Suri swallowed. "We need to talk about the Glen."

Kol scanned her again from head to toe. "What happened over there?"

She knew the silent question in his gaze. Did you make a deal for your soul? Are you whole again? But he had no idea how bad it all really was.

She took a deep breath. "We couldn't stop it. The massacre. We thought they'd poisoned the wine, but we were wrong. It was the food."

"Shit," Kol said.

"How many dead?" Viantha asked.

"Around thirty," Suri said, glancing at Nadrian for confirmation. The redhead wasn't looking at her though, his eyes glazed as he stared at nothing. "Enough, probably."

"Who?" Scilla asked.

Suri waited. Nadrian had to be the one to say it. To explain who he now was. He blinked, his attention coming back to the room and she gave him what she hoped was a reassuring look.

Nadrian dropped back into the armchair. "Both Xianyu and Nuo are dead."

Viantha's sharp intake met Scilla's muttered swear.

Kol just froze.

Nadrian chuckled humorlessly. "You're looking at the new Fae King. Long live me, I guess."

No one spoke for three breaths.

"You're joking," Scilla choked. "You're *King*, now? You said you'd never do it."

"I didn't want to. I thought they didn't want *me*. But they asked me. More than that, they begged. And I—I can't fail them again. I couldn't say no. It was too risky to allow Lingyun any chance to claim the role of Consort."

"The King of the Fae. The Son of Life. The Seer of Time. Heiress to the Water Guild," Scilla said monotonously, pointing around the room. "And me. Where's my title?"

Suri smirked. "You might be a Daughter, now."

"I have to share that title, though," Scilla replied.

"How about Gouger to the Seer?" Suri retorted.

Scilla barked out a laugh as the rest of the room flinched. "Fuck that. Maybe Waris is looking for an apprentice."

Suri laughed. "Witch-in-training, I could see it. You just need some jars of organs and you're all set."

She grinned. "Are you offering?"

Nadrian tutted in false reproach, but there was a smile beneath it. "You two are something else."

Viantha looked a little pale.

Kol stared at Suri's smiling mouth. Heat met with curiosity. Fear? His brow tensed as he pulled his bottom lip into his mouth. He must have worked it out. Xianyu was dead. Her soul, freed.

He dropped her gaze and walked over to Nadrian and offered him his hand. Nadrian took it, and Kol pulled him to his feet and into a hug.

"I know you're older than me," Kol said. "But I'm proud of you. You'll be a great King."

Nadrian sniffed over Kol's shoulder, patting him on the back. "You're just glad to have another King on your side."

Kol chuckled and leaned back, shaking his head. "Take the compliment, Nadrian."

"Over my dead body," he said. "Or Xianyu's, as it were."

Scilla groaned and Suri held back a laugh.

"Too soon?" he said.

Kol nodded. "Yes, brother. But I am glad you are right enough to jest."

"I'll have to return to the Glen as soon as Lera's siege is over."

Kol grimaced. "Ah. The Aviary has you."

Nadrian sighed. "That it does. Just another reason to end this war sooner than later. I'll get increasingly grumpy otherwise."

"What are you talking about?" Viantha asked.

"All the souls Xianyu had captured escaped when he died," Nadrian said. "As part of my coronation, they embedded my soul into the Glen. It works as a power source for the glamours and charms which protect us from intruders. But it's feeding on my soul alone now. The soul coffers are empty, and it's my job to fill them. Ideally, before the spells eke out all the juice from mine."

"That sounds awful," Viantha said.

"It's not so bad," Nadrian said, overly chipper. "I'm pure Fae, it'll take the Aviary a while to use me up."

"Fae souls are worth more?" Suri asked.

"I wouldn't put it like that. But they last longer."

Suri's mind raced as she thought of the war ahead, of life and death magic, of time and souls. "Do you have to have consent to bottle a soul?"

Nadrian narrowed his eyes. "What are you thinking, killer?"

"Wait a moment," Scilla said, staring at her with her hand raised. "All the souls Xianyu captured escaped. Suri, is your soul back?"

Every pair of eyes in the room fell on her.

She smirked. "It's back."

Kol didn't flinch, and she knew he'd worked it out the instant Nadrian had mentioned Xianyu's death, if not before. She met his gaze, unable to prevent her blush, and he simply stared at her. They needed to talk.

Scilla let out a sigh of relief and grinned. "Thank Dio, I've been carrying the guilt for helping you make that deal for weeks."

She laughed. "I'm sorry to have been such a nuisance in your life."

Scilla shrugged. "I suppose I'll forgive you."

Suri tensed, the statement sending her thoughts spiralling. It was just a joke, she knew. She didn't truly forgive her, not for all of it. Not for Barsen, never for that.

Scilla also gauged the double meaning of her words, and straightened a little.

Nadrian put his hand up. "I, for one, would love to hear the end of your earlier thought, killer."

Suri nodded, and tried to work out how to express her idea.

Before she could say anything, Kol cleared his throat. "I'm going to pay Rasel a visit. You lot can bring me up to speed later."

Suri furrowed her brow. "Are you sure that's a—"

But he was already moving. He left without a glance back, and she watched the door close behind him.

"Where's he going?" Viantha asked.

"Probably to beat the shit out of Rasel," Nadrian said.

Viantha's expression twisted. "Maybe he needs help."

The three of them studied the princess. She could tell Nadrian had half a mind to refuse her, but Scilla had no such reservations.

"I'll show you the way," Scilla said to her, then nodded to Suri. "We'll meet you at Kazem's later."

Viantha took in Scilla's casual acceptance with surprise, and then quietly followed the general out the door.

Nadrian threw his hands up in confusion. "I don't know how I attract such bloodthirsty friends."

"Because you're so mild-mannered," Suri quipped.

"You know me so well," he said, placing his hand on his heart. "Now tell me your plan for filling my soul trove, killer."

26

Through my rigid instruction, he learns the true names and properties of flora now, too. Under him, I have learnt what it is to hold warmth within.

Unknown author, est. 2nd-5th century

A rap at her door had her out of bed before the fourth knock had fallen. Her head pounded from the three Ice-bolts, and she cursed herself for not drinking more water before she'd passed out. She paced down the stairs, her comfortable clothing still warm from the bed.

Kol never came to Kazem's, and didn't respond when she tried to reach him through his silk after, and she decided to take the hint. Despite her tiredness and the drinks dulling her head, all she could think about was whether he was on the other side of the door.

Instead, though, Jem stood there, an awkward look on his kind face. He showed no signs of change, though she realised it was wrong to expect him to look much older in the weeks she'd been gone. It was still hard to fathom that this man who looked perhaps even younger than her, was nearing one hundred and twenty. The same age as Mother Edi, and there wasn't a single line on his face.

Suri smiled. "Hi, Jem."

He nodded, something strangely close to a bow. "It's nice to have you back."

"It's good to be home."

Jem smiled at that and held an envelope out to her. "This came for you a few days ago."

"For me?" she echoed, taking the paper. It was worn and smooth, with only her name written on its front.

"No one opened it, of course," he said, frowning. "But it has no seal, no royal mark. The men in the desert city described the bird it travelled on and it is none that I know."

Suri smirked at that. "You know many birds, then?"

Jem's cheeks warmed. "I studied with Axri'don for many years as a scout."

"I see," she said. "Will you take on his role?"

"That is up to the council," he replied. "First, we must discover if it is safe to travel through the Gate."

She'd forgotten that part, how Sotoledi's creation of this place, this sanctuary for thousands of the dead from the Wrath, had come at a price. None of those brought back could travel through His Gate to the ruined city. They were alive, but trapped here. Trapped in their bodies, forever unchanging, and trapped on its shores, hemmed by rough waters.

Now, with Kol's soul freed, they aged once more. But whether it was safe for them to cross through, no one knew.

Suri pulled her lower lip into her mouth. "Wait before you test that."

Jem narrowed his eyes. "Do you know something?"

She shook her head. No, she knew nothing at all. But if they could get rid of Sotoledi, that would surely undo this magic. It was better to test it then, when all of this was over. "Just hold back. There is too much that isn't known."

He studied her, but nodded. "As you say, my lady." He bowed now, in full. "I will leave you to your letter, but if you ever have need for distraction, I am at your disposal."

Suri smiled, even as her body tensed at his deference to her. "Thank you."

Jem left, walking back down the wooden pathway towards the centre, and she closed the door. She looked down at the letter. Who would have cause to write to her?

Suri grabbed a knife from the pocket of her trousers, which she had thrown over the padded seat last night a moment after she'd walked in. She sliced open the letter, sealed with a blob of tar-black wax, and pulled the letter out, reading it quickly.

S
I've moved your brother out of the city. The two women had to come, too. They're safe, for now.
We caught wind of a raid against his place. This was no little gang dispute, this was the city guard. I don't know why the King is after him, but you owe me. Big.
T

Suri sat down, the words blurring as she blinked and read it again. And again. A horrible clawing feeling gripped her heart, and her fingers felt suddenly cold. Esra was in danger again, and she couldn't help but feel it was all her fault somehow.

T could surely only be the Tanner, and the two women had to be Aisha and Mother Edi.

May had done what she'd asked by protecting Esra, and Suri would be sure to reward her for it. Though why the city guard was after Esra, she had no idea either.

What could her brother have done? Or what had Tanner done to force such a thing? He was supposed to be safe there, and now, he was on the run again, being held in some place she couldn't even reach. May left no address, no indication of their whereabouts. Suri had to trust her, and by the Gods, she didn't.

She needed to speak to Kol. Suri ran upstairs and grabbed the seeing silk from her bedside, pulling it over her eye. She thought of him, so easily, for she had been thinking of him for weeks. A strange sense of vertigo hit her as the silk revealed his viewpoint, sands far below, stretching for miles. Good, he was actually wearing his damned silk. "Kol?"

"Suri?" he replied, his voice caught a little by high winds. In the distance she noted something, a sandy haze. She would have guessed it was a sand storm, but it was small, something approaching in the distance.

"Wait there, I'm coming to you. There's news of Esra."

He didn't immediately respond, and she nearly put the silk down. But then he looked back to the ruined city on the other side of the battlements. "Good. A royal visitor is arriving, and I wouldn't mind some back up."

There was something odd in his voice, something he was holding back. He seemed detached from her and she didn't understand it. They needed to speak about this, about her feelings and her soul, and she wasn't going to let him run away this time. "I'll be there soon."

Suri removed the silk as she focused back on the room around her. She looked down at herself, taking in her socks, bed trousers and soft cotton top, and sighed. A royal visitor probably meant she should change.

Aisha must have stocked her dresser, she didn't imagine Scilla had the time or care to pick out dresses this fine, or carefully lay the matching filigree belt over its hanger.

Maybe it was time she dressed for the part she didn't want.

Suri pulled out a dress with layers of thin fabric in white, pale blue and the occasional touch of darker blue. There were even green tones, giving the effect of a coming wave. It fit her perfectly, cinched with a silver belt worked carefully into an undulating pattern.

She washed her face and brushed her dark hair, holding it back from her face with matching silver clips.

Staring into the mirror, Suri gave herself a moment. Her skin had darkened a little from the travels, the sun she seldom saw in New Politan now dusted her arms with a light tan and a few new freckles dotted her shoulders. Despite the constant movement, she had eaten reliably and with good hardy fare. Her cheeks were no longer sallow, the darkness under her eye brightened. Even neglecting the cosmetics on the table nearby, she looked better than she ever had.

She lifted her black leather eyepatch and took in the sight. Her good eye, grey and assessing, took in the absence of the other. With the skin around the wound completely healed, she looked fearsome, but not horrifying, with the purple amefyre eyepiece sitting perfectly in the wound, staring into the mirror just as readily. A line just above and below the setting was scarred in a small jagged line, but if it hadn't been there, someone could have thought that she was born this way. One silver eye, one purple.

Her hand trembled slightly as she placed the eyepatch on top of the dresser. This was who she was. There was no one in Akdaria or the ruins of Ucraipha who would take her amefyre from her. This was her home, and this was her true face.

But this armour she wore now, disguising herself in beauty, it felt unnatural. Seeing the bright blue reminded her of Axri'don, always the most colourfully dressed in any room, and when he turned that sparkling charm in her direction, it was like the first summer's day after a rainy spring. It also reminded her of Queen Lera. They both used their appearance as a weapon, turning it against those who didn't see it often. Surely, to an untrained eye, looking good and being good must be married to each other. How could someone look that angelic, and be evil? How could someone resemble the Gods, but be the cause of all that suffering?

The thought gave her comfort; what she wore today was not a new lie. A thief, a murderer, a woman with monstrous thoughts and little patience, could still wear this. She could look like the flower, but be the poison under it. She followed in the footsteps of many liars who looked like the sun-kissed ripples of the sea, but acted like the swirling undertow beneath.

Suri left her rooms, and made for the sandy city.

If she had thought herself conspicuous in the city yesterday, alongside Nadrian with her court pin, it had not prepared her for the level of staring she endured now that she was dressed as a lady. As she walked through the wreck of Ucraipha, its newfound population would stop in the street to watch her pass. They would whisper to their friends, pointing her out. She found herself fighting with every step to keep her chin up and try not to do anything embarrassing, like step on rotten fruit or fall over.

Even worse, they would not accept her help. A bag of grains tumbled from the back of a wagon in front of her, and she stepped forwards to help, only to receive gasps as others dashed forwards to help first.

This wasn't just a strange form of armour, it was a shield from being useful in any way. To them, she was a noblewoman of their King's court. She'd never felt so immobilised in her life, and she'd been in a cage.

At least in the cage, people saw her for who she really was.

She made her way through the streets to the battlements, seeing the attempts to make a home in the fallen city. Dyed cloth hung over the entryways, clothes dried in the dry heat of the mid-morning and traders sold small luxuries: herbs and spices, jewellery, and dyed soaps.

At the city wall, she climbed to the very top, far above the entrance. From here, the city looked almost normal. Some of the roofs were dilapidated, or caved in at places. But the landscape of networking buildings and streets, its disuse disguised by the constant flow of people, looked like a thriving metropolis.

The battlements were higher than they needed to be. The city was encircled almost entirely by mountains and cliffs, set into the empty space within as the perfect natural fortress. The one point of entry, the gateway, was built as high as its cliffs, the builders so spoiled by the lack of breadth of their task that they performed a feat of height instead.

"If any city is built for siege," Suri murmured to herself. "This must be it."

They must have been at least fifty feet up. As she'd climbed, corridors sprawled out at lower levels, carved with arrow slits and manned by a dozen archers. At the top, men stood all along the narrow city wall and then beyond, onto the cliff-heads themselves. They seemed at ease, a few on watch, but largely in reserve, waiting for the army that had yet to arrive.

The wind flowed through her hair, whipping it around, the battlement itself only rising to chest height with nooks descending to knee height.

It was a clear day, and she could see two towers in decent focus, with two others fading into the deep horizon, the wind intermittent and a welcome respite from the worst of the midday sun's burning heat. Again, she saw that approaching thing, and now identified it.

Two slow-moving carriages bounced over the sandy path on wheels not equipped for the terrain, kicking up dust as they moved towards the city. She narrowed her eye, trying to glean any more information, but from this distance, she could not make out even a colour with any certainty.

The voice from behind her made her jump. "You found me."

She turned, and saw Kol stood behind her, the bird Sama'yon perched on one leather-bound arm. He was back in his usual outfit, dressed in encompassing black from head to toe, with the hood pulled so she could only see his eyes.

With his imposing height, and now the huge bird he carried, she remembered how intimidating she had first found him. Now, all she could fixate on was how much she desired him.

"I did."

"You removed your eyepatch," Kol said, his voice rougher.

Suri only nodded as a creeping insecurity pulled at her. She resisted the urge to cover her damaged eye under his scrutiny.

He did not look away. "If it's not obvious to you, you look beautiful."

"Thank you," she said, her voice barely a whisper. There was so much she wanted to say. "Kol, can we—"

"Have you guessed our visitor?" he interrupted.

She glanced at the bird still perched heavily on his arm. "No, I haven't."

Kol pointed to the carriages, and she followed his hand. "They should be here in half an hour."

"Who?"

"If my scouts are to be trusted, it is the fire princeling and a group of his favourite soldiers."

Fear lanced through Suri as she recalled the note. "Shaedon rides here?"

"I believe so," he replied.

Suri turned to him. "Then you should see this." She pulled the note out from one of two hidden pockets in her dress, something she was certain he himself had requested. "It came whilst we were away."

Kol whistled and Sama'yon pushed off from his arm, cawing and spinning in the warm air, his powerful wings pushing him into the sky until he was barely a dot. He reached out, and she passed the paper to him. Their fingers brushed, and a jolt went through her body despite the leather covering his fingers. He pulled his hand back from hers immediately.

She watched, her heart pounding from a mixture of fear, rejection and pure uncertainty as he read the note.

"Shit," he said, simply, flipping over the paper as he checked if there was anything else to it.

"Why do you think they'd go after Esra?"

He looked up at her, guilt clouding his face. "I think I know why, though I was hoping they wouldn't find out before I could meet them."

"What is it?"

"I rode here from Lartosh as fast as I could," he explained, looking a little pale. "I needed to give my people as much warning as possible."

Suri realised what he meant. "You didn't glamour."

His eyes tensed and he shook his head. "Someone must have seen me."

"And the North thought you were dead. We made a whole deal with them based on it."

Kol nodded. "I imagine they're not pleased."

"Is that why they're coming here?"

He sighed, holding up the paper. "Before I saw this, I was hoping they were coming to witness. I sent them a letter of my own, ostensibly from Scilla. It told them of Lera's declaration, and asked one of them to come to the city to see the truth of it unfold."

Suri grimaced. "So, are they here for peace, or to chew you out for lying?"

"I suppose we are about to find out." Kol held his hand out. "And today, you look far more the part than I do. Welcome them with me?"

Suri placed her hand in his and stared up at him. His skin glowed ever so slightly.

He was hard to behold at times. Not only his beauty, but now knowing who he was, the son of the woman in white who walked through time, and Diophage, a man long thought to be a god. How could she even stand so near to him? How could she lay claim to any part of him?

"Kol."

He swallowed and his faint glow faded to nothing. "Let's go."

"We need to talk."

He walked towards the stairs, pulling her behind him. "After we speak to Shaedon, you can tell me anything you need to."

Suri bit her lip. "As you wish."

He glanced back at her as he started down the stairs, but soon turned his head away with a small shake.

What did it mean? Did he no longer want this?

They descended to the bottom in silence, and he pulled her out into the sunshine as the guards pushed open the gate to allow for the first carriage to enter.

A flame-coloured banner flowed from the back, settling in a flurry as the carriage wheels creaked to a stop inside the main courtyard. A hand moved behind a curtain inside, as the footman hopped down from the carriage driver's seat to open the door.

Suri gulped in a breath, straightening her back.

"It is him that should be at attention, not you," Kol murmured in her ear. "Keep your head high and stand beside me, Seer of Time."

Shiny boots hit into the dusty floor. His tunic was orange and finely spun, complemented by dark brown trousers embroidered on each side with red trim. His red hair was in loose waves about his irritated face.

He looked around him at the old city of Ucraipha and clearly found it wanting, along with the diaspora of citizens who had stopped to watch his arrival. Finally, he turned his assessing survey to the two of them, appraising Kol first with a sniff.

When he looked at her, she could see there was a second where he didn't recognise her, where all he saw was the pretty dress, and silver clips, and he dismissed her as little more than a decoration. His judgement returned to Kol for half a breath, before training on her face once more. His cheeks went rosy, and she bit back a wolfish grin.

His address was perfunctory. "You're not dead, then."

"No, I'm not," Kol replied.

"I do not like to be lied to," Shaedon said.

"I was dead in that arena. What you saw there was no lie." Kol let that sit in the air for a calculated breath. "But death is not so permanent of a condition when one has mastery of it."

The Prince of the Forgelands sneered. "And yet you come to us, asking us for favours, when you do nothing but trick and lie. Little wonder most of your allies are gutter rats and deserters."

Shaedon's eyes fell on her when he spoke the last few words.

She only raised an eyebrow. She'd heard far far worse, and he did not frighten her. "Prince Shaedon. A pleasure to see you again."

Shaedon rolled his eyes, but then his face whitened, and it wasn't her doing. She didn't need to look at Kol to imagine the expression contained there, as it was written in the Prince's fear.

Kol took one step forward. "You will greet my Mistress of Coin as befits her station, your Grace."

Shaedon swallowed, and a moment passed, locked in tension. Suri watched his guards put their hands to their hilts, and beside her, the two white guards touched their scimitars. No one spoke, as the Northern Prince considered his next words.

Eventually, he nodded to her in recognition. "Always a pleasure to see a Northern face."

She nodded back at Shaedon. "The pleasure is all yours."

A smile appeared on the Prince's face, as if by muscular instinct more than choice, but his face soured as he truly heard her words. Still, the hands at the hilts relaxed.

"Prince Shaedon, thank you for coming all this way in these dark times," Kol said. The sentiment rang true, even if there was an undercurrent of warning there. *You are welcome, but only as long as you behave.* "I apologise for deceiving you, and I assure you my intent for doing so was far more at the expense of Lera's court than yours. I hope you intend to stay, to discover the truth of what is to come."

Shaedon considered his words, and then sighed deeply. "Our course is not decided, and our trust will be hard won. But it was a long journey, and I am tired. My men and I will need rooms."

Suri fought back a smile. He would not fight them here, and he would at least stay the night. It was the smallest of victories, but right now, she could hardly expect more from them. Trust took time, she knew that better than most. This would be tense, but it was a start.

"Of course, we can speak more later," Kol replied easily. "Rooms have already been prepared. Please follow Irun to your lodgings, we will transport your chests."

Shaedon nodded. Irun, part of Kol's white guard, moved forward immediately to gather the Prince's belongings, and several other guards assisted in unloading the two carriages.

They both caught the grumble as Shaedon sulked past them, his shoulders slumped. "There better not be sand in my bed."

His men followed him, members of the guard taking the reins from the carriage drivers and steering the horses off towards the stables.

Suri turned to the man beside her with a wry smile. "Still hopeful?"

"Very," Kol said. "It's a miracle. He didn't swear once or badly insult either of us."

She knew he wasn't joking but she laughed all the same. Kol froze at the sound, and the laughter died as he stared at her mouth with such intensity she found it hard to breathe.

She reached for his hand. "Can we talk?"

He let her hold his hand, but still didn't move. "We are talking."

"Kol, stop it."

"What?"

She made an aggravated noise and finally snapped at him. "You've barely looked at me since you found out I have my soul back, what's going on?"

He looked at her again, his hood-shadowed gaze so penetrating it was as if he was trying to see through to her soul, to prove it was indeed back.

Her mouth went dry as she waited for him to decide his next move. After what felt like an eternity of listening to her heart ricochet against her ribcage, she felt him squeeze her hand.

Kol leant down and whispered into her ear, so close she shuddered. "Come with me."

27

He grows close now, to living in time. I only hope to build a world where I have the instruments to find him.

Unknown author, est. 2nd-5th century

The cavernous room took her breath away as Kol helped her clamber over the rubble separating it from the castle's dilapidated corridor.

Suri tipped her head back to take it all in. There was no roof, the light of the late morning hitting upon her cheeks as she studied the towering walls. Each pillar, supporting nothing on their shoulders, told a story, carved with open-mawed creatures or reed-like flowers with closed buds.

Kol's voice was sombre. "The remnants of Ucraipha's throne room."

The room was also destroyed. Past the missing roof, each pillar had chunks taken from it. A maned beast missed a paw, the eye socket of a winged creature was chipped to nothing, and the once intricate window settings were smashed to pieces.

"The Wrath did this?" she asked.

"People did this." He pushed his hood back and tugged the face guard to his neck. "The pillars and ceiling were once painted with flaked gold. The tiles of the roof were rumoured to be pure gold, but they were merely painted. Didn't stop people from trying, though."

Suri looked to the dais, where a single throne remained of the pair, where a Queen might sit. The other, she imagined, was the one dragged into the main hall. "This throne is still here."

"The stone of it, yes. The jewels encrusting it are long gone."

Suri approached it, and drifted her hand over the curving loops and knots carved into its cold stone face. Across its back, they'd carved a siren with wild hair to drag sailors to an early grave. She touched the woman's eyes, which bore the scratch marks of some tool or chisel. She wondered what gems had sat there. Had the maiden had blue sapphire eyes, or piercing emerald? "It's beautiful."

"And thankfully, too heavy for any looters to bother moving."

He leaned against a near pillar, the light hitting his dark hair and finding the brown in it, humanising him.

But his sombre expression had changed to something darker. Hungry. "Sit in it for me."

Her stomach clenched. "Why?"

His reply dripped with something torturous. "Humour me."

She sat down, never breaking eye contact. She could never refuse him when he looked at her like that, like he could consume her, like she was his undoing.

He pushed off the pillar and stepped towards her, standing at the bottom of the three steps like a desperate man at an altar. "As much as you hate it, little thief. You look exquisite on a throne."

Suri flushed. "Why have you been avoiding me?"

"I haven't." Kol ran his hand through his hair. "I've been waiting for you to come to me, to tell me whatever it is that's troubling you."

"I tried to find you yesterday, in your office. I even checked the prison."

His hand clenched at his side."You spoke to Rasel?"

"He wasn't in a state for visitors," she drawled, giving him a knowing look.

Kol's mouth twitched and she saw the deadly self-satisfaction lurking under it. "Well, you've found me now."

She stared at him and wet her lip, pulling it into her mouth as she worked out how to start. Kol took a deep breath and dropped their tormented eye contact, staring at the empty window to her right.

"Look at me," she said.

His voice was a whisper. "I'm not sure I can."

"Kol—"

"Suri," he interrupted, the glow from his skin gone entirely. He looked resolved, determined.

Her eye flashed with frustration. "I—"

"If you're going to ask me to leave you alone, I don't think I know how. I can try to be... less," he said, folding his arms. "Be whatever it is you need from me, and nothing more. But I don't think I can be away from you. Not fully. Your place is here. This is your home."

Suri didn't follow him at all. When had she ever suggested that? Asked for that? "What are you talking about?"

"You can feel again, now," he said, his body still as the stone at her back. "I know it might not mean to you what it meant to me."

Suri scoffed. He had to be joking. Gods above, the man had no concept of how he consumed every part of her, of how long her heart had been held by him, even when she hated the very idea of it. "Stop talking."

"What do you want, Suri?" His head fell to his chest as he stared at the floor at her feet.

Suri's heart pounded so hard it hurt, but she wouldn't hide it any longer. "You. I want you."

Kol breathed in, a sharp intake of breath, and raised his black gaze.

"The moment I saw you again with my soul back, I could not imagine a worse fate than one stripped of you," Suri said, and her voice barely wavered. "I look for you in every room I walk into. I think of you every minute of my day."

His hand shook at his side.

She breathed a sigh. "It's you, Kol. It's been you from the start. You see me as no one else ever has."

Kol stepped forwards. Suri leaned forward, preparing to stand, but he shook his head. "No, don't move."

Suri swallowed as his iron gaze fixed her to the throne as surely as if he had tied her here.

The glow from his skin shimmered just a little, his face betraying a spark of the sun within. He stepped up the final step, his body towering above her in the eleventh hour sun. In his small shadow, she shivered. The golden rays striking the back of his head painted him a dark vengeful force, an obstruction, a being which blocked out the light. But it was so far from the truth. He *was* the light.

Then he knelt down, and Suri felt the heat of the sun against her face and chest once more. She blinked, her eye lidded as she stared at him, their faces once more at the same height.

The silence between them was weighty, but not a burden. It was a moment they both knew would change everything. It was a folding of a page, a holding of breath, marking the moment in time as neither of them needed to say another word, allowing the scene to play as they both knew it would.

She had said the magic words. She could see them reflected in his dark, ravenous gaze. *I want you. It's you. It will always be you.*

Kol cupped her face and pressed a searing kiss to her mouth. She gasped, before kissing him back fiercely. She couldn't breathe, and yet his air was all she wanted. His lips were insistent against hers, and her heart thundered.

She grabbed his shoulder to pull him closer, but he only broke away with a tut. Her brow furrowed as he chuckled low.

He reached down, and as soft as the first drove of winter snow, he lifted her ankle and pulled the slipper from it. He raised her foot to his mouth so slowly, the sun itself may have moved faster in the sky than he did.

Kol kissed the side of her foot, the sole, the ankle. He pressed soft kisses up her calf, his eyes drinking her in, and they basked in the warmth of the moment and the light. He reached her knee, pressing another kiss there as he pulled her leg up and draped it over his shoulder.

Then he reached his hand under her dress and brushed his thumb exactly *there*. Suri inhaled sharply as he rubbed in a small circle, his mouth curling into the smallest of smirks as he pulled another noise from her.

The glow of his skin warmed into how it was before, that steady subtle shimmer signalling who he truly was. She wondered if he was even aware of it, the beacon of life within him. Others would notice it soon, question what it meant for them, who Kol really was. But she only cared for what he was to her. He was *her* monster, her nightmare, and her salvation.

He rubbed there, five more circles. Ten. Twenty. He dipped his middle finger under the edge of the cloth, touching her entrance. She heard him swallow as she writhed slightly on the throne.

Suri stared down at him as his fingers hooked on either side of her underwear and he raised an eyebrow at her. She nodded, and his mouth twitched again as he pulled her underwear off and tucked it into his trouser pocket. She nearly made a comment about it, some glib joke about him needing to buy her a new wardrobe if he intended to steal half of it, but the look on his face quietened her again.

He stared at her like a man starved.

Once more he put his thumb to her, and he positioned one finger at her entrance, watching her face as he slid it into her tight heat. She twitched, biting her lip to keep from moaning as his finger stretched and played with her. His other hand rested on her stomach, and a lock of his hair trailed across the skin above her abdomen as he watched his finger slide in and out of her. Every part of her skin he touched felt as if it were aflame.

Her head fell back against the back of her ancient, looted throne as her Lord worked her first with one finger, and then two. And ever that pressure at the apex of her thighs, that bundle of nerves sending spasming delight across her body.

It didn't take long for the sensations to become too much, riding that edge of being overwhelming. Her face felt too hot, her body the flint and his fingers the tinder she would happily spark against for eternity. Part of her knew she was coming up too fast, as if taking her breaths too quickly. She wanted to savour it but she couldn't hold on, she'd been imagining his fingers on her for too long.

Suri's breath came in short pants, her ears warm, her legs quivering. He didn't stop, his fingers pulsing inside her as his thumb rounded eager circles. She squeezed her eye shut as she careened to the edge.

And then over it.

White, blinding light. As if death and life just hit her in one blow, and cancelled each other out in a moment of bodily ecstasy.

And then she blinked and the world was back.

Kol put her leg back down, the smooth stone was warm beneath her naked foot. He stood, blocking out the light as before. "Stand up."

She raised her head from the back of the seat. "I'm not sure I can."

His answering smile was wicked. He reached down and put one arm under her legs and the other reached around to hold her back. Kol lifted her in one easy motion, before turning and sitting down on the throne himself, righting her over his lap.

He was hard beneath her, and she wriggled immediately over him, and he moaned. "Fuck. Sit on me, Suri."

Suri moved so she was straddling him, the momentary shake in her legs forgotten to her newfound hunger. She reached down, undoing the button at the top of his trousers. Her fingers were a little clumsy in her need.

"That's it."

She undid the rest of the buttons and worked her hand inside, finding him and caressing its length.

"Gods, Suri," he gasped. "Your hand feels incredible."

"Can I—"

"Whatever you want. Whatever you want," he said.

She pulled him free of his trousers, and he groaned as she held him in both hands, staring down at him and drinking in the sight. Seeing him bare to her like this, feeling the silken hardness of him, was something else. She needed him so badly.

Suri raised herself until she was just above him, and rubbed the head of him against her wet entrance. Back and forth, coating him in her.

"Please," he said, the word falling from his lips like a prayer.

She pressed her mouth to his as she knelt lower and the tip of him pushed inside. She hissed in a breath and he moaned against her mouth, nipping at her lower lip as he grabbed her hips and pulled her down, spearing himself in her to the hilt.

She gasped as he filled her completely, stretching her and giving her barely a moment to get used to his size as he speared her once more. "Oh—"

Kol reached one hand up to cup her neck as he kissed her savagely, rocking up into her again and again. "You feel so good. I knew you would."

Her pulsing nerves hit against the fabric of his trousers, sending shocks of delicious friction through her body as she held onto his shoulders and kissed him back with equal vigour. It was exactly what she needed and still never enough.

The sensation was everywhere, the cold stone beneath her knees, the thickness of him inside her, the feeling of his breath on her face and the sun on her back. There was nowhere else she could be, no space in her mind for any thoughts. It was only this, only them.

His hand at her neck moved into her hair, gripping it, pulling her neck back as he pressed his mouth to it. Kol's other hand moved underneath her, holding her as he thrust into her. She found his rhythm and met it, growing used to him as she pushed herself down on him.

"You're unbelievable," he said.

His moans and her answering whimpers punctuated their desperate and aggressive movements.

"Give me more, all of it," she said. "I need all of you."

His movements got more erratic as he pummelled into her again and again, sighing into her mouth between each punishing kiss. He fucked her hard, as he'd promised he would.

He pushed himself all the way inside, and then once more, burying his face into her neck as he came inside her.

Both of them breathed hard, both still dressed. Him, the desert man in black. Her, the debauched lady, her dress up to her hips and her hair clips fallen at their feet.

At a glance, two nobles entwined on a throne in a loving embrace. In truth, two monsters who had seen themselves in the other, and fallen apart, tumbling together. A pillar eclipsed the sun, casting them into shadow, and neither of them noticed, nor felt the loss of warmth.

28

I invited him to stay, to live with me, and he agreed.
I do not wish to be parted from him, ever.
Unknown author, est. 2nd-5th century

Suri sat up, shivering, the smell assaulting her first. Salt, sewage, acrid smoke, and fish guts. The sounds hit next and it was cacophonous, and she had no idea how it hadn't woken her earlier. Yelling, scrambling, bells, horns and slaps of wood against stone.

She was in a dark alleyway, at its mouth the bright light of day bounced against stone, wooden posts... and water. Suri clutched her body for warmth as she tried to fathom how she got here. The smells, she recognised, the sounds and sights, too. This was surely Lartosh.

How was it possible?

Moments before, she'd been in Akdaria. She'd returned home with Kol and he'd pressed his tongue to her until she'd come undone again, and they had lain there, lazily.

They must have fallen asleep.

She figured she must be dreaming, but this felt more real than any dream she'd had before. If this was a dream, she'd have imagined some different clothes beyond her underwear. She shouldn't feel the cool wind this easily, nor taste the rotting flesh of fish and sour smell of urine.

Suri stood, looking around, waiting for any explanation to become clear. She had no shoes either. A few broken crates were kicked in across the alley, their husk forming some kind of sleeping spot, its inhabitant gone, a rough brown blanket marking their spot.

She swept it up, sending a quick mental apology to whomever's bed she stole from, and wrapped the blanket around her until it resembled a cloak. At least she was covered, if far from proper.

Nothing in the alleyway hinted at how she'd got here. If someone had grabbed her or moved her here, they hadn't hurt or restrained her in any way. What would have been the point? Who could have got past both her and Kol?

She wandered to the mouth of the alley, determined to make some sense of it all.

Definitely Lartosh. She recognised its bells and spires, its wood jetty painted green by the sea, and the endless stream of sailors and traders, hawking their wares and heaving their supplies.

Then she recognised something else.

The time of day, the position of the sun. The grumbling from the bustling crowd, the woman who said she'd lop an ear if her kid weren't more careful, and her orange skirt which she pulled up and out of the reach of the fishmonger's bucket.

This was no dream.

This was the past.

Just as the thought occurred to her, she saw it.

Suri ducked back into the shadows, pulling the blanket up and over her face, just as her own self walked past the entrance to the alley, barely sparing it a cursory glance.

Shit.

Why was this happening?

Had she herself caused this? How did she end it?

Suri waited a moment before looking again, and found herself watching the back of her own head. She was quite tall. She knew she was, but seeing herself from this distance, it was easier to tell. What if someone else put her here? What if there was something she needed to see?

The notion had her moving from her alleyway, bare feet be damned, and following herself through the crowd.

Of course, she realised. The identity of the stranger, that was why she was here. If she could discover who it was, that would solve a mystery. Maybe her curiosity for it had somehow dragged her here unconsciously.

The stranger must have dived from the boat into the water, it was the only way she wouldn't have seen them leave. If she could position herself to watch the other side of the boat, she could discover their identity once and for all.

Suri watched those in the crowd around her, trying to remember what had happened. A person had yelled, she had turned, and someone had hit her and run off.

She looked around for anyone moving quickly through the throngs of people, but didn't see anyone that looked the part. Then she scanned ahead, and her throat went dry as she saw a familiar plush black cloak. Queen Lera, complete with her guarded escort, had just left the large warehouse building ahead and headed for the jetty.

Her own self ten feet ahead hadn't noticed. It would happen now, then. The Queen was on the move, it wouldn't be long until she reached the jetty.

Suri looked around again. Why wasn't it happening? Why was no one moving?

She tried to remember any details about the person. They'd been a similar height to her. And they couldn't have been hugely built, as the barge didn't fully send her sprawling.

A brown cloak.

No. Suri touched her finger and thumb to the blanket around her shoulders.

Gods, it couldn't be. Could it? The one who ran into her, stole from her, brought her to the ship just as Lera's meeting was about to happen.

Queen Lera was close to the jetty now, her guards forcing the constant stream of people aside.

Fuck. It was now or never.

Checking her make-shift cloak was in place and holding onto it with one hand, Suri dragged in a breath and surged forwards. She pushed through the crowd, shoving bodies out the way.

Someone yelled. Loudly.

A familiar head turned, but not quick enough.

Suri slammed past her, her shoulder knocking her past self hard. In the same motion, she reached down, grabbing the purse from her pockets as she pelted away.

It was her. It was *her*.

What did that even mean? How had she done it? But she had no time to think and barely any to breathe as she ran like thunder to the jetty, her bare feet pummeling against the planks. Leading her as she had been led.

Suri ran until she saw the ship, and scarpered along the gangplank. She shoved open the door. Empty. She found the place, that little raised cupboard, and ran to it, even as she heard her own footsteps slamming along the jetty outside.

Prying open the cupboard, she clambered in, pulling it shut behind her as she gulped in a couple of heavy breaths. The coin purse jangled as she rested it next to her, and tried to work out what she was supposed to do next.

She wasn't supposed to be in here. This was supposed to be empty. Suri panicked, pushing against each wall, testing for some false back. No sooner had she pushed the last wall, did her head spin and her vision twinge black. She was supposed to be—Gone.

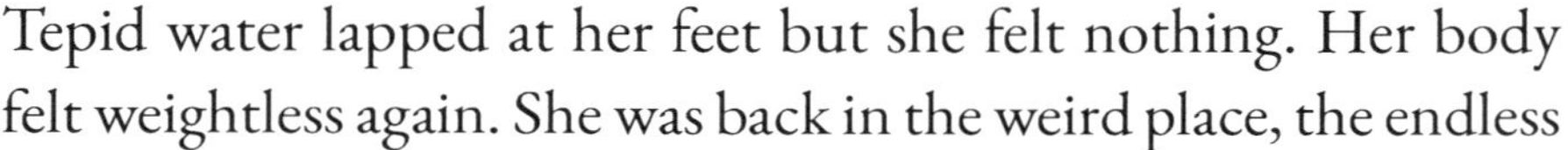

Tepid water lapped at her feet but she felt nothing. Her body felt weightless again. She was back in the weird place, the endless span of almost flat undulating white sand, with pink skies and purple mountains deep on the horizon.

The woman in white stared at her with disappointment. "You should not have done that."

Suri blinked at Cthanda, the whiplash of the change still hitting her. "I don't even know how I did."

Cthanda's tone was just as chastising as ever. "You are a Seer of Time. You are supposed to find the balance in time, not use Time to your own advantage."

"How am I supposed to find the balance if you won't teach me?" Suri asked, embarrassed by the whine apparent in her voice.

"You are on a dark path."

Suri made an aggravated noise. "I don't know what path I'm on at all. Why can't you just tell me what to do?"

"The past should be a guide only, not something to tamper with." There was something Cthanda wasn't saying. "Do not be selfish with Time, Suri. Attempts to change the past have only led to misery and ruin for hundreds of people."

Suri narrowed her eye. "How? Someone tried before?"

"Yes," she said. "A Seer took Time into her own hands. The action she took caused the world to be as it is today. The less said on it, the better. I do not wish to encourage you to follow in her crime."

Suri held her hands up. "I promise I won't dabble any more. Intentionally, at least. I just don't know what I'm looking for."

Cthanda appraised her. "Work on your own relics. Strengthen your relationship with Time. He needs to unlock the prophecy. Help him."

"I don't know how to help anybody."

For a moment, there was silence. And not the natural silence of a pause, but the unnatural silence of pure nothingness. There was no wind here, no sounds of lapping water. There was only the hazy projection of her, ever wary.

When Cthanda spoke, it was distorted, the words not matching with the movements of the woman's pretty peony mouth. "There will come a time when you can make a selfish choice. This is not your world, we are not your playthings."

Suri stepped forwards, and the world warped like a ripple in a storm. "Cthanda? I don't understand."

The voice was disembodied now, coming from all around her as Cthanda's image contorted. "Sometimes to change the world, you need the courage to choose inaction."

"What are you talking about?" Suri asked, but she was already fading. "Please. Don't go."

29

Reader, he told me he loves me. My own heart is fit to bursting. We will be as one being, in perpetual adoration.

Unknown author, est. 2nd-5th century

Suri shuddered and sat up. She was in her own bed in Akdaria, her underclothes dry and warm, her feet clean. Nothing suggested where she'd just travelled, but she was certain these were no dreams. They were visions, some part of her was there in Lartosh just moments before.

Kol wasn't in the bed beside her. He stood on her balcony, stripped to his waist and facing out on the city. Sama'yon perched beside him, watching over the city just as his Lord did.

Suri rubbed her eye and pulled herself from the bed. She might not bear a physical stain of her time, but she felt it in her body and mind: she had not rested, not truly. Padding to the door, she knew she had to tell Kol, but didn't know where to begin. She didn't want to ruin their time with visions of his cajoling dead mother.

Sama'yon, King of the Skies, turned to her, cocking its head and squawking. Kol's back tensed, the muscles flexing, but he relaxed when he saw her. "You should go back to bed. I'll be poor company."

Suri walked out onto the balcony, the warm evening air sticking to her skin as she stared out. No one looked up at them, everyone milling around the city as they normally would.

Kol sighed. "Will you ever do anything I tell you?"

"Maybe one day," she said with a smirk.

His hand tensed. She noticed a small scroll of paper hanging from two fingers. The glow from earlier had faded.

She nodded at the bird. "What news?"

"Lera's troops are on the move. They'll reach the city at dawn, the day after tomorrow."

Suri swallowed. War rode towards them, then. She held his arm, feeling him shiver under her touch.

He turned to her, his eyes a swirling storm of dark brown with hints of gold. As he stared at her, the glow on his skin flared for a moment, and then faded.

"We will stop her," she said.

Kol raised his hand and caressed her face. "You are beautiful."

"Do you not believe we can?" Suri asked.

"I don't know how to stop her without giving her exactly what she wants. Another massacre, bringing her to seven. We need to keep our people in the walls, we can't retaliate. How do you defeat an army you can't fight?"

"I don't know either."

"No one does," Kol said. "We only have two options. First, we hope the world sees what is happening and speaks up to stop it. We can afford to wait a week, maybe two, before I cause the massacre myself by accidentally starving our entire city. The food this island produces is only enough to sustain its own population. Without the Food Guild, all those through the Gate will soon suffer." The grief of that statement fell in a greyness across his cheeks. "Or, fight. Hope to kill enough of them that even if she does somehow bring Sotoledi back, we have the advantage and the edge to destroy him, too."

"How powerful is Sotoledi?"

"No one is alive anymore who knows the answer to that," Kol said. "But he's granted me some of his knowledge, and I can kill tens of people at will. If he created this ability, understood its origins, understood death and amefyre enough to form the Gates in the first place..."

"He could kill hundreds," Suri finished.

"More," Kol said. "Diophage's rage wiped out half the continent when he was still dead. Unleashed, with the power of eight massacres including the Wrath itself, Sotoledi could destroy our entire world."

Suri considered this. "With Nadrian, after you left, I suggested we try to bottle Sotoledi's soul."

"What?" Kol said, more surprised than irritated. "How—"

"If it all goes wrong, if it comes to war. We can find out where she's trying to bring him back, and destroy him the instant he returns, grabbing his soul."

"How would we know where to be? And how would we kill him?"

"I don't know. I don't know any of it. It was just an idea. If we had his soul, he would be nullified. He wouldn't be able to ever come back again, he'd be in body only, an unpowered husk."

"It's a good idea, but I'm not sure how we could be able to execute it."

"Neither am I," Suri admitted. "But maybe we don't need to."

Kol narrowed his eyes. "What are you thinking, little thief?"

"I think the relics are linked," Suri said.

Kol just waited for her to explain.

"I had a vision of your mother," she said. Kol sucked in a breath. "And when I touched her, I saw a flash of her with Diophage back before the Wrath. One of the relics locked into Ruben."

Kol flinched at the mention of the Roanhadham, and the secrets the beast held inside him. "I've seen Ruben's relics before."

Suri watched the people move below her, avoiding discussing that topic any further. "If I can travel through Cthanda to her relics, without touching Ruben... Maybe I can do that again." She spoke the words as much to explain it to herself as him. "If I go through Ruben, to Diophage, maybe I can access *his* relics."

"Travel to Diophage's time?"

"Diophage and Sotoledi were close. He must have knowledge of him, stored something from that time. Maybe there's something we can learn from their past. Something that will help us now."

Kol breathed out. "I suppose it can't hurt. Diophage must have tried to make relics inside himself. But there might be nothing to find out."

"Then no harm done," Suri said.

Kol paused. "Can you do anything in the relics? Touch anything? Change anything?"

Suri paused. Now would have been the perfect time to tell him about the vision she'd just had and how she'd been their mystery ally this whole time. But Cthanda's caution made her hesitant. "Why?"

He smiled darkly. "You could just go back in time and kill the pair of them. Spare us from their playing with our world. Stop the Wrath."

Suri smiled, but it held no mirth. Part of her was glad he had that streak, too, the need and urge to change time, just as she had. But what would their lives have looked like without Diophage and Sotoledi? He was the son of Diophage. He wouldn't exist without him.

"That would kill you. If he never lived to turn himself into whatever he is now, some entity of stubborn ancient magic, Cthanda would never have met him," Suri said.

He shrugged. "Meeting him killed her. It killed a lot of people."

Suri snapped at him, frustrated at his own self-sabotaging behaviour. "You can't know that the alternative would be better."

He held his hands up. "Fine, don't let me play the martyr then."

"I'm not going to let you erase yourself, Kol Aubethaan," Suri said. "Besides, I don't think I can change anything anyway."

It was true, she thought. The vision had been different, she had been whole, perceivable. When she had travelled in Cthanda's relics, she'd been like a spectre. No one could see her, she could do nothing, only watch.

"Well, then," Kol said. "I give you permission to try to find out all of Sotoledi's sordid secrets."

She huffed. "I wasn't asking for your permission."

"I know you weren't." He rubbed his thumb across her bottom lip. "But just this once it's nice to pretend you're in my service, and not the other way around."

Suri laughed. "You are not in my service, *your Lordship*."

His eyes flashed with amusement. "Oh, I think I very much am. I've been on hand and foot at your altar for weeks. I'd struggle to refuse you anything."

She smiled up at him. "Then kiss me."

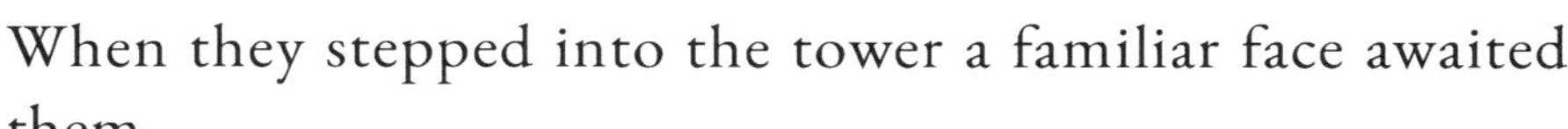

When they stepped into the tower a familiar face awaited them.

A beautiful woman dressed in navy and gold, her long dark hair looking almost black in the dim light of the room, sat in Nadrian's usual chair, smoking what looked like Nadrian's own pipe.

Suri stopped dead in the doorway. Kol stiffened, then strode into the room with only a little more tension than usual.

The woman nodded to them when they entered, and did not stand. "I do not know how you cope with the heat here. It's oppressive."

A scuttling of scalish feet on wood drew Suri's eye to the top of a bookcase. She grimaced as a familiar beady pair of blinking red eyes stared back. The damned blood bat.

"Waris," Kol said. "I wasn't expecting you."

Waris caught Suri's expression with a knowing smirk. "Thank you for letting my Hara accompany you to your quaint little meeting, child. Those hounds looked as ghastly as ever."

Suri stepped forward and the door slid closed behind her as she eyed Hara with distaste. "I hope you enjoyed your snooping."

Waris smiled, bearing her pointed teeth.

"What can we help you with?" Kol asked.

Waris shrugged at him. "Queen Lera destroyed the Healing Fields when she killed your mother. If you're taking her down, I want to be here."

"We're hoping we won't have to," he replied.

"How naive. She's thrown the gauntlet at your feet, accusing you of crimes requiring death. She will not pick it back up."

"You want to help us?" Kol asked.

"I'm considering it," she responded.

"But what about your mists? I thought the blood magic had to be kept... fresh."

Waris clucked her touch with impatience. "I am here to offer you a deal. Take it, and I'll stay and assist you. Refuse it, and I'll return to my mists."

"What deal?"

"I'll protect the city with Blood Mists. A deadly deep fog from the sand at its foot to the battlements of your city gates." Waris pulled another deep breath of smoke into her mouth, holding it before finally exhaling. "Their only way into the city would be to scale its cliffs, something far easier to prevent. Or, firing blindly through the fog. Some arrows may find a target, but they will have no vision of you. Your people will be far safer than they are now."

Kol was careful not to betray his eagerness. "And in return?"

Waris tapped the end of the pipe and the embers jumped. "In return, you provide me with the means of creating such a thing, and the reward that befits it."

"What reward do you seek?" Kol asked.

"You mean to destroy Queen Lera?"

"We do, eventually." He flexed his hand. "Once the world sees her for what she is, we will end her. Though, I have promised her death to Nadrian."

Waris smiled. "Ah, I do not want her death at my hands, as nice as that would be. I want *her*, body and soul. Once the deed is done, my payment shall be her corpse and her festering soul, and your assurance that no one will threaten my mists for the duration of your reign."

Waris opened her bag to reveal three empty soul cages. They were small, barely larger than a man's fist. The hexagonal prisons hung from her hand like expensive baubles from a tree.

Kol glanced at Suri, and she shrugged. She had no want or need for either the woman's soul nor her body. Waris could do with it what they wanted. She did green slightly though, at imagining the Queen's body, hanging from Waris' dilapidated tower, gutted and dancing.

Kol pursed his lips. "Why now? Why help this time?"

"I'm done with these false prophets. The only true magics of our world are blood and souls. The ballad of Sotoledi and Diophage, then the invented and decorated Trio, I want all the nonsense to end. It's smoke, mirrors and lies. Two men who were annoying in life should *not* be able to make this much noise five hundred years later. It's an insult."

Suri raised an eyebrow at the vitriol in the comment. It was more than irritation coming to the surface, it sounded like envy.

"Besides," Waris continued. "This is Aisha's home. I'd rather you bring the Eastern Kingdom back to life and undo the work of those terribly stupid men once and for all."

"Waris," Suri asked. "How old are you?"

Something lit up in her gaze. "That is an incredibly rude question."

Suri rolled her eye. "Then I'll ask the other one. We know the reward. We'll grant you Queen Lera's body and soul, whenever the time comes. But what are the means?"

"A far more polite question," Waris said, with a nod. "I'll need ten corpses, the fresher the better, and of course, unquestioned access to the towers at either side of the main city gate. I would remind you to advise your guards against entering, at all, but frankly, if they die from their shock at the sights within, I wouldn't mind the extra bodies."

"Anything else?" Kol asked in somewhat disgusted jest, his face whiter than usual.

Waris thought for a moment, either not hearing the sarcasm or not caring. She took another puff of the pipe. "Three days."

Suri looked at Kol. "Lera's army arrive in one day."

"Then I recommend you find a way to stall them," Waris drawled, as the words leaked out of her mouth like poison. "And fast."

30

A strange visitor came today, one we cannot rid from our minds. She knew the final piece to complete our puzzles. A rare rock, and a beating component.
Unknown author, est. 2nd-5th century

With the third royal arrival in as many days, Suri wondered if there was any member of the Waterborne family left to play host for. Maybe a distant cousin, or a bastard son.

The cold silver of her hair, sleeker than Suri thought possible, reached close to her waist as Ressa walked beside Scilla in silence a few paces ahead. The woman had been travelling for two days from the Pail, and yet she looked as fresh as anything.

Scilla and Suri greeted her at the city entrance. Suri had tried to get out of it, throwing Nadrian under the cart in her place, but no one could find him that morning at his usual haunts, and Kol had to speak with his citizens. So she'd been nominated to represent the court.

As the coach pulled up, her whole body had tensed. No sooner had Viantha escaped her imprisonment at Suri's own hands had she been sold down the river by the Northern Kingdom to the Storm Pan. Ressa had been at that ball, asking after her daughter. She must have known that her daughter had in fact been taken prisoner by a city gutter rat like her, but she hadn't been in the throne room that day. Ressa had never actually seen her.

The driver opened the door, and there she was, dressed in a silver metallic fabric which caught almost blue in the light, delicately nodding to both the colours of the Water Guild, and the silver of Kol's court. The dress was not the usual style of courtiers, instead it fell down in a column without shape. A black clasp pinned her hair from her face and she wore only one item of jewellery, a pendant of amefyre.

The two of them, by contrast, were more practically dressed. Scilla wore her navy general's tunic and trousers, and Suri wore her riding gear. She had little urge to attract the attention she had the day before, and planned to track down Ruben as soon as this painful meeting was over and done with.

Ressa stepped down from the coach, studied her and Scilla with something approaching disdain but somehow more polite. "Where is my daughter? I want to be taken to her immediately."

Scilla ducked her head. "Of course, Guild Leader. We have prepared rooms if you would like to wait for her there."

Ressa nodded. "Fine. Take me there."

Scilla tasked Suri with fetching Viantha, telling her where to look. Suri followed behind Scilla and Ressa for a moment, watching the effortless beauty of Viantha's mother and the way she didn't seem to even notice the stares of the desert folk, and then broke off at the second junction.

Viantha was on this side of the Gate today, knowing her mother was to arrive imminently. Kol had asked her to be part of the greeting party, but she'd been reluctant and he hadn't pushed it. Suri weaved through to the very edge of the city where the buildings had yet to be cleared of debris. Except for one small house, that is, a complete non-descript set of walls where the sand had been carefully pushed away from the entrance.

Suri pushed open the door, finding a simple room with a broken chair. "Viantha?"

Something clattered to the ground in the next room. "Who is it?"

"Suri."

"Oh." Viantha appeared in the doorway, taking her in. "I didn't expect you."

"Your mother's asking for you."

Viantha flinched. "Great."

The heir to the Water Guild made no moves to come closer, and Suri stood with her hand holding the front door, unsure what to say next. So she asked the obvious question. "Why are you here?"

Viantha didn't seem surprised by the question. "Creation. I needed a space to focus."

"In the middle of nowhere?"

She smiled, only a hint of it, but still something. "In Akdaria, it's harder for me to focus on creation. There's so much water there, in the air, on the leaves, in the pools. When I try to pull water from somewhere else, my magic feels like it's resisting me. It wants to pull from an easier place, to move instead of invent."

Suri looked around in understanding. "And there's no water at all out here."

Viantha nodded. "I asked Scilla to find me somewhere to practise, beyond even where the city folk were living. I didn't want any water other than that in my own body to be anywhere near."

Suri tapped the side of the door with a finger. "And how's it going?"

Viantha shrugged. "Slowly. I can create small amounts, but it hurts my head and makes me weary."

"Well, if the dam is freed, then perhaps you won't need to create anything."

"I think we will. For Kol."

Suri froze. "What do you mean?"

"For the prophecy. I think the Daughters of the Earth need to create life."

"Do you think you know how to fulfil it?" she asked genuinely, finding she lacked her usual jealousy. Kol was hers, and she was his. The prophecy was now a problem for all of them to solve, not something threatening to take him from her.

"We have the Son of Life. He seems to be able to emit light, though I don't think he knows how to control it. If he can create light at will, that could be important. We have a Daughter who can create water. Me. A Daughter who can create plant life: Scilla. Perhaps human life, the ability to save someone from the brink of death, too, is a Daughter."

Suri mused. "Aisha?"

"Her, or someone like her. If we all combine our powers somehow, Diophage may release this land from its curse. I can't think of any other powers linked to life."

"It's a good idea," she said, truthfully. "When can we do it?"

"I wanted to write to Aisha, but Scilla told me she's moved," Viantha said.

Suri nodded. Wherever May had taken Aisha, Edi and Esra, was anyone's guess.

Viantha sighed. "I suppose it would be too dangerous for her to travel from the North right now anyway."

"Yes, it will have to wait until after the war."

There was a strange silence then, and she wondered if either of them truly believed there *was* an 'after the war'.

In the awkwardness that followed, Suri tried to smile. "I'm going to see if I can discover anything from the past. About Diophage, Sotoledi, maybe the prophecy."

"I wish you luck," Viantha replied, but it lacked warmth.

"Thank you."

The moment hung between them again.

Suri cleared her throat. "Shall we?"

Viantha frowned, but it didn't seem focused on Suri. "Let's go speak to my mother."

Suri pushed through the curtain and knocked on the ajar wooden door behind it. "We're here."

Scilla's voice came back immediately. "Come in."

Suri pushed the door open and Viantha stepped through, her shoulders back and face stiff.

Ressa's rooms were possibly the nicest the ruined city had to offer, a little grander even than Shaedon's. The stonework was undamaged, the windows polished, and the furniture lovingly crafted by the local carpenters. Thick quilted linens covered the carved teak bed in the far end of the room, the wash basin was pure silver, and the curtains would be better described as tapestries. Clean, woven rugs in every warm shade of red, yellow and ochre covered the floor.

Scilla sat on a stool next to a tray of untouched wine, her posture stiff and uncomfortable. Suri caught her eye and gave her a small nod, which was returned with a slight grimace. Neither of them were natural hosts.

Ressa drew in a tight breath and took two steps towards her daughter, then stopped herself. "Viantha."

"Mother."

Ressa glanced between Suri, who'd now stepped into the room behind the heiress, and Scilla, who stared at Viantha from her perch, then back to her daughter. "You look well. Are you well?"

Viantha's voice was pure ice. "I am no longer imprisoned, if that's what you mean."

"Viantha, dear. You must know, I had sent messengers, scouts. I suspected Lera was involved, but I had no proof. As soon as Kol confirmed your presence in the Storm Pan, I appealed to all the Guilds."

"So Kol tells me," Viantha said.

Ressa's face hardened, and she looked at Suri and Scilla again. "Might I speak with my daughter alone?"

Scilla stood to leave, but Viantha raised her hand and the general stopped dead.

"Anything you have to say to me, they can hear."

Ressa blinked. "Viantha, is that wise? You do not know—"

"Wise is all you care about," Viantha interrupted calmly. "These women saved me. Scilla, behind you, broke into the Seat itself to save me. Suri," she gestured vaguely to her, "had no allegiance towards me, and yet guided us out of Drameir nonetheless."

Ressa took them both in with surprise, but Viantha wasn't finished.

"Our world is cursed, barren, and cold. Some of that is the Wrath's doing. Some of that is Lera's doing. A lot of it is everyone else, for allowing it. The people here are trying to do the right thing. You will not send them away, I will not allow it."

The leader of the Water Guild rippled with the quiet strength in those words. "So this is your allegiance now? You've thrown your lot in with the desert folk."

"No, mother. I've thrown myself into life. Change. By coming here, I hope you're choosing the same."

Down in the stables, the huge Roanhadham was restless. With all the people arriving, and Scilla and Kol busy in the city, no one had taken him out in days and he turned in circles, scraping his hoof on the wood.

When she popped her head into his stall, Ruben nickered and pressed his nose into her shoulder.

“Hey, boy,” she said, rubbing his nose. “How are you doing?”

He huffed out some air and she smiled.

Resting her hand on his neck, Suri reached into her pocket for her seeing silk eyepatch and pulled it over her eye. It took her no time at all to focus on the object of her mind, he was all she had thought about in days. In a blink, she found herself staring into darkness. But the noises indicated she was in the right place. “Kol?”

A scuffling noise reverberated in her head, and a moment later she could see. It was still dark, the room now full of smoke. Ah, he was in Kazem’s. “Suri? Where are you?”

His voice was curious, not angry. There was something solid about it.

“With Ruben.”

“Ah,” Kol said. “Have you seen anything?”

“Not yet,” she replied. “He’s restless, though. Do you think I could take him out of the city walls? Is it safe?”

Kol paused for a moment. “We should have a day yet before Lera’s troops arrive. But be vigilant, please. Stay within sight of the walls. Ruben knows to protect you, he’ll bolt back if he sees anything.”

“I’ll be careful.”

“And Suri?”

Her hand faltered on its way to removing the patch. “Yes?”

Kol’s voice was as silken as the material on her face, dripping with sin. “Come to my office when you’re done.”

Suri flushed. “I’ll be there.”

She heard his answering chuckle as she removed the eyepatch.

Ruben nipped lightly at her hair.

"I know, I know," she said. "We're going."

The stablehand helped Suri to kit out the Roanhadham for a short ride as Suri stewed on what was to come, and tried not to let Kol's request distract her.

They rode out of the city, the guards opening the gate for her without question. It might be the last time she left these walls in a week or more, depending on how the war went. She might never leave again.

She leaned down to touch Ruben's neck, asking him in her mind to stay close, and stay safe, and then she let her eye flutter closed, and the time slipped away.

31

We have set off, him and I, to find the truth of our pursuits. We have decided to go east, into the fertile flats. There is amefyre in their mines.

Unknown author, est. 2nd-5th century

Once more, Suri found herself in that first relic. A warm field, with the girl sat in the white dress. Instead of keeping her distance, like last time, Suri stood directly beside Cthanda. She could not feel the coarse grass against her ankles, and the mud did not move underfoot, the breeze ruffling Cthanda's hair doing nothing to her own. She waited in her static watching state, breathing deeply, until the air changed.

There, in front of a gleeful Cthanda, the wind distorted, as if forced to part around an obstruction. If Cthanda was to be trusted, Diophage's spirit wavered before them.

Suri reached out. Not just to grab, but to search, to discover. She reached the air as she had reached for Ruben, as she had reached into the Time Circle in the Glen. With a calm curiosity, with a need to know.

Her hand brushed the queer pattern in the air.

And then the field fell away, much like the Glen, melting into something else before her very eyes.

Only, she recognised this place.

Even so changed from how it was now, the well flared her memory, the stones only a small degree less weathered.

She stood before the cottage in Drangbor. But its walls were firm, its windows filled with pocked glass, its grasses managed and path clear of debris. The thatch on its roof looked freshly laid. Was the roof thatched before? Suri found she could not recall, and the memory of the present day nearly wrenched her from the moment.

It was a struggle, being here. It weighed on her mind, like trying to swim straight down against her own natural buoyancy. She had to work to breathe and to keep her mind focused, threads of both the relic and her life above trying hard to pull her away.

She steadied her breath. Staring at the cottage, she worked through why she was here, *when* she might be. This was not one of Cthanda's relics, she'd come here through Diophage, which must follow that she was now inside one of his relics. Had he lived here?

The curtain twitched and Suri moved to one side, the movement harder than it should be, before recalling that of course, they would not see her. Right? The living memory of Cthanda had never perceived her. But Diophage was incredibly powerful, and this was their time, the time of the two ambitious Fae who broke the world in pursuit of their own legacies. She should not assume the same rules would apply to him.

Suri approached the front door of the cottage. Footsteps sounded and Suri forced herself quickly around the side of the building, pressing herself to the wall.

Someone left, their footsteps light along the path. Suri risked a glance.

A woman with dark wavy hair, much longer than hers, walked away from the cottage. The lady wore a white dress and a strange black veil, which fell to her waist at the back and obscured her face. She passed around a corner and out of sight.

Diophage had captured this moment. Why? Suri had to know. He must be inside, for this to be his memory, his relic. Whatever had just passed between the two of them had to be relevant.

Summoning her courage, she moved around the corner, her head beginning to pound with the effort of concentrating on this tether.

The door lay open in the woman's wake, and two voices spoke inside with intensity. Two male voices. She had heard both of those voices before. One had haunted her for a decade.

She stepped inside, and what she saw nearly made her lose her grip on this reality entirely.

A fire crackled gently in the swept fireplace, extra logs stacked beside it, and a simmering pot hanging above its flame. Paper, strangely shaped glassware, and half-melted candles covered the table. Along one counter, books filled every available inch of space, piled high enough to block out half the window's light. Along another, a curious collection of rocks were carefully arranged, free of any dust.

This was not a hide out, nor a lair. This was a home. A loved one.

The two men didn't look around at her entrance.

A man with brown hair and a full beard stood, his fingers held to his mouth. He smiled, his voice animated. "To think, all this time, amefyre was the missing ingredient. Can it truly be the key to your travelling archways?"

She'd heard that voice before in the relics. This was Diophage. The God of Life.

Across from him, a clean-shaven man with shockingly white shoulder-length hair sipped at a steaming mug, a flea-bitten blanket over his legs. "I suppose it is worth a try. There are a handful of minerals I have yet to test."

Suri did not need relics to know this voice.

Diophage only nodded. "I can ask at the market this coming rest day."

Sotoledi put his mug down and stretched out his legs under the table with a yawn. "Why would the wise woman come to us? Why now? And what she said about your work... Of the need for a living vessel?"

Diophage shrugged, his manner so at ease it made Suri want to vomit. "It held a strange logic. We don't know all the ancient magics of this world yet."

"Clearly," Sotoledi said.

"So? The market?"

Sotoledi shook his head and stood, drifting a finger over a well-worn leather-bound book. "He won't have anything for us there. Amefyre is only native to two places in this land."

Diophage rolled his eyes. "Are you testing me again?"

Sotoledi laughed, an easy barreling noise she had never heard. "That depends on if you know the answer, Dio."

"Amefyre is native to the northern mountains," Diophage said, in a mocking tone which held no true cruelty, as he used tongs to move the pot off the boil and placed it on the cooling tray below. "And found in the caves along the eastern coast."

Sotoledi moved up beside him and Suri inhaled sharply, the pounding in her head reaching a boiling point of its own.

The God of Death touched Diophage's shoulder, and Diophage reached up to hold his hand back. "So you *have* been listening."

Diophage grumbled. "Sometimes."

Sotoledi leaned closer until he was embracing him from behind. "It's time for a trip."

Suri reached a hand out, trying to steady herself, feeling desperately for anything that might anchor her here.

Somehow, her hand caught. Just for a moment, she felt something ceramic brush against her hand. And then it was falling.

The cup shattered on the floor.

Sotoledi whipped around, and she saw something in his eyes she recognised. Fear. He stared at her, then around her, at the very air she stood with no focus, enough to know that even her brief touch had not rendered her visible. "Is someone there?"

She gasped, and felt herself pulled from the moment, sucked like liquid as the relic fell away. Her vision warped, Cthanda's field distorted around her in vivid colour, and then it all went black.

Time later, she awoke.

The Roanhadham beneath her whinnied. Somehow she'd managed to stay astride him, most likely thanks to the beast and not her own luck. She heard his heartbeat thick and fast, her face pressed to his neck.

She pushed herself up, looking around. They stood a hundred feet from the city wall, empty dunes around them basking in the fading orange and purple hues of twilight. It was empty out here, the refugees long now inside the walls. The city on the eve of a siege.

Diophage had locked that moment inside him. The moment the Fae men thought they might play at Gods.

The moment that changed it all.

A voice came from the pile of clothes discarded on the floor. She leant over the side of the bath, the steaming fragrant water dripping over the pile as she fished for the silk.

She found it, and put it to her missing eye. Again, the voice came through.

"Suri," Kol said.

"Yes?" she replied, closing her good eye to let his sights dominate her own. He walked through the streets of Akdaria.

"Where are you?"

She smiled. "The bath."

"I'll be outside in five."

She sensed the tension in his voice so easily now, as if it was her own. "What is it?"

He sighed. "We're going to the prison."

Why would they need to go there? Then she recalled. "Rasel?"

"Since the swelling went down around his mouth he hasn't shut up. He's been talking Nadrian's ear off half the day."

"What does he want?"

"Apparently," Kol said, with no small degree of disdain. "To help us."

"Horse shit," she said. "You'd believe that mudstain about anything?"

"No," Kol replied. "But whatever he has planned, it involves you."

Rasel wanted to help *them*. How did that make an ounce of sense? He'd made his way into the city, followed them into Akdaria and frozen them, not to mention drugged her and carved her with blood symbols. There was nothing he could say which would make him trustworthy to her. The man was a serpent, like his harpy mistress.

Suri stood, her anger heating her even as the cool air hit her wet body. "I'll be ready in two."

When Kol arrived, she was already waiting on the doorstep, her hair dripping. He offered her his arm and she took it, and they walked fast towards the prison.

The prison was on the highest level, up by the canopy. It was the easiest place to defend, and the hardest for the prisoners to run from.

"Why is Nadrian on Rasel duty, anyway?" she asked, as they navigated their way up to it.

"He volunteered," Kol said. When Suri raised her eyebrows, he shrugged. "He didn't think Scilla or I were capable of the... *restraint* required. We nearly killed him last time as it was."

"Probably a wise call."

Kol smiled. "Nadrian's clearly grown some sense along with that shiny new title."

Suri understood Kol wanted to kill Rasel for what he did to her back at the manor, but Scilla? There was comradery there, loyalty, but surely she would not kill for her misfortune.

She asked as much.

Kol's smile dropped. "Rasel used to hurt Viantha. Before she was named heir, he near-tortured the girl into an early grave."

Suri breathed out. "Shit."

Kol nodded.

They stepped into the prison, but when they reached the guarded door, Kol stopped Suri. She stared up at him.

"Are you sure you're ready for this?" Kol's question was soft, but his eyes were dark and his jaw was steel. "After what he did to you."

Suri rolled her shoulders. "I'm ready."

"Try not to kill him."

She grinned. "And let him off that easily? I wouldn't end that rat's life if he was begging for mercy."

Kol stared at her with something approaching reverence.

"What?" she asked.

He licked his lower lip, and grabbed her hips. She took a quick breath and placed her hands on his chest.

His throat bobbed as he bent to her ear. "Your cruelty is unfairly attractive, little thief."

Her stomach flipped. Fuck. Did he have any idea what his words and simple touch did to her? "Is that so?"

He pressed a kiss to her neck. "Do you want me to show you what you do to me?"

She was certain one day he would undo her with nothing more than that voice. She raised her mouth to his neck, pressing one kiss to it, before lifting her lips to his earlobe. "Later. Open the door, your Grace."

He pulled back and pressed a smiling kiss to her mouth. Short, sweet, not enough. Never fucking enough. "As you command."

They both straightened themselves, the sight of Kol's hand on the cell door enough to sober them both. Rasel wanted something from them, and for some reason he was stupid enough to ask for it. The least they could do was hear him out before subjecting him to a long and painful death.

Kol hesitated for just a fraction, then turned the handle and opened the door.

Rasel sat on a chair nailed to the floor, his hands strapped behind his back. His face was a mass of purple, only his hair and constant cravat kept him so easily identifiable. One eye was swollen shut, his nose looked broken, and his mouth was a puffy mess. Still, he acknowledged their presence, raising his chin and giving them both a nod.

Suri didn't know how to feel. It wasn't quite pity, but there was something odd about seeing Rasel debased in this way.

The cell itself was clean, recently sloshed with water and mopped. His clothes were free of blood, they'd clearly changed them since his beating.

Nadrian stood when they entered, leaving the bowl he'd been holding on the stool behind him. They were feeding him, then. Because Gods forbid the man go on a hunger strike, and kill Suri that way. "Welcome to the party."

Kol moved to stand beside Nadrian, not taking his eyes off Rasel. "What's this all about?"

Suri closed the door behind them and leaned against it, watching the room. Why she had to be here, she had little idea.

Rasel swallowed, the action thick. He grimaced as his throat bobbed, the swelling around his mouth pinching. "I came here because I need your help."

Suri raised an eyebrow. Kol's own face must have been a matching picture.

"I know," Rasel said. "Do you think I'd ever come to you for help if I had any other option? I'm not a fucking idiot. But I figured, since I'm a dead man walking either way, I'd at least make one last attempt at prolonging my sad existence."

"How can *we* help *you*?" Kol asked.

"Well, for one, you have to keep me alive," Rasel said. "And that makes you the only people in these lands trying to do that."

Kol hissed. "There are worse things than death that we can do to you. I can torture you to within an inch of your life, every day of your miserable existence, keeping you just healthy enough to live until we can find a way out of your fucking bond."

"Promises, promises," Rasel said, the words hollow as he kept his face as still as possible. "But hear me now, if you do nothing, and Lera makes it to eight massacres, there's a good chance both Suri and I will die."

Suri straightened. "What are you talking about?"

Rasel swallowed again, his voice rasping. "The eight massacres open the window between wherever Sotoledi is and here. But for Sotoledi to walk through it, for him to be strong enough to come through, he needs power. He could drain every soul he's ever taken to nothing as he steps through."

Kol narrowed his eyes. "And how is this our problem?"

Suri remembered, then, the dancing blue light in Sotoledi's tower. Ah. Her voice was cold when she spoke. "Sotoledi has Rasel's soul."

Kol looked at her.

"I saw it in the tower," she explained. "I saw his soul."

Kol swallowed, the realisation now hitting for him, too. "If Sotoledi comes back..."

Rasel nodded. "My soul is probably gone. Destroyed. Depleted."

"Is that the same as death? If your soul is completely destroyed, does your body still live?" Kol asked.

"I don't know," Rasel said.

Suri wrung her hands, her gaze piercing into the snubbed brother's hopeless eyes. "Bringing Sotoledi back will kill your soul, and maybe you. And through the blood bond, maybe kill me."

"Yes," Rasel confirmed. "That's pretty much it."

"And you knew this?" Suri asked. "Why would you help Lera to do something which would destroy you?"

Emotion flickered on Rasel's expression for the first time since they'd walked in. The whole time he'd seemed resigned, but now that old fire came back. "I didn't know. She still doesn't know that I know. She told me she would discredit Viantha, and that

Ressa would be imprisoned, too, for siding with you pagans. In her new world, I would be the Heir of Water." His lip curled. "But the whole time, she knew he had my soul, and what her new world would do to me."

"Boo hoo," Nadrian said. "Queen Lera betrayed you. Join the club. She treats everyone as a pawn, you should know that more than most."

"Everyone is a pawn to someone," Rasel said. "At least as her pawn, in her court, I had a chance."

"Then Lera cannot get her eight massacres. We knew that before, and we know it doubly now," Kol said firmly.

Rasel chuckled, but the sound only lasted a few seconds as he winced from the pain. "Lera will get her eight massacres. There is nothing now that will stop her."

Nadrian folded his arms. "She's only on six. If everyone sees—"

"You don't understand," he interrupted. "If you do not give her the massacres, she will kill her own troops."

A horrid quiet fell over the room as his words sank in.

Lera's words from the ship rolled back to her. When she'd asked for troops from Dabri'yon, and the Kans Queen had asked her how many she needed... Her response was simple. *'How many can you afford to lose?'*

Only now, the awfulness of that showed itself.

"She wouldn't," Nadrian said, but even his conviction was lacking.

Rasel just stared at them, as if they were stupid.

"She would," Kol said. "If she was sure everyone would assume I had killed them. The Demon King, wasting half her army. I'd believe it."

Rasel nodded. "She will get her eight, one way or another."

"So we're doomed then," Nadrian said. "She'll get eight massacres, bring back Sotoledi and probably kill you two in the process."

"That's why I came here," Rasel said, and he nodded in her direction. "You got Kol's soul back."

Suri stiffened, looking at Nadrian.

Nadrian raised his hands. "I said nothing."

Rasel smirked without mirth. "When I go to the tower now, it's dark. Empty. The soul that had blazed from its top is gone. You took it, didn't you?"

Suri sighed and nodded. If Rasel was right, and they were dead men walking, there was no real reason to hide it.

Rasel leaned back. "He was relying on that as his main source. Maybe before, he wouldn't have needed to use the rest of us to make it back."

"How do we stop him?"

"You have to do it again. Go in, retrieve my soul. Maybe it'll be enough so he can't come back at all. Or maybe he still will, but at least we'll both live long enough for him to slay us like men."

Suri shook her head. "No, you don't understand. The last time, I tricked him. It won't work again. He won't let me in without something in return. Maybe not even then."

Rasel's smile pulled against his fleshy bruised cheek. "Well, you better figure something out. You don't have long. Only until Lera gets bored of waiting for you to starve."

A knock came at the door at Suri's back. She flinched away from it, then turned and opened the door.

Jem stood in the doorway, his expression grim.

"What is it?" she asked.

"Her army has arrived."

32

We located the stone in Ucraipha, a new and bustling city growing quickly. He wishes to stay here for a few weeks, and test his new theory.

Unknown author, est. 2nd-5th century

An hour before dawn, Suri stood on the clifftop to the left of the main gate. The army moved slowly, still some distance away.

It was a nightmarish sight, a dark mass of movement, the torches the only way of conveying the sheer number of them, stretching back hundreds of yards, almost as far as she could see.

Word came on the wings of bedraggled birds, with twenty of them dropping their burden of text into the city.

Lera's stance was clear, the tight script as hateful as the message it contained. Lingyun's handiwork, most likely. It was hardly even a list of demands, its language closer akin to a religious decree, and just as sanctimonious.

To the citizens of all Peregrinus,
The Lord Kol and his unseemly court of pagans have committed endless atrocities against the lands of Peregrinus. One hundred years ago, his deliverance caused the deaths of thousands. For decades, his men have laid ruin upon the Drameir Road, and only weeks ago, he murdered hundreds in the north.
Now, we discover he has lied to the world again, faking his own death so that he could escape the allegations against him. How many more need to die before we say it is enough? Before we conquer our fear of him, once and for all?
In the name of all that is good, under the eyes of the Trio and in the presence of the honourable Queen Lera of Drangbor, we demand each active member of Kol's court be tried, questioned, and if deemed guilty, hanged by the neck until they are dead.
The royal army of Drangbor hereby places the Lost City under a peaceful annexation until the tyrants are brought to justice.

"Do you mean to reply?" Suri asked.

Kol stood beside her, staring out as the wind whipped against his cloak and through his hair. "What is there to say? She will play out the farce of the peaceful siege and let us all starve inside the walls. Dellon cut us off five days ago, I imagine she thinks our city is already on the brink of revolt. Shaedon is here, Ressa is here, Allis'don is watching. Let everyone see the monster she becomes when her patience runs dry."

"So we wait it out."

"For as long as we can. Lera only has six massacres. We will not be forced out by hunger for another week yet at least. There is time for her to blunder, for the world to see the truth as we discover how to end her."

"We should get some rest, Kol," Suri said.

"But then you'd miss the show. It's nearly here."

"What show?"

"The show that might buy us the two more days Waris needs. By my calculations, it can only be another hour," he replied enigmatically.

A throat cleared behind them and they both turned.

Shaedon stood, his clothes rumpled and hair unkempt, but at least he wasn't visibly drunk. He didn't even look hungover, she realised. He looked sober, and very tired. "Kol." He addressed him, before nodding to her in acknowledgement. It was more than she expected from him, though she imagined less than her status required. "I heard the news. The army has arrived. What do you know?"

"Prince Shaedon. You heard quickly." Kol waved his hand towards the view, inviting the fire prince forward as he held out the note. "See for yourself."

Shaedon took a couple of nervous steps forward towards the edge and grabbed the note from him. Kol and Suri stood a full six feet from its precipice, a low barrier of piled rocks shielding the edge.

Shaedon stopped a couple of paces further back. It didn't seem to be Kol he feared, but the height. He scanned the note quickly with a frown, then he stared out at the mass of torchlight approaching them. "So many."

Kol nodded. "Yes. Reports indicate the Queen has secured additional troops from Kans."

Shaedon blinked. "Dabri'yon gave her men? But her own army would surely be more than sufficient. Does she mean to scare you with this show of force? Make you back down?"

Kol shook his head. "On the contrary. I believe she means to destroy us completely."

Shaedon frowned. "She announced it would be a peaceful annexation."

"And that is why you are here," Kol said. "To witness."

Shaedon folded his hands in front of him. "Quite."

"And when Queen Lera seeks to bring Death to these lands, you can see whose hand the bloodied stone sits in."

"The rumours of the killings, the massacres... There is nothing to suggest Lera is behind it. You only have speculation," Shaedon said, but his voice held little conviction.

Suri laughed, and the fire prince fixed his gaze onto her. It was as if he'd forgotten she was there, and now she had made noise he looked at her like a piece of curiosity. "Are you calling me a liar?"

Shaedon swallowed, tucking a red curl behind one ear. He looked uncertain and yet affronted. "That was not my intent. Though you'll forgive me for not believing the word of a thief and a murderer over a Queen."

Kol gritted his teeth.

But Suri was quicker. "Ah, of course. Though in my limited experience, I've yet to meet a royal without blood on their hands. And far more than you can find on mine. Pray, how many men have you sent to the mines, your Grace?"

Shaedon crossed his arms and looked at Kol, his ears reddening. "I will not be spoken to in this way."

Kol shrugged. "Then walk away, but see what happens here. And above all, *asari ith vulturis*."

"I don't speak your pagan language, Demon King," Shaedon replied, but the bite of it was lost to his exhaustion.

"It means 'beware the harpy'," Suri cut in, glancing at Kol and basking in the warmth in his gaze. "Or, in other words, try not to die."

Shaedon sniffed. "Then try not to starve us, King of Sand."

Kol just watched on, amused, as Shaedon turned and walked further from the edge, a shake still in his knees as he walked back to the city wall.

Then Kol chuckled, his eyes sparkling with mirth.

"What is it?" Suri asked.

He stared at her. "You amaze me. You're utterly fearless."

Suri stared back, her heart in her throat. Sometimes it was overwhelming, just to look at him and see him looking back at her. There was so much unsaid, so much she wanted from him. "That's not true. I have fears."

Kol shook his head, and pressed a kiss to the top of her head. He murmured against her. "I hope to discover them one day."

She wanted that, too. For him to know all of her, under every star and in every season. She wanted him for hours, days, years. She could see an entire life stretching out before them.

And Lera wanted to take that all away. Take the future she desperately craved.

The realisation had been circling her ever since she got her soul back. Even when she was lost without it, cold in her heart and mind, she still reached for him like a tether. Something to pull her out of the drowning weight of nothingness.

She was in love with Kol.

Suri wrapped her arms around him, and he pulled her in tight, pressing another kiss to her head. Every part of him warmed her, filled her with more security than she'd ever known.

Home.

They stood there, embracing on the cliff overlooking the approaching army, for several minutes. She wondered then, if he loved her, too. It was a doubt, a niggling fear like a small fish clinging onto the giant oceanic behemoth that was their impending doom. It was a silly fear, a selfish fear, but one she held nonetheless.

If she spoke those three words, what would he say?

Maybe he would say them back, and for a moment the thought was so tempting it made her heart judder and a lump rise in her throat. She almost wanted to shout it out just for the chance of hearing it back.

But the idea that he might not, silenced her.

What if he wasn't in love? Would she be able to love him, knowing that he didn't feel the same way? She still would, she knew. It wasn't something she could turn off. But to stay with him if his feelings didn't match hers would be painful.

Then Kol made a noise and pulled back. "Look, there."

Suri turned and followed his point. "What?"

"The show I promised. Right on time," Kol said, quietly into her ear.

He stepped behind her as she squinted, wrapping his arms around her again from behind, watching over her head.

What was it?

Something fast-moving and frothing white approached in the far distance, coming from the south-west as the army moved in from the north-west.

The noise came next.

A low rumbling which grew and grew as the white wall approached, coursing down a path in the sand. Then it grew closer, no longer a white object on the horizon but a serpent of white and grey, catching blue in the pink of the dawn.

Gods.

It was water. The Dam was destroyed, and the river was coming home to the Parched Lands.

The rumble became a roar. The army's torchlight faltered as they appeared to come to a halt, watching the same scene play out before them.

Then the sun tipped over the sea line at Suri's back, warming it and catching on the white torrent as it flowed into its old banks. The water flowed furiously past the city's entrance, cutting the city off from Lera's men with a barrier of water, as it made its way past and flowed out of sight behind the cliffs.

"It's beautiful," Suri said.

"It's the start," Kol replied. "Life will come back to the Parched Lands, Suri. I will make it true."

Suri stared at the mass of people caught on the other side of the river. In the growing light of dawn, their numbers were truly horrifying. Thousands moved towards their cliffs. "They've stopped."

"Not for long."

When Nadrian found them half an hour later, they hadn't moved. They were suspended in that moment before the war truly began, before the siege reached the river's banks.

He let out a low whistle. "Would you look at that? That is sure something."

"Morning, Nadrian," Kol replied. "Here for the view?"

"Kol, the people are worried," he said, studying them.

Suri watched Nadrian back, noting how grey he looked, his eyes dull, his cheeks sallow. He looked like he hadn't slept in several weeks, but she'd seen him only hours ago.

"You look terrible," Kol said, loosening his hold on Suri as he moved around to her side.

"It's the distance from the Glen," Nadrian said with a sigh. "It's starting to pull on me."

Kol placed a hand on his shoulder. "You should fly back."

Nadrian shook his head, glancing between them. "I'm not leaving you."

And he meant them both. He meant the city. He meant their little court.

Suri frowned. "It'll kill you—"

"It's fine," he said. "I can manage it."

The moment hung between them, and then Kol nodded. There was a risk here to all of them, but bigger than that: this could break their very world. Who knew what power Sotoledi could bring back? He could kill them all, raze this place to the ground. Nadrian would probably rather die before he ran to the Glen.

"What's the word in the city?" Kol asked.

"People saw the water, and the troops. They're scared."

Kol nodded. "I'll go speak to them."

Nadrian grimaced. "What will you say?"

"Whatever I can to bring them hope, without lying to them."

"That'll be a short speech, then," Nadrian said.

Kol couldn't hide the small smile that crept onto his cheek. "Astonishingly helpful, as ever."

"That'll be my epitaph."

Kol shook his head, but the creeping smile prevailed. "From now on, no one leaves the city without my express permission. Give the orders to the gate."

"Will do," Nadrian said. "I'll take the Seer with me, keep her out of trouble."

"Hey," Suri responded, affronted. "I like trouble."

Nadrian smiled. "Which is why I'm going to ensure the guards take a good long look at you, and expressly know not to let you go anywhere."

Suri huffed and rolled her eye. She had no plans for a dramatic escape, but she had to agree it was something she had a history of doing.

"He's got you sussed," Kol said, grabbing her hand and squeezing it. "I'll find you later?"

"You better," Suri replied.

His face glowed slightly. "Goodbye," he said. Then under his breath, he whispered. "*Nen alerisee f'ith sotele.*"

"You've hardly returned," Suri said with a smile. "We've been here all morning."

Kol laughed and then patted Nadrian on the back, leaving back towards the city. Gods, she loved him. It was going to kill her when it ended.

Nadrian watched him walk away, and then moved to sit on the very edge of the cliff. For a second, her heart fluttered with fear for him, but then she remembered his wings. She blinked, looking for what her mind hid from her, what his glamour concealed.

The huge golden wings came into view, the golden light of the morning sparkling on the tips of the feathers. He rolled his shoulders, and the wings rolled in an arc, the membrane flaring and settling. "You two seem happy."

It was only an observation, but it made Suri prickle. She didn't want to be private about whatever they were to each other, but she hadn't spent enough time with just him to know how to be, much less to know how to be around anyone else.

But it was just Nadrian. She could talk to him. "We are," she admitted.

"Good," he said. He pulled a piece of fruit out of his pocket, and handed it to her.

"Thanks," Suri said, taking a large bite into the crisp fruit.

Nadrian drummed his fingers on his leg. "Has Kol ever told you about a vision he had as a child?"

Suri swallowed the bite, taking another smaller one before answering. "When he gave his soul to Sotoledi?"

"Oh, so he has told you about it."

Suri narrowed her eye, confused at this line of conversation. "He has. Well—I'm in it. I've been there, I saw it."

Nadrian's surprise could only be genuine. "What?"

"In Rasel's manor, drugged with tea, I saw the tower," she explained. "I saw Sotoledi reach for Kol, only he was younger and afraid. I ran for him but I couldn't get to him in time."

She still flinched thinking of it, remembering his face white in the moonlight, how scared he had looked. Afraid was putting it mildly. Kol had been terrified, looking at that clawing hand like a nightmare come real. And she hadn't been able to help him.

Nadrian though, stared at her with his mouth hanging open. "That was you? You're the light in the darkness? It literally is you. You're her."

She shrugged. "I guess so. Light in the darkness." She tasted the words. "Is that what he called it? That memory?"

He shook his head. "It's what he calls you. The light in the darkness." Nadrian laughed to himself. "I figured it was a metaphor. You're a symbol of hope like his vision had been, and you reminded him of her. But you're actually her."

"He doesn't call me that, though," Suri said. What was he talking about?

Nadrian stood up, the humour alight on his face as he explained. "He's been telling me about seeing the vision of a goddess, one he would call The Light in the Darkness, ever since I met him. And now he says it to you." Suri must have scrunched her face in confusion, because Nadrian sighed. "*Nen alerisee f'ith sotele*. It means 'the light in the darkness'."

Suri made a strange strangled noise. "But he told me—"

"He lied."

33

I long to go back to our home. I miss my books, but I do not wish to rush him. He enjoys the company of society far more than I do.

Unknown author, est. 2nd-5th century

The day passed with a strange sense of normalcy for Suri.

With the leaders focused on the war on the other side of the Gate, Jem had been put in charge of keeping order in the green city. He wanted her advice, as limited as it was, and she happily took up the grunt work of passing messages around and checking on Rasel.

As evening fell, she swam for an hour in the leaf pools before changing into new garments and going to Kazem's bar. She told Kol where she was, and he arrived not long after. One drink later, they'd left, falling into each other's embrace again and again until sleep took them. They both felt pent up, frustrated, waiting for the war to begin. At the same time, she wished she could freeze this final moment of calm forever.

The enemy was moving again, and word had come from the guards that they were setting up at the banks, testing the best places to cross. It wouldn't be long now before they found a solution and then it would begin in full.

In the morning, Kol stretched out beside her. He'd taken to spending the night at hers, and she realised she didn't actually know where his own quarters were. She'd seen his office, of course. But where did he sleep?

She rolled over and asked him as much.

He shrugged, looking a little guilty as he matched her posture, rolling towards her and staring at her face in the morning light. She didn't wear her eyepatch at night with him, and he never looked at her as though there was anything damaged about her. "I have rooms near the centre of town, but I rarely sleep there."

"Why not?"

"They feel cold, vacant. The amount of space makes me feel uncomfortable. The rooms feel lonely," he explained.

"Then where do you sleep?"

"Right now?" he said. "Here."

She scoffed. "And before that?"

"The scout hut."

Suri paused. "The hut. Where you put me when I first arrived in the city?"

He nodded.

"Jem said you might stay a night there when you got back to town, but I didn't realise it was that often."

Kol smirked. "Well, either he was being kind, or he wasn't aware. But I'd stay there most nights."

"Why?"

"As a child I lived in tents or houses filled with families. We were running from Lera's troops for a decade, and taken in by strangers for most of those years. Even when the search grew less intense, it felt strange to be in wide, open spaces," he explained. "They would only remind me of the desert, of constantly checking over my shoulder, searching for troops on the huge horizon. After I gave my soul and we came through the Gate... The mess of trees felt like safety. It was overwhelming in its closeness, but somehow it felt more secure. The scout's hut was one of the first buildings we made: a small storage area to leave tools and materials. I would stay to oversee, and then I would stay because I liked the smallness of my world there."

"And then what of recently? When I was staying there?"

He shrugged. "I'd stay in my office, or sleep on the sofa in Scilla's quarters, or Nadrian's, or Axri'don's. "

"I had no idea," Suri said. "You should have said."

He shook his head. "Don't fret about it. I put you there. Partly to give you your space from the rest of Akdaria, but also because it was somewhere I knew you would be safe. It... helped me to know which walls were around you."

Suri stroked his cheek.

"Besides," Kol said. "You were driving me so mad then that I hardly got any rest anyway."

"Sorry," Suri grinned.

"You're not sorry at all, little thief," he said, then reached out to pull her body on top of his.

She laughed. He rubbed her back and pressed his face into her hair, kissing above her ear.

They lay like that for a time, holding each other.

Then Kol groaned. "I have to go. Waris has been trying to understand your bond with Rasel, to look for a way around it. I need to see if she's made any progress."

"Has she told you anything?"

"Only that it's unlikely she can tamper with it."

"We don't know if Rasel was telling the truth," Suri said.

Kol stroked her hair. "I know. I know. But if there's any chance he was." He stopped, and Suri pushed herself up with her hands to stare down at him. Kol's face was grave, the morning light hitting his cheekbones. "I can't lose you again."

Up on the battlements, Ressa and Viantha stood side by side. On either side of them, three others stood, their matching blue robes identifying them as the members of the Water Guild who had arrived with Ressa.

There was a distance between them, and not just in the six feet gap between their bodies, but in their posture, in the way they spoke to each other in clipped fragments.

Suri paused beside Scilla, who watched the pair from a distance. "What are they doing?"

"Manipulating the water," Scilla explained quietly. "Whenever the troops try to cross or throw down some kind of bridge, they make the water swell, or catch them in a tide and pull them downriver."

"That sounds like a lot of work," Suri replied.

Scilla nodded. "It's tiring. Even between the eight of them, the weight of the constant movement is a burden. They won't be able to disrupt them forever."

Suri watched one of the manipulators point out at a cluster of guards approaching the water's edge, and the others murmur quickly between them. They waited until the men were up to their waists, barely a quarter across, and then Ressa's command came. A short, quiet 'now', was all it took, and the manipulators focused. Some twisted a hand, some threw both hands in the direction. Ressa and Viantha barely moved, but Suri saw the tension in both their faces.

The men yelled out as the water around them swelled up to their necks. Suri squinted, trying to see from this distance what was happening. Two were pulled under the water, and then resurfaced, coughing violently. The group threw themselves back towards shore, swimming to the best of their ability before clawing their way out on their hands and knees, staring back at the water with shuddering gasping breaths.

"Do they know we are manipulating the water?" Suri asked.

Scilla folded her hands across her knees. "I'm sure Lera has worked it out. Groups try to cross so often she must be testing their limits, trying to wear us out."

Suri studied Scilla, but the woman wasn't looking at her. Her dark gaze was locked onto Viantha, and it was one of concern and fear.

Kol had assigned Scilla to protect Viantha, but Suri knew that look. There was far more to that look than any bodyguard should hold.

"You care for her, don't you?" Suri asked.

Scilla finally looked at Suri. The general's expression was hard to read. It was stern, but soft. She looked exhausted, but not in any way defeated. "She holds me in the palm of her hand."

Suri nodded. "Does she know it?"

Scilla sighed. "She's suffered so much. If it's easier for her to shut me out, I will not press."

"What if she is never ready?"

Scilla glared at Suri, a familiar ripple of irritation. "I do not think it such a burden to love without knowing if that love will be returned. It's enough."

"You're a far better person than I am," Suri said.

Scilla rolled her eyes. "I have been a member of this court longer than you. All we have ever had to our name is hope. Now I have a new hope, that one day I might live long enough to deserve the love of that woman. It gives me something to fight for."

Suri took Scilla in from head to toe. She remembered the time, just before Scilla had taken her eye, when she had thought that they were two sides of the same coin. Two women, on opposing sides of a conflict, both blinded by their need for revenge. By what they needed to take from each other to make the world right.

Now here they were, two women sat on the same side of a battlefield. Scilla said all she had ever had was hope. What part of the coin was Suri, then? Fear. Always, fear. Ever terrified that someone would try to take the things she'd fought so hard to get.

"I'm in love with Kol," Suri told her, with no idea why she was telling Scilla of all people. They were never truly close.

Scilla raised an eyebrow at her. "When did you work that one out?"

"I think when I saw him after my soul was back," Suri said.

Scilla's mouth twitched. "Then you were the last to know."

"What do you mean?"

"I saw your face when Kol stepped into the arena with us that day." Scilla clenched her fist. "You are one of the most selfish people I know. You always choose you. But that day, you would have died for him for a chance at making him better."

Suri's own mouth twitched even as her chest panged. "I'm scared."

Scilla shook her head, another withering look settling on her fine mouth. "You're both completely insane for one another. You owe it to yourself, and what is to come, to say it before it is too late."

34

He has made progress, implanting a thought of a time long past into a ready subject. Yet still, he will not leave.

Unknown author, est. 2nd-5th century

"Tell us everything you know about bringing Sotoledi back," Suri said the moment her and Kol walked into Rasel's cell later that day.

Nadrian was there again, sitting on the stool next to Rasel.

They were back to this, asking Rasel for anything he knew that might help them. There was nothing Waris could do. The blood bond was carved following every tenet of blood magic. The only way she could override it was to carve something new in hopes it might alter the meaning of the words. But to do so, she'd have to carve a bone knife from her own body, and she would not attempt it on a wish and a prayer that it might assist them.

"What do you want to know?" Rasel asked without surprise.

"She gets the power of eight massacres," Suri said. "Then what? Is there a ritual? How does He pass back?"

"The deaths will have already happened, so a full ritual won't be necessary. The ritual was a way to channel the past massacre, to use fresh death to try to tap back into the Wrath."

"What will happen instead?"

"Lera will choose a conduit to channel these deaths through. If the conduit isn't strong enough, she'll choose another, and another, until someone is strong enough to bear the deaths."

"A priestess?" Suri pressed.

Rasel shrugged. "Probably. It seems to be more about mental strength than physical, so one of those devotees is likely the best option."

"So there's no use in killing the conduit," Kol said.

"No, she'll have several," Rasel said. "Even if all of them die, she'll kill half her army again finding someone who can survive it."

"How long will it take for the conduit to channel them? How long did it take you?" Suri asked Kol.

"A few minutes, maybe," Kol said, with a frown.

"What about the other side? What happens to Sotoledi in that time?" Suri asked.

"I don't know," Rasel admitted. "We call on him to take the power of the deaths, offering them to him. He speaks back to us. Maybe he is pressing on our world just as we are pressing on his."

"He'll be distracted. Maybe after the eighth, as Lera tries to use a conduit to channel them, I can slip into His world and retrieve the souls," Suri suggested.

Kol shook his head. "Too risky."

Suri sighed. "If anyone can think of a single plan that is less risky, I'm ready to hear it."

"We have our first plan," Kol said. "Convince Lera the world is against her, and make her back down. We have our back up plan, wait until Lera starts to kill her own. Right now, she still has to do it twice. Everyone will see her true nature, then we end her before the conduit can channel the deaths."

"It's all temporary," Suri said.

"It gives us time to come up with some other way to stop her," Kol said.

"Or it gives her time to perform the last massacre somewhere else, and channel Him there when we have no control over it, where there is no possibility of us stopping Him," Suri snapped, her frustration leaking through. "We don't win by killing Lera. Give it a year or two, and Dellon will decide it's his turn to be Sotoledi's favourite. Or Dabri'yon will kill a hundred people across the Shale and bring Death back there."

Rasel, Nadrian and Kol fell silent.

"No," Suri said, her voice quieter again. "It has to be here. It has to end. I won't let anyone live in fear of that fucking Fae any longer. He destroyed your life, He's whispered into the ears of starving children for years. It's here. Now. While we are watching, so we can destroy Him once and for all."

Nadrian stared at her. Then he nodded. "She has a point."

"I know. She always has a point, she's infuriating like that," Kol said.

"Sotoledi needs to be destroyed. And we can't kill Him in the shadow world, so He has to come here. We need to end it," she said again.

"If the weasel isn't lying to us, then you won't be ending anything if he comes here," Kol said, his own anger flaring. "You heard Waris. His soul dies, you die."

"Then I need to go and get it back."

Kol's nostrils flared and his eyes flashed. "Sotoledi will kill you."

"I won't go alone," she said.

"Who?" he asked.

Suri pointed at Rasel. "Him."

Kol scoffed. "You want to go into Sotoledi's world with *Rasel*. Are you kidding?"

Her expression was resolute, with no pinch of humour. "We need you, Viantha, and Scilla for the prophecy. He's the only one with no value here."

Rasel raised an eyebrow. "Ouch."

"And the only one with nothing to lose," she continued, shifting her focus from Kol's growing despair to Rasel's cold look. "You're a dead man walking, you said it yourself."

Rasel grumbled but didn't object.

"What's more," Suri said, walking towards him. "You won't desert me in there. You need me to stay alive. If you even tried to fuck me over, it would kill you in the process. You're my greatest ally right now, because He can't offer you anything you could possibly want more than your own life. Which means you have my back."

Rasel watched her, his jaw clenched. He scanned her eye and the patch over the other one, then he nodded.

"How are you going to get it back?" Nadrian asked.

"We still have the seventh massacre. That gives us some time. But if Rasel is right, and Sotoledi might be distracted by the call of the conduit, then the moment Lera attempts the eighth massacre, we'll enter the shadow world," Suri said. "One of us will call Him, and the other gets the soul."

"You say that as if it will be easy," Kol said, and the pain in his voice prevented her from turning around. She couldn't see his face right now, or know how annoyed he was.

"Not easy," she replied, still watching Rasel. "Just our only option. It has to work, because otherwise we both die."

Around her, everyone stopped, thinking of any possible way around it, and finding nothing to grasp onto. Suri simply stared at the man who had bound her to her own death.

Nadrian eventually sighed. "Of all the people to pick a fight with, of course, we pick a god."

"I'm sorry." Suri stepped back out into the early evening air. The dropping sun peeked through the gaps in the canopy and warmed her face. Kol hadn't spoken in over a minute. "I know you wanted to decide this together."

"I was in there with you. We talked about it. I'm not angry at you." Kol stared at the ground, stopping outside the prison entrance. "I'm angry at myself."

"What?"

An anguished noise fell from him, and it made her heart hurt. "I wish it was me. I wish I could be the one to save your life. But you have to save yourself, again."

She touched his shoulder, and he flinched slightly, still not looking at her. "Because you have to save the world."

He raised his eyes then, and the storm in them took her breath away. "I don't care about the world if you're not in it, little thief. You're the light. My light."

She smiled sadly. "*Nen alerisee f'ith sotele.*"

He jumped. "How did you—"

Her smile became a little more real. "Nadrian told me. You're a liar, Kol Aubethaan."

Kol smiled back, and then it faded, the warmth drifting from his face. "Then you know how I felt about you from the start. How I still feel. How important you are. I can't—"

"I will come back," she promised. "I'll get Rasel's soul, and I'll come back to you."

"I can't lose you." Kol brushed her hair from her face, his mouth tight with pain. "I know it's selfish, I know I should focus on Sotoledi, but all I can think about is you."

"No, I'm the selfish one. Rasel is a plague. Letting his soul wither into nothing would be what the eel probably deserves, and well worth my life." Kol started to protest, but Suri continued, determined to say what she wanted to say to him. What he had to hear. "But I want to live. Not because I'm apparently some important Seer, or because I want to achieve something important for the world. I want to live because I'm finally happy. I'm finally home."

Kol breathed. "Suri—"

"I want to eat, drink, and sleep here," she said with a small smile. "Laugh with my friends, see my brother again. Dance. Play, have fun. Mostly though, I want more time with you."

"That's not selfish, Suri," Kol said, studying her. "That's human. You deserve to be happy."

"You make me believe that. You make me not feel so monstrous." Suri drew in a breath as she forced herself to truly be vulnerable. "I'm in love with you."

She looked down as the words tumbled from her so quickly she couldn't tell if they came out clearly or in a garbled mess. She breathed in and out, her heart pounding, as if beating the rhythm of a chant. *Please don't break it.*

"Look at me." He touched her chin. "Suri, look at me."

She released her breath and jutted her chin back up.

Kol stood before her, shining like the sun above.

"You're glowing," she said in wonder.

"Say it again. Three words, darling," he purred.

"I love you." It was easier the second time. The words were already known, her heart was already on the line.

His smile was even brighter than the light as it beamed out in every direction. "I love you, too."

It didn't matter what happened in the coming days. It didn't matter if she died. She still had this, forever. The love of the Son of Life, the love of the Lord of Death. Her monster, her saviour, her undoing.

He was hers.

And in every strand of hair, every burst of joy, and every loathsome part of her, she was undeniably his.

35

His study requires people, mine does not. Mine is a study of geology, place and structure. We have agreed that I will return alone, and he will follow.

Unknown author, est. 2nd-5th century

The next day, Suri stared over the battlements once more. Viantha slept, her head resting on Scilla's lap, with a half-eaten roll in her hand. The water heiress had stopped for a rest from the constant water manipulation, and passed out in under a minute.

In the middle of the river, a ten-foot-high wall of water surged for several hundred feet in either direction.

"How long can they hold that?" Suri asked.

"A day, at most. Maybe long enough for Waris to finish her preparations," Scilla whispered, so as not to wake her sleeping charge. "But their side doesn't know that. For all they know, they'll never get through to us."

Suri smiled. “Optimistic.”

Scilla scowled. “Is it too much to hope that they just turn tail and leave? Probably. But as soon as they get to the other side, this strange war becomes too real. And I’d rather not see a single member of this city dead.”

“And him?” Suri asked, pointing to the red-headed man standing behind the manipulators, watching with an unblinking focus. Shaedon hadn’t moved a muscle since she’d arrived.

Scilla shrugged. “He seems to be taking his witness more seriously than any of us expected. Won’t get near the edge, but he hasn’t left since yesterday.”

“Has he said anything?”

“Little. But he watches her,” Scilla said, nodding to Viantha, lightly snoring in her lap. “I don’t like it.”

Suri stared at the sleeping princess, remembering back to the ball. It felt like a lifetime ago now, but it was only a matter of months. “They were to be married once.”

Scilla touched one of Viantha’s dark curls. “All the better for it that they weren’t.”

Shaedon lurched forwards as he pointed outwards. “Look there.”

Suri pushed herself to her feet in an instant and struggled to make sense of what she was seeing beyond the wall of water. It looked like a full battalion was stepping into the water, dressed in shining bronze armour, their spears and swords clenched in their tiny fists warping softly in the haze of water.

“Dabri’yon is sending her troops into the wall,” Scilla said.

Viantha stood a few paces back from Scilla, rubbing her eyes. She looked more tired than ever as she took in the scene.

"Again?" Suri asked.

"It's different this time." Scilla looked sick. "Usually it's a handful. This is hundreds."

The first line walked into the wall of water. The second then walked into it, pushing the first group forward, and so forth, the next line of soldiers blocking the previous line's escape. Suri watched as those at the front tried to turn back, but they were just pushed further into the water. There were eighty men already in the water, with more behind, trying to get across the thick wall to the other side of the river, yet struggling to move within it.

"Wrath's piss," Suri said. "She's drowning them."

"Drop the wall."

Suri swivelled at the sound of his voice.

Kol stood firm, staring at Ressa as he gave her the command with unwavering focus. The water manipulators didn't halt, didn't loosen their grips, looking to Ressa for a decision.

When had he arrived?

"They'll turn back," Ressa said, shaking her head, not looking back at Kol. "Lera will command them back."

"She won't," Kol growled. "If they die in our water, we'll have killed them. She'll have exactly what she wants."

"They won't kill their own. It's a game of wills," Ressa said.

Scilla took a step towards the Water Guild Leader and one of the resting manipulators stopped her, pressing a hand to her chest. The general glared at him, but raised her hands. "Ressa, they're dying. Drop the wall."

"Not yet. She'll call it off," Ressa said, but her voice seemed less certain now.

Shaedon said nothing, only staring between both sides with a wary assessment.

Suri looked down at the scene below once more. There were five lines of men in the wall of water now. Those at the front clutched at their throats as the water distorted them into dark gasping creatures.

Kol yelled. “Ressa—”

“Mother. Listen to Kol.”

Viantha’s interruption was measured and calm, and yet Ressa flinched, even as her brow furrowed in strained concentration.

The heiress stepped forwards, and no one moved to stop her as she touched her mother’s shoulder. “Drop it.”

Ressa shuddered, and finally nodded. She fell to her knees as the other manipulators gasped in relief, staggering as the strain of the wall peeled off of them.

The water in the distance released, pushing the men back to their shore.

Two men didn’t gasp or splutter, but lay face down on the water’s settling surface. Dead.

A dark-haired woman appeared then, walking from the encampment. Suri had never seen her before, but could tell from this distance she was a noblewoman from the breadth of her skirts, and the gleam of sun bouncing off her bronze headdress.

She shouted, and the noise of it carried to them on the wind, even as the words were lost. Dabri’yon, it had to be. Her men reformed on the shore, staggering and soaked.

“Are you seeing this?” Kol asked, quietly, almost to himself. His gaze was on the gathered men, his silk over one eye. He nodded at something she hadn’t heard.

Shaedon and Ressa muttered to one another as Scilla stood behind Viantha.

Dabri'yon's bedraggled men were back standing, formed in six lines as their two fallen soldiers bobbed on the river's surface.

They waited for what was to come. The water manipulators had so little energy left, half of them looked nearly dead on their feet. If they all pressed at once again, they would surely find their way across.

Another shout.

Suri expected them to stride into the water, but they only moved their arms. As one, they pulled out their swords. Pointing them up and out, as if presenting them to the sky above.

The third shout sounded, and this time she caught the word. But it wasn't of their tongue.

Again, the men did not take a step. They turned their blades, and pierced themselves, skewering the metal straight through their exposed necks in one smooth motion.

They did not fall in unison. Instead they crumpled: tidelessly, irregularly.

Suri's ears rang as hundreds of Dabri'yon's men lay dead. She watched the monarch return to her tent. The other Kans battalion stood as still as the eye of the storm, not reacting as their kin died.

Suri only turned to Kol. His silk was still on. Allis'don, she hoped, had seen it all.

That conversation from the boat swept back to her like a breaking dam in her own mind. *"How many can you afford to lose?"*

This was always the plan. This was always the seventh massacre. The eighth, by Lera's design, would be their starvation. And yet, that would take far longer than she thought. How long would it be before she killed her own troops, too, out of sheer impatience?

A day? A week?

Lera had hoped to paint them as the villains once more, as she had since the Wrath one hundred years ago. But the Queen had miscalculated. Suri took in the shock on Ressa and Shaedon's faces. This time, the world was not blind.

Lera's troops stepped over the bleeding corpses from Kans, approaching the river once more. Gods, would they not give them even a second?

"Water Guild. We can't stop now. We still need more time to prepare our final defences," Scilla said, cutting through the mutual horror. "Who among you has the strength to push them back?"

Ressa stepped forward, her eyes glazed over with exhaustion.

"Get some rest," Viantha said to her mother, touching her arm. "I'll take over."

Scilla's eyes tensed.

Ressa blinked. "There is work to do."

"You are dead on your feet. Sleep. The war will still be here when you wake up."

Ressa frowned, then nodded. "As you say."

Viantha watched her mother stagger away from the edge of the cliff, then turned back to the recovering manipulators. "You heard the general," she said. "Push them back. We'll make waves instead, slow them as much as we can. This river is the last line keeping the people behind us safe."

Around her the manipulators simply nodded, rolling shoulders and shaking off their weariness as best they could.

Viantha hummed a soft and melancholic tune which was almost an infant's lullaby. She moved her hands forward, and back, undulating them with the rhythm. The others fell into the same motion.

Waves formed and washed the troops back. Viantha kept humming, kept the rhythm perfectly aligned. But it was Scilla who caught Suri's eye. The general stared at Viantha with an abject awe the likes of which Suri had never seen. This was more than admiration, it was veneration and reverence.

The general stepped up beside the line, and Suri saw her attention fall on a disturbance at the bank. Three men had somehow made it to the other side, coughing up water on the near side of the bank. One of them had a rope tied around his waist.

That was not good. Already, she saw the men on the other side of the river, holding the rope, gesturing. More would be across in an instant.

"He's not in range," Kol murmured.

It was only a matter of time before the river fell, Suri figured. They had done their best to keep the troops from their walls for as long as they could.

Suri opened her mouth to express this to Scilla, but found her locked in complete focus. Scilla stared at the man with the rope with an intensity Suri didn't quite understand.

Then something tugged on the rope.

A vine appeared, wrapping around the rope and yanking the man back into the river. He screamed as it pulled him back towards the middle, his head dragging under for a moment and then resurfacing. Then the waves took him, pushing him back to the opposing shore.

Suri darted her eye back to Scilla. The general looked grey with exertion, her hands quivering and her shoulders hunched.

"Was that you?" Suri asked.

Scilla nodded. "Yes."

Viantha had stopped her vigil on the waves, letting the others lead for a moment as she stared at Scilla with something oddly joyful. "What you did there, that was pure creation. There's no life there. You brought that plant from nothing."

Scilla smiled. "I had a good teacher."

They were keeping them back, even now. Delaying the siege, keeping the army from their doorstep. But it wouldn't be long before they found another route. Lera had sent troops along the river last night, their lights twinkling off down the far bank, men who would find another place to cross, somewhere beyond the realms of the Guild's manipulation.

They couldn't keep the war away forever, but every moment gave Waris more time to construct the mists. Every time they pushed Lera away, instead of attacking, they won allies. She might have seven massacres, but there was still hope.

36

Finally, as the weather turns to chill, I am back under the Drangbor sky. I am itching to see how this amefyre could turn our fortunes.

Unknown author, est. 2nd-5th century

The room at the base of the gatehouse tower looked like someone had stuck a boar with a knife, pulled it free, and let the panicked beast run itself in circles as it bled to death. There was no pattern she could see, only blood everywhere, staining deep into the furniture and the bottoms of the curtains. The floor, at least, was stone, but that only meant the blood atop it was more obvious, sitting in stagnant, congealed pools.

Suri expected something foul, and still clapped a hand to her mouth and nose to prevent the instant desire to retch.

Waris was in the corner, muttering to herself on all fours as she knelt over a bucket, her hand playing with something inside it.

"Lera's men will be across the river soon," Suri said through her fingers. "Please tell me you're nearly ready."

Suri refused to look up, keeping her eye on the witch. The drip, drip, drip of new blood told her all she needed to know about what was above her. The bodies Waris had asked for were those who had died naturally since entering the city, and Kol had told the families they'd been buried out in the sands, as was the custom. She wondered how they would react, knowing they were strung up as puppets in the towers abutting the city wall.

Waris didn't even seem to notice her, still muttering into her bucket.

Suri closed the door behind her, and Waris jumped slightly, but didn't look up. "Waris?"

She looked at Suri then, her head moving unnervingly fast, and Suri pressed her back to the door. "What, what?"

"Is it done?"

Waris bared her teeth in what one could consider to be a smile. "Only the finishing touches left to go."

"Do you—Is there any way to help?" Suri asked with a large pinch of trepidation.

Waris stood, and as she did her hands came out of the bucket, dripping red. "I need to exit the city. You can trot back up the stairs and motivate those Guild idiots to keep them back for another hour."

"Why do you need to be outside the city?"

Waris pressed her wet hand to her chest in a mockery of surprise. "Oh, would you rather have the deadly poison mist *inside* the walls?"

Suri gritted her teeth. They needed her, they needed all of this. Her work would save many lives. "What are you going to do out there?"

"Coat this blood in a line outside the city walls," she said simply, pointing to the bucket.

"I'll get Nadrian," Suri replied. "He can fly you down and back up when you're done. The gates are sealed, we need to keep them that way."

"Fine, fine," Waris said. "How is your time walking going?"

Suri straightened. Did Waris know? Or was she simply guessing? She was a Seer of Time, after all, it wasn't much of a leap.

Waris merely raised an eyebrow.

"I'm struggling to control it." Then she sighed. Waris might be one of the only people that understood the truth of her magic. "I found myself in my own past."

"Did you do anything fun?" Waris responded, with no surprise.

"I—I changed my own past. Cthanda told me it was wrong. But I don't know how I even got there. What if not changing it would have been worse?" Suri asked, letting it all fall out of her.

Waris sneered. "Cthanda was always a preachy Seer. For a woman who held the title only a handful of years, she has Diophage's knack for not releasing her hold on this world. I say, do what you want. Blood, souls and time. The only limit is your own humanity. What you can live with, and what you can't."

"But I'm supposed to be balanced. Neutral."

She laughed, then, and that was somehow scarier than all the blood and corpses in the room. "That's what the world will tell you. The Fae love that line, it's got them out of helping far too many times over the centuries."

"So what am I supposed to do?" Suri asked, feeling like a toy caught between two snapping dogs.

"I suppose their line is true to an extent," Waris mused, ignoring Suri's frustrated question. "You don't owe good or evil your allegiance, if you can even tell one from the other. Your allegiance is to yourself. If you're able to point to a single person who is wholly good, or wholly bad, please show them to me. There's your balance. People have it, inherently."

Suri scoffed. "I think most people would disagree with you."

"That's the value of centuries for you, child," Waris said. "I do not care."

Waris wrapped her arms around Nadrian's shoulders, a sloshing bucket held in each hand. Her smile crept across her face, and once again she reminded Suri of a spider. "Be careful, boy. I don't want to spill my paint."

Nadrian shuddered, but nodded. "I'll keep you as steady as I can."

He let the warm wind of the day fan at his huge golden wings, catching in them. Then he stepped off the edge of the cliff.

Suri darted to the space they'd fallen from, gnawing a fingernail as she watched them float down to the sand below. They made it safely, and Waris removed herself from the Fae King, moving to one side of the city gate and dipping her fingers into the first bucket.

One of the water manipulators was in a bad way, her hands out of sync with the others. Sometimes the waves would falter, and the men in the river would near the halfway point. They didn't have long until the manipulators had nothing left to give.

A minute after Waris' first bucket was empty, and she was past the halfway point, it happened.

Suri was too far away to assist, if she even knew how.

The knees buckled first. The manipulator's head fell forward, her arms lost their grip on the two either side of her. She fell to the ground. The one to her right, on the edge, knelt down, trying to pick her up.

The others groaned with the strain. A quick glance at the river showed the waves slowing, the men heaving through the water making headway.

"Leave her," Viantha said. "Join back, quick."

The man followed the instruction, stepping over the woman passed out on the floor to grab back into the line.

But it was too late, the strain was too much. Another, a man at the far left of the line let out a shout, grabbing his head and falling to his knees.

The line collapsed, none of them able to take the weight of the water with so few of them. Viantha stood alone, raising her arms, screaming at the river. But she was barely moving it.

Scilla moved towards her. "Viantha, stop."

It was over, the water manipulators were down.

Suri yelled out to the handful of guards. "Raise the alarm. Get the archers up here, *now*. The river is lost."

Two guards saluted and bolted down the stairs, their shouts echoing in the stairwells as they raised the alarm.

"Viantha," Scilla said, grabbing her around the waist. "You'll kill yourself."

"The witch needs more time."

The water princess was right. Suri looked down at the sand below to see Waris still had a third of the blood line left to paint. Without the mists, the battlements and the city beyond would be in full view of Lera's archers. They were outmanned by far, and needed this to ensure the next massacre wasn't their own people.

Nadrian had noticed the first line of men already pushing closer to the bank. He spoke to Waris, the words too low and distant to make out. Waris did not speed up, following her same pattern and rhythm.

Scilla pulled at Viantha again. "You've done all you can."

"She won't die because of me."

"The old bat is centuries old and more than half mad," Scilla argued. "*You* are not dying for *her*."

"But—"

"No," Scilla said, and she lifted the princess up. "You're leaving this damned wall. You have played your part."

Scilla turned, the princess in her arms. Viantha's face now turned towards her, and Suri noted the deep blue under her eyes, the line of dried blood under her nose and her chapped lips. As soon as her focus was pulled away from the river, all her energy sagged from her. She relaxed into Scilla's arms, her eyes shuttering closed.

Scilla addressed Suri as she made for the stairs behind her. "Do you have energy?"

Suri nodded.

"Then turn your beats to those poor souls," she said, flicking her head to the groaning water manipulators. "They're sick with exhaustion, heal them enough so they can stumble to a bed."

Suri nodded again. "You keep her safe."

"Naturally," Scilla said, and then left the heights.

Suri followed her instructions, kneeling beside the first woman who had collapsed. She was conscious now, but her breathing was shallow. Suri focused on the beats, but all the while she watched below.

There was nothing she could do now. They couldn't order the gates open, there was no time to unseal them, and if Waris ran out of time, they would need all the help that barricade could give.

She had to trust that Nadrian would get them both the fuck out of there the moment Lera's army got into range.

The first men had reached the other side of the river now, and without the waves, more ran at the water, wading and swimming across. They threw ropes, and tested the wooden bridges they'd held back. When no ripples and tides threw them back, more and more were placed. Within a handful of minutes of the first manipulator falling, fifty were across, and hundreds more piled towards the shore.

Three hundred feet separated them and the city gates.

Around her, city guards in red, black and white ascended onto the battlements with bows strapped to their backs. They positioned themselves quickly and without comment, filling every gap along its walls.

A guard in white looked at her. She had seen him before, but didn't know his name. "What are your orders, my lady?"

"You are in command of these men now," Suri replied. "If they come into range before those two below have made their escape, fire in at their feet. Do not shoot to kill, we must end this without death, if we can."

He nodded. If there was any confusion around her orders, he showed nothing, only passing the information down the line and raising his hand upwards.

Waris had made progress, but there was still some distance left to paint, and they were sitting ducks. She'd need several minutes more to finish it. But she wasn't going to get that time.

Nearly a hundred men had reached the other side. Most stayed to assist with the ropes, bridges, and pulling the others across. But a group of soldiers ran immediately towards the city, pointing towards Nadrian and Waris. A clear target.

Suri's hands shook as she watched it unfold, her mind split as she tried to keep her breathing steady enough to maintain her focus on the beats, whilst another part of her screamed at Nadrian to run for it. She could see his gaze, flicking between the approaching force and the blood witch still calmly painting her line.

The men slowed, barking commands carried on the wind. From the way half the men knelt, Suri guessed at the intent.

Waris and Nadrian were in range of Lera's archers. They strung their bows as the other half started running, charging towards Nadrian with brandished steel.

Beside her, the white guard flicked his hand, and their own archers knocked their bow just as the men did on the sands below. In the distance, at the water's edge, another squadron of fifty ran towards them.

The white guard motioned again, and the arrows loosed. As she'd instructed, they didn't aim to kill, and the arrows sank into the sand around Lera's running footmen. One speared into a leg, taking the man down in the sand.

For a moment, the backline of archers faltered, unsure if they should turn their weapons to the sky, or remain fixed on the pair out the front. The men running staggered to a brief halt, one of them grabbing the fallen man as two others ran for cover behind a rocky outcropping.

Waris was nearly done. Another thirty seconds and she'd be at the city wall.

But then one of the front men barked an order. The running men reformed, and ran once more. The kneeling men behind launched a volley straight at Nadrian and Waris.

Fifteen arrows flew towards the Fae King and the Blood Witch, and Suri couldn't tear her eye away.

Waris didn't even look up, didn't stop what she was doing for even a moment, as three arrows careened into the sand less than five feet from her. Nadrian moved faster than she'd ever seen, beating his wings to throw himself backwards as the rest of the arrows thudded into the spot he vacated.

The white guard motioned and another hail of arrows fired down near the running men, but it didn't stop their flow this time. They were only seconds away from engaging Nadrian. Twenty swords against a batshit witch and a single Fae.

"We can't fire at the front line again, my lady," the white guard said. "We could hit Nadrian and the woman."

Waris painted the final touches, the blood smearing onto the place where the city wall met the cliff face, forming a perfect red shallow arc.

"They'll leave," Suri told herself. "They're going to get out of there."

Nadrian grabbed the witch just as the next hail of arrows soared into the sky, and the first man swung his blade in an arc so close to his wing, she couldn't tell if he'd been hit. Then, he pushed them into the air like an arrow himself, gusting the wind under his wings and sweeping them over onto the battlement.

Suri ran towards them as she pushed past the archers to sprint along the stone. She found them, sprawled on the floor, their bodies shaking.

Then Suri clapped her eye on Waris.

She was laughing. No. Cackling.

And then the mists came up and the army disappeared behind its milky fog, sealing the City of the Damned within its clutches.

37

I write to him often as I manipulate the gem. The woman was right, there is something to this material, something powerful.

Unknown author, est. 2nd-5th century

"They'll send word if something else happens," Suri said, watching Kol fiddle with his seeing silk.

"I know that," Kol said, before taking a large swig of his Storm Bitter. "But they're at seven now. It only takes a moment. It's been a week since Dellon cut us off, she must have been expecting us to walk out and surrender. Instead, we've locked ourselves in further, penned by the mists. We've surprised her."

"Surely, that's a good thing," Suri said. "She's on the back foot."

Kol shook his head, drinking again. "Animals like her mistake a surprise for a threat, defence for a fight. All Lera needs to do is give an order and her men will fall on their swords, and Sotoledi will be freed to do her bidding."

"Better her men than ours. Our people are safer now. And as soon as she acts, the world will see it. We will stop Sotoledi and show the world who Lera is, all in one moment."

After the mists had come up, they took the brief window of opportunity to come back to Akdaria, and it was like stepping into another world.

Kazem's bar around them pulsed with music, purple lights and the smoke of many pipes. Here, it still hummed with new life, its inhabitants free of the shackles of the frozen states. They knew of the war, and the threat it carried if Lera ever breached the city walls, but it felt distant to them, an untouchable force through an untouchable Gate.

Kol was doing everything in his power to make sure the location of the Gate remained a secret, though she knew there was a contingency plan for evacuation through it, should the need arise.

Kol rubbed his face. "That's why I need to be up there, waiting for her next move."

"But if we stay up there all day waiting for that to happen, you won't have the energy to do anything about it when it does. You should be sleeping right now."

"I can't. I can't let my guard down." His eyes locked on her throat as she swallowed some of her Icebolt. "You should be sitting with Rasel right now, not me."

"I'll go soon," Suri replied. "Someone needs to make sure you're sane."

He shook his head. "How are you so calm?"

Suri thought about it. She didn't really know why she was coping either. "Maybe because I've never known peace. I'm used to eternal chaos."

"I want you to know peace."

"Then let's take Lera and Sotoledi down once and for all." At Kol's despairing look, she pivoted. "What news from the Guilds?"

"Metal and Water are fully with us now, after what they just witnessed. Kans, too. The men from the great houses saw it all, as did Allis'don. Whatever Lera might claim, to put your own men to death is no custom of their lands. If Dabri'yon attempts to sail home, there will be a mutiny waiting for her."

"And Shaedon?" Suri asked, draining the rest of her Ice Bolt.

Kol frowned. "Trickier. He was horrified by what Dabri'yon did, and he sees how we do not fire upon her troops, even though we are in range. But Lera will claim she had no part in Dabri'yon's act. He also said raising the mists was a clear act of aggression."

"They're there to defend the city," Suri replied, her own anger seeping through.

"He also suggested we should have negotiated with Lera."

Suri scoffed. "Her letter said the only option to save the city was to volunteer our heads for nooses."

Kol shrugged, finishing his drink. "I think that would have solved a lot of the North's problems."

"What's it going to take, then?"

"If Lera kills her own men, too. That might do it."

Suri leaned back in her seat, folding her arms. "It has to come to that, then."

Kol's look only grew blacker. "If she wants to take control of the battlefield, if she wants to decide when it happens, killing her own is safer."

As Suri watched him, something deeply sad twinged in her belly. How was any of this fair? She got his soul back, and then got her own soul back. And now, only days later, they stood to lose it all? Her entire life was going to be destroyed because of Lera.

No. If she had to die tomorrow because of this heinous excuse for a harpy, she wasn't going to spend her last night with the man she loved talking about her. This was about them, and what they deserved.

Suri narrowed her eye. "If you had to guess, how long do you think her patience will last?"

"A day? Two?" he replied, his voice empty.

Suri reached her hand for him. "Then come with me."

"Where?" he asked, staring into the bottom of his glass.

"Let me distract you."

He sighed. "Suri—"

"No," she interrupted, and it came out more like a bark, rough and gravelly. He looked at her then. She squeezed his hand. "We need this."

He paused, and then nodded. "Lead the way."

"Will you give us a moment?" Suri said, addressing the handful of people having a night swim.

They left in an instant, grabbing their clothing and making their way back towards the city. The leaf pools were so peaceful at this time of night, the moon casting its glow on the black cups of water, the breeze ruffling light around them.

Kol watched her, bemused. “You want to swim?”

“Take your clothes off.”

He raised an eyebrow. “As you say, little thief.”

Kol removed his shoes, then stripped off his trousers, before pulling his tunic off over his head. He stood in his undershorts, staring at her.

“All of them.”

“You first,” he replied.

She smirked, and shed her clothes without a moment’s hesitation, until she stood before him completely naked in the moonlight.

Kol stared at her with that black gaze. “The power of the moon on your bare skin should be outlawed. You live to torment me.”

She took a step towards him. “How is it torment when I will happily let you take whatever it is you need from me?”

She saw how he strained against the fabric of his shorts. He removed them, and took a step towards her. “Then come here.”

Suri shook her head. “We haven’t had our swim yet.”

He groaned. “I don’t need the swim. I need you.”

Her eye flashed. “Then catch me.”

His jaw flexed as she turned and ran, leaping off the edge of the platform and onto the first leaf. The texture underfoot was familiar now, and Suri did not slip. She jumped to the next leaf, and the next. She’d just steadied herself on the pad of the largest leaf near the centre of the pools when a shadow came up beside her.

Kol knocked her down before she could even gasp. She landed hard on her back, and he was immediately over her, staring down at her ravenously as he rubbed against her thigh.

"Caught you," he said.

He breathed hard, his eyes dark. She arched her back.

"What will you do now you have me?" Suri asked, reaching her hand up to touch his face.

Kol grabbed her hands and pulled them above her head, holding both of her wrists in one hand. He pushed her legs apart with his knee, positioning himself in between her thighs. With his free hand, he rubbed his thumb roughly over one nipple before reaching further down to guide himself towards her, and met her gaze as he speared all the way inside.

They both gasped as he filled her to the brim.

He thrust into her, over and over, using his fingers to rub circles above her entrance. She writhed beneath him, but he still would not let her hands go. He only watched with a black gaze as she bucked beneath him.

"Is this what you wanted?" he purred. "To fall together where anyone could stumble upon us?"

"Almost," she said.

His jaw flexed as he stilled, deep inside her. "Tell me what you want."

Suri smiled at him, but it was anything but sweet. "I want you to take me how you need to. Fuck me like I'm yours."

He growled. "You *are* mine."

"Prove it."

Kol's eyes darkened to a Gate-like void as he drank her in from head to toe.

Then he released her hands and flipped her over. He thrust into her hard from behind, slamming his hips into her again and again. The pace was deliciously punishing and she revelled in it, falling into his overwhelming desire.

He murmured curses against her body as he fucked her until she forgot where they were, what was going on, who they were fighting. It was all-consuming, it was all they could be, all they could think about.

Kol buried himself inside her as he came, biting down on her shoulder. She pushed back, meeting his final thrust with her own movement, and then they collapsed, lying down across one another. He rubbed circles on her again, and she came only a minute later, her body already close to the edge.

They lay on that leaf in comfortable silence for a time, watching the moon as they listened to the sounds of their breath.

"I can't lose you," he said eventually.

"You won't," she replied. "I won't let myself be lost."

"If there comes a time, when you have to choose," Kol said. "Don't be a hero, don't save the world. It's you that I need."

Suri smiled. "Have you met me?"

Kol leaned over, staring down at her with his head propped on one elbow. "I have met you. And as much as you like to think you're a bad person, you're not. But I'm asking you to do the wrong thing, if it means saving yourself."

She reached up, ghosting a hand over his lower lip. "You won't lose me."

Kol frowned.

Suri rolled on top of him, pressing a kiss to his jaw. This time, when their bodies joined, it was slow and languid. They poured their love into each other, until they could not hold any more.

38

The first snows had already fallen when he returned. I welcomed him with open arms, and he told me of all his successes.

Unknown author, est. 2nd-5th century

Suri stepped into the prison cell, and the guard closed the door behind her. The floors were recently swabbed and still damp.

Nadrian turned to her from his perch on the stool. A stool which was much closer to Rasel than it had been last time. "Ah, killer. Is it time?"

Rasel's face was decidedly less swollen, his mouth almost back to normal. Under the puffed redness though, the black and blue bruising became much more obvious. His white-blonde hair looked cleaner and he seemed strangely at ease. Maybe he'd just made peace with his likely death.

She glanced at Nadrian, whom she now noticed was holding two hands worth of cards. "Not yet. But Kol thinks it's imminent."

Nadrian swept all the cards into one hand, and tapped Rasel's arm. "We'll call this one a draw, then."

Rasel sighed. "But I was winning."

"I would have beaten you with my next card," Nadrian replied, a mischievous glint in his eyes.

Rasel rolled his eyes. "Because you're cheating."

Suri folded her arms, shaking her head in disbelief. "Really, Nadrian? You're playing cards with him?"

Nadrian stood and pocketed the cards, giving her a purposefully obtuse look. "What would you prefer I play with him?"

"Nothing at all?" she suggested.

He widened his eyes. "But then I'd have to talk to the man."

"I'm right here," Rasel said.

"I know that. If I said it behind your back, that would be cruel gossip," Nadrian told him. Then he turned back to her, and his expression sobered a little. "Are you... Do you want me to stay?"

She waved her hand. "No, I'll be fine. Get some rest while you can."

"Have you got everything you need?"

She took the two small glass bottles from her trouser pocket. "Two vials of Fae blood and a terrible plan."

"We've had worse odds," he said.

"Have we?"

"I don't know," Nadrian replied. "It just felt like a nice thing to say."

She couldn't help it, she laughed despite it all. He smiled back at her and opened his arms. She stepped into them and it turned from friendly to sombre in a moment, both of them holding on too long.

When Suri pulled back, she gave him her best attempt at a stern look. "Take care of yourself. You're a King now, you have people waiting for you."

He tapped her nose. "And you, Suri. Try not to do anything too stupid."

"No promises."

Nadrian shook his head as he opened the door. "At least you're honest."

"Can I ask you something?" Suri asked after nearly two hours of silence.

Rasel slid his eyes over to her. "I can't exactly leave."

"Why the blood bond? Why would you link our lives?"

She'd wanted to ask since she first understood what he'd done to her. And what better time to ask when they were both probably on the verge of death.

Rasel closed his eyes, weariness falling over his expression. But he answered her nonetheless. "Kol never liked me. Even before you stole Viantha from the Storm Pan, he wanted me dead. I knew it was only a matter of time before he came for me. But he seemed to care for you, since he rescued you from the Altar. Say what you like about the Demon King, I knew he would protect his own, and so he wouldn't kill me if we were linked.

I obviously had no idea just how *much* the man cared for you, which was an unexpected boon."

"But you never expected Sotoledi would drain you dry."

"Obviously," Rasel drawled.

His cravat still looped around his neck. Someone must have done that after they cleaned him, and she wondered if it was at his request or for their own sake, so no one had to see the mess of skin beneath it. Her own memory of it was hazy, but she remembered the jagged, torn lines on his neck. Had Sotoledi done that? "When did you give him your soul?"

"Maybe ten years ago, when I was around your age."

She frowned. "Why?"

"Because he asked me to," he said simply, a hint of dark humour trickling into the words.

"What did he offer you?"

"Exactly what you would expect. Power, riches, glory."

She curved her brow. "Not enough to make you heir."

Rasel's face soured. "Ressa wanted any excuse. She never liked me, even as a child. Even when I tried to prove my worth to her, again and again. She never saw my value."

"Did Lera?"

Rasel met her studying appraisal head on. "Yes."

Suri sniffed. "She saw how she could use you for her own means."

"Don't act so high and mighty," he spat. "I could say the very same of you. When have you ever treated me as anything but a tool."

She opened her mouth to reply, but found she had no answer. He had a point. In the desert, she had lied to him and Manira to gain passage across the desert. She had approached him the night of Scilla's raid, not out of love for him, but to use his body for some semblance of comfort. Then in the Seat of Drameir, what had she done? Flirted with him to distract him, stole back her earrings, sold them back to him to buy her freedom. Her trip to his manor had been for the sole purpose of learning his way to bring someone back from the dead. To take his secrets by any means necessary.

She had treated him as something to use at every single opportunity.

Rasel didn't seem to get any satisfaction from her silence. He merely sneered at her. "See? You are not so different."

Suri was about to respond, to argue that he was using her just as readily, when her seeing silk eyepatch spoke to her.

"It's happening."

She blinked and focused on the sound of his voice. "Kol?"

He came into focus, and through his eyes she saw it all. The men writhing at the edge of the white fog, their skin covered in boils blossoming all across their skin, spreading like fungus, distorting them.

Kol gagged. "Lera just sent two hundred troops into the mists."

She could only see ten, those at the edge, not fully obscured by the fog's maw. Suri covered her mouth. "Oh, fuck."

"If you're going, it has to be now, Lera will start channelling them soon," Kol said.

Suri nodded, her stomach churning. "I'm with Rasel, we'll go now."

"Get his soul, and come back to me. Steal it from under his fucking nose." Kol turned away from the sight below, turned back towards the ruined city, looking out to the sea beyond the cliffs. Somewhere, on an island far in the distance, beyond his vision even on the clearest days, was Akdaria. "I love you, little thief."

She bit her lip, holding back a sob. "I love you, too. And I'll see you soon."

Suri pulled the eye piece from her head and set it on the stool, breathing hard. Rasel's watchful gaze was not the sneer she expected. His face was sad, if anything. She stepped behind him and clicked the key into his wooden manacles, dropping the chain holding him into place, but not releasing the cuffs themselves. This was their deal. They would let him move freely, as he needed to in Sotoledi's world, but he would not have his ice.

Suri moved back around in front of him, appraising him warily as he groaned and pulled his arms around to his front, stretching them out and rolling his wrists.

Even like this, without his ice, he could attack her, attempt to overpower her and make a run for it. But then he would lose his only chance to save his own life. She had to believe that was what mattered to him most.

Rasel rolled his shoulders and stood, stretching out his legs. Then he held his hand out, palm outstretched. "Let's do this, then. One last play in the dark castle."

Suri pressed one vial into his hand, but she didn't release it. "Find the tower. Get your soul back before He's pulled through. I'll distract Him."

Then she sat at the edge of the room, back pressed to the wall, and took off her amefyre piece by piece, until she was left with only the eyepiece. She could already feel him, the cold grip of him and the welcoming sigh, like a breath on the back of her neck.

Rasel sat down in front of her, and unstoppered his vial of blood. He raised it up, and she let herself take two breaths, and no more. To think more would be to panic, to realise how slim the odds were.

Then she slipped the eyepiece from its socket and opened her own vial. She scrunched her good eye shut as she tipped the contents into her mouth and swallowed.

And everything went dark.

39

Today, he showed me how to read him, and I could not fathom how much he had trapped.

Unknown author, est. 2nd-5th century

Sweet, conniving Suri. You've been shutting me away, closing my eyes. Have you come to return what you stole?

"No," Suri said, the wall at her back no longer cold. It was no longer anything at all, just grey spongy resistance. The cell around her was bleaker than ever, cast in its monotone of blacks and whites. "I've come to offer my own soul. Come and find me."

Now, why would you do that?

She could still see Rasel. In this place his appearance was more shocking than ever, his hair practically glowing white, his bruising near black. He sat before her as he had a moment ago, and tried to speak, but it came out in a blur, as if he spoke to her from underwater, and she couldn't hear it.

"My reasons are my own," she replied to Sotoledi. Then to Rasel, she nudged his knee with her hand. He didn't feel like a real person, it was as if pushing against a thick shadow. "Go."

Rasel only blinked, his eyes glazed over. Was Sotoledi in his ear just as firmly? What was he saying?

Then he stood and bolted from the room.

His manacles would stop him from using his ice magic, but with no amefyre and no soul, would he even remember what he was trying to do? Would he hold onto his sanity long enough to save both their lives?

There was nothing for it. She had to trust that his self-interest would win against whatever promises Sotoledi would make in his addled mind.

I know you're not alone. I've missed my ice prince just as truly. He's been very quiet. Where have you been holding him?

Suri ignored the questioning. "You don't have enough power to come back. Rasel's soul, the other souls you have, it won't be enough. You need mine."

You don't know that.

"Neither do you. You've never crossed back over before. You're guessing. But with my soul, you would have enough power. You know you would."

And what do you wish for in return?

"Come down from your tower. Come to me, and I will give you my terms."

Sotoledi did not reply immediately. It was not silence however, but a sensation of waiting. She felt His pregnant pause as He breathed into her skull.

Tell me, do you know yet? Do you know who you are?

She shuddered. “The Seer of Time.”

Then, tell me, Seer. Is this it? Must I trust you now?

Trust her now? What did He refer to? He craved some answer from her, some certainty she had no knowledge of. She felt Him grasping into her mind, searching for some unknown thing. How long had He known she was the Seer?

She tried to shut her mind from Him, shuddering away from the scraping of claws against memory. She focused only on what she could see, on the shadows and the light. “Trust me now, and come to me.”

Suri walked out of the prison complex, finding before her the grey vista of the city.

It was unnatural to see Akdaria free of colour. It was one thing in New Politan, where the colours of the city were bleak at the best of the times with rock walls and rain-covered cobbles. The hints of life He stripped away could just as easily have been caused by the fog of morning. But here it was wrong. This was a sanctuary, a swirling green pulse of life.

And worse, His tower rose from one of the trees, curling into the black of the swirling sky overhead. He tainted every facet of her home.

Do you recall the first time we spoke?

“I was a child.”

Sotoledi laughed as thunder cracked overhead and the swirling sky darkened. Tendrils came down from the sky, seeking her. *I will come to you, as you once came to me.*

Suri did not expect Him to be so agreeable. She offered her soul, yes, but why did He trust her? He surely knew her to be on the side of life? To be against His followers, against Queen Lera.

She planted one foot on the windowsill of the prison building behind her, wedging her fingers into the grooves of two planks higher up. In her normal world, the planks would cut splinters into her hands, but here, everything was formless and fuzzy, her muscles didn't feel real, the world didn't feel real. It was a shadow of what had been. She pulled herself onto the roof of the prison and sat down, looping her arms over her knees and staring out at the realm of nothingness around her. She really didn't want to die here. If she was going to die in this war, have it be with her friends, with colour and life around her. Not in this landscape of nothing.

This place, it belonged to them, it belonged to her. She wanted to punish Sotoledi for corrupting it.

Was it all Him? Every action that Lera had taken, every betrayal, buy out and underhanded deal. Killing Cthanda, causing the Wrath, blackmailing Axri'don and getting him killed. Her own eye. How much was His influence? What would the world look like without five centuries of Sotoledi's will?

Suri could feel Him. The thrum was back, only now it didn't feel like a phantom heartbeat, pulling at her. Every thrum of this world, pulsing its darkness into hers. It felt like footsteps.

Thrum. Thrum. Thrum.

Her palms tingled. He moved towards her, she could feel it as firmly as a rope tied between His black heart and her own.

No, she decided. He spoke to her, and she had blamed Him for it once, accusing Him of causing the darkness that swayed her. But her actions were her own. His influence only existed, because people craved the darkness He promised. Greed, lust, power... He satisfied it all.

Then she heard it, a voice. The word rumbling with the thunder. A woman's voice. No, a Queen's voice. *I summon you, Sotoledi.*

The tendrils looping through the darkness shuddered. The thrumming skipped a beat. The city beneath her fell a little out of focus, as if looking at it through thick glass.

It was happening. Lera was calling to Him. The barrier between their worlds was collapsing.

Where was Rasel? Was he in the tower? She wondered if he remembered why they were there at all.

The Queen calls for me, Seer.

"Then come quicker, or die passing through."

As you say.

Once more, Suri didn't understand why He listened to her. She realised, then, she had believed her threats and demands would fall on deaf ears, that she could not truly be able to distract Sotoledi.

But He came like a lamb to slaughter, with barely any nudging. Why? Surely, He could not fathom Rasel's purpose. He would not allow himself to be drawn from the one thing that could bring Him home, for her sake.

Darkness lurched in front of her, a dark window like the void of the Gate yawning open on the roof beside her. From it, stepped Sotoledi.

Suri scrambled to her feet as He walked onto the roof beside her, His eyes as black as Agata's and as cold as Lera's.

Like Rasel, His cropped white hair glowed bright, but no bruises marked His perfect face. She remembered then, His hair in the vision of the past, down to His shoulders. When had He cut it?

I am here. Tell me, sweet Seer. What do you see for my future?

His mouth did not move. Even standing before her, He spoke into her mind.

She stared at Him.

Was this why He entertained her? He had discovered her identity and now sought to know His fortune, like she was some common street teller. "I do not have that power."

He seemed undeterred by her reply, unwavering. He only cocked His head to one side. *How long do I have left? Will I feel the rays of the sun on my face? Will I feel grass again? Will I touch a lover's skin again?*

She stepped back. "I cannot know. Why do you ask this of me?"

I have languished here for centuries on the promise of more. On the promise of an eternity. Soon, I will be free. Living once again. Was it ever really my choice?

For the first time in weeks, she heard something new in that voice. Pain, anguish. She didn't understand why He spoke to her like this, what He could possibly want from her. She knew only the past, and barely that. How could she tell this god-pretender anything He didn't already know?

She narrowed her eye, knowing she should entertain His psychosis as much as it unnerved her. This conversation was the distraction Rasel needed. "Every action you have taken is your own."

Sotoledi laughed, then. Still, His face did not move, He laughed into her mind, and she shivered, the sound of it bouncing around her bones. *Tell me. If I gifted you the blade of your own destruction, and the instructions to use it, would I be to blame if you fell upon it?*

"Why are you asking me this?"

His voice was angry now, and edged with despair. *I trusted you as you asked of me, I came to you. Answer me.*

Suri thought quickly, her heart pounding as loudly in her ears as the waves of thunder cracking the sky overhead. "You would be, in part. But the person holding the weapon always has the choice. They could have always chosen differently."

So it was free will, then? I am here because of myself.

His despondency terrified her. She didn't understand what was happening, why He thought she would have anything useful to say. He'd been alive for five centuries. How could she help Him, and why would she want to? "Your actions are your own."

And even if I would make the same ones every time, am I still choosing them?

Suri frowned.

Sotoledi gasped and took a step back. He hinged His neck back, opening His jaw wide. A dark plume of smoke rose from His gaping mouth, spiralling into the blackness all around them. He closed his mouth, meeting her gaze once more. There was no emotion there, nothing to indicate a feeling. His voice in her mind was just as empty. *Rasel has taken his soul back.*

Gods, Rasel had actually done it.

She needed to get out of there, now.

Sotoledi stepped back into the black void He'd entered from. *If that is what you came for, it is done.*

She blinked, understanding nothing of their interaction. "You're letting me leave?"

I cannot take your soul now. To do so would risk my very existence. And I do so hope to feel the sun again.

'What do you mean?"

I will see you on the other side, sweet Suri.

The blackness rocked around her, throwing her so firmly she closed her eye.

Heat warmed her skin, the rough lacquered wood of the uneven prison roof bore into her back. She sat up and saw a city enveloped in green. She was back.

Why had He allowed it?

There was no time to attempt to understand Sotoledi's words, His riddles. There was only time to run. He would be coming back any minute. Would He be summoned right into the battle? Or would He be summoned here, where they'd entered His world?

She needed to warn someone. Sotoledi would try to come through with or without the souls, and Rasel was free somewhere in the city.

Suri had only the confidence to know Rasel would not kill *her*. But loose in Akdaria, in the middle of Lera's war, who knew what he would try to do. They had beaten him, tortured him. All he needed to do was get his manacles off, and he was lethal.

Without her amefyre, her head pounded. It wasn't the normal thrumming, the whispers of dark deeds and temptation. No, it was an approaching stampede. The beat was louder and louder, whistling in her ears.

Suri pushed herself off the roof and slipped back inside the prison. She pushed past a confused-looking guard into the now empty room.

"How did you get out?" he murmured, and she could barely hear it over the din in her head. "I didn't see you two leave."

She snarled at him, pointing towards the exit. "Warn everyone, Rasel is out, and he's dangerous. Find him before he gets his manacles off."

The guard nodded and ran.

She swiped her amefyre up as the stampede became cacophonous. She placed the jewellery on and slipped the eyepiece in. The deafening noise in her head lessened to an ominous rumble.

Suri lifted the eyepatch and called towards Kol. He didn't answer right away. She called out for him again, trying to see through his silk, to hear what was going on. But there was only the rumble and the darkness.

Then the noise stopped, suddenly. The sharp relief of it hit discordantly against the sensation that something was very very wrong.

"Kol?" she tried again.

This time he heard her. "Suri? You're alive? Gods, is it done?"

"It's me. I'm alive. Rasel got his soul back."

Kol sucked in a breath. "I thought I might never hear your voice again."

The silk moved and she saw what he could see. And she could hardly believe it.

It looked like the other world. *His* world. The sky above the Parched Lands crackled with dark energy, the clouds full of storms, blocking the sun's rays entirely. Thunder broke, and lightning spurred out across the growing darkness.

Kol grimaced. "The ceremony is done. Sotoledi is pushing through."

40

My own progress is slow. He brought with him a fever which refuses to pass, and my focus is on getting him well.

Unknown author, est. 2nd-5th century

The web of wooden pathways was empty as she ran towards the Gate, as were the stairs down to the forest floor. She didn't understand why she was still alive, why Sotoledi had not pulled her soul from her chest there and then. She didn't understand His questions, nor His melancholy. She'd never heard Him like that before.

But the God of Death was coming back, and she would be damned before she let Him kill her friends.

Suri stepped through the Gate.

Again, that lurching coldness pulled at her, that dark tugging at her stomach. The echo of a woman's scream far, far away. Her body churned with it as she completed her step, finding herself back in the sandy city. She sprinted down the dusty corridor and burst through the door into the nondescript house above.

It was empty. The guards who had posed here to disguise its entrance were gone.

A peel of horns sounded from outside, warning everyone off the streets. She knew Kol was up on the cliffs, so that's where she needed to be. At his side, protecting him.

Suri ignored the horns and pushed out into the street. But here, she was not alone.

Sotoledi stood before her, standing in the empty alley.

The man, for He was a man at this moment, turned to her, His face tipped to the sky. "There is no sun."

His flesh looked pierceable, the flush of real blood gracing His cheeks. Sotoledi was back. Was He mortal?

Suri froze in the dusty street. "You have pulled the cloud here."

Thunder cracked in the grey mass overhead, a puddle of darkness swirling above, deepening like spilled ink. "Did the wind always feel like this?"

"You have pulled that here, too."

He turned slowly, His palms outstretched. "It is unnatural, this punishment. Why is grief only venerated if never acted on? Why must it be felt in the silence, in the void? If one brings someone back from the edge of death, they are a hero. If another brings someone back when that edge has already passed, that is a dark thing. Why? Why is one only a paragon of life for operating within its constraints?"

Suri had no reply.

Sotoledi lanced her with His gaze then, and she realised His eyes were no longer black, but back to how they were before. Light blue, darker at the edges of the iris, with milky white around them. "He died before me. It was supposed to be together. We created eternity within our magics, sealing ourselves in concept, and were forced to live it apart in prisons of our own creation."

Suri's head hurt. "Diophage?"

Sotoledi closed His eyes. "His love for me faded after he died. He found another that awakened him in memory and time. My love never faded. It only twisted. All the bad things I am came from the best parts of me."

She couldn't help the bubbling sympathy, but she pushed it down, her hand drifting towards her pocket.

"I am tired. I am angry," Sotoledi said. "Perhaps that's the final lesson. It is all irrelevant. We all become what the world has made us in the end."

Suri's heart leapt. She recognised this voice, this darkness, this creeping doom. She felt for the familiar handles of her knives. "You don't have to. You can change."

"No," He said. "No, I don't think I have that power."

From the black storm above, dark shadowed fingers sped down towards them. Sotoledi tipped His head back, and opened His mouth, reminding her of a young child in winter inviting the first flakes of snow onto a waiting tongue.

This was it, He wasn't going to turn back. Suri pulled both knives out and ran towards Him.

When she was less than ten feet from Him she launched the first, changing her grip on the second. It hit firmly into His chest, and she heard the sickening thunk of bone and flesh.

He didn't move, or flinch away. She closed the final step of the gap, ready to lunge and force her other knife in, and then His hand shot out, and knocked her hard.

Her body slammed down onto the ground, her ribs rattling and her head spinning. She pulled herself up, her body screaming as she forced herself into a crouch and grabbed the knife back off the floor.

Sotoledi stretched His fingers wide as the darkness descended and embraced Him. A tendril clawed into His mouth, and His body shook.

Suri stepped back and thought of Kol. "Kol, He's here. He's back. I couldn't stop Him."

"Shit. Where is he? Where are you?"

"The Gate. The Gate inside the city."

"He's behind the mists?" Kol choked, his question answering itself as he saw through her eye. "I'll do what I can."

Sotoledi's feet came off the ground as she lost the connection with Kol.

It wasn't flight, it wasn't that same intention or grace. The tendrils pulled on Sotoledi as they surrounded Him and filled Him up, plucking His body like their puppet. He writhed, kicking like one of Waris's bodies.

His back twisted, cracking in an unnatural way, but still He didn't stop moving, His body contorted, reformed. His bones broke, elongated and stretched, filling the gaps of flesh with black wired smoke, pulling Him towards the sky.

Suri focused, trying to imagine the very centre of Him, where His heart must lie even as He spasmed and grew into something built from a nightmare.

She breathed, lifting her knife beside her face. Her heart pounded, but her aim was true. The knife glinted in the air, whistling and turning once, before implanting deep into Sotoledi's chest, or where it should have been.

And nothing. Nothing happened.

Something shifted inside her, some horrid knowledge rising to the surface. She tried to suppress it, ignoring the feeling.

The flesh body that once had been Sotoledi was now nothing but a dark wraith. Where hands had been, claws now were. His face was little more than a gaping black mouth.

Then He turned that gaping mouth towards the wall. People ran towards them, guards moving like ants across its top. Sotoledi let out a horrible croaking noise, and His tendrils shot off from Him, sliding through doors, slamming through walls. Suri stood, frozen in the street as she heard the screams. A moment later, the tendrils pulled back. A body slammed through a wall, the material giving way to the overwhelming force of the darkness pulling against it.

Eight bodies.

She scanned them, trying to work out if she recognised any of them, but she was barely able to see each face before Sotoledi dragged them into His body, feeding them into His widening maw.

This was the feeling. This was the thing she didn't know how to watch. She was useless. Sotoledi had come back. And now everyone was going to die.

He wasn't killing her. She didn't understand why. Maybe He knew that making her watch was somehow worse.

Sotoledi pulled ten more from their homes. With each gaping screech, each movement, He expanded and became more and more monstrous.

The tendrils grew, becoming pillars of darkness which broke through wall after wall, pulling flesh back through into an ever growing phantom. Suri struggled to find anything left of the man who had stood before her only a handful of minutes ago.

The huge mouth, bigger now than her entire height, swivelled to look down at her. One of the giant arms reached for her then, and she ran. But it was faster and stronger, and she only made it two scrambled steps before its iron grip clutched her, raising her weight off the ground.

He pulled her in close and she didn't make a noise, paralysed by the impending sensation of her own death. Something halfway between fog and smoke emanated from the hole in His face. But He did not consume her.

He only held her there, locked in the consuming black, her arms pinned to her side as it gripped her from hip to shoulder. She could not move, could barely think.

He started moving then, the thin tendrils now stomping legs. Eight of them attached back to that grotesque body, like some sort of insect, skittering across their world. He did not drop her, nor eat her. He held her beside Him like a toy, as His legs broke through the roofs of the ruined city, lurching Him towards the city wall and the mists beyond.

Screams filled the air as He lifted another body, throwing it into the aching hole. She caught the eye of the woman, someone she'd never seen before. She saw the terror as she died.

Then something dived straight for them. A bird? No. Suri flinched, but had no hand to shield herself with. She felt the brush of a feather as the constriction around her loosened. Suri opened her eye to see Nadrian whipping back around for another attempt.

The Fae King circled around, dodging one of the giant insect arms. Another flailed towards him and he ducked it, diving in again. He swept towards her, and she saw the glint of a sword before he plunged it deep into the knuckle of the arm holding her, wrenching it out again as he passed.

The hold on her loosened, and she thought it might drop entirely, but it reformed around her. Nadrian circled again.

"Leave me," she called to him.

"Fuck you," he yelled back.

"Get them out," Suri said. "He won't kill me. I don't know why but He won't."

"Suri—"

"Get as many people out as you can. Kol, Vi, Scilla. Please."

Nadrian hesitated in the air. She could tell he was about to go. There was a hint of a reluctant smile on his face. She could almost hear the grumbled acquiescence now.

But she never did.

Because a tendril ripped through him so fast it tore through his very body.

His face contorted with shock, and then nothing at all, as the arm ripped back through the hole in his chest and let him fall twenty feet to the floor below.

Suri didn't know if she screamed. She couldn't hear anything. Everything in that moment had stopped. She felt her body moving as the insect moved on. It wasn't real. She felt the air on her cheek, and yet her world had stopped turning.

It was a sick joke. Just a sick joke.

No.

Nadrian couldn't be dead.

He wouldn't die without a quip, without some sardonic line. It wasn't real. That wasn't supposed to be it.

The next time she felt capable of understanding her world again, the gaping mouth beside her was as big as a small house, and someone was screaming at her.

Suri blinked, her mind far from her body, her heart in suspension. It took a while for her ears to stop ringing, for her to understand what was happening.

Then she heard him. Kol.

He was shouting. The silk. The silk was still on her eye.

"Suri, please talk to me," he said.

"I'm here," she lied. She'd never felt less *here* in her life.

"Thank the fucking Above," he said. "What happened?"

"Nadrian—"

"Don't," Kol interrupted, his voice empty. "I saw. We need to get you free."

"You can't," Suri said. "He tried. Please, just leave me."

"Can't do that," he said. "We're already here."

Suri focused, and saw he was telling the truth. From his vantage, it was truly horrifying.

Two dozen guards fanned across three roofs in Sotoledi's path between Him and the city wall. Despite their added height, the beast was huge. There was nothing known to their world that could begin to describe it. Its body, for it no longer resembled anything of a man, was a huge rounded shifting black mass of twisted claws and ebony vines, pulsating. From it, nearly twenty offshoots now plunged and writhed like legs beneath it, each the width of two men.

And there, next to its heaving and rumbling cavern of a jaw, was a small white figure, dark hair whipping in the wind, barely visible in its clutches. Her, through his eyes. A girl in a storm.

She shuddered back into her own sight, seeing Kol and his small retinue of elite guards manning the roofs below. They looked pitifully easy to crush.

And yet, when the first leg lanced down, they dodged it, and three of them managed to slice into it at once. She heard the beast beside her shriek and pull the leg back.

"You hurt it," Suri said in wonder.

"Just hold tight, little thief," Kol said. "I'll make sure you're safe again."

They lanced another leg, and then another. Soon, Sotoledi had pulled four of His legs back, a low hiss escaping Him.

Then it was quiet, and she could not breathe. Her ears filled and her vision swayed.

Water. Water encased her head and shoulders, gripping around the blackness.

Steam bubbled all around her, and she shut her eye as she felt the water heat. The grip of the beast loosened as Suri struggled to hold her breath. She had not breathed deeply before it surrounded her, and even the few seconds were enough to make her chest feel tight.

Yet her legs were dry.

Viantha.

Viantha must have created a bubble of water around her, much like she had around Rasel. The tendrils trembled around her. She felt their need to escape the water, to get out of the substance as quickly as it could.

The grip loosened again, and her body slumped downwards.

Then she was free.

She fell through the bubble, and into the air. Her right shoulder hit something, and glanced off it, and then she landed heavily on the roof of a building.

Her ears rang, her breath was quick in a winded ribcage. But she was alive, and the horrifying insect passed by above her, blocking out the remaining light and hissing as another one of its legs was sliced.

She sat up, quickly taking inventory of her injuries. She'd hit some sort of fabric roof before hitting the stone, and it had broken her fall a little.

Suri stood, her ankle painful but bearable, her ribs would be bruised too, but she could move. She couldn't see Viantha, but she laid eyes on Kol. He was only two rooftops away, and running towards her. He leapt from one roof to another. She moved to the edge, waiting for him.

She watched him look to his left and saw him stop.

Suri followed his line of sight.

No.

A black arm of darkness raised Viantha into the air.

Suri couldn't watch. So she watched Kol instead, and it was worse. She saw him flinch, saw her death ripple across his face. Any twinkle of hope or defiance left in his expression died.

A Daughter of the Earth, a key to life magic, dead. The woman Scilla loved, gone. Nadrian alone was too much, far too painful for Suri to bear, but this loss, this had ruined any hope they had for the future, for bringing life back to these barren lands.

Kol looked at her then, and the ghostly expression on her face made her mind up as surely as anything.

This was too much loss. This could not be borne.

She was so useless. Weaponless and fragile. But she had something no one else had.

Time.

There had to be some way she could use it.

Suri started running. She ran to the edge of the roof and gripped its ledge, finding a windowsill to clamber down to before dropping to the dust.

Kol called to her but she kept moving. She needed to get somewhere away from the fight, somewhere where she could think and focus. Maybe she could change this, reverse it all before she was lying dead, too. Before the grief caught up to her and made her blind.

Cthanda had warned her she was on a dark path, telling her not to change the past. But how was she supposed to live with this? Supposed to bear it? She had to do something. Surely, there was some tweak she could make, something that would prevent all of this horror.

She would fall at Cthanda's feet and beg her for her help. She was supposed to help her son bring life back to this world, she couldn't let half the Life Court die. Cthanda would help.

"*Nen alerisee f'ith sotele.*"

The words floated around her. Kol spoke to her, a whispered call.

"I have to do this," she replied.

"Whatever it is you feel you must do, I will not stop you. Just know that I must do the same."

"Kol?"

"There is nothing I wouldn't do to keep you safe," he said.

Suri jumped over a pile of debris, ignoring the still hand she saw beneath it. None of this was real, she would change it. "I'm going to fix it."

"I'm happy I got to love you, before the end," he said. "I hope we find a way to survive this."

Then she couldn't see him anymore, couldn't hear him. He must have put down the seeing silk. Suri stopped dead and turned, searching for him on the rooftops just as a tendril slammed towards her.

She dived, throwing herself to the floor as it pounded through the wall behind her. Rubble fell over her as she crawled forwards, the dust coating her lungs. The tendril ripped back and away, holding someone in its grip.

Suri didn't look, couldn't look. She couldn't risk recognising them.

She kept moving, scanning for Kol.

Instead she saw something else, flying over the mist-locked wall. Her heart leapt, caught with a stiff hope of it being Nadrian. But it wasn't. The wings were not golden, but pink, and the look on its bearer's face was nothing short of triumphant.

Queen Lera. In flight.

Sotoledi's power had made her whole. Was the harpy still under those wings? Was this just a better mask? Or was she now the beautiful ageless winged queen in flesh as well as glamour?

She found Kol, then. He was in the path of the all-consuming beast, shirtless, his torso a blank canvas against the clawing darkness all around him. There was only one reason why he would have removed his tunic.

He disappeared in a swirl of darkness and reappeared again, stepping out of shadow on top of the rumbling beast. She saw his back, bleeding from where he'd ripped out every last chunk of amefyre. His battle cry joined the wail of the black formation he rode.

He was not the Son of Life at this moment. No. This was the Prince of Death, trying to kill the one who had shackled his soul for eighty years, the one who had sunk His claws into every part of him.

There was no silverwood to contain Kol, no cell, no constraint on his power. The monster and the man painted themselves against the sky, and then the battle began.

He was choosing to lose himself. He would risk everything human left in him, his life, his morality, his very self, in order to fight Sotoledi. To protect them all.

Suri's own anger rose like a bile in her throat. It was as hot as fire, the coals of it waiting for a spark and finding it now.

She now knew exactly where she was running, and what she would do when she got there. She wasn't going to allow this to happen.

How was it that those who chose to follow Sotoledi could destroy every facet of her world? They could break every single little rule. Every moral. They used blood and souls as playthings, and massacred hundreds in pursuit of their goals. And because of it, because they didn't follow the rules, they were going to win.

Who did the rules help? Why did she ever listen?

She was livid with everyone else playing at Gods, everyone else who turned the world to their own meaning. What was the use in the power to change anything if you weren't able to use it?

Suri reached the empty stables and burst inside.

Ruben watched her as if he'd been waiting for her to arrive.

Suri leapt over to him, and he didn't move. She touched a hand to his nose and he breathed softly into it. Something about that feeling made her want to break entirely. Soft, warm air tickling her hand. Reassurance even as the world outside the stable window fell apart, as the aching yawn of the beast killed the city.

The beast was slowing, though.

Kol crouched atop it, holding his hand to its body, and the body began to writhe. The legs flailed, some extinguishing into smoke, others pausing their relentless feeding to stabilise it. Two reached upwards, grabbing fast towards Kol.

Then he flashed away again into smoke and appeared on the other side of the beast. Again, he held his hand at the beast and it writhed, letting out a shriek so high-pitched she could barely hear it. Whatever Kol was doing, however much death he was forcing into that beast, it was hurting Him, but it wasn't stopping Him fast enough.

When Queen Lera swooped towards Kol, Suri's anger shifted into something worse. Something that bubbled and burnt. Something had been growing since she was a child. An all-consuming bitterness.

It was there before Sotoledi, before she ever killed Clacker. It was there from the beginning, because it was her. But it was different this time, because she wasn't powerless anymore.

When she saw Kol fall, his arms stretched towards the black sky above like a fallen star as his body plummeted to his dying city below, her resolve only hardened.

Something had given her power. Something had allowed her to become this, someone with the power to change the world.

And she was going to use it.

She stroked Ruben's nose. Then she took a shuddering breath, laced with every foul emotion she'd ever had to know, and slipped into that first relic.

This was her world, too.

41

His health worsens, and the doctor tells me he doesn't have long. It cannot be so, there is no sun in a world without him.

Unknown author, est. 2nd-5th century

Suri ran as the field materialised around her, crossing its sun-baked grasses and long-stemmed daisies without a downwards glance. She paused in front of where the spectre of Diophage would appear, breathing heavily. She refused to look down at Cthanda: she didn't want to find Kol in her features or speak with the woman who told her not to use this power. It was hers.

Her hand shook with rage as she tried to keep a rein on her anger and failed.

As soon as a hint of him appeared, Suri focused on her breath and closed her eye. Her rage was honed into such a sharp point, so fine a purpose, that the world slipped away in an instant.

When she appeared again in front of the stone cottage, her blood boiled ever hotter. The people in that room had taken everything from so many people.

It ended today.

Sotoledi would die here. Five hundred years of torment, over. He didn't want to live without Diophage? Fine. He shouldn't live at all.

She didn't know what her actions would change, but He had done enough. Taken enough. How many had Lera killed in His name?

Suri didn't stop, didn't think, letting her twenty years of rage, embedded deep within her, spring to the surface. It was deeper than her blood, this anger. Losing her soul had not taken it. No ancient magic could survive in the face of her ruined happiness, and she would ruin the world with it.

She pulled open the door as two men stared at the woman in white. She'd just finished saying something that Suri had not caught.

"Who are you?" Diophage asked, childish wonder alight in his eyes.

Suri ignored the people and focused on her surroundings. She needed to work out how she had knocked that cup before. There must be some extra level, some way of forming herself. From the doorway, she spied a bread knife on the counter behind Sotoledi. She took one step, and then faltered.

The woman in white replied to the men. "There will come a time when you will meet me again. I won't know you at first. But you will have to trust me again before the end. Follow what I have said today, and you will live for hundreds of years."

No.

Why?

It didn't make sense.

She knew that voice.

Then the woman in white turned and stared *through* her to the door beyond. Suri staggered back a step, stumbling back from the door.

Her hair fell in soft waves to the bottom of her ribcage. Under the veil, a soft mauve painted her lips and her one silver eye was shadowed with brown.

She looked at peace and healthy. But it was her. The woman in white, the one who told Sotoledi and Diophage about amefyre.

Herself.

How? *Why?*

It was a bucket of water across the fire burning up her skin.

Suri couldn't fathom it. She watched herself leave the cabin, striding towards the treeline. She had to know, she had to understand.

Suri trailed after her, her hand raised to grab her own arm. But she only wafted through it.

No. Why couldn't she do it now? Why couldn't she do anything? Suri tried again, tried to pull at the woman, shout at her, hit her, trip her. The woman only kept walking, her pace steady as they dropped out of the sight of the cottage and into the trees.

Suri screamed. She knew her grasp on this land was fading, the pain in her head slowly ramping. And she'd done nothing, achieved nothing.

She ran after herself. She scrambled at the floor, desperate. Maybe she could pick up a stone from the ground to throw it. Something. Anything.

The woman stopped dead in the centre of the path.

Suri froze, watching her.

"I cannot see you, or hear you. But if you are here, as I once was, listen to me now."

Once more, Suri's very world tipped on its axis as her own self addressed her. Why would she have done this? Was she herself responsible for all of it? Had she created Sotoledi and Diophage? The questions pummelled her, racing her mind with the one repeating motif. Why? "I don't understand—"

"I know what has happened, and what you must change," she interrupted, speaking over Suri in such a way it was clear she had not heard her. "But if you change this moment, you lose it all. This has to happen, all of it, exactly this way, for the world to exist as it has. Without Sotoledi, Kol would have never given up his soul, if he even existed at all. Barsen would have never been there that night. Think it through. Without everything that has come to pass, you would never have found love."

Suri watched her own back, her own shaky breath shuddering her shoulders.

"This is the path Cthanda warned you about. This is the change we are destined to make. We created this world, more than we ever realised. I am selfish. Maybe you will make a different choice when the time comes."

Suri's grip on this moment was warping, the trees around her whistling with an unnatural breeze, the high-pitched whine hurting her ears.

"To change what really needs to change, to stop Sotoledi before he kills those you love, remember why you're doing it," her voice told her. "Diophage was always driven by love. So, too, is his magic. If you want to use it, let your love drive you and not your hate. Your time magic has always been strongest when Kol is by your side. That is no coincidence. Think of his love, think of him. Change the outcome."

Suri's voice broke out of her as the world sucked away. That same, never ending question. "Why?"

Suri gasped, finding herself pulled back to the world she could not believe was real. She lay on her back, the horse watching her from above. Ruben nickered, his hooves stomping with distress.

"I'm fine," Suri lied.

He dragged his hoof against the wood of the stable door again. She stared out of the window. Sotoledi had reached the city wall and was picking bodies from its top.

The mist was gone. In the time she'd been in there, something had disrupted it. The city would be overrun in minutes.

All she could hear was screams. Was anyone she loved left? Jem? Scilla?

It hardly mattered. Kol was nowhere to be seen, and the doors into the city were buckling under the weight of the siege beyond it.

Suri pulled herself up, and opened Ruben's stall door. The intelligent creature stared down at her.

"You should go," she said. "I don't know if I can change it, but I'm going to try. If I can't, you need to run through the gates as soon as there's a gap. They'll be in the city soon, you might make it through."

Ruben watched her. Something in his expression made her certain he understood her.

But he didn't move.

"Go on," she said, hitting his back lightly with her palm. "Get out of here."

Ruben huffed, and sat down beside her, folding his legs up and lying on the floor. If a Roanhadham could look exasperated, this one did.

"Fine," Suri said, sitting back down and leaning against his warmth. The stable roof shook as a tendril ripped into its adjoining building. She took a deep breath.

She had to change this now, before He grabbed her again, before Lera could find her. If they killed her, this would be all the world ever was.

Diophage created relics with love. She had to seek out love.

Even the thought of Kol made her want to cry. Somewhere soul deep, she knew he was dead, and the knowledge of it nearly crippled her. She would usually push that away, repress the horrible surge of emotion threatening to choke her. But she didn't. She allowed herself to feel the love she had for him. Even tainted with grief, she still found some joy in it.

He was the only one who had truly known her darkness, and loved her all the same. The warmth of his arms, the security of being in his presence. He would never let her fall, not if there was something he could do about it.

Gods, she loved him. She didn't know what to be without him. Before him, she'd had purpose, but everything she'd ever done served her.

Had she really changed, though?

She sat here now, trying to do the one thing Cthanda told her not to do. Mess with her own past, just to create an existence where Kol was still alive, where the man she now needed more than air was back.

Maybe falling in love had made her more selfish than ever.

She thought of the last time they'd spoken, before it all went wrong. Sat in that cell, him telling her he loved her. The hope that it wouldn't be a final goodbye, his faith that she'd make it back.

Outside, the noise of splintering wood, and a huge creak. A low cheer in the distance and the sound of approaching metal. The army was through the city gate. They were coming.

Suri's eye drifted closed.

If this was the end, at least she had something to think fondly of.

Ruben's body was replaced by something hard and cold. She opened her eye, turning her head to find a wall at her back. She swivelled back, taking in the prison cell around her just as Rasel and her other self both disappeared.

This was it, the moment she'd been thinking of, the last minute of calm before it all went to shit. She was here again.

Suri stood, holding the wall for support. It chilled her palm. This wasn't a shadowed world, a muted and feelingless version of some past event. She could *feel* it, just as she could in Lartosh.

Did that mean?

She strode over to the table where she'd left her eyepatch before going under. Her fingers shook as she reached for the cloth.

The silk folded under her fingers, its soft fabric still a little warm. Her breath escaped her in a cry. She was here. She was really here.

How could she change it? How could she fix what had happened? They needed a warning, they needed time.

She remembered how Viantha's bubble of water had made the beast scream. Maybe that was the solution, maybe they couldn't defeat death with more death.

She placed the eyepatch over her eye, her voice thick with emotion. "Kol?"

The slight pause made her stomach turn. Was he dead here, too? Was it already too late? Could she really change the past?

"Suri? What's wrong? I thought you were—"

"No time," she interrupted, her voice strangled as she swallowed back the tears. Even the sound of his voice made her want to collapse. But she couldn't, she had to change it before it was all too late. He was alive here, but not for long, death was coming for him. She would not survive watching him die again. She couldn't let it happen. "It's Sotoledi, He's going to appear by the Akdarian Gate. You have to end Him as soon as He comes out."

"How—"

"You only have minutes," she said, cutting him off again despite how much she needed his voice in her ear. "Get Viantha and Scilla and get there *now*. Use life magic. He seems weaker to it."

"We're on our way."

Suri gasped in a breath and started running for the Gate as she had before. Her other self must be in Sotoledi's world right now, talking to Him. Was it enough? Was it enough to warn them?

She ran, her heart pounding. Maybe if she got there fast enough, she could lay a trap for Him, too. What would happen to her, when her other self arrived? Would she just disappear, as she had in Lartosh? How did she know when she was done? How long could she hold on?

The questions muddied her mind, her confusion spiralling her head as her feet pounded over the wooden bridge.

Please, let it be enough. She didn't know if she had the energy to keep going back. She was so tired. So drained. With every blink she saw Nadrian's death. With every breath she saw the light die in Kol's eyes as Viantha was consumed by death.

This would end differently. Please, please, please.

Once again, Suri burst from the cell, and the guard looked at her with curiosity, but did not question her. She ran for the Gate. Maybe if she could get there before Sotoledi, she could block the Gate, or kill Him before He changed into the monster. Something, anything.

Minutes later, the Gate appeared through the green forest at her feet, as she leapt over a root and back into that clearing. A strange sensation came over her as she looked at the Gate. Something foreboding, worse than normal. It was just a step, and then it would be over.

Suri took a deep breath and walked into the Gate.

And felt it tear her apart.

42

He is gone. The rain falls on the roof and I cannot understand it. She promised we would live for centuries.

Unknown author, est. 2nd-5th century

Suri was weightless, her body suspended in a nothingness that clawed at her even as it refused to let her go.

Every part of her was wrenched in an agony she'd never felt before. If she had limbs, if she had a body, it was as if they were being pulled from her repeatedly, second after second she was reformed and torn apart.

A voice reverberated as it punished her eternally. *Only one can pass through.*

The echo of the scream in the Gate's void now was not quiet. It was all consuming. It tore into her ears before she realised that it was not an echo.

It was Suri's own voice.

She begged everything for it to stop, for it to kill her instead. She couldn't live with this torture, the constant pain of a thousand deaths without the solace of the end.

A lifetime passed there, or was it several? Or was it only an hour, a minute? A second. She did not know. She hardly knew her own self anymore, there was no thought but that the pain had to stop.

Something passed through her, some other body, something foreign to her, and she flinched from it, not able to do anything as it ripped through her.

Then, time later, a thousand more deaths of pure agony later, another body stepped into her world of endless suffering.

Surely another lifetime had passed, but just as surely only another second.

This one she knew as her own. This one she reached for, grabbed at, clutched around the waist and pulled herself within. Clawing, aching, reforming.

Suri fell through the Gate back into the City of the Damned. She screwed her eye tight, unable to believe that the pain was over. Her body felt normal, but she knew that could not be true.

She panted, not knowing what day it was, what time she was in.

Eventually, Suri opened her eye. She looked at herself, expecting a mangled mass of flesh. But she was unmarred. She didn't know how it was possible. She had felt every part of her flayed away, every inch of skin torn and boiled. How could she be whole?

She heard a shout from outside and flinched. But it wasn't the voice of an aching beast, it wasn't the crack of thunder.

It was Scilla. Scilla was outside.

Suri pulled herself to her feet, once more shocked that her body did as she intuited. She moved like she always had, as if nothing had happened. But some part of her had been ripped away in that Gate. Maybe a version of her was still in there, suffering and clawing for eternity, because she had decided she could not live in that other world.

She pushed open the door at the end of the corridor, a souldeep fear rising within her as she climbed the steps. Please, please, please.

The pounding of her own heartbeat pulsed in her ears, saliva coated her mouth. Nausea mixed with dread as she opened the door.

She stopped still, and a tear rolled down her cheek.

Sotoledi was there again.

The man in the dusty, empty street, as those same horns blared out around them, warning the people inside. Except this time, He did not wait ready to coat her ears with riddles and nonsense.

His body was off the ground, suspended in a bubble of water, and He thrashed.

Something burst through a wall, and Suri had the sickening feeling it was one of His tendrils, but then it wrapped around Sotoledi's wrist, hard. She saw it for what it truly was. A vine. Four more burst from the sand around Him, securing His other wrist, His ankles and encircling His neck, holding Him deep in the embrace of life.

Pure creation. Life in the desert.

Suri found them. Viantha, Scilla and Kol stood on the flat roof of the building across, holding hands.

Kol's eyes flicked from Sotoledi and took her in. He smiled in relief, as the morning sun framed his dark curls like a deity. Then he did what he was born to do.

Kol shone. He closed his eyes, his lips still turned upwards in the hint of a smile as he raised his free arm. Then the light poured from him as if he were the sun itself.

Suri steadied herself on the doorframe as she watched him until her eye started to ache from the blinding light. Then she watched him some more. Finally, she turned her eye back to Him.

The light had hit Sotoledi, the rays penetrating in His watery prison and streaming onto His body. He thrashed harder but the vines held Him firm. The water poured into Him and the water started to bubble, heating as His pale skin turned to ash in the light of the Son of Life.

Sotoledi looked at her, then.

The man, the fae, the god, the beast. Her tormentor, and at times, her only friend.

He watched her with an expression that cut her to her very bones. Confusion, as if He was nothing more than a boy lost in a wood. Sadness and betrayal, as if she was the one who had killed Him. Recognition, that she was the one who had made Him.

She looked for relief, but found none.

His body fell apart, and all she could think was how He had got His wish. He had felt the sun on Him, before the end.

Then He was gone.

Consumed, nothing but wet ash in water. The vines had no purchase. The light had no target. All that remained within, was a hint of purple light.

"Hold the water," Kol said as he jumped down. He approached the orb of water, then reached a small glass object into it. The purple light dimmed, and Kol closed the contraption. It was only when he extracted it again that Suri was able to understand. He'd used one of Waris' soul cages.

Kol stood, holding a prism of magically-created water and the soul of a quasi-god. And then he laughed. He raised his voice, projecting it into his silk. "Nadrian?"

"Tell me it's good news."

Hearing Nadrian's voice through the silk broke what little resistance she had left.

Suri exhaled a wavering breath, no longer able to fight the sob that escaped.

Kol looked at her with love and confusion. "The God of Death is no more. Unleash everything we have on Lera's men."

43

I feel him everywhere. I know he is somewhere, if only I could reach it. Our story isn't over, it cannot be.

Unknown author, est. 2nd-5th century

Suri's legs buckled and she crumpled to the ground.

She sat holding her knees, every nerve in her body needing to throw herself at someone, to feel the world and believe that this was real, but raw emotion rendered her unable to move.

Something had changed within her. It was as if a small serpent had lived inside of her for her whole life, deep in her very bones, and now it had died. Whatever it fed off, whatever it needed, died with it.

Scilla and Viantha clambered down from the roof as Kol stared at the soul in the glass with an odd look on his face. She remembered him as a boy, standing before the dark tower, holding his own soul.

She rocked forwards, her hands shaking. "What just happened?"

Kol turned towards her, his grin radiant. "You're brilliant. How did you know Sotoledi would appear here?"

Suri stared at each of their faces. "He is dead. You're alive. You're all alive."

Kol knelt beside her. He touched her hand and she grabbed onto him, pulling herself into his lap as he let out a surprised groan.

Gods, he *felt* real. He smelt real, that same mixture of rain and embers she'd adored from the first intoxicating moment. His arms came around her, loving and secure, and that felt real too.

Kol smiled against her hair. "Because of you. Because you can see the future. You told us where to be, you saved us."

"No," Suri said. "It wasn't the future. It happened. I saw it... I lived it, it happened. You died—you all—"

"I'm alive, little thief," he said, stroking her hair. "You warned us, we're all here. It's all fine. I'm so glad you're here. I thought I might lose you."

Scilla nodded to her as she dusted sand off her knee. "Yeah, thanks for the heads up."

"I didn't warn you of the future, though," Suri said, her voice oddly high. "I changed the past."

Kol laughed, the noise free from the horrors of what should have happened here. No. That was a nightmare. This was the truth, *this* was what should have happened. "Does it matter?"

"I don't know." Her insides were scraped hollow, her emotions were a war of ecstasy and devastation. She pushed herself an arm's length back and stared into Kol's eyes. "Are you sure you feel normal?"

"Normal? Not at all," he said. Suri's heart pounded as she searched his face for pain, injury. But he just smiled, and his eyes danced with constellations like they had back in the Fae Glen, as if tens of stars were locked in his gaze. "In this arm I have the woman I love, somehow the most powerful Seer of Time there has ever been."

Suri scoffed.

"In the other," he lifted his hand up behind her. "I'm holding the soul of an ancient fae who has been venerated as a God for hundreds of years. It's not really my normal state."

They had actually done it. She had done it. The world was right again, and she was in Kol's arms. The beast was never here. She pressed a kiss to his mouth. "I've got a story to tell you later."

Kol kissed her back, his hand gripping her neck. "I look forward to hearing it."

A slow clap came from the doorway behind Suri.

She flinched, swivelling in Kol's lap as Scilla drew her sword.

The dark, poison-laced voice came next. "Touching, but aren't you all forgetting something?"

Rasel stood, watching them with a combination of bemusement and irritation. With no manacles.

"Get behind me," Kol said, moving Suri by the waist as he stood in front of her protectively.

Viantha raised a hand but her brother only raised his arms.

Rasel tutted. "Relax, relax. I'm not going to try anything with all of you here, how stupid do you think I am?"

Suri stumbled to her feet.

Scilla spat on the floor at his feet. “How stupid do you think it would be to trust you, now that you have what you want?”

“Fair,” Rasel said. “But still, why are you all acting like this fight is already won? Lera’s still breathing. Just across your walls, there’s a whole army there waiting for you.”

“I’ve given the order for the men to attack.”

“They’re fighting?” Rasel asked, and something ravenous took over his expression as he took a step towards the wall.

“Where do you think you’re going?”

Rasel blinked. “Where you should all be going. To kill Lera. The moment she realises Sotoledi is dead, she’ll run for her precious green hills.”

Kol pressed his hand to the man’s chest.

Rasel sneered at him. “What’s it going to be? You can’t kill me. If I try to hurt anyone else, those two will have me on the floor before I even breathe.” He pointed to Scilla and Viantha. “Let’s go kill the bitch, once and for all.”

Suri folded her arms. “I hate to say it, but I agree. We need to pay Waris for the mists. If Lera leaves now, we might never get this chance again.”

Kol sighed. “I *did* promise her death to Nadrian. The more the fucking merrier, I guess.”

He dropped his barring hand, but didn’t move, and Rasel stepped around him. With Rasel in the lead, Scilla and Viantha watching his every move, and Kol and Suri taking the rear, they walked in a strange procession through the tangled mess of sandy alleys as the horns still blared overhead.

Soon, they turned onto the main street. It was empty. Yesterday, this had heaved with people, queuing for rations, refilling their canteens from the well. Now, everyone hid inside their homes, hoping the siege would end peacefully.

No huge beast shadowed overhead and already the storm clouds were clearing. It was eerily quiet, so much so that they could hear the tumbling of a single piece of paper as it skittered across the road ahead of them in the light wind.

It was a straight shot from here to the city gates.

Suri cleared her throat. "Queen Lera can fly now, so she might be a little harder to kill. Keep an eye on that mistline."

They all looked at her, bewildered.

Scilla narrowed her eyes. "Since when?"

"That," Suri said, a wary hint of a smile ghosting across her mouth. "Is a very confusing question to answer."

Kol grabbed her hand. "Oh great, she's doing it already. Less than two months in the role and the Seer is talking in riddles."

Viantha smirked, her eyes on the city wall ahead of them. "Let's go kill a queen."

Scilla touched the water princess' shoulder lightly. "*Asari ith vulturis.*"

Kol pressed a kiss to Suri's hand, and echoed the saying.

Beware the harpy. One last time.

They walked along the empty misted battlements, until they reached the manned cliff head. Here, past the mist, the battlefield below was chaos. Now that Sotoledi was gone for good, Kol's guard could try to force a retreat.

The archers rained arrows down on the hordes of troops below, but they held their shields above their heads and staved off most of the blows. The rocks came next, small boulders and pieces freed from the city gates themselves, pushed free from the cliff tops. They tumbled down, catching speed, bouncing off the jagged cliff face and slamming home into the first clutches of men.

Still the men stood.

Suri considered this was their whole plan. Take casualties in their stride, keep reinforcing the gaps with new men, and hope that the number of their living bodies would outweigh the amount of arrows the city had, or the number of boulders. Of course, she thought, they expected Sotoledi to arrive and destroy the city for good.

Shaedon and Ressa stood on the cliff head, too, watching the events with grim solemnity. Apparently the Queens killing their own men was enough evidence for Shaedon to finally fall on their side. She only hoped that went for Thandul, too.

The winds were strong, whipping their clothing and forcing them to shout to be heard by one another. Sotoledi's storm had not disappeared upon his death, the clouds taking their time to disperse.

Kol whistled, and Sama'yon flew to his wrist. He fastened a note to the bird's foot, and the jewel-toned king of the sky squawked, diving down into the army below.

"What did you write?" Suri asked.

Kol shrugged. "I told her Sotoledi is here. That we surrender."

"You think she'll fall for it?"

"I've learnt not to underestimate the royal need to gloat."

Nadrian folded his arms. "Based on your own experience, your Grace?"

"Fuck off, your Grace."

Nadrian laughed. "Oh, I get it now. It *is* aggravating."

"I hope that means you'll stop."

Nadrian clutched his chest. "It's like you don't know me at all."

"Archers," Scilla yelled down the line. Heads swivelled in her direction. "The Queen may soon make flight. Be ready to fire at will on my command."

"Kol's right," Rasel agreed. "If she thinks she's got you under her thumb, she won't be able to resist pressing until you break."

Viantha shuddered from behind him, her body tense as she watched her brother. The others eyed him with suspicion, too, but no one questioned his presence.

Kol grimaced. "Let's hope so."

"Is there a plan?" Shaedon asked, his face whiter than usual but his mocking tone entirely gone.

"That was my plan. Now, we kill her when she comes."

Scilla nodded. "If the archers don't get her, we can."

"Rasel could freeze her solid," Suri said. "The drop would kill her."

Kol shrugged. "So long as there's a body left for Waris to play with."

Nadrian smiled. "Well, that's a grim thought."

Ressa touched Viantha's shoulder, making her jump as she swept her eyes across the group of them. "There is a lot of power here. Let's purge this world of her."

Scilla pointed down to the encampment on the other side of the river. "Movement from the leader's tent."

Suri squinted, trying to focus her eye on the scene below. A group spoke, but it was hard to make them out. That was, until one of them moved, and she saw the back of a very large pair of wings.

"Is that her?" Shaedon asked.

A moment later she shot into the air, her pink wings stretched, pushing her deep into the sky.

"That's her," Suri breathed.

But she didn't come towards the wall. She only flew upwards from the tent, still a good five hundred feet away from the wall and the archers that manned it. Suri doubted that was a distance they could hit, and much less when it was a moving flying target.

"What's she doing?"

"Getting a line of sight above the wall," Viantha deduced. "So she can decide if you're lying about Sotoledi."

"Probably counting the number of men we have up here, too," Scilla said.

Lera gained more and more height, still not moving any closer. Maybe she wasn't so easily lured after all.

"Wish me luck, then," Nadrian said, and he dropped the glamour to his wings.

Suri noted Shaedon's soft grunt of surprise, and some gasps from the water manipulators.

"What are you doing?" Kol asked.

"Being a good subject," Nadrian said. "Acting as juicy bait."

"Don't be stupid," Suri said, swiping her hand at him in admonishment. She couldn't lose Nadrian again. Not now.

But Nadrian danced backwards and onto the very edge of the cliff. "Ah, but that's what I've always done best."

Then the Fae King smiled at them all, and stretched out his arms and fell backwards off the edge.

A moment later he appeared again, already moving faster than she could have imagined. He whipped through the air as if he was the wind himself. She hadn't realised quite how much speed he would have without carrying a passenger, and it was astonishing.

Lera still rose, and Suri realised that this could be it. If the Queen kept her eyes locked ahead, searching for Sotoledi, she may not notice his approach. Nadrian could end it, in the air, right here and right now. In seconds, it could be done, her body tumbling to the floor and hopefully squashing Lingyun in the process.

Her heart pounded in her ears as Nadrian closed the distance as fast as an arrow.

But Lera stopped. From here, Suri could not see her face. She could only notice how her wings flapped as she turned in the air.

Nadrian knocked into her, but her turn in the last second sent them both tumbling through the air before their wings righted them.

He yelled something at the Queen, but the winds were too much and Suri could not make it out. Then his golden wings flipped and he turned back towards them.

Lera gave chase.

Suri smiled. Yes, you wrinkly harpy witch. Follow Nadrian, follow him here and meet your fucking fate.

But her smile dropped as she realised two things.

First, somehow Lera was gaining on Nadrian. This must have been her first flight, and yet her wings were moving with shocking speed. Had this been another part of the deal with Sotoledi? Not only powerful and beautiful wings, but as fast as the crackling lightning?

And second, Lera was armed.

As she closed the distance to Nadrian, she pulled from her hip a bone knife with a dark blade.

Kol looked at Scilla with wide eyes. "The archers. Can you—"

Scilla stood with her hand aloft, a grim expression twisting her brow. "I can't order them to fire, they're too close together and moving too fast. He'll be hit, too."

44

A strange thing happened after my love was taken. The rock I held felt different, warmer. It is a sign. I know he is somewhere, I only need to get there.

Unknown author, est. 2nd-5th century

Suri watched in horror as Nadrian sped towards them.

Did he have any idea how close Lera was? He had a head start on their hunt, but she was close, too close. She was twenty feet from his heel, and he was over two hundred from them.

"I'm in range, you daft prick," Rasel grumbled to himself. "Duck, let me get her."

She glanced at the ice prince, and found him waiting, his hand held up in front of him and a frown on his face. If she believed him capable of any warm emotion, she might think he was concerned for Nadrian. More likely concerned the man would ruin his chance for revenge against Lera.

Nadrian only needed a few seconds, and then he could pull to the side and Lera would be right before them.

A hundred feet.

They started yelling at Nadrian to move, duck, do anything at all. The wind swallowed their words, only leaving their waving forms and terror. Nadrian must have seen, but he kept towards them, making straight for the wall.

Fifty feet.

Move, she begged him. Stop the chase, please. Rasel, Viantha, Scilla, Shaedon and Ressa were here, waiting. Duck to the fucking side.

And then he did. When he was twenty feet from the wall and she could make out the grin of anticipation and exhilaration on his face, he twisted in the air, his wings tucking in as he swanned gracefully into the start of a barrel roll.

But she had caught him. Lera's knife plunged deep into his calf as he spun. They were close enough now that Suri could see the blade was not merely dark. It was dripping with some black ichor, and as it sliced deep into the back of Nadrian's leg, she saw the liquid bubble and froth.

Nadrian's face contorted with pain.

And then he was falling. Not diving gracefully, but dropping like a boulder out of sight.

Scilla screamed and slammed her hand down. "Loose!"

Lera's gaze took in the scene before her with alarming alacrity, registering every one of them in a flash. Her hair was damp with the moisture in the winds, her face as pink as her wings with exertion. Her lip, coated in a thin layer of sweat, curled in a snarl, and even that glistening plate armour did little to hide the anger staining every facet of her beauty.

She swivelled in an attempt to dodge the incoming barrage. But not quite fast enough, because the first arrow to hit Lera's chest was not one made of wood and metal. It was one made of ice.

Lera's eyes went wide as the first barrage of arrows soared just past her, or clattered into her plate armour. None caught her wings, but they didn't have to, because Rasel's power had lanced into her side.

A layer of thick ice coated one wing and half her ribcage.

Then she dropped, feet away from where Nadrian had dropped moments before.

"Fuck," Shaedon said, still the furthest from the edge. "You got her."

"Wasn't a direct hit," Kol replied. "Stay alert."

Suri stepped forwards. "We have to check on Na—"

Kol grabbed her, pulling her back to his side. "After."

But Rasel had already taken a few steps. "I'll check," he said as he glanced over the edge. His white hair fell over his brow as he craned to look down at the rocks and sand far below.

Ressa called out to her son, holding her hand out. "Wait."

Rasel turned to look at them, still bent over the edge. "I—"

Then Lera shot up past him, grabbing a fistful of his hair and wrenching him upwards and away from the wall by the scalp. She pulled Rasel clean off the ground as she screamed into his ear. "Traitorous fucking snake."

Suri's mind went cold with dread. It hadn't been enough.

She pictured Nadrian, lying dead at the bottom of the cliffs as Lera now held Rasel's life, and therefore her own, in her hand.

Scilla held her hand up in an instant. "Hold your fire."

In the same moment, Kol threw his arms out and growled. "No one attacks."

"Why not?" Shaedon asked quickly, without taking his eyes from the pair. He held a ball of blue flame in his hand. "I say, burn them both. What's he to us?"

Lera hovered in the air, holding Rasel, studying their group with a rising rage. She may have noted their guests before, but now she was livid. A damp strand of perfect golden hair had caught in her mouth. "I am disappointed to see you here, Prince Shaedon."

Kol's eyes were pure black as he ignored Lera's taunt. "Rasel has to live."

Shaedon just nodded, even as he did not meet Kol's eyes.

Lera tilted her head. "Is that so, Kol? It does not surprise me to see you alive. You were always bound to be a liar, the bastard get of a whore."

Kol kept his eyes on Rasel, his body completely still.

Suri couldn't think, couldn't breathe.

The Queen held the ice prince, and Suri's own life, twenty feet from the edge. She didn't even look like she was struggling, keeping him aloft in one hand and clutching her dark blade under his chin with the other, just above the fabric of the ever-present cravat.

"Don't kill him, Lera," Kol said. "Let's talk about this."

Lera cackled and the knife pressed closer. Suri flinched, imagining how it would fizz and bubble the instant she broke the skin. "Impressive, Rasel. You've managed to make them care enough for your ugly, insecure soul that they won't kill me. I'll admit, I was hoping for a better bargaining chip than a backstabbing eel like yourself, but it seems you're enough after all."

She didn't know about the blood bond, then. Lera thought their care for Rasel stemmed from something akin to morality. She overestimated their goodness vastly.

"Though for a nation claiming they want peace," Lera continued. "You've certainly amassed quite the force to kill me. Give up now, Kol, and I will let Rasel and the rest of your pitiful retinue live."

Suri assessed the situation and could think of nothing. It was too far to jump, and what would that truly achieve, anyway. Without Death's power, Kol couldn't get to him with the shadows and transport him away. Sotoledi's darkness, along with his ability to kill at will, was gone now. There was nothing, no avenue to rescue Rasel. If Queen Lera wanted to kill him, nothing could be done.

Lera must have interpreted their mutual silence for consideration, for she smiled. "This is your only chance to save your people. He is coming, and his retribution shall be magnificent. Die here, Kol. Die here to save them all."

Next to her, she felt Kol stiffen, and then relax.

He grabbed Suri's hand and squeezed it, but even that reassurance was not enough. Despite everything and all she'd changed, she would probably die here, because of Rasel motherfucking Waterborne.

"Let us discuss this," Kol said carefully, his voice oddly measured. "Rasel lives. Everyone with me lives. In exchange for my life."

Suri's heart seized. No. He would never consider it. Kol wouldn't do that to her, to his court, to their world. They needed him. To lose him was to leave the desert in eternal death, and to leave her as lost as she had ever been.

"Yes," Lera said, beckoning him with her knife. "Come forth and I will end you before the god we both serve."

Kol nodded, and then glanced up. "And yet, I do not see Sotoledi in our city, or in our sky."

Lera shook her head. "What of it? When he does come, you shall all fall."

"Oh," Kol said. "He has come."

The harpy queen glanced over the wall, and then growled. "You lie. Now come to die before I drop your new friend."

"I do not lie. Your Sotoledi is closer than you think," Kol said.

Lera narrowed her eyes. "I grow tired of your games. Maybe I should let you all perish in his darkness after all."

"Scilla," Kol said, keeping his eyes on the Queen. "Bring Sotoledi to me."

Scilla nodded.

The Queen's wings beat steadily, but she blinked a few times, the tiniest betrayal of her confusion. Rasel twisted in her grip and Kol hissed as the blade nudged the skin, so close to slicing through. Some sort of poison must coat it. Queen Lera had fought most of her battles dirty, and it seemed this was no exception.

Scilla passed the cage to Kol.

Kol lifted the soul cage, the purple light in the drowning water. "Here he is."

The Queen's face froze. "It is impossible."

"Reach for him in your mind," Kol said. "Speak to him. He is not there."

The Queen snarled, even as her grip faltered on the ice prince. "He is coming."

"He is dead. Come here, and I shall give him to you." He lifted the cage forward, holding it in his outstretched palm in invitation. "Perhaps there is still power in it."

"What are you doing now?" Suri whispered to him.

"This is a trick," Queen Lera said, but she glanced up at the clearing sky overhead. "He is coming, he is coming."

Kol murmured back to Suri under his breath. "Doing what a good king should."

Suri stared at him in utter confusion. "What?"

The Queen looked at the soul in the glass. Then looked at all of them, lingering on Shaedon. She took in the city, still so intact. The impenetrable mists. Her eyes fluttered closed and she muttered something to herself.

The anger and disbelief told Suri everything she needed to know.

The Queen had finally realised she had lost. Her despair was subtle, but it worked its way out, in the tensing of her fist, the flinch behind her eyes, the tightening of her jaw.

And like all scared things, Lera would lash out against the only target she had. Rasel was going to die, Suri could feel it.

Suri wondered then what she herself looked like, what expression was written on her face, and the answer was too easy.

She knew it was a mirror of the queen's. Everything she saw written there lanced her tenfold; anger that she had tried so hard to change the world and utter disbelief that this was how it was going to end. Their bitterness united them just as it would always keep them apart, too similar to ever be at ease even as they approached their joint deaths. They despaired together in that moment, their lives hanging over a precipice and their destinies on the brink of destruction.

There was no way Lera would let Rasel live. And there was no way they would let Lera survive once the deed was done. The Queen, the prince and the thief would die together.

"Lera, let's talk about this," Kol said, choosing his words carefully. "Let Rasel go."

Her eyes landed straight back on Kol, and the sheer rage in that gaze filled Suri with a sickening premonition.

"You want him?" she said, her hand quivering. "Fine. I'll let him go."

Then she dropped Rasel.

The last thing she saw was his horrified expression as he fell out of sight.

Suri's scream was swallowed by Scilla's repeated order. "Loose!"

Her heart lurched out of her chest as her knees buckled.

But Kol grabbed her, wrapping his arms around her and holding her firm against his chest. "Stalling, Suri. I was stalling."

She buried her head in his chest, knowing these were her final moments. "What?"

"Look."

Suri turned her head to see an arrow lodge heavily into Lera's neck. This time, more had found their mark. The Queen tried to fly away but Ressa and Viantha moved as one, and her mouth gaped open as a gurgling, choking noise spouted from her. They harnessed the water within her body to pull her forwards like an invisible thread between them. Lera held her throat, water already bubbling out of it. So much water, pouring from her mouth. More arrows hit her, one slicing just under her chin as she drowned from the inside out.

Her wings shuddered and failed, and her body collapsed onto the cliff edge. Scilla lunged forward to grab her leg, hauling her firmly onto the plateau as Lera's pink wings shrivelled to black, and her body turned to that form she had so desperately tried to hide. The hag, aged and decrepit, her hands curling into calloused talons as black as her heart.

Queen Lera was dead. Water still flowed from her wrinkled mouth, the mother and daughter leaving nothing to chance even as it was clear the woman was already gone.

Waris revealed herself, running down from the misted battlement with a feral grin and a glass chamber swinging from each hand.

But it wasn't Lera's death that Kol wanted her to see, nor the Blood Witch ready to capture her soul. It was the sight beyond it.

Movement in the distance, the light from the parting clouds catching on the golden feathers as he landed on the opposite cliff head. And the man he cradled, his white-blonde hair visible even at this distance.

Nadrian and Rasel. Gods, Nadrian had caught him.

Even from here, she saw Nadrian stumble to the floor as Rasel placed a hand to his shoulder, shouting something.

Scilla cried out and covered her mouth. “Permission to tend to Nadrian, your Grace.”

Kol nodded, still clutching Suri to him. “Of course.”

Viantha grabbed the general’s arm, dropping her concentration on the drowned Lera. “Let me.”

“You must be tired,” Scilla replied, touching her hand.

“I’m a better healer than you on my worst day.”

Together, hand in hand, they ran down the city wall towards Nadrian.

Shaedon stepped back, speaking into his seeing silk. Ressa sat down on the floor, staring out at the battlefield with exhaustion in her eyes.

Kol turned to a white guard. “Write a note to Lingyun and Dabri’yon. Their false god is dead, and so is the Drangborian Queen. There is nothing but their own deaths left for them here.”

Waris spoke words in the Old Tongue over Lera’s body, and Suri saw the faint outline of an orange light escape from her chest. Waris captured it easily, staring at it with satisfaction. Suri tried not to think about what it meant that her and Lera’s soul were the same colour.

It was over. Truly, entirely, over.

Kol looked down at her. “How are you, little thief?”

She stared up at him, counting every star in his eyes. “I’m alive.”

He smiled. “That’s a fantastic start.”

Her thumb ghosted across his cheek and a hint of mirth found its way into her pattering heart. "What are we going to be wary of now the harpy is gone?"

Kol chuckled and leaned down, pressing a kiss to her nose. "With you around, there will be something unpleasant coming our way soon enough, I have no doubt."

Suri rolled her eye. "Just because something is true, doesn't mean it needs to be said."

Kol clicked his tongue. "I'll remember that one. Though, if what you said earlier is to be believed, I think it is everyone else who should be wary."

"Of what?"

He pressed his mouth to hers in a quick but passionate kiss. He pulled back only an inch, breathing the words onto her face with wonder in his eyes. "Of you. You are terrifying."

She smiled. "Do I terrify you?"

Kol laughed, and a hint of light touched his features. "Every moment."

"Good."

45

Death powers it. I know this now. I built something, a door. It does not move me far, but soon, soon it will take me to him.

Unknown author, est. 2nd-5th century

The army was completely out of sight in less than two days, with only scattered fabric and disturbed sand to indicate they'd ever been there. The dunes were empty as far as the eye could see and the reports from the towers indicated the retreating troops were close to the Pananti foothills.

Nadrian's recovery, however, took a full week.

Suri sat by his bed on the sixth day. It was the first time she'd been in his bedroom, and for a man eager to brag about each and every conquest, his room was surprisingly tasteful. He held rooms in the centre of Akdaria, very similar to her own. The upper floor was a welcoming nook, with thick brown and red rugs, a soft blue armchair nestled between two full bookshelves, with more books haphazardly stacked beside it. His dark wood bed with linen sheets captured the natural morning light, streaming in through large windows.

"I'm so bored," Nadrian whined, lying on top of his sheets dressed in a red silken robe.

Suri tutted. "Your fault for being such juicy bait."

"You took what should be a lethal dose of hill snake venom into your system," Agata said, dampening a cloth in the ewer across from him. "You're lucky to be alive, and very lucky to be bored."

"I am aware, but that does little to alleviate my symptoms," Nadrian said. "Is there truly nothing exciting happening?"

Suri shrugged. "The troops have nearly left."

"I know that already," he sighed.

"The gates opened yesterday, and we've constructed a temporary bridge so people can leave without swimming."

"Old news, killer," Nadrian said, and he pulled a pillow over his head with a groan.

"I'll be back later," Agata said to her. "Make sure he gets some rest."

"I'll try," Suri replied. "Thank you."

Nadrian sniffed as Agata descended the stairs, his words muffled by the pile of feathers encased above him. "I'm not sleeping without gossip, every babe needs a story."

"You are so stubborn."

"I'm waiting."

"Rasel wants to stay here," Suri offered. "He asked Kol last night."

Nadrian froze, then removed the pillow from his head. He stared contemplatively up at the ceiling.

"You knew that, too?" Suri asked. She wasn't sure how she felt about the request. On the one hand, she wanted to refuse him out right. He was a mess, inside and out, and he'd caused the world a terrible amount of pain. On the other, it was useful having him nearby, where they could stop him from dying.

But she didn't understand why he *wanted* to stay, when no one here liked him.

"Not exactly. But he told me he would ask," Nadrian replied, his face clouded and hard to read.

Suri clucked her tongue. "Did you tell him to?"

Nadrian slid his gaze over to her. "I wouldn't say that. I more suggested to him that with the bond linking his life with yours, Kol would never let him out of his sight. So his choices were to live here as a free man, or live here as a prisoner."

Suri thought about that. She hadn't fully considered that Kol wouldn't *let* him leave if he tried, but it seemed obvious now. "Can we trust him, when he's only asking to stay alive?"

"Everyone is only trying to stay alive," Nadrian responded. "Rasel's just more upfront about it."

Suri paused, the words hitting something inside her. She kept going back to that moment by the cottage, listening to her own voice guiding her. Someday in the future, she would have to make that same decision to set everything in motion. She'd told Kol snippets, pieces of what had happened, what she'd seen. But she hadn't told him that part, she hadn't told him that she had steered Sotoledi and Diophage towards the discovery that would change everything.

No. She couldn't begrudge Rasel for looking out for himself.

Nadrian nudged her and she blinked, not realising she'd been staring into space. He smirked. "Come on, there's got to be one thing happening that I don't know."

Suri racked her mind, trying to distract herself as much as him. "A group has been approaching the city from the Forgelands since the day after the siege ended."

Nadrian's eyes widened, and she smiled, happy to have found something new. "A delegation from Thandul?"

"That's what we assumed, too. But Thandul's delegation was spotted at the outermost tower only today. In the full regalia, five carriages decked in gold. This group is days ahead and travelling light, they'll reach the city tomorrow."

Nadrian frowned. "Could it be Aisha? Esra?"

Suri nodded. "I thought that. But there's apparently nearly a dozen of them."

"Interesting," he said, then he winked at her. "Thank you."

"I live to serve." Suri bowed from her perch and returned her eye to him, flinching slightly at the warmth there. She still couldn't look at him without seeing the moment he died. The giant black creature, punching through his chest like he was nothing more than a doll.

He grabbed her hand. "And you?"

Suri held his hand back, staring down at it. "What do you mean?"

"I know you saw something back there," he said, and she stiffened. "Something happened, something in that place with Sotoledi, or after. You saw something. I can see it's haunting you."

She took a breath, letting it fall, shaking from her body. The urge to cry nearly overwhelmed her. She knew she'd allow herself to feel it all one day, but she couldn't break down yet. It was too recent, too confusing. "I—I can't talk about it yet."

"I get that," Nadrian replied.

Suri said nothing, feeling the morning sun on her back as she tried not to think about it, reminding herself that *this* was the real world.

He patted her hand. "I need to make my way to the Glen soon. I'll finish my healing there, where I'll be stronger. But you are always welcome. You'll be a guest of honour."

She looked up and met his green gaze. There was no joke in his eyes, nothing playful about the invitation. He meant it, wholly and solemnly. And she knew she would always be protected in the Glen so long as he was its leader. Her whole life, if his predecessor's lifespan was anything to go by. She nodded, no hint of humour in her voice either. "Thank you, Nadrian."

He studied her. "And thank you, for whatever you did there. I know you saved us, somehow. The way you looked at me... it was as if I was a ghost to you made flesh again. And yet here I am. So thank you. Even if you won't talk about it."

Suri swallowed and the memory of her grief was so raw and real then that she struggled to hold back a sob. But she only nodded, her one eye shining with an unshed tear.

"There you are."

Suri straightened at Scilla's voice, still towelling off her mostly dry hair. "Here I am."

Scilla looked jittery, but not distressed. If anything, she looked excited, though Suri had seen excitement so rarely on Scilla's face that she hardly knew its likeness.

Swimming in the leaf pools had been one of the few ways she'd managed to distract herself from everything. Ducking her head underwater and blocking out the noise, bathing in the warmth of the day, listening to the chatter of those around her, it kept her grounded. She'd just dressed and was about to go find Kol when the general arrived.

"Come with me," Scilla said, and walked off without a backwards glance.

Suri slipped her shoes on, throwing the towel over a wooden fence to dry before trotting after her. She caught up to her and touched her elbow. "Where are we going?"

"The group from the North arrived."

Suri blinked. "Oh. Who are they?"

Scilla turned to her. "Look, I hate surprises, but this is something you really ought to see for yourself."

Oh, great. As if she hadn't had enough surprises to fill a lifetime.

When they got to the Gate, Suri paused. The behemoth had not ceased to exist on Sotoledi's death. Its magic continued, still transporting them between Akdaria and the ruined city as before.

But now, it terrified her.

What if she stepped inside, and was lost again to that eternity of pain? And even if she wasn't, she knew she would hear the echo of that scream. One she was certain now was her own scream, that version of herself trapped in its endless void, reverberating back through time itself, haunting her each time she passed through.

"Suri?" Scilla said, waiting beside the Gate. "What is it?"

Suri met Scilla's eye. "Would you step through with me?"

Surprise froze her expression, but only for a breath. She narrowed her eyes in a curious study of Suri, but held her hand out nonetheless and did not ask. "Of course."

Suri nodded and breathed out. She could do this. After Lera's death, the distraction of the day had been enough to let her stumble back through to Akdaria. But she hadn't returned, hadn't set foot in the ruined city in the week since.

She couldn't see its walls without picturing them destroyed, couldn't look at the sky without seeing *His* shadow. But she took Scilla's offered hand, and they walked through together. Scilla pulled her through and she barely had time to register the scream or the feeling of a hand at her stomach. That's what she told herself, at least.

Once through, she released her iron grip on the general and they walked through the dusty city together. Scilla was carefully silent.

Suri spoke to keep her mind off her surroundings, her tone forcibly light. "I'm surprised Viantha isn't with you. I haven't seen you apart in a week."

Scilla nodded. "She was there when they arrived. I didn't want to tear her away."

Who was *they*? "This better be a good surprise."

Scilla smiled, then. "One of the best."

They mounted the stairs to the main throne room and Suri touched Scilla's arm. Scilla stopped, glancing down as they stopped beside the heavy door.

"I'm happy for you," Suri said, dropping her hand. "I'm happy for you and Viantha."

Scilla nodded. "Thank you. I'm happy for you and Kol."

Suri took a deep breath, her heart pounding. She needed to say it, it was far overdue and she was done waiting until the last possible moment to apologise. "I know you'll never forgive me. But I'm sorry for Barsen."

Scilla's warmth spilled away, and Suri saw the grief touch her eyes before she schooled it away into nothing.

Suri swallowed. "Sorry, I shouldn't—"

"I forgave you already," Scilla interrupted. "When you went into Sotoledi's land that first time, when you were willing to risk everything for Kol and for this court."

Her heart thundered in her chest and her hands shook. Forgiven? Gods, she didn't deserve it.

Scilla forced a smile onto her face and touched Suri's arm. "Barsen would have liked you. I'll never forget him, and sometimes when I think about him, I can't help but wish things had gone differently. But I don't think we would be here right now if it was not for you. So I find I cannot hate you. And I have chosen to forgive you."

Suri couldn't stop the sob, then. It was a small one, a crack in the wall she'd been building her entire life. Her eye welled up and her breath hitched in her throat. She stuck out her hand, sniffing back her emotion. "Friends?"

Scilla shook her head. "I dislike you too much to be friends with you."

Suri dragged in a breath.

Then Scilla clutched her hand, tight. "Sisters."

Suri choked, and a tear escaped down her cheek.

Sister. It was a good word. One of a bond bigger than mutual connection. It was a word of blood, love if not always like. A declaration that when it came down to it, they were always on the same side, always standing beside one another against the storm. That they would kill for each other.

They shook on it. Sisters, it was.

Then Scilla pushed open the door.

The scene in the dilapidated main hall froze Suri to the spot, and she could no longer fight her tears.

Nine people stood before Kol's throne, all girls or young women. Kol himself appeared enthralled, locked in his position of wonderment.

One of them stepped up before him and attempted a clumsy curtsy. She was the youngest in the party, and could not be more than nine. She screwed up her mouth, her cheeks flushing red as she stretched her palm out wide in front of her. Her face was near purple with strain, and then it happened.

A small beam of light came from her hand. Not taken, not manipulated from the light of the room. It came *from* her, just as Kol's light came from him. The girl grinned and relaxed, the shine lingering for a moment before falling away. Then she ran to the back of the room, past the other eight gathered and to a shadowed corner where two others watched on.

These, Suri recognised. Aisha stood beside her mother, Waris. They'd been locked in conversation until the girl tugged on Aisha's hand and caught her attention. Aisha smiled down at her, congratulating her in a low voice. Waris looked at the child with faint distaste.

Another person stepped towards the throne. It seemed they had formed something of a line to demonstrate their abilities to Kol, and she was the penultimate, the rest chattering in low voices.

"What are they?" Suri asked, the words barely audible.

"I think you know," Scilla replied.

It was now Suri realised she recognised this face, too, but it was so unbelievable she almost dismissed her suspicion out of hand. The woman was standing before Kol, her face only visible in profile as she held a dead yellow flower.

May Tanner.

The flower was a Northern weed, any ugly thing blooming in the cracks in the walls. Hardy, weathering the harsh springs with impressive fortitude, coming back with each new year. May lifted the flower, so crumpled that she must have taken it straight from New Politan.

Her forehead creased as she steadied her breath, every inch of her attention locked on its petals. And just like that, in a matter of seconds, it bloomed back to life.

Suri scanned the group. With Aisha, there were ten of them, children and grown women alike. All of them fighters, and survivors, with darned clothing and dirt under their nails. All of them were what she had been. Nervous, jaded, distrusting. But together, they were a force. Bonded by the experiences they'd had, forced to find light in the darkest places.

"The Daughters of the Earth."

"With Viantha and I, that makes twelve of us," Scilla said.

"Do you think it's enough?" Suri asked.

"We'll find out. And if it's not, we'll find more."

Something stuck in Suri's throat then. Tears welled in her eye and fell down her cheek. Gods. If not, they'd find more.

The sheer simplicity of that statement rocked her beyond belief, because they could now, because Lera was gone and Sotoledi was gone, and there was time. There was true hope for their futures, and it didn't hang in the balance of the next day or week.

She had the catastrophically freeing sensation that everything might actually be alright, and no idea of how to handle it.

Suri had spent her whole life trying to keep herself alive, determined not to die. Then, her only goal was to stop everyone she cared about from dying, too. The idea they could do something greater, not merely fight to keep breathing, but actually *live*, seized her with such force she hardly knew what to do with herself.

We could *live* here, she thought.

Suri stepped into the room proper, her heart fit to burst from the emotions that wracked her body like waves upon the shore. It was then she noticed two other visitors.

They stood to one side of the hall, watching the girls. As she walked in, they looked at her and her breath hitched, her heart clamouring in her chest.

A young man, his arm no longer in a sling, and a very tired-looking old woman, leaning against a stick. Her old home was finally here, in her new home.

Suri ran to them, throwing her arms around her brother.

"Suri," Esra breathed in relief, clutching one arm tight around her. "I thought the Queen was going to wipe you all out."

"So did we," Suri said, laughing through her tears.

"You were right about finding daughters in the North," he replied. "Life magic loves a survivor."

"I can't believe you found them all."

"Well, I think most of the credit for that lies with May." Her brother gave her a sheepish smile.

"You're telling me the fucking Tanner was the first one you found."

"What, so you can be friends with infamous killers and I can't?"

"I guess I can't argue with that," Suri said. "We have a lot to catch up on."

"And we will," Esra said.

That bubbling and overwhelming sensation rose in her again. There were no Bloodhounds chasing her, no dark forces pulling her under, no queens, princes, or armies at her heels. She had her life, her soul, her lover, her family and her friends, a roof over her head and food in her belly. More than that, she was a rich woman now, a member of an established court. She had everything she could ever need or want.

That other feeling crept up on her again, unwelcome and bone-deep. The belief that she didn't deserve any of it. The feeling fell from her mind as she turned to the woman who had raised her.

Mother Edi raised an eyebrow, carving into the grooves in her worn flesh. "I have a feeling we have much to discuss, too."

She knew something about what Suri had done in the war. If not the exact details, she knew Suri had changed things, that she'd altered time. A shred of alarm flashed inside her, and she swallowed.

Mother Edi smiled knowingly. "But first, I must rest. We have time, after all."

Her tone was playful, a taunt without the sting. Her own power was Suri's now, after all. She knew what Suri was capable of, and certainly she would have her own thoughts on it.

They would speak, that was known, but there was no rush anymore. What was done was done.

Esra touched her arm, and pointed back to the group. Suri watched alongside them as the final girl, maybe fifteen years of age, raised her hands and caught Kol in a personal shower of rain.

Kol laughed, raising his hands to the ceiling. He stood and opened his mouth, catching the created water in his mouth. Suri couldn't help but laugh, too.

46

I can travel near anywhere but to him. It does not matter how many I kill, he is too far away, always.
Unknown author, est. 2nd-5th century

A storm brewed in the distance, fine sand creating the hint of a haze on the horizon. Imperceptible without knowing its existence already, but the far tower's signal had showed its approach plain, and the near tower's warning now flickered beside them.

Kol acknowledged it with little more than a quick nod before returning his attention to the Daughters. The tower was close, and they could easily reach its shelter before the storm hit and besides, they had clear enough tents to house them and shade them from the worst of it if required. Kol's grin held too much excitement to think of seeking shelter yet, he clapped his hands and dropped his bags upon the baking sand, determined that this would be the place where the deed was first attempted.

Attempted was the best word for it, as they had no real belief in their own success, but that seemed to do little to dim the energy.

The twelve Daughters and one Son gathered in a circle. A handful of paces away Suri stood with Mother Edi and Waris, three women whose magic ran on far more ancient lines. They watched on, and Suri fancied them as crones in some player's troupe, prophesying and declaring. They would play no part in what was to come, except to witness.

Suri watched Kol with something lighter than veneration, but no less powerful. He was effervescent now, glowing with the joy of hope even when he didn't mean to, shining on them like a star. He met her gaze as the group of them collected into a circle, and lanced her with a smile so bright it sliced like paper on a thumb.

Kol stepped into the centre of the circle and spoke to those around him in a low voice. He reached out his arms as Viantha led half the women, holding Kol's left hand and Scilla led the others, placing her hand in Kol's right.

It reminded her then of that foul time in the altar, when Queen Lera led the massacre of priestesses and drove many of them to their deaths. But there was no knife here, no collection of blood or offering to a now dead man. This was a celebration of survival and life. They did not swirl in a chaotic tangling of skirts until the bloodletting forced them down. No, from the off it was calm.

The women and girls knelt to the floor.

In turn, each closed their eyes, the youngest cajoled into the movement. Kol knelt, too. As Diophage's son, as the purest Fae blood amongst them, he was the strongest and would take the strain on the magic put upon him by the Daughters. But it was not his words that came forth.

"I thank you all for coming here," Viantha said. "I too, am a stranger to these lands. I grew up in the Pail, in a land known for its warm summers and its five Guilds. Many of you hail from the North, a land known for cruel winters and heavy ales. This place, these sands, this is not home. Its heat is painful, its inhabitants believed to be cut-throat thugs, and its ruler rumoured to be more fearsome than death itself. And yet, you all came here. On a whim, a prayer, an idea that anything could be better than where you came from."

A couple of the younger girls opened their eyes and exchanged a look of embarrassment, as if their thoughts had been laid out upon the sands.

Suri found herself watching Scilla, and the lazy smile resting on her face.

Viantha smiled, too, her eyes still closed. "But what's behind it all is something much greater. We are all here because we have hope. Hope for ourselves. Hope for our friends and families, that we may bring them a brighter future. Hope for our world, that it may be a kinder one. It unites each and every one of us here now. Whether we succeed today, or in a month, or in five years when each of us is grown, it matters little. I love each of you, for you have come here, and you offer your strength in the name of hope."

Scilla blinked, and a tear fell upon her cheek. "To hope."

The murmured echo rumbled around the circle. Kol, too, said those two words, his lips barely moving in the centre of the circle.

The youngest girl's contribution happened first. Strange, the way the light moved. Before, it had appeared from her palm like a personal sunbeam. Now, a small ball of light travelled along her upper arm, seeming to have jumped straight out of her heart and across her shoulder.

Suri squinted. No. It wasn't a ball. The light had tiny legs.

A tiny dancing sprite of pure light ran down her arm, diving headfirst into Kol's waiting hand. The Daughters' eyes were all closed, so Suri looked to Mother Edi with pure surprise written on her face. The old woman looked equally riveted.

Aisha came next. A pink sprite, also dashing down from her chest and along her arm, disappearing into Kol's hand. The rest came forth then, ten more spirits in warm yellows, greens and blues, cartwheeling down the arms and throwing themselves headlong into the Son's embrace.

Kol shuddered, not violently, just in the way of an unexpected chill. His head fell forwards and it looked like he might keel into the sand. Suri took a step in his direction, but Waris grabbed her arm in silent rebuke.

When he raised his head again, the tension on his face was gone. He breathed a sigh of relief. "Mother."

The word was whispered, but in the silence of the circle, it was heard by all. Kol opened his eyes and stared into the empty space before him. Suri narrowed her eye, searching for any sign.

She saw, then, the shadow of them, cast by something invisible to her. A shadow of two people, holding hands, stretching back across the sand.

Kol reached forwards, touching the place where their shadowed form began. His finger touched the edge of it, and Suri heard Mother Edi wheeze in surprise as the world started to change.

"Look," Kol said to the Daughters. Eyes flew open, and hands clutched to mouths as they saw what had begun. Scilla held her hand out, and Viantha took it, and their eyes both shined with joy.

The shadow was gone now. The moment Kol had touched it, the dark mark of them across the sand became something else entirely. Rich, black soil in the shapes of two people.

Kol stood upon the first soil of his new land, and it expanded, the sand changing before their very eyes. "Come," he said, holding out his arms. "Come and make this new world with me. Come and bring life to this desert."

Viantha rushed to his side, laughing as she jumped from the dune to the soil. The moment her feet landed, the soil grew again, spanning another dune. With glee, the other Daughters each stepped into soil.

And there it happened.

The soil took over, as far as the eye could see, changing beneath Suri's very feet. And not just that. From the feet of the bringers of life, grass and flowers bloomed underfoot. Every laughing step would bring fresh life anew.

Hope, in Suri's mind, was little more than sheer determination, a choice to believe even when everything was terrible. It was the hardest thing to hold onto, the easiest thing to slip away. And yet she'd found it. She'd found her people, her purpose. She'd found life.

One Son, finally at peace with himself. Twelve Daughters, bonded despite every odd set against them. And the three Seers who watched them, knowing they were so wholly separate, but feeling a part of it nonetheless.

All of them together stood on the sea of green grass, staring in abject wonderment.

Yes, she thought. We will live here.

47

I am somewhere now. Somewhere cold. He is not here.
Will I ever see him again? Will I ever feel the sun?
Unknown author, est. 2nd-5th century

King Thandul clasped his ring-laden hands as he appraised Kol from across the huge stone table. "You brought my son here, we've witnessed your strength. The height of your walls, the tenacity of your men, the curious allies you have. And now, the life of the land has been restored."

Kol said nothing, waiting for the question. They had cleared the rubble from the corridors in the old castle, and they sat now in what must have been a dining room. Light filtered through a broken piece of the ceiling above. The renovations to the ruined city would take several years at least, but this would suffice for the meeting the North had demanded.

Thandul narrowed his watery eyes. "What is it you seek now? What power will you claim next?"

Kol paused. "I have no desire to stretch beyond my lands. I only want to be the Lord of the Eastern Kingdom, as I have been for decades."

Shaedon looked to his father, silent as the grave.

"Before, the land was barren. Yours was a title no one wanted," Thandul replied, not unkindly. "Now your lands are rich and fertile. Even if your desire is to merely hold its borders, that will require constant work."

Kol raised an eyebrow. "If you suggest that others will vie to take this place from me, I do not doubt it. I have long protected us from outsiders, and I will continue to do so."

Thandul dampened his dry lower lip. "So that's it, you will rule your lands, and I mine?"

Kol smiled. "Yes."

"I thought after your pretty show of force, you would seek to make demands," Thandul grumbled.

Kol narrowed his eyes and stood.

Suri stood with him, and their Northern guests immediately scrambled to their feet.

"I am not Queen Lera," Kol said clearly. "I do not brandish power as a means to subjugate others. If I am called upon to defend my land against intruders, I shall do so without impunity. Know that. But if you are a friend to me, I would hope our lands can co-exist in peace and in trade."

Thandul leaned forwards, his already creased brow warping with obvious confusion. "You have no requests? No punishment for throwing you into an arena, murdering your man, my treatment of your court? Am I to think you benevolent, knowing your reputation? It reeks of trickery."

Suri's lip curled into a snarl at Thandul's implication. Kol stilled her with a warning look, and she forced her twitching hand away from her knife. It had not gone unnoticed, Shaedon's eyes flashed at her movement. Good. He should be worried.

Kol held up two fingers. "I have two requests."

Thandul swallowed, but nodded. "Then make them."

"First, that you give me the grace of time. We need to till our lands, pave its roads, grow its crops, reinforce its mines," Kol said. "Second, when the Eastern Kingdom is restored to its former glory, I request that you be our first trade partner."

Thandul blinked, more of that same confusion lacing his brow. He looked to his son, then, truly, for the first time since their meeting had begun. There was a question in his old eyes. Shaedon gave him the barest hint of a nod.

Thandul sighed, and the years piled onto him as he met Kol's black gaze with resignation. He stuck out his hand across the table. "You have a deal."

Kol took his hand, shaking it firmly.

They both sat in silence as the Northern royalty left the room. She imagined they would stay only long enough for King Thandul to regain his strength and his horses to be well-rested, and then they would be on their way. Their allyship was tenuous at best, relying on the common enemy they had found in Queen Lera. Now she was gone, the Kingdoms of Peregrinus were unsteady, and everyone held their cards closer to their chest. She wondered if the Northern King had any aspirations for the Seat of Drameir. Already the word of Lera's disgrace and demise would be spreading across the lands like wildfire. Her successor was far from secure, with no line established. It was anyone's guess whose stewardship Drangbor would fall to.

Once Thandul and Shaedon were gone and the door closed, Suri rose from her seat and took a new one in Kol's lap. "Leave us," she said to the two white guards.

Kol smirked at her as they waited until they were fully alone.

She tapped his nose. "That was more than a fair deal."

He held her around the waist. "I do not strive for gold now. It only brings suffering and resentment. I've lived with a hundred years of that. Now is a time for peace."

She held his face in her hands, staring into his warm brown eyes, searching them for something. "What happened to the monster I fell in love with?"

Kol laughed, and his grip on her tightened. "Let me show you."

Suri gasped as he lifted her and pressed her onto the table, parting her legs. They moved together as the light streamed in overhead, their bodies clawing from each other the darkness they both still craved.

Nadrian stood on the city wall directly above the city gate, tying his pack to his chest. He pulled on the final knot as he flexed his wings, the beige membranes between them thin enough that some of the pink sunset filtered through, creating deep orange light in its shadow.

Out there, beyond the wall, there were no great plains of sand, but undulating verges of grass and meadow on rich, dark soil.

The water cut through the green like a sapphire snake. They'd strung up a rough wooden bridge, and already trodden paths in the dirt had formed where the citizens had started to make their way back home, ready to start anew.

Nadrian turned to the pair of them. "I suppose this is goodbye."

Kol cleared his throat. "Aren't you missing something?"

He grinned. "A hug from my favourite Son?"

"I'll not begrudge you a final embrace, old friend," Kol said, rolling his eyes. He moved something around from behind his back, the purple glow lighting up the water surrounding it. "But I had meant this."

Nadrian's green eyes widened. "Sotoledi's soul?"

"You've done a terrible job making any soul deals since your coronation," Kol replied, the glass cage swinging from the chain. "It's frankly embarrassing."

Nadrian clicked his tongue. "Oh, I'm deeply sorry for being so committed to *your war.*"

"You're forgiven, so long as you take this as a token of my gratitude." Kol held it out towards Nadrian. The Fae King shuddered, but took it from him, holding it as far away from his body as he could, as if the soul cage was a dead rat. "The power of it should last a century, and take the strain off your own soul. Besides, I'd like it kept somewhere safe. Hopefully the last of its light fades before I die, so none of him is ever released into the world."

Suri had forgotten that facet. If Kol died, every soul he had sealed would be released again. She frowned, wondering where it would go if set free. "With his body destroyed, do you think his soul still holds any power?"

"I'd hope it's useless with no vessel to return to, but I'd rather not test that. Waris might know the answer," Kol said, his grim expression mirroring her own.

Nadrian shivered as he tucked the soul cage into his pack. "That's a problem for the two of you, I'd rather not visit the harpy's dancing corpse."

"It's a problem for another time," Kol said, resting his hand on the small of Suri's back. "For now, its power is yours."

"Thank you, your Grace," Nadrian replied, though the sarcasm lacked its usual bite. He looked at them both. "You'll visit soon?"

"Of course, we will," Kol agreed. "I need to teach her how to dance. She brings shame upon us all."

Suri pushed him away even as the grin crept onto her face. "You're terrible."

"You love me," Kol said as he laughed, and touched her chin with his thumb.

Nadrian grabbed at his chest dramatically. "Poison me again, now."

"I thought you were leaving," Suri teased.

Nadrian stuck out an arm. "Come here, killer."

Suri ducked under his wing and stepped into his embrace. Their hug was brief, though both squeezed harder than they needed to. She would visit soon, that was certain. As soon as everything here was a little more settled, they would party the night away.

She pulled back and met his playful look. "I'll miss you."

He patted her head. "I'll miss you, too. Look after each other."

Suri ducked away as Kol pulled him in for a hug. They held each other's arms, an unspoken accord passing between them.

Then the Fae King nodded, and stared back out at the distant horizon. "Now, to chase that sunset."

Nadrian took flight, beating his wings as he stepped lightly onto the knee-high stone before him and leapt forward into the air. His wings caught him easily and he soared away high over the endless grass field without a backwards glance.

Kol took her hand and together they walked back through the ruined city. Every minute he would stop them, pointing to something he wanted to rebuild, or plants he imagined growing. Along the Main Street, nearly a hundred citizens dressed in their brightest clothes danced in the street, horns blazing and ribbons streaming from their spinning forms.

Suri asked Kol what occasion they celebrated, and he told her it was a funeral. She looked up at him as he weaved her through the laughing crowd with a serene smile. "Strange, to celebrate death with so much life."

"Is it?" Kol asked. "They have to face each other, two sides of a coin. There's no value in life without death."

"I suppose," she replied. "It is hard to see light, without dark."

His smile widened, and her heart skipped a beat.

She'd seen him in so many lights, yet this might be her favourite, his jaw caressed by the fading evening light as ribbons swirled in the background.

He stopped in the chaos of people, holding her hips. "And I find beauty in both, *nen alerisee f'ith sotele.*"

“But your darkness matches mine. Maybe you just find beauty in yourself,” she joked.

“Oh, really?” Kol chuckled, and then ducked down, pressing a searing kiss to her mouth. He moved back and tucked a strand of her dark hair behind an ear, looking at her head contemplatively. “You know, you’d look divine in a crown.”

She rolled her eye. “I'd rather just be your little thief.”

“Can’t you be both?”

“I’ll consider it.”

He laughed heartily then, throwing his head back. “See, you’re a natural. You’re telling me no without telling me no.”

She smirked. “Maybe in ten years.”

“Whatever you say, my darling thief,” he replied. “After all, we have time.”

It was uncanny, hearing those words. The echo of the teasing taunt Mother Edi had given her only a week prior. But from him it was different, from him it was a promise that they would spend their lives together. Something she would have only once dreamed at, something she wanted more than anything else and would stop at nothing to protect. She knew then that she would use her power again, she would make any choice she had to make, for this. For them. For herself.

“Yes,” Suri said. “We have Time.”

Epilogue

The nightmares of the dark beast crawling over the city still haunted her.

Viantha, Nadrian, Kol. She watched their deaths every night, playing out in gruesome horror. It had happened. In some world, under the same sun and the same false gods, they had all died.

But Kol was always there to stroke her back, hold her close, and murmur his love into her ear. He didn't fully understand. She had tried to explain what she had seen before. How Sotoledi had skulked across the sky, his gaping mouth blotting out what little sun tried to peel through the storm engulfing the clouds above. Words didn't do it justice. The only justice that could be done was erasing it, knowing that it had never happened to *this* Kol.

Nearly a year had passed since that day, and every changing season helped heal the hurt of the memory. Suri stared out from the balcony, her eye glazed as she watched Akdaria, its wooden streets pulsing with life under the morning sun.

"I thought you might wear this today," Kol said.

Suri turned, and her breath stuck in her throat.

No. So soon?

"Is that a good surprised face, or a bad one?" he asked, scanning her frozen expression.

"It's lovely, of course," Suri replied, pulling her braided hair over her shoulder. She hadn't realised how long it had grown, over halfway down her back.

"White is the traditional colour for births," he said. "Aisha helped pick out the veil."

"Why the veil?" Her voice trembled.

"Don't worry, I'm not marrying you just yet," he said, his cheeks flushing. "The watchers cover their faces so that the sun may smile on the babe alone. It's another tradition."

Kol laid the outfit on the bed. A white floor-length gown, and a gauzy black veil.

"You pagans and your traditions," she said with an attempt at levity, but her voice quivered still. She didn't know veils were traditionally used in weddings here. That was a good cover for her nerves, at least.

He smoothed down the dress and then turned to her, his arms folded. "What's wrong, little thief?"

"Nothing," she said. "I just haven't eaten today."

"I'll get something sent up whilst I change," he said, his eyes softening.

"Thank you, that would be great."

Kol paused in the doorframe, his hand holding it. "I love you."

"I love you, too."

Kol closed the door and left.

Suri touched her hair again. It was today. This was the day she did the thing she could never take back. The day she was to go back five hundred years, and give Sotoledi and Diophage the information that would change everything.

She'd thought about this moment so many times over the months. Some days, she dismissed it all as some horrible memory. Other days, she hoped she'd misremembered, hoped that the version of herself she'd seen had been some ghostly apparition, or at least several years wiser.

Cthanda's words swirled back to her, the warning clanging in her head like ghoulish bells. *"Sometimes to change the world, you need the courage to choose inaction."*

It was now, it was today. If she didn't go, what would happen?

How many more people would have lived over the centuries without the God of Death? Every death fuelled by Sotoledi could be undone now. Every massacre, every kill using his power. Gone.

All she had to do was nothing at all.

And yet, none of her life would exist as she knew it. Akdaria wouldn't exist, created as it was from the Gates. The Wrath would have never happened. If Kol and her existed, they would not be here. She would never have been his light in the darkness, she might not have killed Barsen, and if she had, Kol would have ended her in the desert.

All of it would be different.

And this, this perfect life, this was all she had ever wanted. To be loved. To not be alone.

"Hey, are you ready to go?"

Suri blinked.

The world fell back into place as Kol stepped through the door. He stopped in the doorway and stared at her. "You look stunning. As always."

"I'm ready, yes," she said, standing up and smoothing down the front of the dress. "Sorry."

That was it, she told herself. It was done now, and she would never go back again.

There were so many changes tempting her, and when she thought back to her younger self, and how horribly dark, twisted, and lonely she had been, she wanted to weep for her own life. She wanted to go back in time and destroy anyone who had ever wronged her.

But then she wouldn't be this. She would never have been desperate enough to break into that damned ball, without the weight of all that shit piled up. Without years and years of debt, neglect, and mistreatment, she never would have ended up right here with him. Anything she shifted now could undo the only life she ever wanted.

He leaned against the doorframe as he took her in from head to toe. "We're not late. What are you apologising for?"

His tone was playful, and she gave him a full smile. But the question hit her hard, as much as she tried to hide it. *What are you apologising for?*

Suri met him at the doorway, and he reached for her chin, pulling her towards him and pressing his mouth to hers.

Once, twice. Three times.

When they pulled apart, she stared up into those dark eyes. This was her world.

Sotoledi, and everything he had ever done to the world, was her folly now. All of his deaths, all that he had coaxed others into, those were hers, too. She was a horrible, selfish, terrible monster. But she was in love now, and she would never let herself be lonely again. Not now, not ever. "Nothing, I'm not apologising for anything."

Kol smirked. "Is everything alright?"

"Everything is exactly how it should be," Suri said.

Kol kissed her again, harder. "Hmm," he said, kissing her again. "How can that be true when we both have our clothes on?"

"You're diabolical."

"Only for you."

She smiled. "Good."

He grinned and grabbed her hands, facing her as he backed out of the room and towards the front door. "Are you ready for this?"

She wrinkled her nose. "I don't spend a lot of time around babies. Will I have to hold it?"

Kol laughed. "I'll do the holding if you promise not to call the baby an 'it'."

"Maybe it's best if I don't talk at all."

"You'll have to say something. It's the first baby since life restarted again," he said with a smile. "And you know our people adore you."

Together, they walked into the bright day hand in hand.

"*Your* subjects pretend to like me because you keep getting drunk and calling me your lady. They have to act nice to me."

"Scandalous lies." Kol dragged a hand through his hair. "Sometimes I refer to you as my queen."

"You do not," Suri said, her cheeks heating.

"It might have slipped out once or twice."

"As long as they don't think you're serious," she said, meaning every word. "I'm far happier without a title."

"Only because as soon as you leave Akdaria you have about eight. There's a bard by the name of Maggory in the outpost spinning all sorts of tales about you. And the guards call you God Slayer."

"You're joking."

"I wish," Kol said. "I don't even have a nickname that cool."

Suri groaned.

Kol pulled her in and pressed a kiss to the top of her head. "Don't worry. I promise not to let it go to your head."

"My hero," Suri replied. "No titles allowed. Just Suri and Kol."

"One exception," Kol said. Suri glanced up at him. He was completely radiant, staring down at her as if she was his kingdom, his city, his whole heart. "You'll always be my little thief."

Suri laughed. Yes. She would be. That was all she ever needed to be.

The End

Join Sandpiper's Newsletter NOW for Free Content and Exclusive Updates

Scan the QR code or go to rasandpiperbooks.com today!

A Small Request

If you're at this page having just finished this book. Thank you very much for reading my debut fantasy trilogy, and pat yourself on the back for getting another series under your belt! Can I ask for a favour?

Please consider leaving a rating or a review.

It doesn't have to be a particularly good one, and I know you're busy. But reviews are everything for indie authors, and most of my author operation is a one-woman show. The simple act of leaving a rating online is probably the best way you can turn this from being a hobby to a career for me.

Thanks again.

Acknowledgements

My first big thank you is to some very generous friends who have given their very valuable time to Amefyre for zero moneys. To Samuel Yearley and Dave Lawson, a huge thanks for your beta reading of the books. Both Sam and Dave are fantastic fantasy authors in their own right and anyone reading this should definitely check them out. Next, to Anna, Tash, Chloe and Taryn for your proofreading and your cheerleading of the trilogy.

Thank you to Saint Jupiter (saintjupit3rgr4phic on Instagram) for the cover.

As with book two, I did most of the editing myself, so if (*cough* when) you find typos, you can heartily blame me.

And thanks are owed, last but by no means least, to you, the readers. It's lovely to have you here, and I hope you enjoyed the ending of Suri's story. Or, really, was it just the beginning? After all, they have Time.